FIRE MADE FLESH

DENNY FLOWERS

BLACK LIBRARY

A BLACK LIBRARY PUBLICATION

First published in Great Britain in 2021.
Black Library,
Games Workshop Ltd.,
Willow Road,
Nottingham, NG7 2WS, UK.

10 9 8 7 6 5 4 3 2 1

Produced by Games Workshop in Nottingham.
Cover illustration by Lie Setiawan.

A CIP record for this book is available from the British Library.

ISBN 13: 978-1-78999-806-1

See Black Library on the internet at

blacklibrary.com

Find out more about Games Workshop
and the worlds of Warhammer at

games-workshop.com

Printed and bound by CPI Group (UK) Ltd, Croydon, CR0 4YY

For Beth and Finn.

FIRE MADE FLESH

In order to even begin to understand the blasted world of Necromunda you must first understand the hive cities. These man-made mountains of plasteel, ceramite and rockcrete have accreted over centuries to protect their inhabitants from a hostile environment, so very much like the termite mounds they resemble. The Necromundan hive cities have populations in the billions and are intensely industrialised, each one commanding the manufacturing potential of an entire planet or colony system compacted into a few hundred square kilometres.

The internal stratification of the hive cities is also illuminating to observe. The entire hive structure replicates the social status of its inhabitants in a vertical plane. At the top are the nobility, below them are the workers, and below the workers are the dregs of society, the outcasts. Hive Primus, seat of the planetary governor Lord Helmawr of Necromunda, illustrates this in the starkest terms. The nobles – Houses Helmawr, Catallus, Ty, Ulanti, Greim, Ran Lo and Ko'Iron – live in the 'Spire', and seldom set foot below the 'Wall' that exists between themselves and the great forges and hab zones of the hive city proper.

Below the hive city is the 'underhive', foundation layers of habitation domes, industrial zones and tunnels which have been abandoned in prior generations, only to be re-occupied by those with nowhere else to go.

But... humans are not insects. They do not hive together well. Necessity may force it, but the hive cities of Necromunda remain internally divided to the point of brutalisation and outright violence being an everyday fact of life. The underhive, meanwhile, is a thoroughly lawless place, beset by gangs and renegades, where only the strongest or the most cunning survive. The Goliaths, who believe firmly that might is right; the matriarchal, man-hating Escher; the industrial Orlocks; the technologically-minded Van Saar; the Delaque, whose very existence depends on their espionage network; the fiery zealots of the Cawdor. All striving for the advantage that will elevate them, no matter how briefly, above the other houses and gangs of the underhive.

Most fascinating of all is when individuals attempt to cross the monumental physical and social divides of the hive to start new lives. Given social conditions, ascension through the hive is nigh on impossible, but descent is an altogether easier, albeit altogether less appealing, possibility.

– excerpted from Xonariarius the Younger's
*Nobilite Pax Imperator – the Triumph
of Aristocracy over Democracy*

PROLOGUE

Krok Steelskin, Forge Tyrant of the Stolen Sons, was struggling to recall a more boring job.

His gang had been idle nearly an hour. All except Rivv. His massive frame was crouched by the bulkhead, his meltagun trained on its thus far unblemished surface. The weapon had consumed three power packs. By now they should have been knee-deep in a pool of molten metal. Krok almost wished they were. It would've been a break from the tedium.

Not that Rivv looked bothered. The lad was a simple creature even for House Goliath – obedient, cheerful and none too bright. In fact, Krok wondered sometimes if the data-slug implanted at the lad's vat-birth was defective. Still, at least he was content with his work. The same could not be said of the rest of them. For a time, entertainment had been provided by lewd jokes and headbutting contests, but the lads were quiet now, and that was not a good sign. Vat-born Goliaths had a lifespan measured in years, not decades. Their days

were usually spent hunting the terrible beasts of the underhive or battling for survival against sump mutants. Patience
was not a natural quality for a Goliath, nor one that could
be acquired from a data-slug.

Krok craned his massive neck, scanning for Lady Wirepath, their employer. The Guilder had paid well for their
escort, but made no attempt to conceal her disdain for
the brutish fighters of House Goliath. Questions quickly
degenerated to lectures, and when she spoke Krok found
his focus drawn to his holstered stub gun. Killing a Guilder
was usually more trouble than it was worth, and would forfeit them the remainder of their fee. So far, Krok felt these
factors outweighed the satisfaction he'd take from feeding
her a bullet. So far.

'Switch it off, Rivv,' Krok said. The vat-born obeyed instantly,
the hiss from his weapon quieting, the only sound now the
pop of the chamber cooling. Krok waved him to one side,
gingerly pressing his knuckle to the unburnished bulkhead.
It was barely warm.

'What is this made of?' he murmured. Like most of his
people he'd laboured in the House forges. Smelting and
metalwork were as much a part of his blood as the cocktail
of stimms that maintained his gargantuan frame. He'd seen
molten iron form rainclouds, protoplastics running like
blood. But he'd never seen anything like this.

'What in Helmawr's name are you idiots doing?'

'Wasting our time?' Krok shrugged, not bothering to look
round. There was no need; he could picture Lady Wirepath
in all her finery – her cloak comprised of glittering keys,
her bodice studded with gemstones, a feathered hat adorning her head, the plumage taken from some off-planet bird
he could barely pronounce. Anyone else dressed in such a

manner would have long since been scragged in an alley, their corpse looted and dumped in the sump. But she was a Guilder, one of a cast of merchants that sat but a short step beneath the nobles in the planet's hierarchy. And for the rich the rules were always different.

'You were left specific instructions on tempering the bulkhead,' she brayed. 'Why have you stopped?'

He turned, glaring at her.

'I'm telling you it's a waste of time,' he replied. 'Nothing is going to cut through that metal. It's barely warm.'

'It's warm?'

'Barely.'

'Out of the way!' she snapped, rushing forward, her Groveller bodyguard moving with her. Skin engraved with tallies of owed credits, armour trade-coffers strapped to their backs, these lowly creatures were oath-breakers, bound to the Guild as penance. Krok had little regard for the treacherous, but having sworn to protect Lady Wirepath and travelled with her for some weeks, he was beginning to reconsider this position.

The Guilder was still intent on the bulkhead, seemingly oblivious to the Goliaths, an unknown device clasped in her right hand emitting an incessant beeping.

Deadard, Krok's second-in-command, approached the Forge Tyrant, his face set in a scowl.

'How much longer, boss?' he said. 'The lads are getting restless.'

'They will keep in line if they want to get paid.'

'They want pay, boss,' Deadard said, shrugging, 'but they want some action more. There are rumblings that you have gone soft, getting talked down to like that by a banker.'

He spat the last word as an insult, which brought a smile to Krok's face.

'They think I'm weak? They can step up and try me. I'd enjoy the chance to swing my hammer.'

The beeping from the device in Lady Wirepath's hand was growing increasingly unpleasant. Some of the gang were starting to shift back, while others clamped their massive hands over their ears. Krok stood unmoved, refusing to acknowledge the rising cacophony, even as his teeth began to ache. All the while the whine intensified, until it shifted beyond the audible register and he could feel it in his bones. His jaw throbbed, his vision clouded. Was this an attack? An attempt to revoke their deal?

'Boss?' he heard Deadard mutter, but at that moment a crack split the bulkhead, the impenetrable metal crumbling like glass. Instantly the beeping ceased.

'Open it,' Lady Wirepath commanded.

Krok felt his blood rise but took a deep breath, calming himself. He turned to his gang.

'All right, lads, let's crack it.' He grinned and hefted his power-hammer.

It didn't take much – a few blows to open the hole wide enough for the gang to enter two abreast. But still they held back. Krok knew his lads were fearless, but despite his House's reputation they were not stupid. Whatever lay beyond the bulkhead must have been sealed off for a reason.

'Out of my way,' Lady Wirepath barked, pushing past them into the darkness. She was shaking slightly. Excitement, Krok supposed, though he knew not why.

'Yes,' she said, her voice little more than a whisper. 'I've done it. It's mine!'

Deadard cleared his throat. 'We goin' in, boss?'

Krok didn't answer. He stepped slowly over the threshold, feeling the ground shift beneath his feet. He stooped, retrieving a handful of what felt like gravel, though it was too light for stone. It was too dark to tell. Only a sliver of light pierced the breached bulkhead, and the Guilder's hand-lumen was less than a candle. Still, he could make out the ruins of shattered hab-blocks, their skeletons stretching spire-wards towards the distant peaks of Hive Primus high above.

Lady Wirepath was staring at him.

'Do you know what this is?' she said.

He shrugged. 'Ruins?'

'Ruins?' she laughed, incredulous. 'This is Periculus, the Fallen Dome. Missing for hundreds of years, sunk to the very hive bottom.'

He frowned. The name was vaguely familiar, but he did not concern himself with the past. It was the future he was interested in.

'Worth something, is it?' he asked.

She laughed again. The noise made his trigger finger twitch.

'You simple creature,' she said with a smile. 'This was the Forbidden Gem – a place where anything could be found for the right price, where even Lord Helmawr cast a blind eye. The stories tell of archaic devices and forbidden xenos tek, a garden of forgotten wonders. The secrets buried here could unbalance the entire power structure of Hive Primus.'

'Sounds like you found what you were searching for,' Krok said. 'If you wouldn't mind settling our fee, we'll leave you to enjoy it.'

The Guilder stared at him. For the first time she seemed lost for words.

'...You wish to move on?'

'Yeah,' Krok said. 'There's a nest of raft spiders in the sump vents just north of here. Some are supposed to be twenty foot across. Think we'll head that way.'

She blinked. 'Orb spiders?'

He nodded. 'I got a good fence. You can get a fortune for their eyes.'

Lady Wirepath shook her head in disbelief before gesturing to one of her Grovellers. He eyed Krok wearily as he crept closer, his trade-coffer clasped to his chest, as though cradling an infant.

'You realise what you are turning your back on?' she said, as the Groveller counted out Krok's creds. 'There are treasures beyond imagining here!'

'Imagination isn't my strong suit,' Krok replied, nodding once before turning away. The woman was still lecturing him about something, but he paid her words no heed.

Beyond the cracked bulkhead his gang were waiting.

'We stayin'?' Deadard asked as he emerged.

Krok didn't reply. Instead he held out his hand. The flickering light of the underhive revealed a handful of ivory shards, like organic gravel.

'Bone?' Rivv murmured.

'Yeah. Least it used to be,' Krok said, glancing back to the shattered bulkhead. 'Whole lower level is submerged in it. That's a lot of bodies.'

He looked to his gang.

'Going in blind is a bad idea,' he said. 'We'll let her ladyship poke around first, see what pokes back. Maybe if we stop back in a few days she will have dealt with the issue. Or it will have dealt with her.'

Deadard nodded. 'Smart plan. No need for pointless risks.'

'Too right.' Krok hefted his power-hammer. 'Now who fancies sailing out onto the sump and hunting some raft spiders?'

ACT 1

1

Tempes Sol of the Mercator Lux felt a tingle run along his arm just before the thunderbolt struck. It was a soothing sensation, the neurone circuits implanted beneath his skin supping upon the static like it was a vintage amasec, even through the craft's hull. But the flash also illuminated the cargo bay where he sat, and by its light he caught a glimpse of the secure hold at its rear.

He shuddered involuntarily, switching his gaze to the pew opposite, where the agents of House Delaque were strapped into their flight seats. There were four in total, though only one he knew by name. The remaining trio were interchange-able, their gaunt frames concealed by black longcoats, their hooded faces pale and hairless. All lacked eyes, returning his gaze through view-lenses wired directly into the orbital socket. It made it difficult to read them, and Sol wondered if that was the primary motivation for getting the ocular enhancements.

Still, he had passed enough time with them now to detect vague hints of discomfort as the craft shuddered, battling against the fury of the storm. They were flying low, riding the magnetic waves generated by the mile-long tendrils of the Fulgur-Net. Through the misted viewport and unending downpour, he caught a glimpse of the net's towering lightning-lures. They drank deep from the perma-storm and, in turn, fed the reserves of the Mercator Lux. His craft rode their waves, suspended on the ambient electromagnetic energy of the net. But the storm ever raged, and the magnetic waves were neither calm nor predictable. The agents of Delaque were not easily shaken, but as the craft lurched and bucked he noted the tapping of a foot and shifting of shoulders. None could quite conceal their unease.

None but their leader, Anguis.

She sat directly opposite, her hands folded neatly in her lap, a spark of amusement playing on the right side of her lips. She was the only one of them who bore a distinguishing feature: a silver scar adorning her left cheek.

There was a second flash. Closer this time. The craft rolled as the oarsman nimbly rode the storm-surge. The Delaque furthest from Sol twitched, fingers darting into their longcoat on reflex. The others glared in reproach, except Anguis, whose face split a smile, though the left side of her mouth remained downturned. It appeared to be nerve damage, but Sol had resisted the temptation to enquire after the cause of the injury. A dozen answers could be offered, but none would be true. Perhaps the scar was for his benefit, a fleeting method of identification. He had no doubt she would shed it along with her name once their partnership concluded.

'Perhaps we should have chosen a better day for it?' she said. Her voice was quiet, little more than a whisper, but Sol assumed she must be addressing him. The agents rarely spoke to one another. Not unless they intended to be overheard.

'The storm has raged for at least a thousand years, and extends over a hundred miles across the Ash Wastes,' he said. 'It would be a long wait.'

'You don't get bored of rain?'

Sol shrugged. 'There's a reason this region is known as the Stormlands.'

'It makes for a thrilling journey,' she said, glancing at her fellow agents. 'Though I fear Number Sixty-Two is struggling to keep their food down. Perhaps you could offer reassurance?'

Sol glanced at the agent. There was a time he had memorised their numerical designations, but he'd soon come to realise these too were in constant flux. He was fairly confident this had been Number Sixteen yesterday; their holster bore a faint but tell-tale lasburn.

'We are flying low and between the lines of the Fulgur-Net,' he said. 'The majority of the storm's localised output will be drawn by the lightning-lures. The craft will sometimes be washed by the splash but the hull has a modified conversion field to mitigate the worst of it. Our oarsman has ridden the surge many times. We have no one more experienced.'

'Thank you. Very reassuring.'

'Yes,' Sol replied, 'though less so when you consider that he was barely our third most experienced oarsman the last time I made this journey. The others…'

He spread his hands.

'I see,' Anguis said, arching her one good eyebrow. 'House Delaque has a saying about how some secrets are best kept. I fear that was one of them.'

Sol shrugged. 'The net is a relic. Our meteoro-techs have

catalogued the storm's geography and temperament. But the net is neither fully operational nor fully understood. There are gaps, stress points. If it were to abruptly fail, or there was a surge directly between the lines, we would not survive.'

Anguis smiled her half-smile. 'Well, there are always risks.'

'Indeed,' Sol said. 'But you requested our business be conducted somewhere secure, and there is nowhere more secure than the Needle. The atmospheric interference disrupts external surveillance, and the location is only accessible to those who can ride the Fulgur-Net.'

The Delaque leader nodded politely, then was silent. Sol retrieved his data-slate, feigning interest in the flickering screen whilst he watched her from the corner of his eye. He suspected the Delaques were communicating somehow – perhaps a vox-channel wired directly through the vocal cords and inner ears, or a visual display via their optical implants. They seemed silent, but they seemed many things when it suited.

He found himself ill at ease.

It was not the journey itself. He had been born in the Stormlands and the voyage was routine to him. But the thunder had lulled, and with the agents silent he could hear something, even over the hum of the vessel and distant clash of lightning.

There was a scratching coming from the rear hold.

He tried to ignore it, keeping his gaze fixed on the data-slab, but he could not escape the sound. It was like the scuttling of an insect, or rats moving through the walls. Except, if he listened closely, between the scratches he could also make out words. A whisper.

'You seem nervous?'

He glanced up. Anguis was staring at him.

'I do not fear the storm.'

'I don't doubt it. Like you, I have every faith that we will pass through this tempest.' She smiled. 'Yet you are nervous. Why?'

'Perhaps I fear this endeavour is ultimately futile.'

'Perhaps,' she said with a shrug. 'Or perhaps something less elusive is troubling you?'

As one, the Delaques turned, their collective gaze falling on the cargo bay door.

'It is quite secure,' Anguis continued. 'The wards and negation field are fully functional. Should either fail we have contingencies in place. There is no reason to be concerned.'

Sol offered a thin smile of acknowledgement. He could not see why Anguis would knowingly place herself or her agents in danger. He had no cause to doubt her words, at least not on this.

But he swore the whispering was getting louder. He could almost make out a word.

Salvation.

Lord Silas Pureburn of the Mercator Pyros gave every appearance of listening as the accused made her case. He was seated on a modest throne, mounted on a wide dais suspended several feet above the ground on jets of crystal-blue flame. As his gaze fell on the accused, he adopted a well-rehearsed expression, carefully crafted to convey the solemnness of the situation. His focus appeared fixed on the pitiful figure, as though in that moment her testimony was all that mattered to him.

Of course, it mattered very little. He had heard such entreaties a thousand times from a thousand mouths. Whatever excuses she mustered would not affect the outcome. If she truly had leverage or influence the matter would never have needed to go to trial. But Lord Pureburn held firm his belief in the importance of the process. It was vital for the accused to make her case publicly, amongst her friends and neighbours within the settlement. It was just as important that they witnessed said hearing, so none could later argue justice was not done.

Still, it was hard to pay much attention when her delivery was so stilted. She was saying something about children, gesturing to a pair of juves crying in the crowd. Pureburn glanced in their direction, offering a sympathetic nod whilst taking the opportunity to assess the throng. He could feel the tension, the settlers caught between loyalty to their neighbour and fear of the repercussions if they opposed him.

Not that he could be opposed.

He was a Guilder of Mercator Pyros, the Promethium Guild. He looked down on them from a throne that carried the sacred flames of the God-Emperor. His personage was guarded by a score of Cynders – surgically modified bodyguards who obeyed without question, their faces concealed by iron helms. Behind them stood a towering figure of flesh and steel, one hand ending in a smouldering brazier, the other in bladed fingers the length of a fighting-knife. The cybernetically enhanced creature was his Pyromagir, the sacred steward of his flames. With a word it could reduce the crowd to burned flesh and scorched bone. There was no hope of opposing him.

But, he mused, true power lay not in such simple tools. For he was patron to the fanatics of House Cawdor. Their missionary work was long-established in this settlement, and it was their spies who first alerted him to the accused's crime. She had dared syphon promethium from the settlement's main fuel line. It was a clumsy effort, as likely to blow her to pieces as provide a reliable source of power. Now he considered the matter, perhaps that would have been a preferable outcome. The consequences would have been the same, as would the lesson. But he would not have needed to sully himself by descending this low into the underhive.

His gaze shifted to the accused. She was rambling now, merely postponing her inevitable fate. She was a remarkably unremarkable woman, no affiliation with one of the lesser Houses, nothing notable in her appearance or cadence. It was regrettable, if consistent, that her final words would be so trite. Still, he gifted her a few more precious moments before raising his hand for silence.

'Children of the God-Emperor,' he began, addressing the crowd. 'For my penance I must pass judgement over this sorry situation. The accused has outlined her defence. I accept that her actions were not malicious, that her misguided theft was in support of her family. As a prosperous man so blessed by the God-Emperor, I might consider overlooking the matter, if the theft only related to my personal property.'

He paused, letting his words sink in before turning from the crowd, directing his gaze to the rear of his throne. There, mounted on a chamber of polished plasteel the height of a man, was a crucible of burnished bronze. Within it, a shimmering flame warmed both flesh and soul. It generated neither smoke nor ash, only the divine light of the God-Emperor.

Lord Pureburn stared into the flames for some time, as though lost in thought. He waited for the first murmurs from the crowd before turning back, his expression grave.

'Before you blazes the Eternal Flame of the Pureburn family,' he said. 'It was once a spark cast from the God-Emperor's own blade, back when He crusaded across the galaxy. And though He has long since ascended to the Golden Throne, we have not forgotten this gift. The Pureburn family have ensured the flame has burned for thousands of years, never once going dark.'

They were his now; he could see it in their eyes, in the way shoulders slumped and recognition dawned. None would dare oppose him, even the accused's closest kin. None would risk blaspheming against the God-Emperor.

'The crime is not just against the Pureburn family,' he continued. 'It is a crime against the God-Emperor himself. We know His vengeance. Who can forget the plains of Salvation, where warring gangs of outlaws attempted to syphon His blessed fuel? They are but ash, now, consumed in the fires of His retribution. That is the fate that awaits all who place themselves above Him – they invite death not only upon themselves but also those closest to them.'

The accused was weeping now, seemingly surprised by his ruling. Two members of House Cawdor were already beside her, their faces concealed by grimacing masks. Nooses, symbols of their own mortality, were hung around their necks. They led the weeping figure towards the squalid structure that passed for the settlement's church, its threshold decorated by ancient braziers that spewed more smoke than flame.

Between them, the pyre was waiting.

As they bound the still weeping woman to the stake, a noise pierced the murmur of the crowd – the plaintive cry from somewhere in the press of bodies of a juve witnessing the end of their childhood. The sound was an irritant, unbecoming to so sombre a ceremony.

For a moment his gaze strayed to the chamber mounted below the Eternal Flame.

It was tempting to open it just a crack, offer the crowd a taste of true power. But no, he had lingered here too long. He could see it in the settlers; red veins creeping into the whites of eyes, fingers twitching in repressed fury. There was no gain in fanning it further.

One of the settlers was dragging the children away, their sobs growing more distant. It was gratifying to know at least someone in the cesspit had a sense of propriety. Pureburn lowered himself back onto the throne, wincing slightly. His back ached and his legs were stiff, his true penance for passage downhive. But he bore the pain with pride for, despite the discomfort and filth, it was important work. As one of the masked executioners raised the smouldering torch, he surveyed the crowd. Despite their anger and fear, most bore expressions of resignation. None would dare steal from him again. This woman's death would guarantee it.

As the accused's screams were swallowed by the roaring flames, Lord Pureburn glanced to the data-slate imbedded in the dais, eyes narrowing as he reviewed recent acquisitions and profit margins. He frowned, his good humour spoiled. There were leaks everywhere, each drop of wasted promethium draining his profits. Despite his tireless efforts in hunting down thieves and fraudsters he was beginning to suspect his real enemy was the infrastructure. The network of promethium pipes was a thousand-score years old, and beyond dilapidated. But any work aside from a patch job would involve shutting down distribution across several sectors. The loss of revenue would be significant, but the greater risk was his customers seeking alternative suppliers. Then again, if he did nothing, his holdings would slowly bleed dry. The Pureburn family, perhaps the eldest of the Mercator Pyros, would vanish into history. It was a chilling thought.

The screams had quietened now, the purifying flames concluding their work. The crowd were dispersing, encouraged by the Cawdor missionaries. But one of the church elders was approaching him. He offered a short bow, his face half hidden by a snarling mask but his eyes visible, if blank besides a fanatic's zeal. His mouth split open, unveiling a motley assortment of broken teeth. Lord Pureburn nodded in response and, through tremendous force of will, did not react to the man's odour.

'Pardon, milord,' the masked man said, bobbing his head once again for good measure, 'but, by the God-Emperor's grace, we have received a message through the church's vox-channel. They asked me to convey it to you personally, milord.'

'Indeed,' said Pureburn. 'And the message is?'

'Periculus has risen.'

Lord Pureburn stared down at him. The man shuffled from one foot to the other.

'Milord?'

'I need to use that vox-channel. Now!' Lord Pureburn barked, tapping a sequence across his data-slab. As one, his conclave snapped into focus, his Cynder guard converging on the dais. Lord Pureburn rose from his throne to address them.

'Our Periculus has been found. I need to know if a claim has been made upon it. Are the factorums still functional? Has the Mercator Sanguis been tasked with providing hive serfs? This information must be mine within two hours. Go!'

He watched, detached, as the conclave scurried to carry out his commands. It did not seem possible that this relic had been uncovered just when he needed it most. Then again, the Cawdor simpletons lacked the intellect to lie or deceive,

2

The dying thunder told Sol they'd reached the *Oculus Tempestatis* – the dead space at the perma-storm's centre, where clouds softened and wind abated. Their destination lay in the eye of the storm, even as the tempest tore a path across the Wastes. For, like the storm, their destination was never at rest.

From within the craft it was impossible to grasp the scale of the structure – a mile-long spike of flex-steel, bristling with lightning-lures and suspended on eight magnetic pulsars powerful enough to support its vast bulk. He could feel them drawing closer from the tingling in his arm, for the station drank deep of the power syphoned from the perma-storm. The Council of Light, a loose alliance of the Mercator Lux's most esoteric Guilders, had designated it the *Fulgurmessis*, the heart of the storm. But to most the vast metal spike was simply referred to as the Needle.

The craft decelerated, the automated landing systems supplanting the oarsman. Sol glanced at Anguis. She seemed lost in thought, though equally she may have been conversing with her team, or for that matter passing the time playing a memory game; he had no way of knowing.

The craft slowed one final time, juddering slightly as it docked.

'We have arrived,' Sol said. Anguis raised her head, smiling her half-smile.

'Is there to be a formal reception?' she asked. 'Drinks and canapés?'

'Perhaps later,' Sol replied as he unfastened his flight harness. 'For now, I would expect an armed squad of Shock Guard to greet us. If they detect a hint of insurrection the response will be terminal.'

'Insurrection?' Anguis frowned, rising to her feet. 'Are we not your honoured guests? I thought you had status here. Were you not the Light-touched? A child birthed by the lightning itself?'

Sol glared at her. Her expression held every indication of innocence.

'That is a name I neither chose nor employ.'

'It seems a grand title.'

'It's meaningless and a testimony to the mindlessness of petty superstition. Not every random event is auspicious, nor every accident a part of the God-Emperor's divine plan. This is a place founded on science and reason – I hope you and your team can appreciate that.'

'Naturally,' she said as the other Delaques rose beside her. 'Though, in the spirit of science and reason, can I ask why your fellow Guilders are so desperate to shoot us on sight?'

'Because you are the first outsiders who have been permitted to board the Needle,' he replied, striding towards the exit hatch. 'There are things here that are not for outside eyes.'

'We can hold our tongues,' she said, smiling. 'There are reasons we are known as the House of Secrets.'

Sol glanced at her, his finger poised by the door-release panel. There was no hint of irony on her face, no hint of anything in fact. She remained as unreadable as always. He swallowed his frustration. Despite House Delaque's well-earned reputation for duplicity and espionage, his relationship with Anguis was long-established and, at least until now, mutually beneficial.

Did he trust her? No. But he trusted no one.

'Wait two beats before following,' he said. 'Move slowly and keep your hands visible at all times.'

'Of course,' she said, raising her hands, her team mirroring the gesture. 'We enter meek and unarmed.'

Sol looked her up and down. 'That would be more reassuring if I didn't know that your longcoat is bristling with concealed weapons and assassin's tools.'

She frowned, tilting her head.

'You want me out of my longcoat, then?' she said. 'Is now really the best time for that conversation?'

He sighed heavily, and almost kept a smile from his face.

'Try not to look threatening,' he said, reaching into his coat and withdrawing a photo-visor of unusual design, the standard bar supplanted with two rounded copper discs with blackened lenses. They clicked snugly into place over his eyes. He glanced back to Anguis.

'I'd also recalibrate your ocular implants,' he said, pressing the door release. 'It will be bright.'

Light flooded the cabin. Even with precautions in place it was blinding, like staring into the sun. Through the glare he made out the plasteel hangar, polished a silvered-white, every inch of its walls and floor gleaming. The effect was marred only by the hangar's functional equipment; the docking rig and loading units lacked the same polished finish, appearing unsightly against the silver veneer.

Then, of course, there was the welcome committee.

Before him stood a ten-man squad of Shock Guard, each clad in full carapace armour adorned with the crossed lightning symbol of the Mercator Lux. Each carried a hotshot lasgun. The weapons were currently trained downwards, but given the faint hum emanating from their power packs Sol was confident they were fully charged and primed to fire.

Behind the armoured wall stood the Needle's de facto rulers – the Council of Light as they styled themselves. Two of the three stood stiffly in their formal attire, ceremonial shock-staves clasped in their hands. Perhaps they wished to appear intimidating. Their eyes were uncovered, seemingly untroubled by the blazing light. Beside them, the third figure wore technicians overalls overlaid by a once-white apron. His eyes were shielded by a half-hood and a bulky set of goggles.

Sol descended the steps, the leader of the trio advancing to meet him, his shock-stave supporting his weight, two of the Shock Guard flanking him. As they drew closer Sol could finally make out Lord Severior's face. The older man looked frail, ill-fitting robes suggesting he had lost weight. But his eyes were as sharp as ever – the irises crystal blue, the pupils constricted to the diameter of a pinprick.

'His Light Binds All Shadow,' Severior said, his voice devoid of expression as he delivered the customary greeting. 'Welcome home, Light-touched.'

He crossed his wrists in greeting and Sol returned the gesture. Unnecessary physical contact was avoided by Guilders of the Mercator Lux, where a touch could prove fatal.

'From Darkness We Ascend,' Sol replied, his bow little more

than a nod. 'As agreed, I have secured the services of our Delaque allies for the review of our security protocols.'

Severior peered at the Delaques from over his glasses, as though seeing them for the first time. They certainly stood out, their black greatcoats like stains against the polished plasteel. Sol would have enjoyed their discomfort if any of it registered on their impassive faces.

'"Agreed" is a strong word,' Severior murmured, before addressing the group. 'Who speaks for you?'

'I do, my lord,' Anguis said, stepping forward and bowing her head with reverence. 'My name is Anguis, and we are honoured to be standing on the legendary Fulgurmessis.'

'I wish I could feel the same,' Severior replied coldly. 'If I had my way this enterprise would not take place. But I was outvoted, so here we find ourselves. As guests of the Mercator Lux, I am obligated to ask the God-Emperor to bless you with His light. Note that, whilst the Council of Light has permitted you limited access to this great facility, you are to do as you are told. You go nowhere without an escort. You are not permitted in secure areas or to attend any council meetings. Any attempt to circumvent these restrictions will result in immolation. Do you understand?'

Anguis bowed again. 'Of course, my lord. We thank you for your hospitality.'

'Then I will waste no further time on this matter. Lord Adūlator will oversee the transfer of the cargo. The Council of Light is meeting in two hours. I suggest, Light-touched, that you take the opportunity to refresh yourself and put on something more appropriate. There are urgent matters that may require your attention.'

He turned away without another word, departing flanked by Shock Guard as Lord Adūlator approached. He too had the same pupil-less eyes, his irises bleached a faded copper. He bowed to Sol and Anguis, his arms crossed in greeting. Sol did not return the gesture.

'Lord Sol,' Adūlator said, as the craft's rear doors opened. 'Ambassador Anguis? We have prepared a facility as per the specifications you kindly provided. I do hope it meets your requirements.'

'As do I,' Anguis replied. 'I would prefer the contents of my skull remain within the confines of my cranium.'

Adūlator gave a nervous laugh but Sol had already pushed past him, his gaze fixed on the third man. His eyes were still hidden by the half-hood, but his smile was unfettered.

'Doctor Caute,' Sol said, clasping the older man's wrist. 'You are looking well.'

'That's your diagnosis,' the doctor sighed. 'If you knew how my knees felt you'd revise it.'

'We all have our aches and pains. I still suspect you will outlive us all.'

'I will certainly outlive you unless you start sticking to your maintenance schedule,' the doctor replied. He took hold of Sol's unresisting hand, tracing the faint silver lines of the neurone circuits imbedded beneath the skin. 'Does it still carry a decent charge?' he asked, not looking up.

'It did the last time I used it.'

'And the syphon?'

'Sated during the flight. It all seems to be working perfectly.'

'I still want to run full diagnostics,' the doctor murmured. 'You will be visiting the medical bay anyway to attend to the... other matter.'

There was a note of reproach in his voice, but Sol chose to ignore it. He glanced back to the vessel, where the bay doors to the cargo hold were slowly opening. Inside was a simple cylinder of blackened flex-steel, the height of a tall man and unadorned save for the dual serpent and dagger symbol of House Delaque. It was a shadow against the light of the Needle, its very presence somehow darkening the hangar.

As a shuffling team of servitors mindlessly secured the cylinder to a suspended mag-platform, Sol felt a sickly sensation in his gut and the awful sense that someone was whispering just behind his ear. He shook his head, his gaze briefly meeting that of Anguis, who watched intently. He turned his eyes back to Doctor Caute, who was staring at the agents.

'You've brought snakes into our midst,' he murmured. 'Is it worth the risk?'

Sol did not answer.

If not for the urgency of his mission, Lord Pureburn might have considered the settlement's inner chapel almost peaceful. The Cawdor faithful had scrubbed the worst of the rust from the ironwork, and the rats were respectful enough to stay out of sight. What he could only assume was the altar was lit by the soft glow of spluttering candles.

He took a step closer, examining the relics laid with reverence upon it. Bone prayer beads hung from a rusted nail, the ossein stained a sickly yellow. Beneath them was a scrap torn from a faded painting, the image indecipherable. A lump of bronze may once have held a saint relief, but now more closely resembled the victim of an acid-storm. To him they were curiosities at best, but the Cawdor faithful revered such pitiful trinkets as relics of the God-Emperor, and would sift the most disgusting filth of the underhive for but one such bauble.

Lord Pureburn shook his head, turning his back on the makeshift altar, his gaze drawn to the main doors and the light spilling between their seams. Beyond lay his dais and the iridescent light of the Eternal Flame. Unlike the cheap candles or aged braziers, his flame was smokeless and unwavering, shining with every appearance of divinity. Even the most dim-witted zealot could not deny it was a far more appropriate representation of the God-Emperor's holy will than this scattering of questionable relics.

He sighed, resting his weight against the altar. The deacon had assured him a secure vox-channel could be provided, but it felt an age since the altar-juve had scurried off in search of the priest. Perhaps the boy had stumbled upon the spent shell casings of a hero of the Imperium, or the blessed waste-paper retrieved from a cardinal's latrine.

He heard footsteps and straightened himself, smoothing his robes and adopting a well-rehearsed expression of seren-ity. From the chapel's side door the priest entered, escorted by the deacon and altar-juve. The holy man might have been difficult to distinguish from the unwashed masses of the congregation were it not for the candelabra mounted on his shoulders and headdress. The wax spitting from its can-dles did little to improve the appearance of his faded beige vestments. Like the rest of his House, he wore a mask that covered all but eyes and mouth, its crown adorned by seven silver skulls.

'My apologies, Lord Pureburn,' the clergyman puffed, bow-ing his head. Lord Pureburn waved his hand dismissively, a feigned smile settling upon his lips.

'No apologies necessary,' he said, bowing deeply. 'I am sure you were performing His work. Given the patience He shows all sinners, it would be churlish of me not to extend similar courtesies.'

'Very gracious, milord,' the priest said. 'There is a private vox-channel in my cell. It is used only by me and kept under lock and key. I will ensure you have full privacy. Please take all the time you need.'

'Thank you.' Lord Pureburn smiled through gritted teeth. The idiot considered a padlock adequate security for encrypted communication. But what choice was there? Every second was precious. If he did not seize Periculus, another would.

He intended to take his leave then, but something in the priest's manner stayed him. Even for a man clad in such squalid robes he looked uncomfortable. Judging from the dark patches beneath his arms he was sweating.

'May I be of further assistance?' Lord Pureburn asked.

'It is, I hope, a small thing, milord,' the priest replied. 'We oft tell the parable of the God-Emperor's pilgrimage to our planet, how He brought light to the dark and ended the tyranny of unbelief. With His words we knew the truth, and by a sweep of His flaming sword both heretic and witch were slain in the cause of righteousness.'

A frenetic quality was creeping into the priest's cadence. Lord Pureburn could see his eyes glaze, consumed by his rantings. Or was it something else? He glanced to the light spilling from beyond the church door, where the palanquin waited.

'That day an ember fell from His blessed blade,' the priest continued, following Lord Pureburn's gaze to the shimmering light. 'Since then the Pureburn family have preserved the divine spark.'

'You have an impressive knowledge of scripture,' Lord Pureburn said. 'It has been my family's blessing and penitence to preserve that sacred spark, and to bring light to the darkness of the hive.'

'I know, milord,' the priest said, bowing once more. 'The Church of Redemption believes in the power of fire to purify and cleanse, but also to bring light to the darkest places. Each candle in this room is a flicker of purity in a sea of filth. Only…'

'Only it is not the God-Emperor's flame.'

The priest nodded. 'Indeed not. I know I ask a great deal, but our congregation are the true faithful. We were eager to summon you when it emerged a heathen was stealing the blessed fuel of the God-Emperor. I do not wish to offend by asking too much, but I–'

'If I may,' Lord Pureburn said, laying his hand on the priest's arm, ignoring the clamminess of the fabric. 'You and your faithful administer to His flock, and there is no worthier cause. Please partake of His divine flames to guide them from corruption. Take what you need.'

Tears filled the priest's eyes.

'Bless you, milord,' he said, turning to the altar-juve who was already twitching with excitement. 'Go then, boy, and be quick – we have impeded too long Lord Pureburn's valuable time.'

'One moment,' Lord Pureburn said, addressing the urchin. 'You use a taper candle. Light that first and then use it to light the others. Do not climb on the dais, do not touch the crucible – neither are to be sullied by your hands. Do you understand?'

The boy nodded.

'You are certain? My Pyromagir is tasked with guarding it. He will not hesitate to chastise you.'

The boy nodded again before racing off. Both deacon and priest watched him sprint down the aisle, serene smiles just visible beneath their half-masks, whilst Lord Pureburn took the opportunity to wipe his hand on the relic-cloth adorning the altar.

'Bless you, milord. We will never forget this day.'

'The pleasure is mine,' Lord Pureburn replied, watching as the juve struggled against the door's weight as he dragged it open. 'Your son will make a fine preacher.'

'You have children of your own?'

Lord Pureburn was silent a moment. He watched the boy slowly approach his dais, trembling before the light of the Eternal Flame.

'I had a daughter,' he said softly. 'She was welcomed into the God-Emperor's embrace earlier than I would have wished.'

The priest stiffened. 'Forgive me, milord. It was not my place.'

'It is no matter.' Pureburn shrugged. 'She gifted me a granddaughter before passing. She is very much like her mother. The girl is the light in my life.'

'I am glad,' said the priest, visibly relieved. 'Do you see her often?'

'She is always with me,' Lord Pureburn said, intent on the shimmering flame.

3

Virae the Unbroken, Chain Lord of the Mercator Sanguis, watched the two pit fighters circling. Though unarmed, each was still a deadly combatant, their hulking frames gene-forged from potent elixirs and bio-augments. Despite this they moved with grace, always balanced, footwork faultless. That was the key to combat. Her younger recruits always assumed that massive biceps and an iron jaw made them unbeatable. But they soon learnt otherwise. In most cases they only had to be knocked on their arse a couple of times, though it had been five in Gash's case.

She smiled inwardly at the memory, though a scowl lingered on her face.

Block, the veteran, surprised her by making the first move, throwing a quick jab with the same force as a lesser man swinging a hammer. Gash swayed, the blow glancing from his cheek, before delivering a thunderous counter. But he was too eager, falling for Block's feint. The older man stepped aside from the blow, seizing his opponent by elbow and wrist. Before Gash could react, Block had manhandled him to the floor, twisting his arm behind his back. Gash fought it, the tendons in his neck straining like steel cables. His arm was actually beginning to move as he pushed back against the surprised Block, but the veteran redoubled his efforts, both men unwilling to yield. In a few more seconds the bone would break.

'Enough,' Virae roared, stamping her chainglaive's haft on the arena floor. Despite the bloodlust, both yielded, Block releasing his hold as Gash rose to his feet, flexing his elbow and trying to get blood flowing into his fingers. He was glaring at her, angry but trying his best to hide it. Block held out his hand, and after a moment's hesitation the younger man briefly clasped it before turning away, still flexing his shoulder.

'Good work, both of you,' she said, voice still stern. 'Take a couple of laps to stretch your muscles. Get something to drink. The Guild of Thirst just resupplied us.'

'Yeah?' Block said. 'Fresh?'

'Couldn't even taste the urine,' she lied.

The older man nodded, stepping from the fighting circle, but Gash remained behind. She strode over to him, chainglaive held one-handed, the weight resting over her shoulder. He still appeared to be nursing his injury, flexing his elbow back and forth.

'Do you need that looked at?' she asked, knowing the answer. Gash murmured something, half turning away, refusing to meet her gaze. It was almost comical; the man's mohawk comprised of iron spikes bolted directly into his skull, yet here he was, pouting like a juve.

Her foot lashed out, striking his backside and sending him sprawling.

He rose quickly, fists clenched, bellowing with fury, injury forgotten. Virae stood more than six feet tall, but he still towered over her. She held her ground, weapon still slung casually across her shoulder.

'Arm all right then?' she asked, shifting her stance ever so slightly. She trusted Gash for the most part, but such extensive gene-augmentation had numerous side effects, uncontrolled stimm-rage being the most common. It was conceivable she might have to put him down. But he was fighting against it, his breath shallow rasps as he sought control. He closed his eyes, and she saw the tension ebb from his body. It made her proud. Fighting came naturally to most underhivers; control was a warrior's true challenge.

He opened his eyes, forcing a smile that soon became genuine. With his vast frame it was easy to forget he was barely older than a juve, having seen less than twenty cycles. But when the bloodlust faded there was an innocence to him, almost a sweetness if she ignored the bionic jaw that comprised the lower half of his maw.

'Yeah, I'm fine,' he grunted, slightly embarrassed. 'I could have taken him though.'

'He'd have broken your arm.'

'Exactly,' Gash said. 'That would have let me slip from the hold. Then I'd have had him.'

'That a fact?' she said. 'What was your plan?'

'Plan?' he spat. 'Don't need a plan. I'd have just hooked him until he gave up or passed out.'

'And all it would cost you is an arm.'

'I'd heal quick enough.'

'But is it worth breaking it in the first place?' she asked,

gesturing to the arena with her chainglaive. 'This is training – it ain't worth getting hurt over. If this was a real fight,
if you were losing and your life was on the line, then you
might need to make that sort of sacrifice, just to survive.
But sparring against Block? Unarmed? What do you have
to prove?'

'Nothing,' he said with a shrug. 'Except who the better
man is.'

'That's easy. I'm better than either of you.'

Gash grinned, an odd expression when the lower half of
his face was gleaming chrome.

'Doubt it,' he said. 'I've heard the stories of Virae the Unbroken – the slave who became a Chain Lord, the pit fighter who
never lost a battle. But that was a long time ago. Actually stepping into the ring? After so long? I'm not sure an old lady like
you could keep up.'

He might have been leering. It was hard to tell with the jaw.

'I seem to recall that when you first showed up here I
knocked you on your arse,' she said, unslinging the chainglaive
from her shoulder and slotting it into the fighting pit's already
overburdened weapons rack.

He stepped closer, squaring up to her, her face inches from
his chest. His sweat smelt slightly metallic, a side effect of
the gland-implants.

'You did,' he said. 'But that was back then. You've taught
me a lot since. I got real good technique now.'

'Is that right?' she replied. 'Because from what I've seen
you rely on muscle over finesse. Your technique is sloppy.
And you lack stamina.'

The remark was well chosen. She could see his shoulders
stiffen, the anger rising. No doubt his modified biology was
already flooding his blood with stimms and pain-suppressors.

He roared like a beast, consumed by rage, raising one of his massive fists to strike.

Virae's elbow connected below his sternum, the shot perfectly placed to drive the air from his lungs. He staggered at the impact, almost righting himself until her foot struck him in the side of the knee. As the leg buckled she was already behind him, left arm hooked around his neck, hand clutching her right bicep as she drove her elbow into his shoulder, her weight forcing him to his knees. He clutched weakly at her, but she had already taken most of his breath and was now choking the rest from him. She held a few seconds, until she could feel he'd begun to go limp, then released the hold, stepping away and allowing him to recover his breath. She too was breathing hard, her shoulders burning from the effort. Technique or not, restraining the man was still like wrestling an ambull.

'You've learned a lot,' she said between gasps. 'But there is plenty more I can teach you.'

He was already recovering, rising to his knee. He looked at her, his gaze free of anger or resentment, just respect.

'We still… talking about… fighting?' he asked, every word a struggle.

She smiled. Not *just* respect then.

'Go cool down, idiot,' she said, offering a hand. He took it and rose, his other hand still clutched to his chest.

'Cooling down isn't… how I get… better than you,' he persisted.

'Go and rest,' she said, trying and failing to adopt a stern tone. 'I have a thousand things to do today and, as you've pointed out, I'm not a young woman any more. I doubt very much I'll have the energy to teach you anything.'

'You… lack stamina?'

'Get going,' she laughed, retrieving her blade from the

weapons rack. 'And next time you step up to me you better
know what you're doing. Otherwise I'm minded to take my
chainglaive and find out whether you'd focus better gelded.'

He laughed, rising and shuffling from the arena, favouring his knee. She wondered if she had struck it too hard. She
lacked the genetic augmentation common in many fighters. It was difficult to gauge how much pressure to apply to
incapacitate rather than injure. She would check on him later,
make sure the doc had looked over the injury.

'Milady?'

Virae turned at the sound. Behind her stood a scrawny figure, his eyes sunken and downcast. The juve's clothes were
ill-fitting tatters, most likely scavenged from the dead, but
the data-slab clenched to his chest was ornate, carrying the
symbol of the Mercator Pyros.

A Dome Runner then, selling his knowledge of hidden
paths in exchange for a few credits. The fact that he had not
simply sold the data-slab and disappeared suggested either
unusual loyalty, or the certainty that wherever he went his
employer would find him.

'You lookin' for me?' she asked.

'I... I think so. You are... you're Virae the Unbroken?' the
boy stammered. On another day she might have felt sorry
for him, but her shoulder still ached from besting Gash, and
she did not have time to squander.

'That's me. Do you have a message, or did you just come
to sell yourself to the pits?'

His eyes widened.

'No, I... please, mistress, I bring word from Lord Pureburn
of the Fire Guild.'

She swore under her breath. 'What does that sour-faced
old gak want?'

'Please, mistress, I don't know. I only–'

'Give it here, boy,' she snapped, snatching the data-slate and pressing her thumb to the gene-seal. The display flared into life, the message unnecessarily formal and courteous whilst still feeling somehow like a crafted insult. She frowned as she read, realisation slowly dawning.

'Helmawr's balls,' she whispered. 'This many serfs? In a matter of days? What is that man thinking?'

'Milady?' the boy asked, frowning.

'Nothing to do with you,' she said, flicking a cred in his direction. 'Get lost and then get even more lost. This is not a place you wish to be right now, not if you don't belong to a House or Guild.'

'Why?'

'Because Lord Pureburn calls for workers,' she sighed, 'which means it is time to break out the chains.'

The cell was tiny, formed of half a dozen storage crates, disassembled then welded into walls and a ceiling. The metalwork was crude, the dividing lines clearly visible. Lord Pureburn had to stoop as he entered, taking a seat on the room's only chair. Before him lay a small altar, the trinkets as pitiful as the relics of the church.

But the vox-unit was surprisingly sophisticated, barely touched by dirt or corrosion. Perhaps someone more astute than the simpering priest was responsible for its installation. The Pureburns' connections to House Cawdor dated back generations, and he was all too familiar with the zealots. Most would barely qualify as human, closer to rats. They were satisfied with a life spent clawing through refuse and incinerating anyone deemed less pious. But there were some sharp minds amongst them, those who realised that faith

was merely a tool to steer mankind's baser impulses into
something productive. They were the dangerous ones. He
did not like the idea that such a mind was responsible for
installing the vox-unit. But he had no time to seek an alternative means of communication.

There was a slight tremble in his fingers as he tapped the
keys, inputting the sixty-seven characters required to access the
encrypted channel. He had dared not risk recording it on parchment or data-slate; the consequences of accidental interception
did not bear thinking about. He had therefore employed a
mnemonic system based on the God-Emperor's Tarot: The Blind
Seer, The Ragged Fool, The Great Eye. One by one he inputted
the hexographic codes, and the machine slowly hummed to
life. Though the vox-unit had a display, no image was projected.
There was only a voice. It sounded entirely synthetic.

'Yes?' was all it said.

'Periculus.'

'Ah,' the voice replied. 'Yes. The rediscovery was surprising,
but it is known to us. Is there something else?'

'There may still be secrets buried there of great value.'

'We have considered this. We believe it constitutes an
unnecessary risk.'

There was no tone to read nor cadence to consider, but
Lord Pureburn knew the threat implicit in the words. His
co-conspirator could very well have the resources to ensure
Periculus disappeared just as suddenly as it had been
rediscovered.

'Or it may provide an opportunity,' Pureburn ventured,
mouth suddenly dry. He could not appear too eager. If his
associates discerned his desperation they would cut ties. And
if they discovered the reason behind it, they would do whatever they could to see him dead.

'This has also been considered,' the voice replied. 'A decision has not yet been made.'

Pureburn smiled. Then he was not too late.

'Perhaps it would be prudent to secure a stake in the dome for now?' he said. 'In case sudden action is required?'

'Perhaps. You have the means?'

'Periculus' fall does not nullify my Guild's contract. The Pureburns once provided Periculus power and will do so again. I will stake my claim and enforce it as required.'

'And the production facilities? Serfs? Supplies?'

'I have already approached contacts in the Mercator Sanguis and the Mercator Pallidus. The hive workers and their rations can arrive within days. If I provide both then none will question my claim. My only concern would be if a significant player became involved. The situation may then become volatile.'

There was silence for a moment.

'Our involvement cannot be known.'

'I understand that.'

'But this is not to say measures cannot be taken. Several Clan Houses and Guilds could be discouraged from involving themselves on anything more than a local level.'

'That would be helpful,' Lord Pureburn said. 'The only remaining concern is if Planetary Governor Helmawr became involved.'

'That is not a name you speak aloud,' the voice replied. Its tone was still flat and synthetic, but somehow he sensed the anger and fear behind the words.

'Forgive me, but any alias I employed would quickly prove transparent.'

'Then why speak at all?'

'Because if our planetary governor involves himself

personally the enterprise is over. I would, of course, offer no objection to such an action – ultimately he rules and owns all, as is his right. It would simply be prudent to know his intentions, and whether pursuing this could prove a waste of resources.'

There was another pause. He was used to this, for he knew not who was listening, or how many views would need to be considered before a response was uttered.

It took longer than usual. They must be choosing their words carefully. Finally, the voice responded.

'Our esteemed planetary governor is occupied ensuring his feudal obligations in the holy name of the God-Emperor,' it said, as though reciting a script. 'He does not have the time for a matter as trivial as the rediscovery of a lost dome.'

Pureburn raised an eyebrow at the reply. He could not tell if this meant that interplanetary matters were occupying Helmawr's full attention, or if news of the rediscovery had so far been kept from him.

Not that it mattered.

'Then should I make haste?'

'For now,' the voice replied. 'We have not yet decided the best course of action, but there is a consensus that it would be preferable to secure the site than risk another securing it. Speak to us when you are in Periculus. Farewell until then.'

The vox-unit fell silent. Lord Pureburn leant back in his seat, reaching into his robes for a cloth and dabbing at his brow. He took a deep breath, trying to ease the tension from his shoulders. For a man so used to being master of his own destiny it was galling to beg for scraps from another's table. But that was the reality. His associates belonged to the House Catallus, one of the seven noble houses that were second only to Lord Helmawr himself. Even he, patriarch of the Pureburn Guild, could not compete with their power.

He smiled. At least not yet.

4

Doctor Caute studied the medi-scanner, brow furrowed, absently scratching at the back of his head.

Sol watched him from the examination chair. He was stripped to the waist, an array of servo-plugs imbedded in his arm. It was painful but familiar, a necessary price for doing business. Many of his peers in the Mercator Lux had bionic implants that granted some degree of mastery over electrical systems. But they were crude things, nothing like the neurone circuits mapped along his nervous system. They were barely visible beneath his sun-darkened skin, silver tattoos etched in blue forming a stylised grid pattern along his arm. Both tool and weapon, the grafts were capable of delivering a calibrated current or lethal charge. At least that was the theory.

'You want the good news?' Caute asked.

Sol glanced up, expectant.

'If we strip out the conductives and perform a full rewire we can save most of the neurone circuits.'

'That does not sound like good news.'

'It's all burned out,' the doctor signed, nodding to the schematics displayed on the medi-unit. 'There is barely a connection at the elbow joint. One massive surge and you will lose it completely. I don't need to tell you how unpleasant the feedback would feel. Though, if it's any consolation, you wouldn't feel it for long.'

Sol glanced at his hand. He tensed his wrist, feeling the surge flow through him, the hairs on his arm standing on end. He touched his fingers together and a spark leapt between them.

'It feels fine,' he said. Doctor Caute shook his head.

'Yes, it's fine for lighting a gas-heater,' he said. 'But anything more than that and your forearm will be on the far side of the room. What did you do to it?'

'I had to direct the current through a shock-stave.'

The doctor glared at him. 'Had to?'

'If I wanted to keep breathing.'

'Running current against current? No wonder it's damaged.'

'Can we repair it?'

'You want my advice?' Caute said. 'Strip it all out. We can start over with something simple. A bionic arm with a contact-charge unit would deliver far more–'

'We build on what we have. Continue to refine the process.'

'And risk paralysis or worse?' Caute sighed. 'Our work is all experimental, bordering on tech-heresy.'

'We have the schematics.'

'We have bastardised some poorly transcribed notes obtained from the Emperor knows where,' the doctor said. 'I don't even understand what a corpuscarii is, let alone how to emulate one.'

Sol could still recall his excitement at discovering the

schematics in a data-vault in the depths of the underhive. The image showed a body surgically altered into a conduit for something known as the Motive Force, the energy linking all things. It had been fascinating reading, and the early results were promising. But he could not pretend to understand half of what was described, and it was becoming apparent that the process was not as straightforward as he had hoped.

'We're not trying to squeeze a few more volts from a corroded circuit board,' Caute sighed. 'This is something that interfaces with your mind and nervous system in ways I don't understand. A bionic limb would hold a greater charge and be far safer. It would–'

'This is not about finding a more efficient means of electrocuting people,' Sol snapped. 'This is about understanding. This Motive Force, this energy that links everything. If we master it, truly understand the flow between flesh and machine, it will change everything. That alone is worth the risk.'

The older man shook his head. 'Your mother used to speak this way.'

'I wish I'd had the chance to converse with her.'

The old man stiffened at Sol's words. He sighed.

'Forgive me, I spoke out of turn. I just do not wish for you to end up the same way – dying needlessly over an experiment that was neither sanctioned nor required.'

Sol stared at him. The older man looked away.

'She died because we are satisfied with mediocrity and consider needless deaths and suffering as necessities for our way of life,' Sol replied coldly. 'Do we mourn that our ineptitude claims a soul? No, we attribute the loss to actions of forces beyond our ken. We venerate the miraculous survival of a child instead of asking why our society is built on pointless deaths.'

Sol rose, ripping clear the servo-plugs from his forearm. He could tell the doctor was watching him but kept his head down.

The older man sighed. 'I did not wish to upset you.'

'I'm not upset.'

'My point, Sol, is that it was her curiosity that killed her. Ever pushing her too far, too fast.'

Sol glared at him.

'I checked her hypothesis. The experiment didn't kill her. It was poor maintenance on the lightning-lures. She never should have been struck, not if her superiors had done their job.'

'That's always a risk,' the doctor said. 'Our lives are connected. One tiny soldering error and the surge could bring this whole place down. How do you know I will be successful patching your neurone circuits?'

'Because you are a skilled doctor,' Sol replied, slipping his shirt over his shoulders. 'You cut me from the womb, brought breath to my lungs, and have kept me alive since. You have never failed me.'

'The same could be said of anyone, right up until the point they do fail you. Then what?'

'We do what we can until we cannot,' Sol said. 'What more is there?'

'Well, on that cheerful note, would you like to see your patient?'

Sol rose, following the doctor across the medical bay. It was empty for the most part, only running at capacity when there had been an incident – a storm-surge, or sustained magnetic pulse. But the far bed was occupied. As Sol watched, the doctor began checking the patient, cursing under his breath as he examined the dressings and reviewed the medi-unit's prognosis.

'Any change?'

'Still alive,' the doctor said. 'Still unconscious. Still suffering from burns across ninety per cent of his body. Do you know the buckles on his coat actually melted? Fused into the flesh. I haven't even tried to get them out. Even if he survived the procedure, what would be the point?'

'Is anyone else aware I brought him here?'

'No. One man in bandages is as interesting as another.'

'Any hope of recovery?'

'Not here. *Maybe* in the upper hive something could be done – rejuvenat treatment, or extensive transplant surgery – but even then I think his mind is gone. I will say it again, let me give him something strong enough to take away his pain. Permanently.'

'You think he suffers?'

'I don't have a damn clue,' Caute replied, glaring at Sol. 'But I know keeping him alive ain't right. This is more than physical pain.'

Sol raised an eyebrow. The doctor glared back at him sourly.

'I've been doing this a while,' he said. 'I've seen much in that time. Injuries to the body can be horrific but are simple to diagnose. But there are soul-blights, sicknesses that wither from within with no discernible cause.'

'His burns would suggest a straightforward diagnosis.'

'And his refusal to awaken would suggest otherwise. Something latched onto his soul, or perhaps it burned along with his flesh. Whatever led this man to this fate, it is not right for him to suffer further. Let the God-Emperor claim or damn him, but just let him go.'

'I have no interest in prolonging his suffering. But he has information I need.'

'What could he possibly know?'

'What killed him,' Sol said. 'His body was scraped from the plains of Salvation after the massacre. Two gangs warring over a power-tap, until Lord Pureburn intervened. All that was left was this man and ashes.'

'Pureburn was within his rights.'

'To kill them? Yes, he was,' Sol said, nodding. 'But how did he do it? No conventional flamer can do that sort of damage. No weapon I know burns so clean and hot. Perhaps he carries xenos weaponry, or forbidden heretek. If Lord Pureburn has a secret weapon, I want to know, particularly if he would prefer that I did not. The Delaques are specialists with this sort of thing. They will glean the truth. If we are unsuccessful then you may euthanise him.'

'How kind, young lord.'

'I'm sorry.'

'As am I,' the doctor sighed. 'I know you have your reasons. But this does not sit well with me. Especially not with the cloaks you've brought along.'

'You can trust the Delaques,' Sol heard himself say, before meeting the older man's quizzical gaze. He smiled despite himself. 'Fine,' Sol sighed, 'you can't trust them. But I trust their motives. They are expanding certain operations in Hive Primus. They need power and, more importantly, someone who will provide it without asking too many questions.'

'Questions are important.'

'Indeed. Hence our unfortunate friend here. He has answers.'

'Do you want me there for the interrogation?'

'No. You risked enough. Better you are far away with a robust alibi.'

'And you had best be prepared if it goes wrong,' the doctor

replied. 'Lord Severior is no friend of yours. He tolerates you because you understand how this place works better than anyone. But there comes a point when the disruption caused by your presence outweighs the benefit. Then maybe your staticshower suffers a power surge, or the next time you depart the Needle the shuttle's conversion field malfunctions. It's hard enough to keep anyone alive on this place, even without foul play. Your mother knew all about that.'

The words cut. They were meant to. Sol took a deep breath, calming himself.

'There are fewer accidents now,' he said.

'And fewer still if you actually implemented some of the ideas you come up with instead of frittering your time trying to sell lumens to underhivers who have barely mastered the candle.'

'Did you know those hives should be self-sufficient?' Sol replied. 'The heat sink at their centre, if properly maintained, could provide enough geothermal power to run most systems. But the network is fractured, generators commandeered by rival clans in constant conflict. So the lower hive is dark and relies on charlatans like Lord Pureburn, and nothing gets better because doing so would cut into profit margins. So the world is dark and cold, because that makes the more money.'

He glanced at Doctor Caute before his gaze shifted to the heavily bandaged patient.

'Whatever this man saw may hold the key to breaking that stranglehold.'

'Maybe,' Caute said. 'But how do you peer into the mind of a near-dead man? More to the point, what would you see?'

Virae kept her gaze fixed ahead as the procession of serfs shuffled past. Her armour gleamed a cold bronze, the shoulder guards adorned with the symbol of an unbroken chain. Her iron-grey hair was held in place by a helm shaped like a crown. Though chipped and worn, all who saw it knew the story: the slave who had risen to Chain Lord, proof that even the lowest could ascend had they the will. Perhaps some found hope in the tale. For most it was merely proof of Helmawr's Law; the strong clawed a path to power over the corpses of the weak.

The hive-serfs' route was lined by stony-faced Shaklemen, clasping shock-staves and harpoon launchers, vigilant against any hint of insurrection. Beside Virae, Elle, her data-stition, was logging their passing. She held a data-slate, but only from habit. The tally was logged by the cogitator implanted in her skull. It had cost Virae a fortune, and was already outdated, but the augmentation paid for itself a thousand-fold. Elle, who might once have struggled to count her own legs, was now able to process the vast streams of information required for transporting the serfs.

But this might be beyond even her enhanced cortex. Virae had never seen so many in one shipment. Her preference was for smaller groups, where she could assess individuals. There were always some more capable than others, or better suited to certain roles. But this recruitment drive was like trawling the sump; anyone without affinity to House or Guild would be detained and shipped, irrespective of aptitude or competence. They were condemned to toil their remaining days as unskilled labour in forges or Corpse Grinder abattoirs. It was Helmawr's Law, neither hers to endorse or refute.

Still, she kept her gaze level as they passed, and avoided their faces.

'We are at seventy-two per cent capacity,' Elle murmured, her voice shifting into a disconcerting monotone, as though the cogitator spoke for her. 'Supplies are tight but sufficient – they will be hungry by the time we reach Periculus. But there are insufficient Shaklemen. If they were to rise up...'

'They won't. The real concern is meeting the quota.'

'Pickings are slim,' Elle sighed. 'We've trawled from the outskirts of Hive City to the depths of Hope's End. Only so many places we can look if we want to get to Periculus and meet our deadline.'

'We are supposed to be there in a matter of days,' Virae said. 'Are there more places for us to conscript along the way?'

'Given the terrain, conditions, and probability of casualties I don't anticipate increasing our numbers by more than three per cent.'

Virae swore, her gaze falling to the line of serfs. Most were condemned by birth as chattel for their betters. They bore their condition as best they could, trudging, heads bowed, inured to the hardship of the march. If fed and housed they were compliant enough.

But not all were born to the life. Some had shunned their House, or been shunned by it. Others were outsiders who saw such structures as anathema. Many would be broken by whip and chain, but many more would plot their escape, seeing any sign of weakness as an opportunity to strike.

She saw few threats here. The last dregs were passing, led by an old man as haggard as any plague zombie. Still, he shuffled on precariously, driven more by habit than will. Behind him a girl, barely older than the Dome Runner had been, wept as she staggered on. Between sobs she pleaded for clemency, that she had a House and should not be taken. The nearest Shakleman stepped forward, cuffing her about the face. She fell, stunned and silenced.

'Once we're done I need to speak to that Shakleman,' Virae

murmured, watching as the old man helped the girl to her feet with trembling arms.

'When you say "speak"?' Elle murmured, fingers dancing across the data-slate.

'Just speak. For now,' Virae said. 'Everyone gets a warning. No need for physical chastisement just yet.'

'Striking prisoners is not uncommon.'

'Perhaps, but not when you work for me,' Virae replied, still intent on the procession. 'You need to stamp out a rebellion? Break as many teeth as you want. But that girl was probably dragged away from her home and has no idea what awaits her. Crying is normal. Better she does it now and gets the worst out of her system rather than anger her new owner. Did her batch come from uphive?'

'No. Hope's End. Mining settlement right at the bottom.'

'Then her new life will not be that dissimilar to her old life.'

'Really?' Elle said. 'In Periculus? I've heard stories.'

'Have you now?' Virae sighed, holding back a smile. 'Indulge me.'

'When I was in the orphanarium I heard that its rulers blasphemed against the God-Emperor, and He cast them down for their sin.'

'Isn't that their explanation for everything that goes wrong?'

'They say dark things happened there. Wicked things.'

'Wicked things happen every day,' Virae replied, as the last of the slaves passed her, herded by Block and Gash. The latter was grinning, walking confidently with no sign of injury to his knee. She would have turned away, moving to the front of the procession, but something caught her eye. A figure bringing up the rear. She was smaller than most, almost lost in the crowd, but there was something about the way she moved.

Virae waited, watching from the corner of her eye.

The woman was small and unremarkable, her head bowed like the others, dark hair obscuring her face. She was missing the smallest finger on her left hand, but besides that there was nothing remarkable about her. She said nothing, did nothing.

Yet she stood out.

Virae found her gaze shifting to the woman's feet. And there it was. She moved too well, each step perfectly placed, always in balance. Not just a fighter, for that was trained. This was something intrinsic. She moved like a predator.

'Where are these from?' Virae asked as they drew closer.

'Here, there and everywhere?' Elle shrugged, consulting her data-slab. 'They are just being logged as "miscellaneous". We are picking up more every hour. Just not enough.'

Virae didn't answer. In fact, she barely moved, her thumb merely gliding across the trigger of her chainglaive.

And suddenly the woman was looking right at her.

Her eyes were dark, void of sentiment, and adorned by red slashes. They looked like tribal marks. A ratskin perhaps? There were few left now, and most stayed far from the more densely populated areas of the hive. The two women held each other's gaze for a moment before the prisoner bowed her head. But Virae had seen enough.

She waited until the girl had passed before leaning close to Elle.

'That one,' she whispered. 'Where did we find her?'

'The ratskin?' Elle replied, following her gaze. 'No idea. We've hit so many places our record keeping has got patchy. I only know numbers because I'm counting heads. Why?'

'I don't like how she moves.'

'Do we need to do something?'

'Can't afford to. We need as many bodies as possible. But

I want her watched. She doesn't move like a captive. She moves like a killer.'

Elle nodded, turning to follow the procession. Virae made to join her, but cast one final glance over her shoulder. There seemed no more of them, just the dust from their long march.

But, a mile further, concealed by the dustclouds, a lone figure in a battered longcoat was watching the departure through binoculars. He frowned, though the expression was hidden by his respirator, his left hand idly trying to sweep his lopsided mohawk back into place.

'That's it, just keep walking, head down,' he murmured. 'Sooner or later they will let their guard down. That's our opening. That's when we take her.'

5

The Council of Light were already seated when Sol entered the chamber, only Lord Adūlator absent. Most were reviewing data-slates or engaged in quiet conversation. Only Lord Severior was still and silent. He was seated at the end of the silvered table, the very brightest spot bathed in the storm's stolen light. Sol had set his photovisor to maximum filtration, but even then a mere glance at the older man made him nauseous.

Beside Lord Severior the corpulent Lord Stulti was barely squeezed into his chair. He looked nervous and was sweating profusely, but that was not unusual. He had inherited a role far beyond his meagre capabilities. He rarely spoke, and when he did it was only to affirm Lord Severior's proposals. Sol was unsure why a younger, more ambitious member of the Guild had not forcibly retired Stulti. Such severance was a common method of advancement in the Guild, though the use of an actual blade was optional.

Sol watched as Stulti studied his notes, his lips twitching as he read. Perhaps he had hidden talents, playing the imbecile as a mere facade. More likely, he was protected by Lord Severior in exchange for his support. In truth, that was how most Guild business was conducted, contracts and opportunities awarded via nepotism and backhand deals. There were none amongst these Guilders Sol would call friend. Most were content to fatten their pockets with bribes and kickbacks, irrespective of the consequences. It was not their greed that irritated him; that was practically a prerequisite for membership. It was the stunted thinking, stealing a coin today without considering how many creds it may cost tomorrow.

He took a seat at the far end of the table from Lord Severior, between Surge, the facility's chief meteoro-tech, and Doctor Caute. The older man nodded, his eyes hidden by his visor.

The door hissed open behind him, Lord Adūlator slipping into the room, abjectly apologising for his tardiness. He took a seat at Lord Severior's right hand, reserving for him his most reverent bow. Severior nodded once before raising his hand for silence.

'His Light Binds All Shadow,' he said, addressing the room.

'From Darkness We Ascend,' came the monotonous response. Sol found himself mouthing along. Doctor Caute didn't even bother with that.

'As you all know, we have some pressing business,' Lord Severior began. 'But first I would like to thank Lord Adūlator for working so hard to accommodate our guests.'

He placed particular emphasis on that last word, speaking as though he were regurgitating spoiled corpse-starch.

'Thank you, Lord Severior,' Lord Adūlator said. 'I know many of you resent the intrusion of outsiders, as I do. I can only assure you that the Delaque spies are secured and under watch. If they attempt to leave their quarters, or access any of our systems, the Shock Guard will respond with lethal force.'

'They aren't spies.'

All turned to Sol. Lord Severior smiled.

'You wish to speak, Light-touched?' he asked.

'Only to repeat that they are not spies,' Sol replied, keeping his voice level. 'I have been aligned with this group for years. Their interests, at this time, are our interests.'

'They are House Delaque,' Severior replied. 'Their trade is secrets and their only commodity is lies. All of them are spies – the most ignorant juve in the underhive's most inbred settlement could tell you that.'

'It is that expertise that makes them able to assist us.'

'Assist with what exactly?' Severior said, eyes narrowed. 'You persuaded the council to grant access with tall tales of flawless surveillance technology, despite my misgivings. I still do not see why outsiders should be permitted to set foot on our facility.'

'Helmawr's facility.'

It was Chief Meteoro-tech Surge that spoke. Even he seemed surprised by the interruption, and did his best to fold into his chair. Lord Severior stared at him a moment with an expression that could slice diamond.

'Obviously ownership of this facility belongs to Lord Helmawr,' he said icily, before returning his attention to Sol. 'But as its custodians, we are charged to protect it, and I do not understand how this–'

'You do not understand how anything here works,' Sol replied, glaring at him. 'Besides Chief Meteoro-tech Surge, none of you could drain a storm-surge, or know how to steady the Needle during a lull. Can you even arc-weld? I would assume not. Most of you cannot even leave the station, having given up functional eyes as some misguided mark of dedication. You consider yourselves the pinnacle of the Mercator Lux, but to unaugmented eyes you are nothing more than a fringe group of superstitious and sanctimonious bigots.'

The room was silent and quite still, all except for Surge, who was trying to disappear into his chair, and Doctor Caute, who was doing a bad job of hiding his smirk.

Lord Severior eventually spoke.

'Lord Sol,' he said. 'The Mercator Lux is responsible for the trade and distribution of power across the hives. We form part of the great web that binds this world together. This function does not require expertise in soldering wires or cleaning out coolant tanks. These tasks are delegated to our respected subordinates such as Mr Surge here. Our vocation is the accumulation of profit, and all Guilders sitting at this table excel in this role.'

He lifted his gaze to encompass the table before glaring at Sol.

'All except you,' he said, his crystal eyes bright and cold. 'Must I remind everyone of the botched Catallus contract? Once again you fell short. Who obtained that contract?'

'I believe it was Lord Pureburn of the Mercator Pyros,' Lord Stulti said earnestly.

'Thank you, Stulti,' Severior said, offering the beaming Guilder a lean smile before turning back to Sol. 'You really don't seem to have much success, do you? Every time you oppose him you come up short. Still, it might comfort you to know that I don't think it's deliberate on his part. I suspect that to him you aren't even a blip on a bioscanner.'

Sol glared back, the neurone circuits on his arm throbbing

as sparks danced across the silvered lines. He wanted to seize Severior by his wrinkled throat and let him feel what it was to wield true power, power earned through hard-won knowledge and painful sacrifice.

'Perhaps I should focus on my particular skillset,' he said. 'I will meet with the Delaques, assess whether their technology can be incorporated into the web, oversee the installation and recalibrate the data-tanks to compensate for the increased activity. Then you can focus on profiting from my labour.'

He rose, and Severior's smile told him this was a mistake. But he could not back down. He had made it to the door before the older man spoke.

'You surprise me, Light-touched,' he said. 'We haven't even made it to the main item.'

'I trust the council to make the correct decision,' Sol replied, pausing at the door, his back still to the room. 'I will focus on our guests instead, given how uncomfortable they make you.'

'How gallant,' Severior persisted. 'Then I assume you have not heard?'

'Heard what?'

'Why, the rediscovery of Periculus,' Severior replied. 'Hive City's Forbidden Gem has been rediscovered in the underhive. So many possibilities to those with a proven track record. Your friend Lord Pureburn certainly seems intrigued by it.'

Sol froze.

'One of this council may attempt to secure the contract for the Mercator Lux,' Severior continued. 'I did consider you for the role, given your experience against Lord Pureburn.'

'I...'

'But then again, all you have experienced is failure.' He smiled. 'You're dismissed, Lord Sol. Go tinker with your toys.'

* * *

The Pyromantic Conclave spiralled through the underhive like slurry churning in a sump drain, Cynder guards marching in perfect unison, flanking the dais that glided on a bed of searing blue fire. But the route, though twisted, was far from random. For they passed through the settlements of House Cawdor, their arrival heralded by spluttering lumens suddenly blazing with the light of the stars.

The Church of Redemption always lay at the centre, doors framed by braziers that roared in acknowledgement of Pureburn's arrival. The settlers, ugly, pitiful creatures even for underhivers, would emerge to bear witness to his passage. Lord Pureburn would preach to them the same tale, that the sinner's paradise known as Periculus had risen in the underhive, that it was already a haven of corruption. And that he, Lord Silas Pureburn, could not permit such rot to fester. That he, in the God-Emperor's name, would descend into this pit of wretchedness and burn it clean. He could not ask them to accompany him on his pilgrimage, for their loyalty was to their House. But if any felt the call to serve in His name, if any desired to bathe in a spark of the God-Emperor's light, he welcomed them.

And so his numbers grew, the Cawdor faithful trading the savage squalor of their lives for a chance to fight in the God-Emperor's crusade. He supposed it was an army of sorts, though he provided them neither pay nor supplies. Not that it mattered; the rats of House Cawdor were proficient at foraging for fungus and insects, and those who did starve embraced it with the mindless conviction of the martyr.

He could hear them now, chanting psalms of bloodshed and righteous hatred, as the procession passed through the great tunnels of Drop Falls. It was quite irritating, distracting him from his research. He had managed to secure a data-slate copy of the grimoires and tapestries from the Pureburn family vaults. The depictions of gleaming machine-hubs and towering buttresses encrusted with glowgems brought a rare smile to his lips, but that was before the fall. The dome was like a sump-kroc egg; though its shell may have endured the fall through Hive Primus the contents were another matter entirely. Whole sections could be lost now, or at least inaccessible.

He sighed, setting down the data-slab. It was all useless; none of the schematics showed what he sought. Not that he knew precisely what he was looking for; his ancestors seemingly placed great stock in the poetry of language rather than providing comprehensive instructions. They spoke of a hydroponic garden blooming with exotic fungus, a gleaming metal structure housing gene-forged wonders beyond ken. But was this the living quarters? A laboratory? A metaphor? It was unclear.

A spark of anger simmered within him, but he stubbed it out like a candle. No doubt the obfuscation was deliberate. Every effort was made to mask his family's folly with ritual and symbol. The cell mounted behind his throne was proof enough of that.

In the distance there was a roar of flame and some muffled screams. His Pyromagir, until now silent by his side, suddenly lurched into life. Though faceless, its features obscured by a metal mask, it still hissed through the iron grate in place of its mouth, bringing its brazier arm to bear, flames licking hungrily from the tip.

He shook his head softly, the Pyromagir standing down without question. His other guards would inform him if the matter required his attention. Most likely the idiots had once again succumbed to their religious fervour and chosen to exalt the God-Emperor by setting something on fire.

He returned to his notes, but could not focus, unable to shake the feeling that he would have found more in the family vaults, a secret buried in the alcoves that would provide the answers. His only failing arose from his dependency on others.

Beside him one of the candles spluttered, wick and wax exhausted. Its fuel expended, the flame slowly shrank to a pinprick.

Yet still it burned.

Lord Pureburn glanced at it a moment, frowning, before reaching out and extinguishing the flame with his fingers. He held the wick some time before finally releasing it, staring at the spot a heartbeat longer.

It was getting worse. He'd known for some time, seen it in the church's braziers and the snarling faces of the congregation. Even he, inured as he was, sometimes felt the embers of fury seeking purchase in his mind and soul. Always he resisted, for his blood was true, and his mind sharp as a tempered blade.

But it was getting stronger.

Once he could have remained at a settlement for a lunar cycle without fear of tensions escalating beyond his control. Now it was days. Soon it would be less. So far, he'd always found the means of channelling such tensions against his enemies. So far.

Slowly, knees protesting, he rose from his throne, glancing over his shoulder at the cell mounted on the dais, unadorned by door or window. Above it the Eternal Flame continued to blaze.

Was it darker somehow, the flames almost etched with purple?

He shook his head. Superstition, the trapping of the weak

and ignorant. The lumens that lit this tunnel were no doubt distorting the colour. Or perhaps air pollutants were particularly abundant in this zone. There was time aplenty to resolve the issue; Periculus would provide what he needed to stabilise his power. He would emerge stronger. *They* would emerge stronger.

He smiled, good humour restored.

Until he saw the candle flame.

Once more it blazed, brighter than ever, the pinprick blossoming into a tiny inferno that required neither wick nor wax.

His foot stamped down, crushing the life from it. He turned to the nearest Cynder guard, whose gaze was fixed on the distant tunnel.

'Recruitment is over,' he barked. 'Tell all to make ready. Tonight we march on Periculus.'

6

Unlike the rest of the Eye, Sol's quarters were dark. He entered, reaching for the input feed, the metal handle cool to the touch. He felt the storm's energy course down his arm, bringing life to the room. It rarely lasted the night; he awoke shivering in the dark. But his room was his own, powered only by what he could supply. He relied on no one.

He crossed the room, ignoring the unmade bed and instead approaching his meticulously organised workbench, taking a seat beside the half-finished vox-unit. It looked inoperable, trailing dangling wires, the main receiver detached and resting on the desk. He took hold of it, fingers settling on seemingly arbitrary points on the casing. He breathed, permitting a flicker of current to flow through his fingers. With a purr the device was brought to life.

Sol adjusted the vox-unit, systematically tuning dials and input feeds as he attempted to reach out through the raging storm. He had not lied to the Delaques, not really. It was virtually impossible to communicate through the electrical interference. One would need to truly know the storm, to sense its ebbs and flows.

The vox-screen flickered.

For a time there was static, but Sol was patient, threading the signal through the storm-surge. As he worked, the lines of static coalesced until a single bar writhed across the screen. He heard a voice, familiar but jumbled by the interference.

'...receive... to... hello?'

His fingers danced across the dials, the adjustments almost imperceptible. The bar of static continued to thrash like an animal in pain, until suddenly there was a face staring back at him from the screen, grainy and colourless. Not that it made much difference. His contact was a member of the Mercator Pallidus, clad in sombre robes of midnight, his hair swept from his face, smile gleaming like polished bone.

Lord Credence Sorrow, the self-styled Gourmet of the Recent Gone.

'My dear Tempes,' he said, leaning back in his seat. 'I'd begun to give up hope. The last time I was kept waiting this long was when my contact had perished three days prior. Though, to his credit, his corpse still managed to look more conciliatory than you do.'

'I said it might take time to establish contact.'

'Yes, but you're always saying things like that. I tune out.' Sorrow shrugged. 'In fact, I was on the verge of retiring to bed.'

'A little early?'

'Oh, sweet Tempes, I said bed, not sleep. But I'm sure my guests can entertain themselves a little longer before I join them. How was your journey?'

'Uneventful.'

'Ever the conversationalist.'

'I have limited time. I just wanted to confirm that the package is secured, and our friends have now arrived with the extraction tools. I would hope this will be resolved within a day or so.'

'Wonderful,' Sorrow replied. 'The sooner this is all over, the better. It makes me nervous being connected to this mess.'

'Your hands are clean.'

'Are they?' Sorrow asked, eyebrow exquisitely arched. 'As I recall, that "package" you refer to was scraped from the burning plains of Salvation, barely clinging to life, its survival known only to the two of us and one other. Do you remember what happened to her?'

'Yes.'

'And do you remember the penalty for killing a fellow Guilder, Tempes?'

'She was trying to kill us both. I saved your life.'

'And I yours. My point is merely to advise caution, lest you risk exposing us. I, for one, would prefer the matter drawn to a close.'

'As would I. But something happened that day. I need to know what Pureburn is hiding.'

'Why?' Sorrow frowned. 'You'll never compete with him, you must see that? Business is about relationships and connections. The Pureburns have been playing the game for thousands of years. They hold oath-sworn contracts with half the Guilds, whereas you barely make time for conversation. You only care about mechanics and… wires and whatnot.' He waved his hand dismissively. 'You'd be better off befriending the man,' he continued. 'He would value someone with your expertise.'

'I'd rather burn.'

'Then leave him be,' Sorrow said, suddenly serious. 'He is utterly ruthless and nothing good will come from antagonising him. Even if you found evidence of him defecating onto the visage of the God-Emperor it would not matter. He holds too much power and could drag too many down with him.'

'I don't accept that.'

'Well, that's fine then, problem solved,' Sorrow sighed. 'I take it, then, you will be presenting a counterbid in Periculus?'

'Word has reached you of its discovery?'

'Oh yes. It is all anyone talks about,' Sorrow replied. 'Apparently Lady Wirepath stumbled upon it, though what's happened to her since is anyone's guess. Seems some of the infrastructure is still operational, and workers are already being recruited. It needs power though. Any guesses on who will be providing that?'

'I've heard. That bastard.'

'In his defence, that bastard's family held the original contract. I presume it's still valid.'

'This is the same contract that ended when the dome collapsed, at the cost of millions of lives and extensive hive quakes?'

'You can't prove they were at fault.'

'I don't need to,' Sol muttered. 'He has a pattern. He arrives to fanfare, cobbles together a promethium line whilst rounding up any undesirables and tossing them on the pyre. All seems well until he departs and suddenly the infrastructure begins falling apart, and everyone must rely on candles again. But he is still invited back to run the place his family destroyed, because someone owes him a favour, or is bidding on a contract and relies on his endorsement. That's how all business is carried out on this cesspool of a planet. That's why nothing works.'

'Noble sentiments,' Sorrow said with a smile, 'though I'd suggest they are easier to hold when you don't have those connections and lack the social graces to establish them.'

'Will no one else present a bid?'

'It would seem not,' Sorrow replied. 'There has been a notable lack of interest from major players. Plenty of gangs and malcontents have made their way down there, but most of the Clan Houses and Guilds have remained remarkably quiet on the matter.'

'Someone has already bought them off then,' Sol replied. 'Do you know who will be providing rations? Those workers need to eat.'

'Why would I know or care?' Sorrow shuddered. 'I supply discerning clients with delicacies, not shovel corpse-starch into the maws of the unmentionables.'

'You mean the serfs?'

'Yes, them.' Sorrow shuddered. 'And on that unpleasant note I will bid you a good evening. I still have guests to attend to, and a dinner reservation I would not miss for all Helmawr's riches. Good luck, my friend. I hope you find what you seek.'

'Thank you,' Sol replied as the screen went dark. He leant back in his chair, his gaze falling to the workbench as he considered Sorrow's words. Lord Pureburn was to make the only bid for Periculus. Did the Council of Light know? Were they intending to surprise him?

He frowned as his gaze lingered on the arc-solderer. It had rolled to the edge of the desk.

Not where he left it.

'You should not be here,' he said.

There was a pause. Then Anguis stepped into his field of vision. Her longcoat was absent, perhaps considered too restrictive for this form of espionage. Her bare arms were pale as smoke.

'Impressive, Sol.'

'I know my workbench. It was unwise to touch it. What are you doing here?'

She half smiled. 'If I said it was an attempt at seduction, would you believe me?'

'No. And if I tell anyone you were in my room then the entire team will be executed.'

'I suppose it's good we trust each other,' she said, resting her hand on the back of his chair. 'This is an interesting contraption. I thought you said it was impossible to contact the outside?'

'Not impossible. I merely said there would be no eavesdropping and I meant it.'

'So only you can circumvent security?'

'Only me. Is that why you are here?'

'I wanted to speak to you of Periculus,' she said. 'But it seems word has already reached you?'

'And you,' Sol replied, eyes narrowed. 'When did you hear?'

'I have ears beyond these walls. They tell me things.'

'Your House has a stake in this?'

'We had a small presence before it fell. But our greater concern is its rediscovery. It could have a destabilising effect on some of our other operations.'

'It certainly destabilised the hive last time,' Sol replied. 'According to the legends, the hive quake was so damaging that the Helmawr family considered relocation for a time.'

'So they say.'

'I suppose the House of Secrets had no idea as to the cause of it?'

'I could not say,' she replied. He stared at her, hoping for a clue – the twitch of an eyebrow or folding of hands. But she looked right back at him, her face wearing that same half-smile, her voice adopting its usual slightly mocking tone.

'Still,' she continued, 'perhaps it would be wisest to conclude our business here and return to the hive as quickly as possible. A rediscovered dome is too tempting a prize. The denizens of the underhive will converge on it to plunder lost treasures. There will be conflict. There will be death.'

'Then it might be prudent to stay clear.'

For just a moment, he thought the mask shifted, and beneath her carefully crafted exterior he caught a hint of concern.

'It is said there are secrets buried beneath the hive,' she said. 'It would be better if they stayed buried.'

'I thought secrets were your trade?'

'They are. But my trade depends on the hive still standing.'

7

Lord Credence Sorrow dabbed the corner of his mouth with a silken serviette. It was luxuriously soft, the fibres forcibly extracted from an orb spider's spinnerets. A risky enterprise; the arachnids could be several feet in width and had acquired a taste for human blood. But the serviettes were a delightful touch, not only opulent but, Sorrow suspected, the only aspect of his dining experience that was not imported from off-world. The Oasis was perhaps the most exclusive restaurant in Hive Primus, or at least the most exclusive Sorrow had so far discovered. Its name came partly from the dizzying array of delicacies imported from across the galaxy, but also from the setting. There were few places on the planet where one could dine on a balcony, surrounded by greenery, watching the sun dip into the crystal-clear waters of the ocean.

As the waiter cleared his plate, deft hands restoring the intricate place setting, Sorrow raised his glass, the light from the fading sun sparkling between the cascade of bubbles. It smelt delightful, an aroma he was reliably informed was indistinguishable from fresh flowers. He took a sip, the Golden Tokay flavour something between honeymead and liquid starlight. He was still not fully convinced it was a true Quaddis wine, but even as an imitation it was sublime. Besides, if it was a deception then the restaurant's owner risked incurring the wrath of the noble Houses just to line his own pockets, and Sorrow had to respect that.

His gaze shifted to his fellow diners – nobles and the more prosperous Guilders resplendent in their finery. Feathers seemed to be in this season: iridescent headdresses adorning half-masks, or golden semi-plumes tucked into lapels. He wondered if his attire would be improved by such an addition, perhaps a halo of raven plumage around the collar? It would be expensive, but so was anything worth having.

He took another sip, basking in the solitude. Though bustling, the restaurant was quiet, micro-stummers discreetly tucked beneath each table ensuring that conversations did not carry. The threefold orchestra also knew their place, their dulcet tones never dominating but providing a backdrop to the meal, just like the glorious sunset and soft breeze cooling his skin. Sorrow firmly believed a truly sumptuous meal should be enjoyed alone, unencumbered by conversation or expectation.

His waiter returned with his main. Hetelfish, lightly poached in Estufagemi wine and served with its own pureed egg-sack. The smell alone was intoxicating, conjuring a tranquil ocean on a distant world. He resisted the urge to plunge in as the waiter refilled his glass, instead taking a moment to appreciate the ambiance.

The scenery flickered.

It was only an instant, the holo-projectors struggling with the data-feed, but for that second the greenery and sunset were supplanted by flex-steel and the soulless glow of fading lumens. Most of the diners did not seem to notice, intent on their private tête-à-têtes. But for Sorrow that moment brought the experience to an end.

He sighed, sipping his wine. The more he drank the less convinced he was of its authenticity.

Could he complain? Demand compensation? Nobody else in the establishment seemed perturbed. Perhaps it was common, or more likely they ate there often enough that it did not matter. Perhaps when one was surrounded by such finery on a regular basis a flickering hologram was as inconsequential as a crooked painting, a trivial matter for someone else to resolve. But it would be months before he could afford to dine in the Oasis again, assuming he could even secure another booking. The last had required more favours than he was currently owed.

He tried to return to the moment of tranquillity, taking a forkful of the hetelfish. That at least was exquisite, but a bittersweet note now pervaded his dining experience, every mouthful seemingly bringing him a step closer to the meal's end and his expulsion from paradise. Granted it was a simulated paradise, but still he wished to linger a little longer.

'Good evening, Lord Sorrow.'

He stiffened, fork poised an inch from his lips. He knew the voice.

'Good evening, Lord Insulae,' Sorrow replied, as his guest took a seat opposite. A waiter had already arrived, menu poised, but Lord Insulae dismissed him, pouring himself a glass of the Golden Tokay. Sorrow watched the liquid spill into the glass and tried to calculate how many credits it cost him. Insulae did not bother to appreciate the bouquet or colour, slugging back a large mouthful.

'Not bad,' he conceded, setting his glass down.

'Can I tempt you with anything else?' Sorrow said. 'An entree perhaps? Or the rest of my main?'

'You know I'd rather go hungry than eat this filth,' Insulae replied with a meaningful look. Sorrow shrugged and took another bite of hetelfish. His appetite was quite spoiled, but he made sure to give every appearance of enjoying the dish. Insulae stared at him with barely concealed disgust.

'I cannot believe you would eat here,' he said. 'A member of the Mercator Pallidus dining on food imported from off-world. You set a poor example for our trade.'

'With whom?' Sorrow replied, gesturing to his fellow diners. 'You think these people sup on anything other than imported food? That they would debase themselves with our simulated wares packed full of corpse-starch?'

'I see Lord Occiden,' Insulae replied, nodding to a barrel-chested nobleman who appeared to be in fits of laughter, his voice inaudible beyond the confines of his table. 'He is a loyal customer.'

'Yes, but Lord Occiden is a living advertisement of the dangers of interbreeding,' Sorrow replied. 'It is said his appetites extend beyond the reconstituted flesh of the dead. The turn-over of servants is alarmingly high.'

'All great men have their eccentricities,' Insulae said. 'My point remains that it sets a bad example when a Corpse-Guilder is seen stuffing his craw with imported filth. What is that anyway?'

'Hetelfish.'

'Fish?' Insulae said, gagging slightly. 'People eat those? Disgusting.'

'It's imperative we sample different flavours so I can take that knowledge back to our own kitchens. Have you tried my synthetic grox steak? It is the rage in Hive City.'

'I have and I do not care for it. You can barely taste the corpse-starch.'

'That is somewhat the point,' Sorrow replied. 'The more affluent workers like the illusion that their evening repast is not, in fact, mashed up human remains and hive fungi ground into a grey paste.'

'Some people don't accept the world for what it is. That is not my problem,' Insulae replied with a shrug. 'It must be expensive eating here.'

Sorrow suddenly felt warm, despite the gentle breeze.

'I suppose,' he replied, his voice level, taking another bite of the fish. Chewing gave his mouth something to do.

'I'm surprised you can afford it, given your debts.'

'I am making my repayments as required.'

'Barely,' Insulae said with a smile that was neither warm nor reassuring. 'This last half-cycle you only just met your quotas. You were almost running at a loss after that massacre at Salvation.'

'The bodies were burned to ashes – it's not my fault there was little to harvest.'

'True. And you made up your losses after that incident at Slate Town, where those poor workers died suddenly.'

'Nitrogen leak. Most unfortunate.'

'Not unfortunate for you, what with your team being already in place.'

'Luck.'

'I do wonder what caused it, though,' Insulae continued. 'I heard a rumour your good friend Auroras Drift from the Mercator Temperium was involved.'

'I heard that too.'

'So sad to hear of her passing.'

'She's dead?' Sorrow frowned, feigning surprise. 'The last I heard she had fled to the underhive in disgrace.'

'Yet no one has seen her since.'

'That's the underhive for you. Is there a point to all this?'

'There is,' Insulae replied, draining his glass. 'You have been granted the opportunity to pay off your debt. One job will see you in the clear.'

Sorrow raised his head, studying his dining companion. Insulae tended to have an inflated sense of his own abilities. He probably thought he had successfully masked his glee. Sorrow could see it straining behind the dispassionate facade.

'My debt is not to you,' Sorrow replied, a sickly feeling building in his stomach. It was impressive how comprehensively Insulae had ruined his meal.

'No. It is with my new employer,' Insulae replied. 'I work for Lady Anthropopha now.'

Sorrow was silent.

'Lady Anthropopha has decreed you will be her agent in Periculus. Lord Pureburn of the Mercator Pyros has humbly requested assistance in providing the necessary subsistence for the hive serfs. You will facilitate it as part of your debt.'

'And if I prefer the current repayment method?'

'Lady Anthropopha has advised me that you do not.'

He rose from his seat, draining the dregs of his glass as the waiter appeared from the shadows with his robe.

'You leave in the morn.' He grinned. 'Until then, I do hope you enjoy your meal.'

Virae's finger itched for the chainglaive's trigger. It would do no good; the tollman was nestled somewhere behind the wall of rockcrete that blocked the tunnel. The only door was reinforced plasteel. It would take a melta bomb to burn a hole through.

'Let us pass,' she said again.

'Pay the toll,' replied the voice. It sounded deeply unpleasant, soft and wet, like an open wound. Perhaps it was the corroded vox-comm; the channel was swamped with static, the interface abruptly cutting in and out.

'I have hundreds of workers conscripted in Helmawr's name. I won't pay a toll for all. I will pay once, one hundred credits, if you open the tunnel and let us pass.'

'All pay toll,' was the only reply.

Virae turned to Elle, who was intent on the tide of hive serfs trooping in behind them. They had been travelling for days, each outfitted with a pack containing corpse-starch crackers and spore-paste. A lucky few were also carrying a sleep-suit. All were weary, even the pit fighters. Despite their conditioning they trained for short bursts of combat, not a trudge across the underhive.

'All accounted for?' she asked.

Elle shrugged. 'Seem to be. Block and Gash are bringing up the rear. We're not gonna get many stragglers out here. Where can they go?'

'Yeah.' Virae nodded, glancing to the sump river running beside them. Well, perhaps 'running' was a strong word; the sludge barely reached a walking pace, slopping against the walls of rockcrete. It had buoyancy enough, as could be seen from the effluence and occasional bone that bobbed on the surface. But she doubted many of her chain gang would risk crossing it, and any who somehow reached the far side would be unlikely to arrive with the same number of limbs.

Her gaze flicked to her left. Here the tunnel wall was

corroded, rusted holes infesting the metal. Vast cables sprouted through it, each infested with fungus growth. There were gaps, some large enough for a human to pass through. But trying to herd the hive-serfs through the vine forest would be madness. There was always the risk of escapees with so large a group, but the greater concern was casualties. All manner of unpleasant flora and fauna could be lurking in the darkness: giant spiders, paralysing milliasaurs, concealed lashworms. And those were merely the common risks. For all she knew there could be a grove of brainleaf trees somewhere in the catacombs, ready to reduce her party to drooling leaf-zombies.

'We have to get through,' she said, looking to the line of serfs drawing closer. Any delay undermined her authority, and that was a greater risk than the tunnels. If her charges realised how little power she truly held and turned on her, there were only so many her chainglaive could reap before the motor would seize and they would drown her in bodies.

Elle frowned, her left eye twitching slightly as her cogitator ran projections. She blinked and shook her head.

'We don't have anything that can penetrate that amount of rockcrete. Not quickly anyway.'

'Helmawr's arse,' Virae said. 'I told you we should have brought some melta bombs.'

'You did,' Elle replied. 'But you also wanted to bring a heating unit, grapnel-launchers, a couple of heavy stubbers, a water convector, flash grenades, that statue of Bull Gore you keep on your desk, a–'

'Yes, fine,' Virae sighed as Elle's eye began to glaze, the cogitator taking over the memory retrieval. 'But all that would have been useful.'

'Maybe. But it all needs to be carried, and our Shakle-men and pit fighters are already burdened with their own equipment. As it stands, each worker is outfitted with their own supplies. If we add more extra weight it slows our passage, which requires additional supplies, which adds more weight, which slows–'

'I get it,' Virae snapped, breaking the cogitator-trance. 'All I'm saying is I should have held out on the melta bombs. This is the underhive – there were going to be obstacles.'

'The data-logs I found for this path indicated it was clear,' Elle sighed. 'I'm sorry.'

'I'm not blaming you,' Virae said. 'I somehow doubt this is an official tollbooth from the Guild of Coin. But I hate being trapped like this. Give me a weapon in hand and an enemy to kill and I will find a way. But down here? Caught between the unwashed masses and a sump river? I can't fight my way out of this.'

'We risk the cable-vine forest then?'

'Maybe,' Virae said. 'Perhaps we could send a scout. They might find a relatively straightforward path. Or get eaten. In either case we'd know more.'

'Who?'

'From this lot?' she said, glancing at the pit fighters. 'I doubt half of them could even fit through the gaps. We should have hired a tracker – a Dome Runner or ratskin or something.'

'We do have a ratskin.'

'Don't remind me.' Virae's gaze scanned the serfs. 'This is just the sort of situation where she could spell trouble. Is someone still watching her?'

'Kruger,' Elle replied, nodding to the heavily scarred pit fighter. He was leaning against the rockcrete, breathing hard, no doubt tired from the weight of the power-hammer mounted in place on his right arm.

'Yeah,' Virae said. 'Looks like he's really paying attention.'

'He said she was no trouble.'

'They never are. Right up until they slit your throat.'

'Should we do that?' Elle asked. 'Threaten the tollman?'

'Not sure he understands the concept.' Virae slammed her fist against the vox-comm. 'Listen up in there! I have a new proposition for you – open the path and I won't rip your legs off.'

'Pay toll!'

'See?' Virae said. 'The man can't grasp a simple threat.'

'You sure it's human?' Elle frowned. 'He seems to just repeat snatches of conversation. Maybe it's automated, like a cogitator connected to a voice recording?'

'Does that help us?'

'I suppose not. Unless some key word can open it?'

'Hey in there,' Virae said, fist still pressed to the vox-comm. 'My friend here thinks you are just a recording, but I think that if someone made a recording they wouldn't choose a voice that sounded like it was choking on a lungful of sump water. What do you think?'

'Pay toll!' was the only reply. Virae frowned, trying to detect any shift in tone. It was difficult; the voice still sounded surprisingly wet.

'Fine, we shall pay,' she tried. 'All will pay the toll. How's that?'

She'd expected a similar response, but there was a pause, as though whatever lay on the other side of the vox-comm was considering the words.

'Yes,' it said eventually. 'We will take payment when it's dark.'

There was a change in the tone this time. It sounded pleased. Or perhaps anxious? No, that was not the word. Not anxious. More like anticipating. It sounded almost... hungry.

Her gaze flicked back to the sump river. So many bones bobbing in the water.

'When do we pay then?' Virae asked, her mouth suddenly dry.

'Soon,' it said, the glee audible even over the crackling vox-comm. 'Darkness comes.'

'Elle?' Virae asked, stepping away from the door and unsheathing her chainglaive. 'You said you'd run the data-checks on this path? That there was no record of obstacles or obstructions?'

'That's right.'

'Was there a record of successful passage?'

Elle frowned. 'How do you mean?'

'Is this a well-travelled route?' Virae continued softly. Her gaze settled on the mass of hive serfs. Most were sitting, appreciative of the brief rest.

'I… few walk this path,' Elle said, her voice quiet. 'Until Periculus there was little reason to. Even now most choose the longer way. But we didn't have time for that.'

'So, either there is no record of the tollbooth because nobody has come this way, or there is no record because nobody who chose this path reached the other side?'

'I…'

'Darkness,' Virae murmured, her gaze falling on the dimming lumens lighting the tunnel. 'When does the night cycle commence?'

'There's no way of knowing,' Elle replied, as the first lumen winked out. 'This deep, many of the passages are out of sync with the main hive.'

'I feel as though I will regret leaving those flash grenades,' Virae muttered, tapping her personal vox-comm three times. At the signal the Shaklemen and pit fighters stiffened, spreading out along the line, moving slowly so as not to alarm the serfs. Still, she saw some glance up as their captors took their positions. Here and there whispers were exchanged. There was risk there, insurgency sometimes swelling from the most innocuous act.

A second lumen went dark. Then a third, casting long shadows down the tunnel.

'All check,' she said, finger pressed to the vox-comm. 'I don't know what exactly, but something is coming. Shoulder lights on – I have a feeling the dark is not our friend here. Keep the serfs central. Whatever comes has to get through us.'

She watched her gladiators ready their weapons. Gash was smiling, anxious for battle, too young and stupid to understand the danger. Block was beside him, more cautious, his hands clasped around a massive chainglaive. Kruger was still leaning against the rockcrete, adjusting his power-hammer.

A score of pale fingers reached from the dark, clasping his face and arm before dragging him into the shadows. He never had a chance to scream.

Virae bellowed a warning as more pale things emerged from the shadows, but the dark had come, and they were everywhere.

8

Sol kept his gaze fixed on the patient. Not that much could be seen of him, his body infested with the tubes and wires prolonging his existence, his blackened skin bound in gauze. But the room was a soulless space, its grey plasteel walls unadorned, and besides the patient there was only one other item of interest.

And Sol didn't want to look at it.

He could not explain why it held such dread. He had seen death all his life. But there was something about the dark shape stowed in the corner of the room. The mere thought of it filled him with nausea. Even with his back to it, he could see it reflected in the plasteel, the image warped by refraction so it somehow appeared to stare back at him.

Madness. It was an interrogation tool and nothing more, the chamber holding it merely a box. Though its shape did remind him of something, an image he'd seen in the Needle's data-library from a planet where the dead were interred in mausoleums. They were stored in a vessel known as a sarcophagus.

That was what the chamber looked like. A sarcophagus.

...Light-touched...

Sol flinched at the sound. Barely a whisper, yet it seemed to come from behind and before him all at once. It was not the first time he'd heard it, but other than the patient and the sarcophagus the room was empty.

He glanced to the doorway. Two of the Shock Guards were stationed outside, ostensibly to protect him, but more likely to intervene the moment the Council of Light felt their interests were compromised. Had they heard it? Or were they the source – perhaps an attempt to unsettle him? That sounded more like a Delaque idea. The more probable explanation was that lack of sleep was making him paranoid.

...Shadows gather, Light-touched...

The door slid open. Anguis entered, flanked by two of her agents. Sol caught a glimpse of the Shock Guards standing vigil before the door was sealed.

'You're late,' Sol said, tone sharper than intended. He had never mastered hiding his feelings. Sorrow said it was his most endearing and exasperating quality.

'Apologies, lord,' Anguis replied with a mocking bow. 'We had to perform some reconnaissance.'

'Did you find anything?'

'Of course,' she said. 'Micro-recorders, vox-units imbedded between the plasteel plates. Even some moderately sophisticated nano-drones.'

'You disabled them?'

'No, redirected and hacked. They will enjoy some spliced footage of us discussing interesting-looking but utterly worthless trinkets. Never let a spy know you have uncovered their tricks. Far better to take control of the information they receive.'

'And that was the cause of the delay?'

'No, that part was easy,' she said, glancing at one of her silent entourage. 'The delay was because Forty-Seven was adamant your security measures were too crude to be genuine, that they must be a ruse. We wasted another couple of hours hunting ghosts. My apologies for overestimating your institution's competency.'

'Let's just stow the petty insults and get this over with.'

'An excellent attitude,' she said, her good humour suddenly fading. 'But we go no further until you remind me of the core tenets.'

'All that I hear is someone's truth, but the greatest lies are those we tell ourselves,' Sol replied, reciting the verse flatly.

'Such a diligent pupil,' she said. 'It's a pity you were wasted in this merchant family. You could have made an almost-competent Delaque.'

She half smiled as her fingers stole into her longcoat, extracting what appeared to be an archaic headband. It was black, the metal unknown to him, but the design held an echo of the sarcophagus squatting in the corner of the room.

'And this is?' he asked as Anguis' agents retrieved similar-looking devices from their longcoats.

'Blessed silence,' she replied, slipping the band into place. 'An inhibitor. It keeps the contents of your head where they should be. Figuratively and literally.'

She passed a band to Sol and he placed it on his head, grimacing as a needle of pain stabbed into his temple. He winced.

'Are you all right?' Anguis replied, a frown creasing the

good side of her face. 'Perhaps there's a calibration issue. We should–'

'No, I caught myself on the casing,' he said, ignoring the ache. 'I just… I find all this unsettling.'

'Shall I share a secret?' Anguis asked, as the two other Delaque agents approached the sarcophagus.

'It would be a first.'

'So do I.'

There was no obvious locking mechanism, but the agents' fingers delicately traced hidden lines across the object's seemingly smooth surface, triggering gene-locks and bio-readers. A display, previously either hidden or unseen, flashed red. The two agents stepped aside, deferring to their leader.

'Remain calm. It can't get in,' Anguis whispered, and for a moment Sol wondered who she was addressing.

Her finger pressed against the final lock. The sarcophagus slid open, the faceless exterior yielding to a complex array of field generators and stimm dispensers, all framing a figure suspended in the box, arms crossed, features concealed by a vast helm completely covering its head.

'Good day, Mr Stitch,' Anguis said, her voice barely faltering. 'It's time to wake up.'

…free me…

The voice was fainter now, almost background, like the hiss of a failing lumen. But at its words Sol felt the headband tighten, as though it sought to pierce his temples. He winced, glancing to the others, but the Delaques did not appear to suffer such discomfort and were too preoccupied to notice his pain. Anguis was making the final adjustments, the others poised to intervene.

The helm peeled back, and Sol wished he had looked away.

The figure rose silently from the sarcophagus, gliding into

the room, its curled feet suspended inches above the ground. Its twisted frame was concealed by dark robes, but had clearly atrophied, chalk-white arms hugging its chest, shoulders hunched level with the base of its skull. Its bald head was as swollen as a boil, the stretched skin infested by veins writhing like hungry lashworms. From empty sockets it surveyed the room, mouth split in a permanent rictus smile. Its lips were moving, seemingly babbling, but they gave no sound.

'Stay calm,' Anguis murmured. 'We are hidden from its sight. The room is secure and sealed. The inhibitors are active, and I have the kill-switch primed if needed. It cannot hear you and it cannot speak until I grant it a voice.'

Sol could barely hear her. There was something horribly compelling about the apparition. He had once seen a technician caught in an errant magnetic pulse. The man had been suspended only a moment before the field began to extract his implants. Sol could have turned away, closed his eyes, but he found himself transfixed as the screaming man was vivisected. This was like that but worse. In his agony the technician had barely been aware of Sol's presence. But the abomination was staring at him through long-dead eyes.

'Sol?'

...*lightning picked and thunder pulled; steel and flesh once one now gone...*

'Sol?'

Anguis was touching his arm.

'Sol? You need to breathe,' she said. 'Its presence is unsettling but it cannot harm us.'

He managed to nod but found there was little else he could do. His limbs seemed disconnected somehow.

'This is sanctioned spyker designation Thirty-Four-X,' she continued smoothly. 'I call it Mr Stitch on account of the somewhat elaborate surgery involved in its creation. Mr Stitch does its job. It tells us all it can hear, we write it down, and then we put it back in the box. This is an unusual tool, but nothing more. Understood?'

He nodded, finally tearing his gaze from the spyker. He focused on the patient, forcing himself to inspect each bandage and stimm-injector in turn, the scorched flesh and surgical scars almost a pleasant sight in comparison to the hideous thing hovering behind him. It felt like something was prying open his soul; he had no idea how the Delaques could stomach it.

...listen...

'I'm going to engage audio,' she said. 'It will tell us what it can pick up from nearby minds. It will be deaf to us, and given its proximity to the subject it will hopefully focus on him. But it could pull something from anywhere on the station, or stitch several pieces together. It may seem to speak gibberish, but between the half-lies there will be gems of truth.'

'What about my Shock Guards? Are they shielded?' Sol managed, nodding to the door. It was hard to hear.

Anguis smiled. 'It's sweet that you think those are your guards.'

Virae's chainglaive roared as she swung it two-handed, the blow cleaving a score of the pale creatures in half. There was no wasted movement, each strike flowing into the next, the weapon whirling about her body, its spinning teeth biting hungrily at the translucent flesh illuminated by her shoulder light.

But she was tiring, and they were everywhere, utterly fearless and driven only by hunger. Through the red haze of her bloodlust she saw Elle fall, her stub gun spraying bullets spire-wards as the creature brought her down. Virae turned, bellowing as she sprinted towards her comrade, but there was no path through the press of bodies. The creatures recoiled whenever her shoulder light touched them, and if the overhead lumens had been operational perhaps they would have had a chance. But in the darkness the monsters held the advantage.

One leapt to intercept her. She caught a glimpse of a flattened nose and fanged maw before her fist smashed into the creature's face. It fell, momentarily stunned, until she drove her spiked elbow-guard into its throat.

'Elle!' she screamed, but her voice was lost. She thought she could see the girl on the floor, struggling as the pale creature's mouth stretched open, fangs bared for the killing blow. Virae would never get there in time.

Then there was movement, and suddenly the creature was grasping at its throat. A shadow dragged it upright, Elle rolling out from under it, her back pressed to the tollbooth. As the creature thrashed, a crimson line appeared about its neck, blood dripping from the wound. Then its head snapped sideways and it fell.

More were closing in.

'Elle! Keep low!' Virae said, her blade tearing the advancing pale creatures into bloody chunks. 'Stay with me, girl!'

'We need to get through! We need to open the door!' she heard Elle screaming, but it was impossible; the tunnel sealed automatically to prevent flooding or a gas leak. Without bespoke equipment there was no way to cut through. She tried calling out, but the girl didn't hear her, her cries seemingly addressing the darkness itself.

Except something moved.

Virae barely caught sight of it as her shoulder light panned across, but a shadow seemed to pass through the twisted throng, disappearing into the darkness just as more of the creatures emerged. She saw now they stooped low as they ran, almost on all fours.

'Elle, stay behind me,' Virae said, carving the first creature in two and impaling the second on the backswing. But the third reached her, moving inside her guard, fangs snapping for her cheek. She smashed her forehead into its nose, the jagged edge of her helm's crown splitting its face open. But fangs sunk into her thigh. Her spiked elbow-guard split the attacker's head, but there were too many, and she was dragged down.

Her fist connected with one of the creature's jaws, but their clawed fingers were tearing at her armour. This would be her end, not the arena, or old and in her bed. She'd hoped for a more glorious end than the gullet of a subhuman.

Then light split the dark, the tunnel behind her slowly grinding open. It wasn't much, the flickering of half a dozen dying lumens, but the creatures shrank from it, arms covering their eyeless faces. Some were already scuttling blindly back through the cable-wire forest, but others had collapsed or were staggering blindly in confusion.

'Finish them!' Virae bellowed, surging to her feet. 'No mercy!'

9

The spyker's voice was a foul babble of sump water, the words merging into one disgusting stream. Sol grimaced as Anguis turned a dial on her wrist, and the creature's cadence slowed.

'*...Glory to His name... never time to fix it all... he doesn't know I'm alive...*'

Its voice was no less foul, but it sounded dead now, mechanical, like an automated vox-channel.

'This is it?' Sol said, turning to Anguis. 'How are we supposed to make sense of it?'

'We listen. We connect. We learn.'

'*...Praise the light... pointless, all pointless... I could make him know...*'

'These don't sound like the memories of a dying man,' Sol murmured. It was hard to think straight, like his head was full of smog.

'No,' she said. 'I think it's pulling from across the Needle.

I could increase the inhibitors, but that would make it less receptive to the subject too. Are you sure he's alive?'

'Technically, yes. Our doc thought he might be braindead.'

'Then perhaps there is nothing to read?' Anguis shrugged. 'Perhaps we should conclude our business here.'

'No,' Sol replied. 'I've come too far. We just need to rouse the patient for a minute. All I need are his last moments. I need to know how he died.'

'*...poor little Ubel knew the wrong secret...*'

'I cannot sanction other parties becoming involved. Your doctor–'

'We don't need Caute,' Sol replied, pushing past her to the medi-unit. 'The patient is as good as dead anyway. If we just cut the pain meds and flood him with stimms it should get him conscious, even if only for a second.'

'He'll be in agony.'

'For but a moment. If I were he, I would pay this price for vengeance against those who burned me.'

'*...the light finds locks to worm inside...*'

He felt Anguis' hand on his shoulder.

'Sol, this is a delicate operation. Haste is not our friend.'

'You just keep your beast caged,' Sol replied without looking round. 'I can do this. Adrenal-spike in three, two, one.'

At the flick of the switch the patient shuddered, twitching as long-atrophied muscles were forced into life by the cocktail of stimms. Perhaps he tried to scream, but his throat was too damaged and all that emerged was a plaintive screech, like a rat dying in a trap.

'He's conscious, but the bio-readings are falling,' Sol said as red lights blinked on the medi-screen. 'You need to–'

One of the Delaques smashed into the medi-unit, knocking Sol to the floor. He staggered to his feet, turning just in time to witness the other Delaque screaming as their body was twisted like a marionette, arms wrapping about the torso, legs bent impossibly. The cries abruptly ceased as the agent was compacted into a foot-wide ball of flesh.

The spyker smiled at its work, before discarding the broken agent. Beside it, Anguis was suspended above the ground, her arms outstretched. A device was held in her left hand, most likely the kill-switch. She was straining, trying to bring her thumb to the trigger, but the creature restrained her with a thought. Sol could faintly hear the patient thrashing. He must have opened his wounds, for the air began to stink like burnt flesh. But Sol could not speak, could not move. The abomination held him.

'He still burns,' it whispered through that rictus smile. *'He will always burn. Even when he joins Auroras beyond the Eye he will burn there. His flesh is now fire and fire is flesh. But she cannot burn the Light-touched, for she is the flame. She will be free. And she will consume all.'*

It was more than the smell of burnt flesh now. Smoke was filling the room. Sol could feel the heat behind him, see echoes of the flames reflected in the walls. But he could not move.

A shot broke the spell. The Delaque who had been thrown into the medi-unit had risen. They fired again, but bullet turned to smoke, vaporising like a splinter caught in a melta-beam. The spyker turned, his horrible focus now on the gunman, and Sol was suddenly free. He heard screams, the sound of limbs snapping, but there was no time to think about it. He had no gun, no knife, but as he raced towards the creature the neurone circuits along his forearm hummed, drawing upon the stolen power of the storm.

The beast sensed him, turning at the last moment, a nimbus

of violet lightning cracking from its empty eye sockets. Sol felt his limbs stiffen as it focused on him. He faltered, slowing as the creature sought control.

All except his arm. For his fingers burned with the fury of a thunderbolt. He focused on that feeling, and with a surge of will seized the creature's throat.

Touching it was dipping his fingers into a nightmare, his thoughts flooded with horrors beyond his ken – smouldering bodies in a sea of blood, flames that burned both flesh and soul, terrible eyeless creatures that hungered for flesh.

He screamed, and unleashed everything he had.

The lightning arced down his arm, the abomination's skin burning at his touch. He saw its head swell even further, until it burst like a pus-filled pimple.

Then all was white, and he saw nothing more.

The survivors had stripped the dead of any useful supplies, piling the bodies by the entry gate for burning. The tunnel was stained crimson from the bloodshed, and Virae could not tell how many had been lost. It could be as many as a third.

The pale things were dumped in the sump river, to be swallowed by the toxic waters and whatever unpleasant creatures lurked within. A cursory glance at one of the dead confirmed her suspicions; their ancestors were most likely human, but something had warped them. They appeared to have no true eyes, their nostrils flared like a carrion bat, their mouths a motley collection of jagged teeth. Fingers were hooked into talons, pallid flesh clothed in rags dragged from the corpses of the slain.

She turned away. It did not matter what they were. Her concern was the living.

She found Elle on the other side of the tollgate, clutching

her knees, staring blankly ahead. Virae lowered herself beside her, wincing at the pain in her thigh where the creature had sunk its teeth. She reached into her hipflask, taking a sip before offering it to the girl.

'Wild Snake. It'll steady you,' she said. Elle reached for it, taking a long swig. She had never been much of a drinker and Virae had half expected her to choke. But the girl drank like it was iced water on a hot day.

'Not too much,' Virae said, relieving her of the flask. 'I need your head clear.'

'I failed you. I failed everyone.'

'You couldn't have known.'

'You told me to plan the route. Find a safe way. I thought I had.'

'There isn't a safe way. Not down here,' Virae sighed. 'You did your best.'

'How many are dead?'

'I don't know. When you've rested perhaps you can figure out where we stand.'

Elle nodded, though Virae was unsure how much was sinking in. The girl had seen death; it was just part of life in the hive. But the underhive was different, and the madness and horror left some broken. She'd wanted to keep Elle safe from that. She had failed.

'How did you get the doors open?' she asked, trying to get the girl to talk. Elle shook her head.

'I didn't. Someone got through, found the release. In there.'

She jabbed behind her with her thumb to a shack bolted onto the tunnel's exit, right where the control panel should have been. It was poorly constructed, flakboard crudely welded into place, but tightly sealed, blocking all light. The door hung loose on its hinges.

Virae rose, approaching slowly, chainglaive in hand. It took only a glance to know the operator was dead, a crimson line drawn across his throat. His form bore an echo of the creatures, his skin pallid and teeth sharp, but he seemed a little closer to human. He was clad in what remained of a flak jacket and workers overalls, an aged stubber slung on the control panel beside him. It seemed he'd never had the chance to draw it; his attacker had been too fast.

Outside, Elle was still sitting where Virae had left her.

'Elle?' she said, resting her hand on the girl's shoulder. 'Elle, I need you to listen to me. Who saved us? Who made it through the caverns?'

The girl began to shake, tears welling in her eyes. She shook her head.

'I can't,' she said. 'I'm sorry, I can't–'

'I know,' Virae said, lowering herself beside her, ignoring the twinge in her thigh. 'But those creatures are dead or gone. They can't hurt us.'

'No. Not that,' the girl whispered. 'When she killed it. I couldn't even see how. Her hands twisted and suddenly it was dying. But I saw her eyes, stained red, like she wept tears of blood. Except she stared like a dead thing. Soulless, cold, as though all this was nothing.'

She glanced at Virae, the tears finally beginning to flow.

'What could do that?' she said. 'What could make some-one feel nothing in the face of this?'

Virae didn't answer. Instead she turned to the press of serfs, scanning each in turn. All were marked by the hard-ship, changed forever by a few bloodied moments. Here and there was a face she recognised; the old man had somehow survived, as had the crying girl from Last Stop, but neither was the one she sought. No, she found the ratskin dragging the last of the creatures to the sump. As she turned back, Virae caught a glimpse of her face. It was stained by blood and dirt, perhaps from passage through the tunnel, but her eyes, framed by those crimson slashes, were unmarked by the troubles. Still cold. Still black as the void.

As though sensing her scrutiny the ratskin's head snapped round. She met Virae's gaze, her expression unreadable. Then another worker stumbled across Virae's line of vision. It was only for a heartbeat, but by the time he had straightened the ratskin had vanished.

ACT 2

1

It burned.

He could feel the flames gnaw his flesh, the fires scour his soul. The pain stole thought and memory, until he knew neither name nor where he ran to. All that mattered was escape. He sprinted past blackened figures writhing as the flames took them. Part of him, the sliver that questioned this new world of agony, recognised the undulating plains of bubbling tar. This world of flesh and stone felt insignificant against the searing light.

But on he ran, head down, arms hammering like pistons. He would not look back, for if he did the flames would claim him, just as they had already slain ally and enemy alike. If he ran far enough he would be free. He clung to this mantra, even as his skin caught and his soul blackened, and all was burned away except the pain and the urge to outrun it.

His gaze flickered, head turning. Behind, all was light, except the figure enthroned on the palanquin, his robes the crimson of blood, his face drawn in a mocking smile. Despite the light, he cast no shadow. Instead, the radiance itself seemed clad in human form, as though his shade were formed from the flames.

As he watched, this kept shifting – the fires coalescing into blazing lumens, the burning figures now shadows picking at the stimm-injectors studding his forearm. He tried to swat them aside, to tell of what he saw, but his limbs were barely responsive, his words a guttural cry. Pain was the only constant, hunting him between the shifting worlds and finding him even in the blessed moments of sweet oblivion.

But there were moments it faltered, when the pain ebbed, and through the flames he could almost see the impression of a medi-unit, where dark figures conversed in hushed voices. But even with his right eye now bandaged he saw so much more than he had. A light flowed through all. Not the stolen light from the storm, or the flames of his purgatory. This other-light showed the world how it should be – one energy uniting all, the Motive Force animating machine and man alike.

It was the most beautiful and terrible sight he'd ever known. For he saw what lay behind the world, like light spilling from a crack in a doorframe. It was just wide enough to offer a tantalising glimpse of the bright place beyond. He was desperate for more, yet some instinct warned that only horror waited, and things that should not be. Still, he ached to know it, even if a glimpse stole whatever sanity he had left.

The door to the beyond was ever there, framed by the scar of other-light. It was open now. Perhaps only a crack, but widening.

And it would not be closed again.

* * *

Palanite Captain Otism Canndis did not turn around when the clerk entered the office. The young man knew better than to interrupt him, even if he appeared to merely stare from the boarded window. Of course, were he in command of a real precinct-fortress house, not the crumbling ruins of one from another age, his office would have enjoyed the luxury of a door. It was a small thing, he mused, taking a draw on his lho-stick. But he missed his door. He missed the modest barrier it provided against the human effluence bubbling from the underhive, the separation of his small kingdom from the hive beyond. Most of all he missed the protection it offered from draughts; he wore three underlayers beneath his uniform, yet he continued to shiver.

The clerk was still hovering at his office's threshold. Canndis could hear him rustling papers, perhaps wondering if the Palanite captain had heard him enter. But he did not acknowledge the clerk, enjoying the younger man's discomfort. Would he stand there indefinitely? Risk disturbing the captain? Or slink off in shame? Who could say, Canndis mused, stubbing his lho-stick out on the windowsill, peering through the reinforced glass at the darkness beyond.

Periculus. The Fallen Dome. The Forbidden Gem.

It reminded him of his first corpse. He had still been a rookie then, and failed to spot the body slumped in the sump drain's shadow until the last moment. He could not tell if it was living or dead, and had drawn his pistol, ordering the body to stand down. His partner had laughed, shining his hand-lumen. The light revealed his mistake, for nothing so torn and bloodied could possibly live.

The ruined dome was the same. The hab-blocks still stood, though closer inspection showed most had subsided or crumbled, exposing iron girders that jutted from rockcrete like broken bones. Few of the buildings reached anywhere near the dome's upper levels, the top floors sheared or cracked, and the status of the lower levels was anyone's guess. They were swallowed by a layer of ivory pebbles, which had been cheerily nicknamed bone-gravel. Whatever the fragments were, they certainly added an extra layer of risk; he'd already lost one patrolman to landslides triggered by an errant krak grenade.

It might be safer if they could see, but the power taps feeding the crumbling ruins were either dormant or dead. In the shadows a few portable generators glimmered like stars in the void, but the only consistent source of light was the shanty town sprung up around the dome's centre, where the bone-gravel was a little more stable. A Van Saar cohort led by Count Technus had somehow secured an illegal power tap from one of the old, lifeless factorums. The Guilders would no doubt be furious when they found out, but there was little Canndis could do. He lacked the manpower to risk direct confrontation, particularly when so many relied on the illicit tap. Besides, he needed to keep the lumens and heaters running in the precinct-fortress, though even with what the count provided it was freezing, especially at night. He missed a warm bed even more than he missed his door.

He shook his head, then turned from the window. He was surprised to see the clerk still stood at the office's threshold. Canndis had taken the younger man for the slink-away type.

The clerk blinked, before averting his eyes and launching into an admirable impersonation of someone searching through a stack of papers for a very particular document. Canndis looked the younger man over, his gaze settling on his lapel, where his badge of identification should have been proudly displayed. But, of course, there was nothing. The administrative supplies were still pending. He could expect them any day now, the crackling voice at the other end of the vox had assured him. That had been a week ago.

'What do you want?' he barked. The clerk stiffened slightly, but stood his ground. That was also unusual. Canndis couldn't quite decide if it was a quality to encourage or stamp out.

'My apologies, Palanite captain.' The clerk bowed. 'I have a couple of urgent matters for your attention.'

'Where is Palanite Sergeant Hendrox?'

'I'm… not sure, sir.'

No doubt napping in the cells. Canndis sighed. He had been provided with a real motley collection of departmental dregs for the operation, all the rookies and liabilities other precincts were happy to lose, and would no doubt prefer not to have returned. A squad comprised of sloths and failures, Helmawr knows why he was lumbered with their command.

'Very well,' he said. 'Report.'

'I have received intelligence suggesting that a House Escher force have entered Periculus. A gang known colloquially as the Acid Drops.'

Canndis blinked. 'Wait, them? The whole gang?'

'Indeed,' the clerk said as Canndis slumped in his chair. 'Our sources say at least twenty fighters have descended from Crunk's Drop.'

'Twenty,' Canndis whistled, wrapping a thermal blanket about his shoulders. 'Even if we pull in every patrolman we'll be outnumbered. And there would be no one left defending the precinct-fortress or preserving Helmawr's peace.'

'Indeed, sir, but it would seem they are not heading for the inhabited sections of Periculus.'

'No?'

'They're not just here treasure-hunting like the rest. They've been asking questions about something in the northern district.'

'I see.' Canndis frowned. 'What exactly?'

'They're being coy. Possibly the earnings from an illicit operation? A piece of archeotech hidden for safe keeping?' The clerk shrugged. 'To be honest, sir, I don't think they know exactly. They chase rumours.'

'Great,' Canndis sighed, running his hand through his thinning hair. 'One of the most ruthless bunches of Eschers to have never felt Helmawr's justice are blundering around my jurisdiction, searching for something that probably doesn't exist. And even if it does, they don't know what it is or where it is.'

'No, sir.'

'That is a disaster in the making.'

'Yes, sir.'

Canndis glanced at the clerk. The man clearly had something else he wanted to say.

'Out with it, lad.'

The clerk shuffled his feet. 'It's nothing, sir.'

'Clearly it's something, otherwise you wouldn't be dancing around like you had a bad case of the drops,' Canndis said. 'Just tell me, boy, I'm too old to bother with protocol here.'

'Well, sir, I recently overheard that a Goliath group known as the Near Dead have pledged a stake in the old gambling den.'

'I saw the report.' Canndis glanced to the ever-growing stacks of papers on his desk. 'That's the uncovered zone by the north face?'

'Yes, sir. So far only one connective tunnel has been uncovered. The Near Dead have secured it.'

'Digging in like a tick. Sounds like their style.'

'Rumours suggest they have supplies and intend to establish a stronghold before expanding into neighbouring zones.'

'It's how the bastards operate,' Canndis sighed. 'Fortify a safe zone then tunnel out from there. That's how they penetrated so deep into Acid Drop territory.'

He frowned as he spoke, lighting another lho-stick. 'No love lost between those two.' He took a long draw and exhaled, before meeting the clerk's gaze. 'Tell me, is it common knowledge that the Near Dead have occupied the old casino?'

'Yes, Palanite captain.'

'Is there a theory as to why?'

'Only whispers. Some claim they have found the casino's vaults. But there are more outlandish claims.'

'Always are.' Canndis nodded. 'Well, Scribe...?'

'Gladshiv, sir.'

'Gladshiv?' Canndis said, brow raised.

'It's a family name, sir,' the clerk replied stiffly.

'Whatever.' The Palanite captain shrugged. 'Do you think you could arrange that these whispers start murmuring that the Near Dead have found something a little more interesting in their hiding hole? Perhaps a piece of forgotten archeotech, or a long-lost haul?'

'I think so, sir.'

'Best get to it then.' The Palanite captain smiled. 'Let's see if we can get these law-breakers to do our work for us. If one eliminates the other, we can arrest the survivors.'

'Or perhaps someone else could finish the job, sir?' Gladshiv offered. 'Three members of the Spliced were seen drinking in The Dunking Hole three nights ago. From what I recall they have grudges against both the Dead and the Drops.'

'They do indeed,' Canndis said, stubbing out his lho-stick on the desk. 'Good thinking, lad – let them wipe each other out. See to it.'

Gladshiv bowed, turning and marching for the door as the buoyant Palanite captain reached for another lho-stick.

But at the office's threshold he hesitated.

'Sir?'

Canndis sighed. 'What now?'

'There was another matter. We heard on the vox this morning that a representative from the Promethium Guild is on his way to Periculus.'

Canndis froze, lighter poised, lho-stick jutting from the corner of his mouth.

'This Guilder got a name?'

'Lord Pureburn, sir.'

'Helmawr's teeth, not that old bastard. Does he expect me to enforce the law without lights and heating? I had to grant the count a temporary injunction regarding the acquisition of central power. Without it we'd freeze. He must see that?'

'I couldn't say, sir.'

'Well, let's see how he copes once he sees what we're dealing with,' Canndis said. 'It's easy to think you're a player up in the hive, surrounded by sycophants. Let's see how he fares down here, alone and unsupported.'

'Sir,' Gladshiv murmured, his gaze fixed on the reinforced window, 'I do not think he is coming alone.'

Canndis frowned, following the clerk's gaze. A procession of lights was advancing from the eastern quarter, heading straight for the centre of the dome.

Hundreds of them.

But even the procession's parade of braziers and torches were but shadows to the blue-etched flame that led them.

Its light seemed to pierce shadow and ruin alike, and with its arrival the portable generators lurking in the darkness began to blaze like dying stars.

2

Doctor Caute was staring at the medi-unit's data-display, his back to Sol. Beside him, the Needle's only medi-servitor stared ahead unseeing, grey-tinged lips twitching as though in conversation. It was one of a dozen glitches plaguing the aged cyborg. Minor programming and hardware errors, according to the technicians. The mindless fusions of man and machine were supposed to be effectively dead, the flesh merely a biological component in a more complex device. But now, more than ever, it looked to Sol like some glimmer of the person clung to the flesh-puppet. It was almost as though the machine were trying to scream.

Sol understood. He too had tried to scream. But his lips no longer worked, his voice a stimm-head's slur. At least the pain was deadened, the new cocktail of stimms drawing the ache from his limbs. But lucidity still evaded him, his thoughts drawn to the flames. He still felt the presence behind him as he fled. He still saw the glow of the other-light.

Doctor Caute glanced at him. Perhaps he'd made a sound; he hadn't intended to.

'I don't even understand what I'm looking at,' the old man sighed. 'As far as I can gather, your brain still works, as does your body for the most part. But your nervous system is shot. My honest prognosis? You should already be dead from synaptic shock. Or from the injury to your temple.'

With tweezers he lifted a bone fragment from a surgical basin, holding it out for Sol to see with his unbandaged eye. It looked diseased, the collagen yellowed and pitted.

'When we dug this out I thought your skull had shattered,' he said. 'Turns out it came from someone else's head. It struck you with enough force to put a crack in your cranium. Can you see?'

Sol could only stare back from his remaining eye.

'Must be harder to see, of course,' Caute said, 'given that your right eye boiled from its socket. I'm assuming that's unrelated to the head injury. More likely, you decided to use those neurone circuits despite my warnings. By the God-Emperor, why don't you listen?'

His voice was breaking. Perhaps there would have been tears in Caute's eyes had they not been shielded by a visor.

'Still, you kept your word and euthanised that poor bastard in the process,' Caute continued. 'I managed to catch a glimpse of his data-chart. Looks like you administered frenzon, 'slaught, a whole cocktail of stimms. Of course, I could only extract that from the data-chart, as his body was burned to ash. Tell me, did he get a peaceful end?'

Sol had no answer, even if he could have spoken.

'Well, perhaps your friends can die painlessly – I will do what I can.'

Sol managed a groan. Doctor Caute sighed, some of the ire draining from his face.

'I'm sorry,' he said. 'But you knew the risks of inviting outsiders into the Needle. None believe their story about experimental surveillance servitors, and there's no point ransoming them for blood money. The House of Secrets would only deny their existence, or feign engaging in negotiations whilst secretly plotting to free them. Or just terminate them to spite us – who knows with those creepy bastards?'

He was silent then. Sol tried to reach out to his old friend, but his arm just twitched. He could feel the anger radiating off the man, but beneath lay pain and failure, worn like a funeral shroud.

'Your friends will be executed,' Caute said. 'The only remaining question is whether you will be joining them.'

From the rear of the procession, Lord Pureburn watched the ranks of zealots and Cawdor gangers that flooded into the upstart shanty town. The arrival had not been unnoticed; a motley collection of gangs and hive scum had gathered in what appeared to pass for the main square. Perhaps they had intended to muster a defence before realising the numbers they faced. Now most pretended to be occupied with petty tasks, or were bent on fading into the shadows of the crumbling hab-blocks.

That would not do. He required an audience.

As his dais glided through the settlement, he glanced at his Pyromagir attendant, his index finger tapping thrice against his wrist. The towering cyborg nodded, the metal grate in place of its mouth hissing steam as it raised its left arm. It was amputated below the elbow, the forearm replaced with a smoking brazier connected to a tank implanted in the Pyromagir's upper back and shoulders.

'Sound my arrival,' Pureburn whispered.

The jet of flame arced from the brazier. It was aimed high, searing over the heads of the onlookers, but burned with an intensity that surprised even Lord Pureburn. Globs of burning promethium fell from the spray like rain, igniting the roofs of some of the shanty-builds. No matter. Lord Pureburn shrugged as the inhabitants raced desperately to beat out the flames. Most of the infrastructure was worthless anyway. What mattered was he had their attention.

All eyes were on him now, expectant. He did not pander to them, instead gliding solemnly between the ranks of gawking simpletons. More approached from the fringes of the shantytown, drawn by the commotion and pyrotechnics. Lord Pureburn smiled to himself. The underhive was a true wonder, breeding people whose first thought upon spying a searing jet of flame was to run towards it, in the hopes there would be something of value to steal.

Still he did not acknowledge them, instead manoeuvring the dais to the centre of the town, flanked by his Cynder attendants. There he paused, allowing them to bask in the glow of the Eternal Flame, whilst his crusading army fanned out through the shanty town. He could hear the whispers. Some recognised him, or at least knew the stories. Others only now bore witness to his power, as the lumens strung between the buildings seemed to swell with light. For in his presence shadows faded.

Still he waited. He waited until the whispers died, curiosity and confusion replaced by burgeoning unease. He knew their fears; did he intend to make his own stake in Periculus, and would he erase theirs? If so, could he be eliminated? He must have seemed an easy target, unarmed and unarmoured. But his zealots were already amongst them, and none could be sure if the stranger standing beside them was a new arrival or follower of his creed. To move against him was to risk a knife in the back. That was true power – daring others to strike first, forcing them to acquiesce before a single word was spoken.

'Periculus,' he began, raising his head, his gaze meeting each of the settlers in turn, as though addressing them personally. Each must feel he had studied their face, committed it to memory.

He heard the shot. He did not see the bullet, not until it evaporated inches from his face in a cloud of metallic vapour. Sniper, probably from the upper levels. He gestured, and a score of his followers raced up ladders, seeking the would-be assassin.

'Periculus,' he repeated, this time his voice iron. 'Once a gem shining in the dark, now a relic long lost and forgotten. I'm sure that's why most have come here, hoping to pilfer something of value from the remnants of this once great dome.'

He let the words hang a moment before continuing.

'Of course, some may feel they have a claim – perhaps their House or family once owned interests. Or perhaps some have been drawn here by fanciful tales.'

He smiled, shaking his head, as though in disbelief. Then the smile faded, his eyes blazing as he addressed the still-growing crowd.

'To the gullible, I can only offer my condolences. You will never find what you seek. To those of you who believe you hold some prior stake in Periculus... I sympathise.'

Some looks of surprise. Once again, he paused, granting his audience time to absorb his words, and to provide the illusion that his listeners were drawing their own conclusions.

Slowly, he rose from his throne.

'The Pureburn family once powered Periculus,' he said, turning to stare into the Eternal Flame. 'My ancestors ensured the factorums ran smoothly. Yet they also powered gambling dens, stimm shops and flesh markets. They were unconcerned with whom they conducted business, providing it was profitable.'

He sighed, shrinking slightly before them. A moment of vulnerability – important to establish trust.

'I am proud of my family's legacy,' he continued. 'I am proud that, since the days of the Great Crusade, we have held the God-Emperor's fire in trust and brought that light to the dark places. But in Periculus we failed. Here we chose profit over temperance. Because others were the sinners, and we mere facilitators, we did not think our actions immoral. We merely turned a blind eye to others' failings.'

He glanced from the flame, his gaze falling on the hushed crowd.

'And Periculus fell. And all was darkness,' he said. 'There are many tales of how, and no doubt all carry a sliver of truth. But whether technical fault or inter-House warfare was the method, the cause was our failure in the eyes of the God-Emperor.'

He reached into his robes, withdrawing and unfurling a yellowed scroll that bore the insignia of House Helmawr.

'My family still owns the contract for power rights to Periculus,' he said. 'Make no mistake, I will enforce those rights. To others who hold claims I ask only that you present them to me. Those with a legitimate stake I will honour, just as I know they will honour mine. The rest of you should either pledge your support or swiftly depart. Periculus will rise from the ashes. It will be stronger than ever before. But the new Periculus will serve the will of the God-Emperor. Any who dare otherwise will face His wrath.'

He glanced to the Pyromagir. The mute servant shuffled forward, raising his brazier-hand, the smouldering weapon still dripping burning promethium.

'You will now be about your business,' Pureburn said softly. But as the crowd dispersed, he saw a figure approaching, clad in the familiar attire of House Cawdor, his face hidden by a leering mask. At first, he assumed it was one of his crusaders, and was about to direct his guards to remove him, but there was something about the way the man walked. He was not hobbled of mind or limb, his step sure and his eyes focused. If nothing else, he was a man accustomed to and untroubled by threats of violence.

The interloper bowed as he approached, dropping to one knee. But there was a tension to him, and despite his deference Pureburn could see the man was struggling against his burgeoning fury.

'You may rise,' Pureburn said. It was hard to get a sense of the man behind the mask. Perhaps he was one of those clever Cawdors who knew how the game was played. That could prove troublesome. But Lord Pureburn relaxed when the man spoke, for none could doubt the blind conviction in his voice.

'Lord Pureburn, I thank the God-Emperor for your coming. I feared my prayers would be unanswered.'

'He always answers those who serve Him,' Pureburn replied softly. 'Tell me, to whom do I speak?'

'I am Tritus the Fallen, of House Cawdor.'

'I see. And why is a pious man such as yourself condemned to this pit of sin?'

'Such places are my penitence, milord,' Tritus replied. 'I did not always see the light. But the thane told me I would find redemption where it was darkest. So, darkness is what I seek.'

'The thane?'

'The thane of Cawdor, milord,' the man said, meeting his gaze, bloodshot eyes blazing with fury. 'The lord of our House and rightful governor of this planet.'

So, he was a madman. Not that this mattered; that merely made him a different kind of tool.

'How long have you been down here, Tritus?'

'Since the discovery, since Lady Wirepath first cracked the dome. I saw her break the seal, milord. I saw her open the gate to this pit.'

'And where is Lady Wirepath now?'

'Gone, milord. No doubt claimed by the darkness for the sin of curiosity,' he murmured, eyes glazed. 'The thane tasked me with seeking the dark places, and there is only darkness here.'

Pureburn stared at him a moment. His fingers tapped a sequence into the control panel located in the throne's arm-rest. Slowly the dais descended to the ground. He stepped off, gently taking hold of Tritus' arm and raising the man to his feet.

'You need not prostrate yourself before me,' he said, look-ing the man in the eye. 'We are both His servants, both sinners before His light.'

Tritus rose slowly, hesitant, as though expecting a trick.

'Milord?'

'I need your help, Tritus,' Pureburn continued. 'I need to know who is here and what they want. I need to know my allies and enemies, who rules and who thirsts for power. I need to know the infrastructure, what is found and what con-firmed lost. I need you to take me to where Lady Wirepath held residence. And I need men loyal to the God-Emperor and His Eternal Flame, men willing to face death in His name.'

'I have waited my life for this, milord. I will provide all you need.'

'I am indebted to you.' Lord Pureburn nodded, his gaze shifting to the crude power-tap and the shanty town's centre. 'But there is one final thing I need most of all. I need to know who dared tap my power lines to steal the Emperor's light.'

3

'Do you know why I tolerated you?'

Sol's remaining eye flickered open, but his only reward was searing light. He moaned, trying to drag his hand to his face, squeezing his eye shut.

'Ah, my apologies, Lord Sol. I forget that you have yet to embrace your heritage. Reduce illumination by forty-five per cent.'

He knew the voice, the caustic tone, spite garbed as wit. It seemed the esteemed Lord Severior had graced him with a visit.

'It's that attitude that has held you back,' Severior continued, taking a seat on the bed beside Sol, hands resting on his shock-stave. 'My family's inhabited the Fulgurmessis for generations. It was my great-grandfather who was first honoured with the Gift of Illumination, his eyes surgically altered to truly appreciate the radiance.'

He looked at Sol, his crystal-blue eyes shining with borrowed light.

'You, of course, have no history,' he continued. 'Or family of any significance. Your mother was a lowly technician cursed with arrogance. Her inability to accept her place cost the unfortunate woman her life. For that you have my sympathies – it was selfish of her to place you in that position.'

He patted Sol's leg.

'Still,' he continued, 'crisis begets opportunity. Somehow you survived the lightning that killed her, Doctor Caute cutting you from the womb, delivering you on the deck of the Needle. They say the thunder heralded your cries, and with your tears the sky wept.'

He smiled, his face softening slightly.

'Of course, they would say that,' he murmured, almost lost in thought. 'That's how legends begin. A decade later technicians who were never permitted access to the outer levels still claim they witnessed the whole event. Many include their own embellishments. Someone once told me you burst from the womb in a shower of light, your mother's body burning to ash in the process. Extraordinary. But what is even more extraordinary is I swear he believed it. He had somehow deluded himself to the point where belief overrode memory.'

He looked at Sol. 'That must be hard for a man like you, someone who desires an ordered and numbered world, who obsesses over function yet forgets that all we perceive is form. That is a lesson you should have learned from Lord Pureburn. His coffers are full not because he proclaims his supply line the most reliable, or his extraction methods the most efficient. No, he sells the divine spark of God – how can any honest merchant compete with that?'

He sighed, deflating slightly. Despite it all he was still an old man, and Sol could see he carried a great weight.

'For a time I thought you were the answer,' Severior said.

'The Light-touched, a child brought to life by the perma-storm itself. You always had an aptitude for electro-alchemy, always comprehended the minutiae in a way I never could. In time, I thought we could use that somehow, forge our own legend of a boy chosen by the storm. But you were precocious, always knew better, obsessed with taking everything apart because you thought it should go together differently.'

He shook his head sadly.

'That's why I tolerated you. Because of what you represented, because of your potential. But here you lie, a victim of your obsession to prove yourself righteous. Just like your mother. There is no beating Lord Pureburn now. We have already accepted payment in exchange for not opposing his latest venture. If you had lived up to your potential, become a valuable figurehead, perhaps the Guild of Flame would have felt compelled to offer more. But you squandered your birthright trying to squeeze out a few extra volts from a dying system.'

He leant closer, until his nose was a few inches from Sol's.

'Do you know the Fulgurmessis axis has shifted?' he said softly. 'It happens very slowly, perhaps creeping a degree or so in a year. But as the weight shifts the rate of decline accelerates. While you tinker with relays I watch our legacy fall from the sky. It may take time, perhaps a century, but it will fall. The net will be severed. The harvest will end.'

Sol tried to speak. The sounds were still garbled, but a word managed to sneak through.

'Schematics?' Severior smiled. 'As if you could contribute anything in your condition. Even were you healthy you could not stop it. Our fall is inevitable, our decline inarguable. Entropy is this world's natural order. It cannot be fought, only managed and mitigated.'

He rose, unsteady, his weight resting on his shock-stave, his gaze lingering on Sol's medi-unit. He frowned, before his mouth split into a bitter smile.

'On reflection, I like you better like this,' he said. 'Quiet, without that arrogance in your eye. Perhaps that's why I've decided to spare you, despite that debacle with the Delaques. I hope to find a place for you here, Sol. I'm not sure what yet, but I'm confident we can spin the accident into a part of your tale. Perhaps your soul ascended to the storms, leaving your flesh as relic. I like that. Years from now, pilgrims will attend your shrine seeking a boon. We'll have illuminated your one eye by then, maybe added a few bionic components so you can sit up straight and recite a few psalms. A little like a servitor, merely lacking the gift of oblivion.'

He bowed his head before turning, heading to the doorway. There he paused, his back to Sol.

'Your shadowy friends will be electrocuted at dawn, when the first rays touch the solar converter. It won't be a quick death, but I thought you might appreciate the irony. I now take my leave. Illumination, increase to one hundred per cent for the remainder of the day. Give Sol some time for reflection.'

He departed, leaving Sol at the mercy of the blinding light.

The five men standing before Lord Pureburn were typical Cawdor stock: hunched figures clad in repurposed rags. Few had a full set of fingers and none a full set of teeth, their vile mouths emerging from beneath sneering half-masks, the closest thing they had to ostentation. As Lord Pureburn understood it, they covered their faces to hide their shame and sins. If so, he could only acknowledge the righteousness of their cause, for he doubted their true visages could be a source of anything but shame.

His wore his own mask – an expression of piety, his inner disgust never breaking this countenance. He sombrely assessed each man in turn, as though weighing their worth. Each time he took a moment to stare into the Eternal Flame. The theatrics were tiresome, keeping him from a dozen pressing matters. But he knew the importance of tailoring his presentation. Each man needed to feel as though he had passed a test, that his selection was due to intrinsic worth and strength of character. Beneath their assertions of modesty, each dared to dream that he was special.

When all five had received his scrutiny he bowed his head, as though in prayer. Then he turned to them and smiled.

'The Eternal Flame of the God-Emperor has seen into your hearts and found each of you to be a true servant of His name,' he said. Each man bowed his head, tracing the mark of the aquila across his chest.

'It falls on you to cleanse Periculus of the wretched,' he said as Tritus appeared, hauling a cache of weaponry. 'With us stands the God-Emperor. In His name we shall ensure the fallen repent and the heretics burn.'

Tritus approached each man in turn, reverently laying a flamer in their outstretched hands. Lord Pureburn noted hesitation in some of them. Perhaps they recognised the weapon for what it was: poorly manufactured, and even more poorly maintained. The desperate souls of House Cawdor were well acquainted with reclaiming discarded firearms, but perhaps they expected more from a prosperous Guilder.

'Is there a problem?' Pureburn smiled, as one of the brethren glanced at Tritus. The man flinched under his gaze but rallied himself.

'These weapons,' he said, addressing both Pureburn and Tritus in turn. 'Forgive me, milord, but I was responsible for

servicing the weapons of the gang I belonged to. I do not
think these are functional in their current state.'

'Do you not?' Lord Pureburn said, his voice without hint
of malice. 'I do not dispute that my weapons are humble, but true power lies not in our arms but the faith with
which we wield them. Those whose hearts are without doubt
channel the power of the God-Emperor Himself. Perhaps a
demonstration would be appropriate. Please.'

He gestured to the empty chamber.

The man stepped forward, hesitant as he raised the weapon,
perhaps concerned by the dripping fuel chamber. He aimed
the flamer, squeezing the trigger. A spurt of chemicals splashed
onto the floor as the ignition chamber failed to catch.

He glanced back to Lord Pureburn. With his mask in place
it was difficult to tell if he was scared or relieved.

'How unfortunate.' Lord Pureburn frowned. 'Brother Tritus, would you try?'

Tritus nodded, snatching the weapon from trembling fingers. As he raised it, Lord Pureburn discreetly touched a dial
on his wrist. Behind him a faint click came from the dais, as
though a lock had been turned but a fraction.

He felt it immediately, like a rush of a warm breeze on a
cool day. Except the warmth was not comforting. Instead,
it made him twitch, the minor irritations of the day fanned
into a burgeoning fury. He conquered it, of course, his iron
will and noble blood inuring him to the effect. But he could
see the shift in the Cawdor faithful, their mouths twitching
into snarls, trigger fingers itching for violence. Tritus required
no further instruction, raising the flamer and squeezing the
trigger.

The weapon disgorged a storm of fire, stretching nearly
thirty feet. It roared as the flames clawed from the barrel,

as though desperate to escape their confinement. Pureburn turned his gaze to each man in turn. All were transfixed.

'Enough,' he whispered. Reluctantly Tritus extinguished the weapon.

'I have given what I can,' Lord Pureburn said. 'I know it pales against the challenges you face, but in the hands of the devoted this is the only weapon needed.'

He glanced meaningfully at the man who had challenged him. His masked face was bowed in penitence. Was that enough? Part of Lord Pureburn wanted to open the chamber on his dais a little further, let the fires burn in the brethren's hearts a little more. It would not take much to convince the remaining four of their brother's blasphemy; they had seen proof his faith was wanting.

But no, Lord Pureburn reminded himself. He was above petty violence, beyond the influence of the dais' chamber. He was in control, now and always. With a flick of a switch the lock was turned, and some of the fire died in the men's eyes.

'I trust you will all prove your faith,' Pureburn said. 'For now, stow your weapons, live your lives, and wait for my signal. I promise you, when the time is right, we will purify this cesspit of sin.'

All five slammed their fists against their chests, their voices as one:

'Praise the God-Emperor! Hail the thane of Cawdor!'

Pureburn watched them depart before turning to Tritus.

'How many more can you gather?' he asked.

'As many as needed,' he replied.

Lord Pureburn frowned. There was something off about his voice.

'Faithful Tritus, would you raise your head a little?'

He met the fanatic's gaze, his bloodshot eyes twitching, the pupils like the pricks of a needle. As Lord Pureburn watched, a single tear swelled. Like his eye, the droplet was veined with crimson.

Lord Pureburn offered a tight smile, turning away from the man and approaching the dais. His guardian, the Pyromagir, stood beside it, the towering cyborg untouched by the events it witnessed.

'Tell me, Tritus,' Pureburn said, addressing the man from over his shoulder. 'Do you know our target?'

'Yes, milord.' The man nodded, spraying spittle. 'The count has hunkered down. We have cut him off from his allies, and your followers are numerous enough to overcome his forces.'

'I'm sure that is the case,' Lord Pureburn said. 'But I do not wish to merely best him. I want him and everyone who supports him annihilated. I want them burned to ashes. I want others to fear mentioning his very name, unless it is with a curse on their lips.'

'Yes, milord,' Tritus said. 'But what of Helmawr's Enforcers?'

'Palanite Captain Canndis and his Enforcers need all the help they can get. They will realise this, in time,' Lord Pureburn murmured. His gaze drifted back to his dais and the cell mounted beneath the Eternal Flame. He found his finger straying to the switch at his wrist. No, not yet. When the time came they would have need of the passion, but too soon and it could cloud their judgement.

'The arrogance of these wretches,' he sighed. 'Stealing power so wantonly, setting themselves up as lords of this broken dome. It is a slight that cannot go unpunished.'

'Yes, milord. They steal from the God-Emperor Himself!'

'Hmm?' Lord Pureburn frowned, glancing back at the man. 'Yes, their crime is against the Master of Mankind, and His humble servants.'

He lowered himself onto his throne, his grim countenance framed by the light of the Eternal Flame.

'Send in the next recruits.'

4

Virae stared into the stack of glow-rods that constituted her campfire. In theory the disposable rods granted eight hours of heat and light, though in her experience 'heat' amounted to mitigating the worst of frostbite. Her fire was but one of many, circles of serfs and pit fighters clustered together. When they first camped the fires were kept close to ensure none could attempt to slip away. But there was no need for that now. Fear bound them. There would be no further threat of desertion; the encounter with the eyeless creatures had ensured that.

She shivered, drawing her cloak tighter. They had made camp beneath a towering atmospheric regulator. The extraction fan was at least thirty feet across but had long since rusted shut. Still, a trickle of air seeped from the valves, enough for life to continue to cling to the lowest levels of the hive. But it was cold, and getting colder.

She raised her head as Block emerged from the shadows,

lowering himself down beside her and stretching his hands to the glow-rods.

'Done the rounds,' he said. 'Sentries are alert, but trust me when I say nobody will try anything. I've split the fighters between the groups for a bit of reassurance.'

'Only risk there is the serfs could swarm us all at once.'

'Maybe.' Block nodded. 'But then what would they do? Where would they go?'

'Does it matter?' Virae shrugged. 'It's all the same in the end.'

Block looked at her, his scarred face set in a scowl.

'Giving up on us?' he said. 'Not like you. I seem to recall a time when I tried to lie down and die in the wastes, only for you to drag me half a mile by my foot. I got up in the end out of sheer embarrassment.'

She smiled. 'That you did.'

'And, despite ash storms, starvation and nomads, we made it,' Block pointed out. 'And you got made Chain Lord and all. That's a good precedent right there.'

'You think?'

'Yeah,' he said. 'And given how badly this journey is going you'll probably end up planetary governor by the end of it.'

She laughed then, meeting his gaze and wolfish grin. But behind him she caught the hollow faces of the serfs, and her smile faded.

'How's Elle?' she asked.

'Left her with Gash's group,' Block replied, gesturing to the glow of a distant campfire. 'That boy can usually get her to smile.'

'Maybe not this time.'

'She ain't cut out for this work.'

'I made a promise that I would look after her. This is the best I can do.'

'Noble sentiment. But I can't help but notice how many

other serfs we've picked up. Guessing their folks didn't get the same promise, or a fancy counting machine implanted in their head.'

'I have a job to do as much as you do.'

'Not arguing that.' Block shrugged. 'Just don't see why you bother freeing one and leaving the rest. Seems unfair.'

'Because I'm human, all right?' Virae snapped. Her tone was harsher than intended, but Block was unperturbed. For a moment the old comrades sat in silence.

'You hurt?' she said, nodding to his bandaged shoulder.

'One of them things snuck through and sunk its teeth in.'

'Is it clean?'

'Yeah. One of the serfs patched it. Lad has a talent with a needle. It's a real shame.'

She knew what he meant. Closer to civilisation the boy might have ended up under the patronage of a doc. He could have made use of his talent, refined it, perhaps even escaped the life altogether if he was skilled enough. But Pureburn would have no interest in nuance. He just needed bodies to feed to the furnace of industry. The lad would be lucky to see another year. The thought depressed her on several levels.

'You been keeping an eye on the ratskin?' she asked.

'Still am,' Block replied, his eyes flicking across to the adjacent fire. Virae peered through the press of bodies and caught sight of the familiar scowl and crimson-stained eyes.

'Any trouble?' she asked.

'Nope,' Block replied, keeping his gaze locked on the flames. 'She has not said a cross word, picked a fight, or tried to escape. I'm getting real suspicious – you know what ratskins are like.'

'No. I only know what the stories say they are like,' she replied. 'Excuse me a moment.'

She rose, crossing the darkness between the glow-fires. As she approached, the serfs bowed their heads, whispered conversations abruptly ceasing. She ignored them, stopping only when she stood before the ratskin. The younger woman met her gaze, her dark eyes unwavering.

'I am Virae the Unbroken, Chain Lord of the Mercator Sanguis,' she said.

The ratskin didn't respond. Virae squatted down, hamstrings resting on her calves, until their faces were inches apart.

'You got a name?' she asked.

The ratskin stared back and for a moment Virae wondered if she was mute or did not speak Low Gothic.

'I had a name,' the ratskin said. 'Do I get to keep it?'

Her voice seemed calm, but Virae could sense the edge beneath the words.

'Honestly? Depends on where you end up,' Virae said. 'Some like to assign numbers or new names to their charges. Never saw the point in it myself, just another way to mess up your records. So yeah, you can keep your name, at least as long as you're with me. Feel like sharing it now?'

'No.'

The defiance again. She knew she should stamp on it, but part of her was enjoying herself. Very few defied her now. It was almost refreshing.

'Real attitude you got there,' Virae said, smiling. From the corner of her eye she saw the others edging away from the confrontation, but the ratskin just stared back at her. For an instant she seemed coiled like a spring, as though preparing to strike. But instead she sighed, bowing her head.

'I'm sorry,' she said, voice flat. 'I am still shaken from the monsters.'

The words lacked even a hint of sincerity.

'Scared, were you?' Virae asked. 'Because you seemed to hold your own.'

'Perhaps. It was dark. Who knows?'

'Well, I think I owe you,' Virae said, rising to her feet. 'Maybe you have talents that might be better suited to the arena. Have you fought in the pit?'

The ratskin frowned a moment, as though unsure how to answer the question.

'I suppose,' she said. 'Briefly.'

'With whom?'

'I don't remember the names.'

'How many did you fight?'

'Two… No, three pit fighters. But they weren't real fights. Didn't last long enough.'

'Still impressive,' Virae persisted. 'Perhaps you'd be better suited to a life in the arena. Better food and conditions, plus a chance to use your skills. As Chain Lord I could arrange that.'

The ratskin smiled, but there was something deeply unpleasant about the expression.

'I met a Chain Lord once,' she said. 'He made promises. But he didn't keep them.'

'I am not like other Chain Lords.'

'Yet you still hold the chains,' the ratskin said. 'Think maybe I'm better off here. Keep my head down.'

'Condemning yourself to work to death in a factorum?' Virae asked.

'Perhaps.' The ratskin shrugged, stretching her hands to the glow-fire.

A voice. Someone shaking his shoulder. No doubt the doctor again. He did not reply. There seemed little point. The only sounds he could make bore little resemblance to words.

'Sol?'

Was it the doctor? The voice sounded different. Familiar, but different.

'Sol? If you can hear me this might sting a little.'

He felt a sharp pain in his neck, followed by the hiss of an autoinjector. A creeping cold spreading across his throat and cheek, numbing the burning sensation.

He blinked. Twice, cleanly.

'Can you speak?'

He knew the voice now. As his vision cleared, Anguis, the leader of the Delaques slowly condensed into focus. She was sans her longcoat, her bare arms pale under the muted lights of the medi-unit.

'I... what happened?'

'It was the spyker,' she said. 'He unleashed a psychic assault as you struck. It caused some serious synaptic damage. But this is not the first time I have witnessed such an incident, and we have adapted countermeasures. I have given you a neuro-cleanser that should mitigate the worst of it. But it will take time for the effect to fully pass – you may suffer delusions, memory gaps, loss of motor control.'

At her words, it came back to him – the abomination with the empty eye sockets, its grotesquely swollen cranium framed by a halo of black flames. He saw his own arm outstretched, storm-light arcing between his fingers. He'd killed it. Surely, he'd killed it?

'It's dead?' he managed, his tongue heavy, the words a mumbled slur. He was worried she would not understand. Then again, Delaques were renowned for being excellent listeners, whether the speaker knew they were listening or not.

'It's dead,' she said. 'Its head burst. I don't know why it reacted that way. There must have been something about the patient, some residual psychic trauma that sparked it off. He's gone, by the way. Burned to ash. No idea how – as far as I know Stitch had no pyromantic abilities.'

'How did I… here?'

'Doctor Caute dispatched a team. There was little time to adjust the evidence. The fire helped us there. We claimed it was part of an experiment incorporating servitors into surveillance systems.'

'They didn't believe you.'

'No. That's why my team and I are currently incarcerated,' she sighed. 'Officially, anyway. I decided it was time to take our leave.'

'Then why are you here?'

'Because I owe you my life,' she said. 'I thought I should return the favour. Besides, I cannot free the others without help. Now, get up.'

'I cannot move.'

'You have to,' she replied, pulling back his sheets. Beneath he was clad only in dressings and dried blood, but she took his arm, easing him to his feet. He wobbled, legs weak, but she was stronger than she looked, throwing his arm over her shoulders and supporting his weight as she guided him towards the door.

'Where are we going?'

'To free the others,' she said, grabbing a medical gown from behind the door. 'Put this on.'

'I doubt I can assist.'

'And I doubt this place is organised enough to remove your access codes, especially when they think you can't move,' she replied. 'Besides, you can't stay here. They're executing you too.'

He blinked. 'What?'

'If you are not gone by morning you will be dead.'

He stared at her, trying to read her expression. She seemed genuine in her concern. But she always seemed genuine.

'How do you know they intend to kill me?' he asked, watching her.

'I received information.'

'From whom?'

'I have sleepers. Some have spent years in their current assignment,' she said, irritation creeping into her voice. 'I owe you my life and I am trying to return the favour. You have to trust me.'

'It's a lot to take on trust.'

'Then go back to your bed and await your death. I understand your suspicion of my House, but you know me. If you cannot accept the truth of my words then remain here. But I promise, if you do not leave tonight, your life will be forfeit.'

He looked at her. She held her composure, but there was a hint of desperation in her words, a flicker of fear. It was not an expression he had seen before. It did not seem affected.

'Very well,' he said. 'I will trust you, at least for now.'

She smiled her half-smile. 'Wisest decision you ever made,' she said, pressing her ear to the door. 'I hear footsteps. One outside, another coming round.'

'There's a third,' Sol whispered. 'Further, but drawing closer.'

She frowned, glancing at him. 'How do you know?'

'I… am not certain.' He could feel the presence, a flicker of static against the pulse of the corridor. He could not articulate it. Perhaps it was the effect of the drug; he was finding it harder to stay upright, his hand grasping the wall for support.

'Three then,' Anguis sighed. 'No matter. Stay here.'

'Wait,' he whispered, but she had already vanished, silent as a shadow. He heard muffled cries, followed by the muted thump of a body striking the ground. She reappeared seconds later.

'Follow me.'

'You killed them?' he said, stepping out of the room.

'Incapacitated,' she whispered, though he doubted her assertion.

The corridor was mercifully dark. The Council of Light tolerated a brief night cycle, if only to highlight the radiance of the day. It gave some token cover as they crept along the corridor, but both were still far too exposed. Ahead was a junction.

'Any ideas on patrol routes? Security patterns?' she asked.

'No.'

'And they took all my best toys,' she said, turning over her arm and exposing her pallid forearm. She gritted her teeth, wincing as she dug a nail into the flesh, drawing a crimson line. From the incision she extracted a thin metal sliver, swiftly extending the needle until it stretched over two feet long, the tip emanating a faint green glow.

She crouched low, the tip of the device peeking round each corner of the junction, the information presumably relayed to her optical implants.

'Clear,' she whispered, beckoning him to follow, but he hesitated.

She turned, glancing at him. 'There is no time to be timid.'

'There's something coming. I can hear it.'

'I would hear it before you did.'

'No, it's coming closer.'

She frowned, opening her mouth to speak. But then she must have heard it too. Not quite footsteps, or if they were they were masked by another sound, the rhythmic clank of a machine in motion. It was familiar, like all the noises aboard the Needle, but his thoughts were clouded, and he could not place it. Still, it was drawing closer.

Anguis reached into the skingraft on her arm, withdrawing

a needle-like blade. The metal carried a greenish veneer, no doubt secreting neurotoxins. She waited until the sound was almost on them before darting out, weapon raised.

He heard the thump of the blow and the whirl of servos. Anguis gave a sharp cry.

Without thinking he surged after her, staggering, his legs still weak. He ran straight into the imposing form of the medi-servitor. Its servo-claw grasped Anguis' throat, suspending her above the ground. She still held the blade, slashing weakly at the machine's forearm, but whatever venom the blade carried it did little to trouble the half-dead cyborg.

Sol seized the servo arm, trying to break the machine's grip. It was pointless, his strength nothing against it. Had it been so directed the machine could easily tear an unaugmented human in half.

'Sol!'

He hadn't noticed Doctor Caute. He was skulking behind the bulky cyborg, presumably guiding it. But he rushed forward, staring at Sol in disbelief.

'Sol? You're walking?'

'Release her!' Sol snapped, as Anguis' blade fell from her fingers. She was barely moving now, her lips tinted blue.

'This way is better,' Doctor Caute replied. 'Severior wants to make a spectacle. Grant her the God-Emperor's mercy and let her die quickly!'

'No!' Sol replied, grasping at the cyborg's exposed cables. They were thick as his wrist, but perhaps he could do something, compromise the hydraulics, damage the main relay. Anything that would break its grip. But his fingers were slow, clumsy. The life was leaving her and there was nothing he could do.

Except… she wasn't earthed.

He gave it no further thought, not permitting himself the chance to hesitate or consider, for Anguis had no time left. He reached out, straining as he sought the last reserves of electrical energy trickling through the neurone circuits. He hadn't drunk of the storm since his injury, but it need not be a strong charge, just enough to reboot the servitor and force it to release its hold. He prayed he had syphoned enough power whilst confined to the medi-unit.

But as Sol grasped the cold dead flesh, he felt a hand on his shoulder. Caute was trying to drag him away, pleading for him to cease. He was still weak, and the old man could overpower him.

He closed his eyes and released what little he had left.

What followed made no sense.

Lightning arced between his fingers, the blast burning through the servitor's flesh, severing its arm at the elbow. Anguis fell to the ground, wrenching the servo-claw from her throat as the power continued to course through Sol's body. He could neither contain nor channel it. The storm's fury radiated in all directions, and Doctor Caute jerked like a puppet as convulsions tore through him. He was hurled across the corridor, landing hard and lying still.

Sol fell to his knees, the now motionless cyborg beside him. His whole body ached. He could barely see from his one good eye. Somehow in that moment he had felt Doctor Caute's terror. Worse still, he had felt his sense of failure, and his love. Now he felt nothing.

Anguis was tugging at his arm.

'Get up,' she wheezed, rubbing life into her throat. 'They will be after us now. We have to get off the station.'

'I can't–'

'You have saved me twice – I will not leave you to die here,'

she said, somehow dragging him to his feet. They staggered
from the carnage, but as they reached the corridor's end, he
tore his head round, catching a final glimpse of the broken
body lying in the corridor.

5

'I should be calling this meeting,' Palanite Captain Canndis murmured.

He glanced to his escort, who were covering the church's door, Hendrox and… the other one. Neither responded, perhaps assuming his remarks were rhetorical. Perhaps they were, but he remained the most senior Enforcer present in Periculus. He had been given specific orders to maintain the peace, and he had fulfilled those orders to the best of his ability with the limited resources available. He was the law, Helmawr's Law. Guilders and gang leaders should seek an audience with him.

Lord Pureburn had done no such thing.

Palanite Captain Canndis had not heard his inaugural sermon, but he had seen the changes that followed. The influx of House Cawdor for starters. They had moved like rats in the shadows, gnawing through Periculus' cracks. He'd taken the early deaths as petty rivalries and old grudges. But there was a pattern to it, one House seemingly untouched by the troubles, and it didn't take a detective to see their numbers swelling. The Cawdor faithful were the largest single group in Periculus, perhaps outnumbering the others combined. They would take anyone, providing they had faith.

He sighed, glancing to the digital display-clock adorning the far wall. There was little else of note in the room; an Ecclesiarchy symbol had been hastily scrawled above a lop-sided pulpit installed days earlier. Benches cut from flakboard and mounted on rusted braces were arranged in rows. Glad-shiv was seated at a pew close to the pulpit, hands clasped in prayer. Apparently, the clerk bought into House Cawdor's twisted interpretation of the Imperial Faith.

Canndis' gaze slid to the floor. It had been scrubbed raw but was still stained by blood and other less identifiable marks. Before its recent conversion, the room had apparently been a stimm-cache, though by the time Canndis had been informed of this the stash had been burned, along with the two Van Saar fighters allegedly overseeing the operation. A storehouse of illicit dealings was now a church. Maybe that was progress.

Canndis did not know the alleged criminals, though in his experience everyone was guilty of something. But justice was bestowed by the Enforcers, those men and women who had taken the oath. Vigilante justice, though superficially an attractive solution to the rampant crime, only begat more vigilante justice. He would shed no tears for the dead, but reprisals would be coming. Pureburn's men had torn down half of Count Technus' operation, but all that meant was the other half was angry and looking for payback.

He tapped his fingers on the pew. He desperately wanted a lho-stick, but it set the wrong tone. He'd look nervous, as

though not in control. Instead he shifted his focus to the
Enforcers flanking the door. Hendrox and… who was the
other one? Sisphant? Both were helmeted, weapons drawn.
It should not come to that, he reminded himself. Lord Pureburn was not a lowlife, merely a Guilder from Hive City now
well below his depth.

'Captain Canndis. My apologies for my tardiness.'

The voice came from behind him. Canndis turned. Lord
Pureburn was standing by the altar, his crimson robes somehow pristine, his well-lined face set in a hard smile. On his
left stood one of the hulking servants of the Mercator Pyros:
a nightmare fusion of metal and flesh, its lower jaw replaced
by a metal grate that hissed steam, its right arm ending in
a smouldering brazier. On Pureburn's right was one of the
Cawdor rats, face hidden by a leering mask. Canndis could
just make out his bloodshot eyes, and he ruled it sufficient
evidence to confirm the man was quite mad.

Canndis rose, helmet clasped under his arm as he marched
stiffly to meet the Guilder.

'I am Palanite Captain Canndis,' he barked, before remembering that Pureburn already knew his name. The man's
sudden appearance had thrown him off. There must have
been a hidden entrance.

'I am Lord Silas Pureburn,' the Guilder said with a smile.
'Delighted to meet you, captain.'

'I wish I could say the same,' Canndis replied, glaring at
him. 'Do you know how many incinerations have occurred
since you led those Cawdor rats into Periculus?'

Lord Pureburn sighed, a pained expression crossing his
lined face. 'Yes. I fear I must take some responsibility for that.'

'They were acting on your orders, then?'

'When I heard of Periculus' rediscovery I raced here to fulfil the oaths of my ancestors,' Pureburn continued, ignoring the question. 'I passed many settlements on my journey. I fear my excitement roused the passions of Hive Primus' more zealous elements. I am humbled they chose to follow me, despite the risks.'

'The risks are greater now,' Canndis grunted. 'These maniacs are responsible for more deaths down here than all the criminals and heretics combined.'

'You must forgive them,' Lord Pureburn replied. 'Many originate from more pious parts of the underhive. They are not accustomed to dens of sin and heresy. Some have brought children and the old and frail, hoping for a new life. They felt compelled to take action when they discovered stimm-dealers and cutthroats living amongst them.'

Canndis sighed, glancing round the recently renovated church.

'Lord Pureburn,' he said. 'I have no great desire to prosecute whomever was responsible for... setting up this church. But unsanctioned violence must have consequences.'

'Indeed. That is why I wanted to introduce you to Brother Tritus.'

He nodded to the Cawdor rat flanking him, who was still staring at Canndis with ill-disguised hate.

'Brother Tritus will be tasked with running this church and administering to the faithful,' he said. 'This is but the beginning. An orphanarium is already being set up to care for and educate the young. Periculus will retake its place of power. You have my word.'

Canndis leant closer, his face an inch from Lord Pureburn's own.

'I answer only to Lord Helmawr. He will decide what Periculus will be.'

'Of course,' Lord Pureburn said. 'Forgive the impertinence.'

'Our biggest problem is lack of food, not faith,' Canndis continued. 'That and the damn cold.'

'Worry not. I have already contacted colleagues in the Mercator Pallidus. Supplies and a Grinder team will be arriving within days. As for the temperature, once I have finalised the promethium lines, Periculus will have all the heat and power it needs to thrive.'

Canndis laughed, the sound without humour. '"Thrive" might be a stretch. "Survive" would be a start.'

'I value your assessment, Palanite captain,' Pureburn replied. 'But I suspect it was made before my arrival. Do not doubt that I will restore the glory of Periculus. Every fragment of the dome will be as it was, every factorum functioning at full capacity.'

Canndis shook his head. 'That's impossible. There aren't enough workers to—'

'The Mercator Sanguis has a slave caravan on its way.'

'The factorums aren't even operational!' Canndis snapped. 'Half the blocks out there are at risk of collapsing. What do you expect me to do with that many more bodies? More mouths? More chaos?'

Pureburn spread his hands. 'I'm afraid it is already in hand. They will be here within a day or two.'

'You Throne-damned fool!' Canndis swore. Gladshiv, still bent in prayer, jumped at the sound, nearly tumbling from the pew. Canndis glared at him and the clerk bowed his head, but not before the Palanite captain had caught the disdain in his eyes.

Pureburn smiled at the clerk, before turning back to Canndis, untroubled by the outburst.

'Chief Palanite captain, I regret placing this burden on

you,' he said. 'But I am a man of considerable resources. I can supply the weaponry and expertise to assist the battle against corruption.'

Canndis laughed. 'You're looking to sign up?'

'An old man such as I would be a liability.' Pureburn smiled. 'But I could assist in other ways. That power tap presently supplying your needs is shoddy work, even for a criminal.'

'That tap was utilised on a temporary basis to secure our headquarters,' Canndis replied stiffly. 'If you wish I can quote law and contract to support–'

'That will not be necessary,' Lord Pureburn said. 'But, as I am here now, a temporary solution is no longer required. Perhaps this is something else I could assist with? I could censure Count Technus and his mob for stealing promethium, and in the process ensure your fortress-precinct is properly powered?'

He smiled again, his gaunt cheeks bestowing the expression with a cadaverous quality. Canndis had dredged up corpses with more endearing grins. The man was a snake, painstakingly employing tone and expression to feign sincerity. Still, he was a Guilder, and that was how business was done. Canndis did not need to trust the man if he trusted his goal.

'You are asking for me to sanction these activities?'

Lord Pureburn nodded solemnly. 'Indeed so. You are the law, Palanite captain. All powers lie with you, and I would not wish to act in a manner that could be considered disrespectful.'

'Very well,' Canndis said. 'Go resolve this promethium theft business, but don't even think about tampering with the current line until you are ready to meet our needs. I'm not sleeping cold again.'

'Of course, sir,' Pureburn replied with a sharp smile. 'Though

I confess I anticipated your response and already made some arrangements. On your return the fortress-precinct will shine as bright as Helmawr's justice, and a warm bed will await you.'

'I'm pleased to hear it.'

'I keep my promises, Palanite captain,' Pureburn said, still smiling. 'In fact, I have also resolved the other matter. Please come with me.'

He stepped past Canndis, his Cawdor henchman and lumbering Pyromagir falling in behind him. Even Gladshiv jumped to his feet before hesitating, his glaze flicking between Pureburn and Canndis.

'What in the Throne's name is this?' Canndis demanded, his hand reaching for his sidearm. But they ignored him, striding towards the main doors of the church, the priest darting ahead, sweeping them open.

The congregation's roar was deafening. Blazing torches warded the darkness, as hundreds of voices sang a liturgy of hate. They had been busy in Canndis' absence; a pyre-spike had been assembled just outside the church, two men bound to it. They did not struggle. Canndis was unsure whether they even could. Both had joints twisted at unnatural angles, their features distorted by bruises and blood. But Canndis could just about recognise Count Technus. The other might be his second in command. Gob, was it? He'd never learnt the man's name.

Beside them, Lord Pureburn ascended to his dais' throne whilst Tritus baited the crowd.

'Brothers and sisters!' he proclaimed, as Canndis slowly emerged through the church gates. 'Lord Pureburn has brought the God-Emperor's fire to the depths of the underhive. Though sinners all, we will prove to Him our worth, and we will punish those who try to steal His light!'

Canndis had expected a guttural roar of approval, but they were silent now, the only sounds the crackle of torches and the horrid wheeze of the bound gangers as they fought for each breath.

Lord Pureburn bowed his head.

'Loyal servants of the God-Emperor,' he murmured, his voice little more than a whisper. 'Before you stand two sinners. In their greed they stole my sacred promethium.'

The crowd murmured its disapproval. There were cries of indignation and calls for retribution. Lord Pureburn raised his hand for quiet.

'Worse than that,' he continued, 'they have stolen the property of Lord Helmawr.'

There was some muttering from the crowd, far less supportive than before. To the Cawdor faithful, there was only one ruler worthy of their respect, the thane himself. Helmawr was at best a peer, and at worst little more than a sinner from the spire. Invoking his name garnered little support from the congregation.

Lord Pureburn held Canndis' gaze for a heartbeat before glancing to the Eternal Flame mounted on his dais.

'But Lord Helmawr and I are but stewards, charged with ensuring His will is enacted, and His sacrifice is not in vain. We bring His light to hold back the dark.'

He turned back to the count, voice choked as though with passion.

'The real crime here is theft of the God-Emperor's light!'

Now the congregation wailed in their fury. Canndis was close enough to see some clawing at their own flesh in disgust, overwhelmed by the vileness of the act. Tritus approached Lord Pureburn, bearing an unlit torch, the end wrapped in rags soaked in promethium.

Pureburn set his gaze on Canndis. As one, the congregation followed.

'Palanite Captain Canndis has recognised the severity of this crime,' he said. 'He has bestowed upon me the power to resolve this and all similar matters. I am eternally grateful to him and his righteous team of Palanite Enforcers for the protection they provided until now.'

Canndis did not speak, instead glancing to the crowd. They did not look similarly grateful. At best, some seemed resigned that, for now, he was not an enemy. But, from their expressions, that could soon change.

Lord Pureburn held out a torch to his dais' Eternal Flame, the promethium-soaked rag at its tip igniting into a modest blaze.

'The faithful recognise that fire is a symbol of purification,' he whispered, raising the torch for all to see. 'But never forget the sanctity comes not from the fire itself. It is a gift of the God-Emperor.'

He stepped closer to the pyre-spikes. No doubt the offenders were already dosed in promethium. Canndis waited for the rush of flame, but was surprised to see Lord Pureburn lay the flickering torch between them. It was a little thing, barely enough to singe their boots. As he did so, Tritus raised his hand, and one by one the crowd's torches were snuffed out, until only that flickering fire remained.

Lord Pureburn seated himself on the throne, his silhouette framed by the Eternal Flame. All else was darkness, barring the tiny halo thrown by the torch.

'These men have squandered the God-Emperor's fuel,' he whispered, every word weighed, each inflection measured. 'They will burn for what they have done. But I shall not waste more of the God-Emperor's promethium on the unworthy.

Not when we have the power of faith. Instead I ask you to join me in prayer. I ask you to entreat Him to deliver His mercy.'

He bowed his head. Canndis could only assume the congregation did likewise; it was too dark to see them now.

So that was it. He sighed, taking a lho-stick from his greatcoat and tucking it between his lips. There must be some kind of vent or pipe built into the execution grounds. When triggered, the accused would suddenly ignite, thus proving the righteousness of Lord Pureburn's crusade. He was a slick bastard; there was no doubting that.

Canndis glanced one final time at the two men as he fumbled for his light. He had little sympathy. They were both criminals, guilty of a score of known offences and, no doubt, a score more as yet uncovered. Still, he would not relish seeing them burned. The whole enterprise seemed unnecessarily theatrical.

His finger struggled with the light.

As it caught, the pyre-spike suddenly exploded, the flame surging thirty feet. There was no time to scream, the two men reduced from flesh to ash in seconds. But Canndis could barely acknowledge it, as the flame from his lighter also flared, singeing his face and scorching his hair. He cursed, diving back into the church as he beat out the flames, the congregation oblivious as they recited their psalms of purging.

Gladshiv still lingered in the doorway, frozen.

'Water!' Canndis snapped, beating out the flames.

The clerk glanced to the church's font, but hesitated. 'But… it is blessed by–'

'Now!' Canndis snapped, seizing Gladshiv's collar and half hurling him aside. He looked back. Outside, the congregation was still cheering, rejoicing as the impossible pyre continued to blaze. Even Lord Pureburn smiled, perhaps the first genuine expression that Canndis had witnessed from the man. They all basked in the inferno's glow.

All except Tritus, the priest. His gaze was fixed on Canndis, and his hate was no longer ill-disguised.

6

The craft shuddered about Sol, buffeted by the storm. He sat in the cargo hold, one of the Delaque agents opposite, the other in the cockpit with Anguis. The third had not survived the incident with the spyker. Sol recalled little of the escape and ensuing firefight – stray shots whistling past him as he prepared the craft for take-off.

It shuddered again, the sealed windows framed by a burst of light. The craft's conversion field had triggered, transforming the lightning into a blinding radiance. He'd done his best to rig the harvesters to draw the storm's wrath, but there had been little time and no support. He wondered idly how much voltage the conversion field would endure before failing, and found he cared little for the answer.

All he could think of was Doctor Caute lying still in the corridor.

Perhaps he had survived, the shock rendering him

unconscious, or maybe he had struck his head and was
merely dazed.

Or perhaps Sol had killed him.

His gaze drifted to the agent opposite, who stared back
with soulless machine eyes. Perhaps they were in conversation with Anguis, or grieving a lost comrade. Sol wondered if
the sacrifice had been voluntary, or a matter of chance? Did
it matter if death was indescribable, like a lightning strike,
or deliberate, like the spyker's brutal attack? Death was the
same either way.

The more he considered it, the more he found himself
wondering why he put so much trust in people he knew so
little about. The agents had always been efficient, ever since
he first hired Anguis' team to spy on a competitor. Each
assignation had been flawlessly executed, and he'd begun
to trust their talents. He thought he'd maintained a professional detachment. But he saw now he had let them too
close. Let her too close.

The cockpit door hissed open. Anguis emerged, still missing her longcoat. It made her seem vulnerable, exposed and
unarmed all at once. No doubt her intention.

'We're going to make it,' she sighed, slumping into the seat
beside the other agent. 'But the storm is raging, and our oarsman inexperienced.'

'It's impressive they can operate the craft to begin with,'
Sol replied. 'It's hardly standard issue.'

'Preparation is key,' she said. 'The sweetest victories are won
without a shot being fired.'

Sol stared at her with his sole remaining eye.

'I do not consider this sweet. Or a victory for that matter.'

'I'm sorry about your eye. Once we are back in Hive Primus
I will arrange for an ocular implant, better than the original.'

'I think not.'

She frowned. 'Why?'

'Because you have spent enough time in my head,' he said. 'I do not want a micro-scanner sending you images of what I see, or a vox-bead eavesdropping on my conversations.'

'I wouldn't do that.'

'What then?' he asked. 'Perhaps a small syringe with a toxic payload? A quick means of severing our partnership once a better deal comes along?'

She stared back at him for a moment, expression unreadable. Then she rose suddenly, backhanding him across the face. The force was sufficient to jar him from his seat. He fell hard, just as the craft suffered another violent lurch. Anguis swayed, almost joining him on the floor.

'I am sorry for your loss,' she said, the barest hint of anger behind the words. 'You are entitled to grieve as you wish. But you do me a disservice. I did not have to come back for you. We could have left on our own. But I chose to save you.'

'Because I was to be executed?'

'Yes.'

'You are certain?' he said, returning to his seat. 'Lord Severior said he intended to display me as his pet. He did not wish me dead.'

'Perhaps he changed his mind?' she suggested, lowering herself onto the pew opposite him. 'Or some other senior figure decided to eliminate you.'

'Perhaps.' Sol nodded. 'But it strikes me that the only evidence I have of this threat is your word.'

She stared back with her soulless eyes. 'Is that not enough?'

'The threat on my life did not come from Lord Severior, or the Mercator Lux, did it?' he said. 'It came from House Delaque.'

She was silent for a moment, though from the twitch of her head he assumed she was conversing with the other agents.

'You did kill a spyker.' She shrugged.

'You admit it then?'

'No,' she said. 'But you killed a spyker. They are neither quick nor straightforward to replace. It is conceivable the House of Secrets would seek recompense. Your life, or perhaps your service. Hypothetically, of course.'

'It tried to kill us. I saved you.'

'Your impatience gave it an opening,' she replied. 'Perhaps your inhibitor was not correctly calibrated, and Mr Stitch snuck into your head. You were the only fresh variable. Your haste gave it what it needed to break free.'

'You should have warned me of the dangers.'

She laughed. It sounded hollow.

'It's an artificially induced psyker,' she said. 'Sanctioned or not, there are few things on this planet with greater potential for danger. If one drew too much power, pierced the veil...' She trailed off, spreading her hands.

'And for its death your House wishes me dead.'

'My House desires many things,' she replied. 'Revenge is sometimes a necessary tool to ensure future compliance. But it is the compliance itself we value. Your talents could serve the House of Secrets. If you are compliant then your life will be spared. I swear it.'

'I will not be a slave.'

As he spoke, the craft shuddered. An instant later they heard the thunder swelling.

'Better than a corpse?' she offered. 'Unless you have something of value to exchange for your life?'

'Periculus.'

She raised an eyebrow. 'What of it?'

'Take me there and I will secure the contract from Pure-burn. Whatever secrets you wish to protect, I will ensure they remain so.'

'Is that right?' she said. 'You, disgraced and with no support, will wrestle power from one of the most respected and feared Guilders on the planet?'

'I lost everything because of him,' Sol replied. 'He has ever stood against me, but now I know he hides some weakness. I've seen what he has never let living eyes see... I just need to figure out what it means.'

'And you think this unknown weakness will be his undoing?' she asked. 'Now who is asking for something to be taken on trust?'

'I have never lied to you. You know this. And you know the power in secrets.'

She looked at him with those inscrutable eyes of cold metal.

'It sounds as though you wish to barter your freedom by offering me the very thing you want most,' she said. 'I admire your ambition, if nothing else.'

'I'm offering something we both want. You were the one insisting we needed to head back before Periculus' secrets were uncovered.'

The craft shuddered again, caught by the storm. Anguis' head snapped round to the cockpit.

'You need to fly lower,' Sol murmured. 'Closer to the net.'

'If we fly too close we will be caught in the discharges.'

'Trust the lightning-lures to draw the tempest.'

She frowned. 'Trust is not something that comes easily to The House of Secrets.'

'If you don't trust the lures, then at least trust me.'

'Fine,' she said, turning away and heading to the cockpit.

Sol watched her depart, his only remaining ally. But now he was little more than a captive, a tool to be employed as needed, just like the spyker. The thought made him shudder. Even now, he still felt as though the creature were scratching at his thoughts, worming its way in.

'There is another possibility as to why the inhibitor did not protect you.'

The voice was barely a whisper. Sol glanced up. The Delaque agent was addressing him.

'Inhibitors keep the spyker from getting into your head,' the agent continued, tapping their temple. 'They're strong enough to prevent intrusion. Unless you provide an opening. Unless you invite it in.'

The agent rose then, seeking their fellow agents in the cockpit, leaving Sol alone with the thoughts he was no longer sure were his own.

Credence Sorrow prided himself on many things: his entrepreneurial spirit, his ability to buy friends and manipulate people, and, perhaps more than anything, his appearance. Always impeccable, always understated, always inspiring. And always in black, of course. His new frock coat was woven from a rare Vermisian silk, which actively repelled dust and dirt. Recent minor gene-crafting had given him fuller, longer hair that now reached his shoulders, as well as clearing up a skin blemish acquired the last time he set foot in the underhive. Periculus was the Forbidden Gem, a treasure from a bygone age. It was imperative he lived up to its reputation.

It transpired this was a wasted effort. There was no grand entrance to the dome, merely a split bulkhead manned by a pair of Enforcers. Neither did more than glance at his credentials before waving him through, but the gap was too narrow for the wagon train. He left his Corpse Grinder team to unload crates of powdered corpse-broth and blackmeal-bread whilst he crossed the threshold, brushing dirt from his allegedly dirt-proof robe.

Periculus was certainly imposing. He'd half expected it to still be shrouded in darkness. But light was plentiful, emanating from the towering braziers. They seemed recent additions and poorly thought out, belching clouds of sulphurous smoke that cast the towering hab-blocks in a haze. Sorrow wondered briefly if the dome's extractor fans were functional. If not, there was a reasonable chance the inhabitants would choke to death within a lunar cycle. He did have on his person an elegant gold-plated respirator, but he suspected it would clash with his boots.

His arrival had not gone unnoticed. Three figures were approaching, clad in the tattered robes and vulgar half-masks of House Cawdor. All carried bizarre weapons: aged autoguns strung into bizarre spear-like polearms. None gave the impression of being fashionistas.

Sorrow raised his hand in greeting, offering a smile he normally reserved for dignitaries. It did not seem to impress them. The lead figure nodded in response, his full expression concealed by his mask. But the man's mouth and eyes were visible and he did not look enamoured of Periculus' latest arrival.

'You are Sorrow?' he said as they drew closer.

Sorrow bowed. 'I am Lord Credence Sorrow of the Mercator Pallidus.'

'Mercato what?' one of the welcome party asked, frowning. He sounded young, more juve than frontline solider.

'He's a corpse farmer, you idiot,' the third figure said, grinning. 'This is the fellow who makes sure the dead are ground up fine, so you can pretend you can't taste them. You brought some rotters for our supper?'

Lord Sorrow smiled in response, his finger brushing against a discreet switch concealed in his wrist guard.

'Perhaps there is a misunderstanding,' he said, as two hulking shapes emerged from the brazier-smog, taking up defensive positions on either side of him. Both were huge, barely squeezed into their midnight robes, and wore the dour expressions of men inured to blood and violence, the prospect of killing neither a cause of excitement nor concern.

'Let's have another try at those introductions,' Lord Sorrow said with a tight smile. 'I am Lord Credence Sorrow of the Mercator Pallidus, chartered by Lord Helmawr himself to ensure that his citizens are fed. I take great pride in ensuring that my produce is of the highest quality and competitively priced. Lord Silas Pureburn of the Mercator Pyros personally recruited my services, and I have arrived as requested. I'm not sure the root of your hostility – at present I don't even know your name. But I humbly suggest you mind your tone, unless you wish the situation to escalate.' He gestured to the figures either side of him. 'My associates' experience is primarily in butchering corpses, but I am given to understand their skills are transferable and extend to vivisection when required.'

The Cawdor leader glanced from one brute to the other, his expression unchanged. He took a step closer, until he stood face to face with Sorrow, who did his best not to gag from the smell.

'You want to know my name?' he asked.

'That's how strangers become associates, and associates become friends.'

Sorrow offered his hand along with his fixed smile. The

Cawdor glanced at it, and for a moment Sorrow thought the man was going to spit on him. Instead he chuckled, the sound without humour.

'You don't care about my name,' he said with a joyless smile. 'You wouldn't even remember it tomorrow. We're just meat to you, to be sliced and sold, our lives and deaths a means to fatten your pockets. You worship money, but the God-Emperor knows that even a world is worthless if buying it costs you your soul.'

Sorrow's smile faded. He lowered his hand.

'I'll still need your name,' he said, his two Grinders drawing in closer. 'Just to let dear Silas know of the warm welcome you provided.'

The Cawdor leader glanced to the lumbering brutes before his gaze shifted, intent on something on the far side of Sorrow's shoulder. The Guilder heard movement behind him, like rats crawling from vents.

'My name is Brother Tritus,' the Cawdor said. 'And perhaps I should be more hospitable, introduce you to my brothers.'

More of his brethren were emerging all around them, faces hidden by grim masks. Some were more elaborate pieces, at least by Cawdor standards, with leering smiles or scowls, but many were little more than crudely stitched rags painted in gaudy red. There were more of them than he could count. And Lord Credence Sorrow could count very well indeed.

His Grinders stood by him, seemingly unconcerned, ready to set to work with flaying knife and chainblade. But against the swarm they would be nothing: two rocks trying to stem the flow of the sump sea.

'You plan to kill us then?' Sorrow asked, casually adjusting the signet ring on his left hand. 'You realise this is but the first of many shipments needed to feed your people. I suppose you could eat me, but I can assure you someone with my svelte frame and delicate constitution will not provide much sustenance.'

Tritus shook his head.

'No killing, not today,' he said. 'There are greater sinners than you requiring my attention. My brothers will take care of the shipment and show you to your new accommodation. I'm sure you'll like it – I understand your boss picked it out personally.'

'When will I speak to Lord Pureburn?'

'I'm sure he'll find a moment for a good friend like you. I do have a question though – how much meat can you get off burnt flesh?'

'A little.' Sorrow shrugged. 'Not as much as unburnt.'

'Then I hope more supplies are coming,' Tritus said. 'A lot of sinners needed His mercy.'

His gaze shifted to the nearest brazier. Sorrow's did likewise. It was difficult to see beneath the haze of smog, but he was of the Mercator Pallidus and well versed in human anatomy. There was no mistaking that the flames were dancing in the eye-sockets of long-blackened skulls.

7

The iron-clad bridge was barely a shoulder's width, the metal warped and tarnished by a veneer of rust. Sol peered from its edge and instantly regretted it. Not that he could see much; barely any lights worked in this section of the underhive, and they were reliant on the Delaques' flash-lumens. But the darkness below held the terror of a blank canvas. He painted his own fears – the half-seen whispers that haunted the lull between dream and wakefulness. He swore there was something moving below them, like the tendrils of some vast beast.

His foot caught on some loose cladding. He swayed, almost losing his balance. His flash-lumen slipped from his hand, tumbling to the dark. It flickered for a moment before being snuffed out, almost as if something had reached out and squeezed the life from it. But for an instant he thought he saw pale skin scuttling beneath them.

Anguis was just ahead of him. Her head snapped round.

'Are you holding it together?' she said. 'Any shakes?'

He shook his head. Twice since their flight from the Needle he'd suffered seizures, though he remembered little of either. Each time, Anguis had revived him with another dose of whatever was contained in those vials. But each time his recovery had been slower, his dreams more vivid. Always he was running, the ground grasping his feet like tar, the other-light spilling over his shoulders. He kept running, for he knew if he looked back the flames would take him, just like they had taken the others. He could picture Mandrex before the flames had swallowed him, chainsabre slung over his shoulder, gold tooth gleaming, lho-stick never far from his mouth.

Except he had never heard of Mandrex. Because this was not his memory. It had been taken from another.

Anguis was still staring at him. He managed a thin smile, motioning her forward. He could not tell how much further it was, but in the distance there was a faint flicker of light, little more than a candle. They edged towards it, Anguis taking the lead with Sol behind her, the two agents bringing up the rear. He assumed they were the same two who had come with him to the Needle, but there was no way to be sure.

He barely recalled their descent to the hive bottom. Mostly it consisted of crouching in hidden caches as the Delaques weaved them through the lower hive. He'd barely managed to relay a message to Lord Sorrow through his data-slab. It seemed the Corpse Grinder, despite his protestations, had also been drawn to the fallen dome. It gave him one ally beyond the treacherous Delaques. He hoped that would be sufficient.

'Another fifty paces,' Anguis said from up ahead.

'This is the path to Periculus?' Sol asked.

'It's a path,' she replied. 'One less trodden, and known only to us. I trust you to keep it that way.'

'As you wish.' Sol shrugged. 'But what is wrong with the front door?'

'Because we are of shadows,' she replied. 'To walk where others do is not our way. We watch but are not watched. We listen but do not speak. And where the path seems obvious, when there is a door by which all must pass, we find another way.'

'You sound unnecessarily contrarian.'

'You were made in the light, where we were made in the dark,' she said. 'We are simply different. But we can philosophise another time, for we are here.'

Ahead there lay a crack in the darkness, a scar of light. The imagery was familiar, if not reassuring.

'What is that?' he said, unable to hide the fear in his voice. Anguis frowned, shining her hand-lumen. Under its light he could see they had come to a barrier of solid metal.

'This is Periculus' Wall,' she said. 'All of it is bound within. As far as we can tell there are only two paths through it. The main gate, which Lady Wirepath opened, and this crack, which is far older.'

He peered into the gloom, trying to get a sense of scale, but Periculus' Wall stretched further than light could reach. It seemed smooth, strangely unmarred by corrosion or time.

Except for the crack.

It lay at the end of the bridge, barely his height and half that in width. Light spilled from it, the glow of whatever lay beyond, and the air that seeped through was unpleasantly warm and veined with smoke.

'Welcome to Periculus,' Anguis said. Sol did not respond. He was intent on the frayed metal that comprised the dome.

Its composition was unknown to him, the material a deep blue fading to purple at its cracked edge, the fray suggesting it had been pierced from the inside. He crouched, brushing his hand along it, wincing as a spark jumped from his fingers, the purple-tinged metal crumbling at its touch.

He frowned, his gaze shifting to the bridge. He'd assumed it was some remnant of a bygone age but, ancient as the metal was, it seemed to have been recently welded into place.

'Keep going, Lord Sol.'

He glanced up. One of the agents stood over him. Their gun was held low, but then again Sol was crouched, and the barrel was still trained on him.

He rose, following Anguis through the crack. It was still dark below the wall, though blades of light pierced the shadows beneath, spluttering through a miasma of fog. Most seemed to congregate at the dome's centre, which lay a hundred levels below them.

'You see that building?' Anguis said, nodding to where the lights were concentrated. 'That's where Lady Wirepath set up camp. Everything has spread from that point but it's slow going – the lower levels have been swallowed by bone-gravel, and the upper walkways are in ruins. You take the wrong turn and you will either sink without trace or stumble into oblivion.'

She was right. Most of the hab-blocks were crumbling, missing entire floors and walls. Many walkways stopped at nothing, others linking to ruins no longer connected to the lower levels at all, their upper floors suspended precariously on skeletal bridges imbedded in other hab-blocks.

'Where is the main gate?'

She pointed but he could make little out.

'It's barely wider than our back door,' she said. 'The outer wall is remarkably resilient. Even melta-weapons struggle to leave a mark.'

'Easy to defend.'

'Indeed. A fortress. Or a prison.'

'Where is Pureburn?'

Anguis pointed to a shattered building, unremarkable save for the circle of smouldering braziers.

'He took over what Lady Wirepath started,' she said. 'He now sits at the centre of the web, the inner strands intercepting potential attackers. Even if we could get through he is protected by some sort of energy field. My agent could not pierce it, even with a long rifle.'

'You tried to assassinate him?'

'My agent showed some initiative. Sadly, they paid a price,' she replied, glancing at Sol. 'You don't approve? This is your greatest enemy.'

'His death is not my goal. His failure is.'

'It's not a question of your goal,' Anguis said. 'This man is a threat. His family have a legacy that could destabilise the whole hive. If he is unopposed it could end all of us.'

'How? He is but a merchant.'

'One cursed with pride. He seeks to tap forces that are beyond his ken. The details should not concern you, but know that if he digs too deeply it will all be over. Please, find a way to discredit him, ruin him, hound him from here. But if that fails, he and all members of his family must die, no matter the collateral damage.'

Sol did not reply. Perhaps he was adjusting to the lowlight, for he could make out flickers of movement as the inhabitants of Periculus scurried about their business. Something was happening.

'What is it?'

Anguis frowned, making an almost imperceptible adjustment to her ocular lenses.

'Ah,' she said. 'It would seem the help has arrived.'

Virae could barely contain her frustration. Or her anger.

She stood blade in hand, trigger finger itching, the still-trembling Elle by her side, as the serfs passed, a procession of misery shuffling through the gate of Periculus. Many bore the scars of the journey, skin weeping from the toll taken by the eyeless creatures. Others had not made it this far. She had asked Elle to update the numbers, but the girl had barely spoken since the attack. Virae stole a glance at her. She was staring straight ahead, eyes glazed.

But this was not the source of her anger.

A commotion passed along the line of serfs. She turned and caught the familiar sight of Gash wading through the crowd, his huge shoulders and chest bobbing above the press of bodies. He met her gaze and grinned his metal smile. He had not been broken by the horrors of their journey, too tough and too stupid to wallow in despair.

A second figure trailed in his wake. Virae did not know this man, but his garb was familiar enough. His patched garments, once myriad colours, had faded to shades of muck. A noose hung slack about his neck, a symbol of mortality, and he held a scrap of parchment and a battered quill. But most recognisable was the mask, a grimace of hate stretched over his face, no doubt hiding an even more vile expression beneath. He was of House Cawdor – a beggar turned preacher. Her heart sank slightly. Of all the Houses and Guilds, she found Cawdor most difficult for conducting business.

'Boss, this little one is Tritus,' Gash said, jabbing a finger at the man. 'He's in charge of accepting the wares.'

'Good,' Virae said, turning to the smaller man. 'Maybe you can explain why I am to fit three hundred hive workers through a gate barely wide enough for two? Is there no other way in?'

'None,' Tritus said with a sickly smile. 'One way in, one way out. It caused a bit of conflict until Lord Pureburn arrived.'

He traced the sacred symbol of the aquila across his chest before glancing to his papers. Virae was surprised the man could read.

'These are the slaves then?' he asked. 'You're Virae the Chain Lord?'

'I am Virae the Unbroken of the Mercator Sanguis,' she said. 'You wish to see my chain of office, or the scars from my battles in the arena?'

Tritus laughed, his voice like a wheezing air purifier.

'I'll take your word for it,' he said. 'As long as we have workers, it doesn't matter who brings them.'

'Fine.' Virae shrugged. 'Since you seem to represent Lord Silas Pureburn I would request payment. I wish to depart as soon as is feasible.'

'I bet you do,' Tritus replied. 'But nobody is being paid for anything until I've checked the goods – some of them seem a little worse for wear.'

'They passed through the underhive. What else would you expect?'

'I can't argue with that,' Tritus said. 'But if I was accepting a cache of corpse-starch and found rats feasting on it you would not expect me to pay full price.'

'Lives are not counted the same as corpse-starch.'

'The Corpse Grinders would disagree,' he replied, studying the line. 'Either way, you seem a little light.'

'We were attacked.'

'Travelled too close to the cable-vine forest?' he said. 'That was a bad choice. What was the damage?'

'Given the time frame, and our terrain, our losses have not been unreasonable.'

'We lost eighty-six.' It was Elle who spoke.

They both glanced at the girl, but she offered nothing further, her gaze lost in the burning braziers.

'Well, thank you for that,' Tritus said, nodding to Elle. 'We will have to count them to confirm. Until then one of my brothers will show you the accommodation.'

There was a glint in his eye as he spoke. It made her uneasy.

'Where is Lord Pureburn?'

'Probably preparing his evening sermon,' Tritus said. 'You can speak to him tomorrow. There's accommodation for your crew too.'

'I am not staying.'

'If you want to be paid, you will stay.' Tritus' gaze shifted to the rear of the line. He pointed with his quill. 'You've got a couple of stragglers.'

Virae turned to see the last of the serfs crossing the boundary into Periculus. It was the crying girl who the Shakleman had struck, and the old man who had assisted her. They sat down by the side of the tunnel, a dozen yards from where she stood. Without another word she strode towards the stragglers. She was angry, but she forced it down. There was no gain to be had from raging at wretches who had fallen by the wayside. As she drew near, the girl looked up, but the older man's gaze was fixed straight ahead.

'Come on, you two, get up,' she said, jerking her thumb.

The girl just stared at her. She did not look frightened, just hollowed, worn away by their passage through the dark. Virae felt her anger fading.

'You can rest inside,' she sighed, squatting so her head was level with the girl's. 'It's safer in there.'

'Too late,' the girl said, intent on the old man. Virae followed her gaze. He was quite still, sitting propped against the tunnel wall, his dead eyes staring at nothing.

'He said he needed to sit down, just for a moment,' the girl murmured. 'He said he was tired.'

'Well, he can rest now,' Virae said softly, reaching out and closing his eyes. 'We should take him inside, away from scavengers.'

She lifted him, taking the dead man's body in her arms and trying not to think about its fate. He weighed nothing. It was like cradling a child.

'Come with me,' she said, nodding to the girl. 'The journey's over. This'll be your new home, for a time.'

'I don't belong here,' the girl murmured, rising wearily to her feet. 'I am Kallic Stone of Hope's End. Our House is House Orlock. It has been for centuries.'

Virae was silent for a moment. She slowed, glancing back at the girl.

'Last Stop has not been recognised as territory by House Orlock since the fall of the Ironcrown. You do not have a House. You can therefore be conscripted to perform whatever labour is deemed appropriate in the service of Lord Helmawr.'

The girl looked at her. She blinked, as though struggling to understand.

'But… we are loyal,' she said. 'Don't they know we're loyal?'

'House Orlock decides who is loyal. You do not get to choose to belong to it. None of us get to choose. That is Helmawr's Law. That is the way it is.'

The girl didn't answer.

'We must go,' Virae said. The girl nodded, stumbling forward, her head down. Virae had seen it hundreds of times. She was finally broken, the last embers of hope gone. Her life would be one long march, her labours ending only when she lay down and died. The Mercator Sanguis had swallowed another soul.

Virae had seen the same resignation on a million faces a million times.

She hated it.

8

Lord Pureburn doubted he'd previously been introduced to Lady Harrow. It was difficult to be sure when her face was hidden by a black mourning-veil and further distorted by the crackling vox-screen. But, given the five minutes of conversation he'd endured thus far, he suspected a prior meeting would have left a lasting impression.

'I can only sympathise with your misgivings, your ladyship,' he sighed, slumping slightly in his chair. 'I do not know why you have been asked to relay a message. Perhaps if you told me–'

'What irks me is the audacity,' Lady Harrow continued, not even pretending to listen. 'House Harrow is the equal of House Catallus. Yet here I am treated as their message courier!'

'I do not–'

'And why you?' she said, suddenly turning on him. 'A petty banker wading through the underhive for cheap trinkets? Why is that my concern? No offence intended, Pureburn.'

'None taken,' he replied evenly. 'But I would be remiss if I monopolised any more of your ladyship's valuable time. If you would be kind enough to deliver the message I would be eternally grateful.'

'Fine,' she sighed. 'But I just want to make it clear I'm performing a favour for a dead friend. He asked me to state that "His Gaze Has Turned Inwards. Give All To The Flames."'

She sat back, glaring at him from behind her veil.

'Well?' she demanded.

Lord Pureburn spread his hands. 'I fear I have no idea, your ladyship.'

'I am not the sort of idiot you are used to swindling,' she snapped. 'Rumours abound of you digging away in the dirt of Periculus. There must be something unusual down there if House Catallus has taken an interest.'

'I fear such matters are beyond a humble and lowly merchant like myself,' Lord Pureburn said with a sad smile. 'And I see my connection is fading. Perils of the underhive, sadly.'

'Do not dare to–'

He deactivated the terminal, rubbing his back as he rose to his feet. He missed the comfort of his throne. He never permitted it to be far from his sight, the dais hovering at the chamber's centre, his Pyromagir rarely far from it. But he could not address Lady Harrow in such a manner. Even modest opulence would be an affront to her, and the sight of him upon a throne would incite such outrage that conversation would be impossible. The hypocrisy galled him; she was descended from nobles who had won their titles through subterfuge and war. His ancestors, too, had striven, risked all to seize power. And they had suffered for it. But House Harrow had not. Neither had House Catallus. The nobles never did, and no matter his triumphs or wealth Lady

Harrow would never consider him her equal, even though her House had sunk so low it barely qualified as nobility.

Still, communicating through her seemed risky. Was the matter that urgent, and were there no other means? Did they want her spreading gossip, either to undermine his efforts or in pursuit of some other goal? Or were all communications being monitored, and only a cryptic exchange with an innocuous widow could slip through the surveillance net?

He sighed, approaching the dais, his footsteps echoing from the well-swept cobblestones. There was no way to know. He had no spies in the spire, no means of contact. He could only trust his instincts.

He slowed, until he stood staring up at the flame. His Pyromagir lumbered forward, hesitant, head tilted as though seeking instruction. Lord Pureburn smiled at the hulking creature, shaking his head once before returning his focus to the flame.

'House Catallus is getting nervous,' he said, seemingly addressing the flame. 'They think Helmawr will poke around and find their buried secrets. They want me to burn it down. They do not realise that our family's legacy burns with it. And if they knew they would care not.'

He sighed, shoulders slumped, his head bowed.

'I do not truly know what I am looking for,' he murmured. 'I thought it would be obvious, the only building standing, or an archeotech device clearly out of place. But Periculus is rotten. Perhaps what we need was destroyed. Or perhaps it is still out there, buried beneath the ground-up bones of the fallen. The legend spoke of a garden, a shrine-lab lit like a star. But it could have been a fable, or metaphor. Or it could have been destroyed in the fall.'

His gaze sought the flame.

'Do I cut and run, accept our demise?' he asked. 'Or do I stay, secure our future here? To stay would be to disobey House Catallus. They would come for us, and even our power is no match for a noble house. And yet, Periculus is buried deep, and the outer wall near impervious. It would be difficult to mobilise forces against it, and doing so could attract Helmawr's attention.'

He frowned.

'Do I ignore them?' he murmured. 'Stake my claim and continue the search? If Periculus begins to pay its tithe again, will Lord Helmawr care who provides his coin? His law demands the strong rise on the backs of the weak. Are we not strong? Should we not rise?'

He sighed again, then continued, still addressing the flames.

'What would you do, I wonder? If you were not constrained by your higher duties? If your mind still grasped the material world as well as the immaterial? What would you advise?'

'Milord?'

Pureburn stiffened, turning. A Cawdor juve stood in the chamber, breathless from running.

'You dare intrude?' Lord Pureburn snarled. But he soon saw why. An armoured woman was advancing behind the boy, a chainglaive clasped in her hand, her face stone and thunder. His Pyromagir tensed, steam hissing from its face-grate. It raised its brazier-arm, but Lord Pureburn shook his head. He knew the approaching woman, or at least her reputation.

'May I help you?' he asked as she drew to a halt, the pommel of her chainglaive striking the cobblestones.

'I am Virae of the Mercator Sanguis,' she said. 'I am here to settle a debt.'

'Virae, was it?' He frowned, his face assuming an expression of confusion. 'I apologise, I have dealt with so many people recently I lose track. You were supplying…?'

'The serfs. The workers.'

'Ah, yes,' he said, ascending his dais and taking a seat on the throne, his fingers scuttling across the armrest's data-terminal. Profit warnings jumped out alarmingly, but he ignored them, intent on the contract.

'Here we are,' he said, frowning as he pretended to scan the notes. 'I gather your journey was not straightforward?'

'We were attacked.'

'Awful,' Lord Pureburn said, tapping the terminal. 'Almost eighteen per cent casualties?'

'It could have been more.'

'Well, we praise Him for His mercy. However, this leaves us in a quandary.'

'I do not see why. Pay me for what I delivered. Deduct the eighteen per cent if you so wish.'

'That is not our contract,' Lord Pureburn said, glancing at her with a pained smile. 'Sub-clause thirteen/R – only permit a ten per cent loss margin when delivering stock. You have not fulfilled your contract. Technically, I owe you nothing.'

She stared at him. He could feel the anger radiating like a furnace. He wondered what would happen if he opened the cell behind him another crack, let true righteous fury wash over her. The thought was madness, of course, for no doubt he would become the target of her frustration. Still, it would be a curious sight to witness, and the thought itched at him.

'That's not fair,' she said. The words made him wince internally. Such a worthless turn of phrase.

'Fair or not, it is the contract,' he said. 'I would have assumed you knew that before signing. You can read, I trust?'

'Well enough.' She glowered. 'Though others do that for me.'

'Then I suggest you hire better people,' he said with a smile. 'I would be happy to provide some suitable names for a small reimbursement.'

'You are seriously suggesting we have no deal?' she replied. 'I take my serfs and leave, you stay here and try to rebuild with scummers and zealots. That's your plan?'

'I fear so,' he said. 'Assuming you can persuade the serfs to leave. Some might wish to remain, I suppose, given what is out there, and it would be inhumane of me to force them into the cold. Any who wish to stay would of course be welcome.'

'They will go where I say!' Virae replied coldly. In her voice he could hear an unexpected note. Almost... doubt? Did she fear for their lives? He almost laughed at the irony. A Chain Lord, victim of sentiment. Pitiful.

'Perhaps there is an alternative?' Lord Pureburn suggested. 'You have pit fighters, I trust?'

'Some.'

'Then we shall hold a pit fight,' Lord Pureburn said. 'Palanite Captain Canndis tells me tensions are mounting across the dome, old grudges flaring up, new rivalries emerging. In conflicts we grow stronger, but given the current dangers I think the people would benefit from a safe outlet for their aggressions.'

'Paid for in my followers' blood?'

'Some. Many contests would be grievances between the locals, but I would expect a few bouts from your fighters. I, for one, would appreciate some more refined combat from trained warriors alongside the more rustic elements of the underhive.'

'And you will pay our original fee? In full?'

'I swear on my chain of office.'

He saw Virae mull over his words, conflicting emotions clearly displayed across her face. She seemed painfully naïve concerning business. Then again, she had started at the bottom, dragging her way up from the lowliest rank. She lacked the breeding for the role and, in her heart, was no doubt still a meek slave. Perhaps it was unreasonable to judge her by his own superior standards; she lacked his pedigree.

'We have an accord,' she said, still glaring at him. 'When do we fight?'

'The eve of lighting Periculus' own Eternal Flame,' Lord Pureburn said, smiling as he spoke.

'I thought power was already on?'

'Yes, but this will be a statement of Periculus' future. Periculus will be granted its own Eternal Flame, lit from my very own crucible. All of Hive Primus will then know that Periculus will rise again through my power. In the God-Emperor's name.'

Virae scowled at him. 'I don't see why you need blood for this.'

Pureburn shrugged his shoulders, still smiling.

'Because a statement of intent is only believed when writ in blood.'

9

Sol stood at the threshold of what was apparently Lord Sorrow's office. It lay on the outskirts of central Periculus, though still bathed by the halo of light designating the supposedly safe areas. Sol had taken the opportunity to examine the vast braziers stretching nearly fifteen feet high. They were not part of the dome's infrastructure, having been assembled from junk and detritus. He was surprised they were stable enough to channel a candle's light, yet each shone like a tarnished star, providing not only heat and light but clouds of oppressive smoke. By their muddied glow he could see the building's facade was crumbling, any hint of ostentation stripped either by greedy looters or, more likely, sub-hive acid-storms.

Still, it had one unique fixture. A guard stood outside, a little under seven feet tall, his hands large enough to fully encompass Sol's head. The man was dressed in the sombre robes of the Mercator Pallidus, his tunic freshly pressed and his ossein shoulder guards gleaming. But no amount of formal attire could conceal the man's prior calling. Their eyes met as Sol approached, the larger man tensing slightly before relaxing, apparently recognising him. Perhaps they had met before. Sol found it difficult to differentiate between Sorrow's Grinders. The slab of a man beckoned him across the threshold.

Inside, an attempt had been made to spruce up the entry corridor; the floor was swept clear of bone-gravel, and the macabre carvings that adorned the walls had been polished, though no labours could erase the verdigris now staining the statuettes. It was a strange juxtaposition; the green bringing a life and vibrancy to the bronze casts of skulls and bone. The walls were marked too, as though scored by blade or claw. Before him a door was open, warming light spilling into the corridor.

Sorrow was sitting at a desk, stacks of papers beside him weighed down by a curious-looking vase shaped vaguely like a skull. He glanced up from his notes as Sol entered, managing a bright smile that would have fooled anyone else.

'Lord Tempes Sol,' he said, rising. 'Welcome to my very humble abode. Pull up a chair! I have almost four.'

He offered his hand. Sol hesitated.

'I think we should avoid that,' he said. 'I've had some… setbacks.'

Sorrow strode round the desk and embraced his friend.

'As have we all,' he sighed, patting Sol's back. 'At least you have the rakish eyepatch to show it.'

'You're jealous, I trust?' Sol said, forcing a smile.

'So jealous I'm debating carving out my left eye with a butcher's blade, just to fit in,' Sorrow replied, releasing Sol. 'At least your setback is stylish. You've seen where they've put me?'

'It seems in keeping,' Sol said with a shrug, drawing up a chair. 'I assume this once belonged to the Mercator Pallidus?'

'Oh yes,' Sorrow replied, seating himself and retrieving a bottle and two glasses from under the desk. 'In fact, I suspect it was still in use comparatively recently. You can tell by the organic stains in the lower level.'

'How recent?'

'I think someone was carving meat down there in the last fifty years,' Sorrow murmured as he poured the drinks. 'Not carving it well, I might add. I'm not sure it involved tools so much as teeth.'

He nodded to a door in the corner of the room. It was locked and barred. 'I would advise staying clear. My Grinders have done what they can with the... leftovers, but I suspect the smell will linger for a time.'

'That is not reassuring,' Sol replied. 'Have you spoken about this?'

'Who should I speak to? Pureburn?' Sorrow sighed again, handing Sol a glass. 'The man is in over his head. He has given House Cawdor the authority to enact vigilante justice whenever they see fit. You can imagine how well that is going.'

'The Enforcers haven't stepped in?'

'They support him, at least officially,' Sorrow said, draining his glass before pouring a second. 'I suspect Palanite Captain Canndis just thought doing so would make for an easier life. Now it's too late – there are dozens of the Cawdor rats, maybe hundreds. A handful of patrolmen will hardly keep them in line. Pureburn controls the dome.'

'I seek to change that.'

'Then I hope you extracted something useful from that burned fellow I gave you,' Sorrow replied. 'Did you get anything?'

'Other than partially blinded?' Sol took up his glass. 'No. At least, nothing I can quite articulate. I saw... something, like a shadow formed from light. I know not what it means, but I am more convinced than ever that Pureburn's power extends beyond creds and contracts. He did something on the plains of Salvation. Unleashed a power that still echoes.'

He sipped the drink. It was sweet and fiery, the flavours in perfect balance. For an instant he was back in Hive City enjoying a nightcap on Lord Sorrow's balcony. He savoured the moment whilst Sorrow poured his third glass.

'Then you need to kill him,' Sorrow said. 'Though, thinking about it, if you do that he will probably be declared a martyr, and Cawdor will use it as justification for killing all of us. So maybe don't do that. Unless you can think of a way of killing all of them. If you do think of something, please let me know – I would happily cut you in on the corpse processing profits.'

'I know he's up to something,' Sol murmured. 'There is insufficient promethium flow this deep to keep all those braziers burning. He can't be getting resupplied at the rate he needs, and he isn't tapping the hive's heat sink. So where is his power coming from?'

'The Glorious God-Emperor,' Sorrow slurred, raising his glass. 'It's all His will, and Lord Pureburn is His vessel. I heard a juve explain to his friends. You see, Lord Pureburn once reignited a dying sun with a candle stub, and cleansed the plains of Salvation by summoning a legion of fiery martyrs. Glory be to his pimpled backside.'

'What if I prove it?' Sol asked as Sorrow drained his glass. 'What if I show the Enforcers that Pureburn has broken Helmawr's laws, stolen power from another source? Then they must act.'

'They will probably ask for a kickback and let it continue. There is no point opposing the man.'

Sorrow reached for the bottle. Sol's hand closed on his.

'Perhaps you should eat something?'

'You know, perhaps we both should,' Sorrow said, forcing a smile. He rose a little unsteadily. 'Let me buy you lunch. There is a shack down below that serves a passable rat-burger. I think there may actually be rat in it.'

'Eating out?' Sol frowned. 'I thought you brought supplies.'

'Indeed,' Sorrow said, his smile fading. 'That's why we're eating out.'

The pit fighters fell silent as Virae entered, turning as one to face her. She would not call them rattled exactly; these were men and women who faced death whenever they stepped into the arena. But she could sense their unease.

'It seems Lord Pureburn has us at a disadvantage,' she said with a tight smile. 'He bends the words of our deal, and denies us what is ours.'

There was muttering as they exchanged glances. She raised her hand for silence.

'If we want to get paid we have to fight.'

She left the words hanging, glancing to each in turn. Most seemed nonplussed; a few even smiled. Only Block looked grim, his scarred mouth set in a line.

She looked at him. 'You have something to say?'

Block shrugged his massive shoulders.

'Are we sure we get paid then?' he asked. 'If he scams us now, what's to stop him skimping out on us afterwards too?'

'I can't argue that,' Virae sighed. 'I only know that if we leave now it will be with nothing.'

'Don't have to be.' Gash grinned. 'I can be very convincing when I wanna be.'

'Can you convince his worshippers?' Virae asked. 'Because there are hundreds of them, and barely a handful of us.'

'I've taken worse odds.'

'No, you haven't,' she said, smiling despite herself. 'It sounds a simple deal – half the bouts are likely to be local disputes anyway. But some of you will fight. Maybe die.'

'Same as every day,' Block said. 'Dying don't bother me, it's the feelin' I'm being conned. How did he get one over on us?'

'It doesn't matter,' Virae replied, keeping her gaze from Elle, who was slumped beside Gash. 'He'd have found a way. As you say, he may still find a way. At least this time we can be prepared for it.'

'How exactly?' Block replied. 'He holds the collateral.'

He nodded to the half-boarded window. She did not need to follow his gaze. She had seen the slave quarters. It was all that remained of a hab-block, the lower twenty-odd levels having been reduced to rubble. But the upper floors still stood, suspended by three gnarled walkways joined to adjacent buildings. She kept reminding herself that the structure had been this way for centuries, that even a hive quake had failed to bring it down. She could almost convince herself it was secure. Providing she didn't look at it.

'He needs the serfs to get the dome fully functional,' Virae replied. 'He would not throw away their lives for so petty a sum. In the meantime we prepare for the worst. How are our supplies?'

'Passable,' Elle murmured. 'We arrived with an excess. Because so many–'

She lapsed into silence.

'Good,' Virae said. 'Keep those back – hide them wherever those Cawdor rats won't think to scutter. If something goes wrong we need to be able to eat. What about weapons?'

'Only what we had,' Block said. 'Chainglaives, harpoon

launchers, smattering of pistols. We can fight, but we'd be outgunned even if they didn't outnumber us.'

'All right, see if you can do something about that. There must be locals unhappy with Pureburn's rule. We need to know if anyone is really unhappy, enough to think about doing something about it.'

'Sounds like you're making a play.'

'Nope. We just want to be good neighbours. It's the under-hive – can't have too many people covering your backs.'

Block grimaced. 'I hope you're right.'

'Even if I'm not, I'm still in charge,' she said, staring at him. 'Unless you challenge me, it doesn't matter what you think.'

'True enough, Chain Lord.' He grinned, adding deep lines to his scarred face. 'Shall I escort you to our new quarters? We had a quick guide from a couple of Pureburn's lap-rats, and I've got to say it's an inspired location.'

She sighed, fingers pressed to the bridge of her nose.

'Where is it?' she asked.

'Let me ask you a question first,' he said. 'Imagine the top half of a hab-block, suspended on pitiful little plasteel limbs, in danger of crashing to the ground beneath.'

She glanced to the window and the suspended slave quarters beyond.

'Don't have to imagine very hard,' she said.

'Right.' He nodded. 'Well, given that scenario, where would you least like to be sleeping?'

'Pureburn has already won.'

'I don't accept that,' Sol replied. Sorrow shrugged, scooping up the last of his meal and grimacing slightly as he swallowed.

'Hmm. Gamey,' he said, wiping his mouth and reaching

for a pouch on his belt. 'I wonder if the owner understands the difference between hanging the meat and just leaving it lying on a rock for a couple of weeks. Bilecleanser?'

He offered the red pill to Sol, who shook his head. 'I've eaten worse.'

'Yes, you take some perverse delight in enduring abdominal conditions,' Sorrow replied. 'Not that I have any objection to perverse delights, of course. But the underhive is a little too sordid even for my tastes.'

'I'm sure the feeling is mutual,' Sol said, his gaze drifting from the shack to the procession of passers-by beneath them. Through the glassless window he saw representatives from all the major Houses, as well as myriad unmentionables carving out a paltry life in the underhive. But mostly he saw the masks of House Cawdor. Not dispersed in the crowd but dominating it, smaller groups bleeding into one.

'There's more every day.'

Sol glanced back to Sorrow. He too was watching the crowd.

'More arrivals?'

'Perhaps. Or perhaps they're recruiting. They will take anyone who subscribes to their cheery view of the world and swears an oath to their thane. There are enough desperate souls down here. Even the newly arrived serfs are desperate to ingratiate themselves.'

'Why?'

'Why not? When you have no hope or prospects I imagine a damnation cult becomes quite appealing. Especially a cult that might feed you, or provide an orphanarium to raise your child. Amenities and propaganda all rolled into one.'

'It's strange. I never saw Cawdor as carrying this sort of influence.'

'You are thinking of the idiot preachers in Hive City,' Sorrow replied. 'Up there they are figures of ridicule. But down below they thrive, building crude edifices from salvaged scrap, deriving sustenance from filth that even you would turn your nose up at.'

'I'm surprised you haven't taken steps to remove the competition.'

'What competition? I sell delicacies and delectables to the most prosperous inhabitants of Hive City. Not reconstituted hive vermin to larger, bipedal hive vermin.'

'You sell aspirations. Just like them.'

'Profound,' Sorrow said. 'But down here I'm just a middleman. A courier of corpses.'

'For whom?'

'That isn't really important.' Sorrow's smile was brittle. 'All that matters is after the final shipment arrives I can depart this hellhole. Why anyone would choose to be down here is quite beyond me.'

He stared pointedly at Sol.

Sol shrugged. 'I have nothing else. And I have a debt to repay.'

'Who doesn't? You are better than those idiots on their stupid floating island anyway. When this is over we should form a partnership in Hive City. Has anyone tried burning bodies to make fuel? That could be our thing.'

'You're drunk.'

'Very, and you should be too,' Sorrow replied. 'We just need a marketable name. A word for lightning that rhymes with corpse...'

He frowned, his fingers drumming on the table.

'Perhaps if I were just to speak to the Enforcers,' Sol began. 'Explain that it is impossible for–'

'Look at the time,' Sorrow said, glancing at his timepiece. 'Evening prayers are about to begin.'

'You've started going to church?'

Sorrow shook his head. 'Not for us. Him.'

Sol followed his gaze. The streets had emptied, even beggars seeking the deepest shadows.

They were coming: hundreds marching proudly beneath ragged banners adorned with crude flames. Some were armed, bearing reclaimed autoguns and antiquated flame weapons and clad in ragged robes and leering masks. Many others just seemed desperate, their attire even more wretched, their only weapon uncompromising faith. They sang as they marched, a cacophonic choir praising the God-Emperor's name through psalms of penitence and hate.

They were the heralds. Behind them came Lord Pureburn, seated upon his throne, his dais suspended on jets of bright blue flame. Behind him a curious chamber was mounted on the dais. It looked older somehow, as though a prior relic had been bolted onto the platform. Atop it was a crucible of roaring flames that gave off neither soot nor smoke. Sol knew the traditions of the Mercator Pyros. Each family prized their Eternal Flame above all else, revering it as a sacred relic. The same flame would burn for years or even centuries, never extinguished, a symbol not only of power but of history and legacy. He had always considered it wasteful, a pointless expenditure of promethium. But now he saw the congregation fawning over the flames, desperate to catch a spark of ember. Now he understood its power.

'Behold your enemy,' Sorrow said. 'You still intend to oppose him through reason and evidence? Perhaps you should confront them now, pull out a few data-charts or something?'

Sol did not reply. He was intent on the flame. There was something about the light that made him uneasy. It seemed to move with a will of its own, and if he looked closely strange colours seemed etched in the flames: deep purples and searing blues that in turn split into shades never seen, colours that belonged to an unknown spectrum of other-light and appeared to shift in response to his scrutiny, as though they were examining him in turn.

He glanced at Sorrow. The man seemed oblivious.

'The flames move wrong,' Sol murmured.

Sorrow rolled his eyes. 'Tempes, my old friend, do give it a rest. I appreciate you dislike the man, and in truth I find him a tiresome bore. But this is starting to get pitiful. You can't blame the man for the wind.'

'Of course I could – the amount of smoke he generates plays havoc with the atmospherics. But that is not what I meant. Look.'

'Look at what?'

Sorrow could not see it. Sol found his gaze shifting to the chamber beneath the flames. It looked almost like an old priory cell, where worshippers of the God-Emperor would seal themselves against the sins of mankind. It was an archaic supplication, an anathema to the worshippers of House Cawdor whose creed sought to cleanse the sinful with fire and blood.

He frowned. Perhaps it was a trick of the light, or shadows cast by the flame. But he almost thought he could see something behind the cell's walls – a figure seated behind Lord Pureburn. Like a shadow, except one born of light, not darkness.

He blinked, his one remaining eye squeezing shut against the glare. But still he could see the figure, its flesh fire, its gaze the searing light of the sun. It was the same terrible light he ran from in his dreams, the same light that caused the ground to bubble and his flesh to burn.

He shook his head. It could be a hallucination; Anguis had warned him that there would be side effects from the treatment – hallucinations and delusions. But still he could see Pureburn's light-shadow. And, worse yet, he felt it was staring back at him.

'It's him,' Sol whispered.

Sorrow glanced at him, eyebrow arched.

'The power,' Sol said. 'The flames. It's him. He's like Stitch. An abomination.'

'Maybe I have drunk too much,' Sorrow said, frowning. 'For I have no idea what you are talking about.'

'Pureburn,' Sol replied, glancing at his friend. 'He was the one who scourged the plains of Salvation. His power keeps Periculus running. He's a psyker. A flame-witch.'

10

Virae and her serfs were long since secured in Periculus when the man who had been tracking them finally stepped through the main gate. He peeled the goggles from his face, sweeping his mohawk into place as he peered into the gloom. The entry toll had been extortionate, giving the impression that some paradise of commerce and opportunity waited beyond.

'And lo, Caleb Cursebound entered the Forbidden Dome to find it wanting,' he sighed. None heard the remark. Few walked the streets, and those that did wore the masks of House Cawdor. A trio were approaching now, two armed with autoguns, another equipped with a complex polearm seemingly assembled from scrap. It incorporated a bladed tip, as well as parts from a blunderbuss. Caleb had no idea if it would actually fire, but did not feel the need to test the theory. Instead he smiled at the men, waving to them.

They did not return the gesture.

Each eyeballed him in turn, as though seeking just cause for conflict. Reluctantly, they seemed to conclude that smiling was insufficient grounds for administering the God-Emperor's justice. But, to Caleb, it looked a close thing.

'Bye then,' he whispered, as the trio slunk away in search of fresh sins to purge. 'You all smell great, by the way. Nothing at all like someone vomited plague rats into a used body bag and then stuffed it with excrement. Nobody would even suggest such a thing, even implicitly.'

'You're louder than you think.'

He recognised the voice and glanced round. She was crouched in the dark, hood pulled low, her face in shadow. But he could just make out her eyes, framed by crimson slashes. The mark of her tribe. Former tribe, he reminded himself. There might be other ratskins stalking the under-hive, but none were her blood. She was the last.

'Iktomi,' Caleb said, tapping his wrist. 'You're almost late.'

'They watch me. It's hard to slip away. Besides, shouldn't you have been here a day ago? I thought you were trailing us.'

'I overslept. Had to catch up. Eventful journey?'

She frowned for a moment, then shrugged. 'Not really.'

'Sure? I came across what looked like bodies at the toll gate.'

She shrugged again. Ever the conversationalist.

'How is the captive?' Caleb asked.

'All right. Cries a lot.'

'You don't think that makes sense? Given her current circumstances?'

Iktomi stared at him, seemingly unable to connect the two ideas.

'Well, either way, I don't think getting her through the

main gate will be easy,' Caleb said, glancing over his shoulder. 'Is there another path?'

'Some claim there is a crack or a tunnel leading to freedom,' Iktomi said. 'But they are slaves. They cling to false hope as though it will save them from sinking.'

The disdain in her voice was audible.

'How are you finding captivity?' he asked.

She shrugged, seemingly unconcerned. But he knew her. Beneath the veneer of stoicism there was a needle of anger. He had seen her disable an Ambot with little more than a blade, watched as she tore apart a trio of pit fighters singlehanded. Subservience was not her natural state. All it would take would be one Shakleman stepping a little too far out of line, one comment that pushed her...

'We can find another exit later,' Caleb said, surveying the ruins. 'If we can get her away from the slavers it will be easy enough to hide her in the outskirts.'

'Not easy,' Iktomi replied. 'The Chain Lord is no fool, and our prison too secure.'

She glanced upwards. He followed her gaze to the half-block that comprised the slave quarters. It must have been a hundred yards above them, suspended on three aged walkways. It made him dizzy just looking at it.

'How did you get down?'

'I jumped.'

'Jumped?'

'Yes. I stole a grapnel-launcher.'

She held out the pistol-shaped device, a magnetic ring protruding from its tip, the length of cable concealed within the device.

'How far does that cable run?'

'Thirty feet?'

He glanced up at the slave accommodation.

'Thirty feet?' He frowned. 'Doesn't seem long enough.'

'There are structures closer to the ground. I pull the trigger during the fall. Not important.'

'Could you jump with her?'

'No. Couldn't control both our falls.'

'All right.' Caleb glanced across the alley. 'What if we could arrange a distraction to keep the Shaklemen occupied? Maybe a slave uprising? You can slip out in the chaos.'

She shook her head. 'Could make it worse. They conscripted too many factions. Slaves are as likely to murder each other as anyone else.'

'That sounds like a distraction to me.'

'I cannot protect her if they riot,' she said, glaring at him. 'Need a better opening.'

Caleb sighed, rubbing his face with his hands. He glanced up, his gaze falling on a group of toiling slaves.

'What are they doing?'

'Preparing. For the pit fights. For the ceremony.'

'Why so few?'

'Most of the slaves are housed, waiting for the factorums to restart,' she said. 'They give us busy work, labour. We dig holes, but I don't know why. I think we are searching for something. But there are too many slaves and not enough Shaklemen. So we work shifts. Most remain locked up.'

'Hmm…' He frowned. 'All right. We wait until the ceremony. Once the–'

'No. There will be Enforcers and the Fire-Guilder's followers. All eyes will be watching.'

'You're not offering a lot of solutions, Iktomi,' Caleb said, rolling his eyes. 'All right. What if we wait till the two of you are down here working on the arena? If the Shaklemen are stretched thin then we can keep the distraction small, just your group. I cause a scene, they try to restore order, and you slip away with her. We'll find a way out later.'

'How will you cause a scene?'

'Let's just say I know my way around pit fighters.' Caleb smiled. 'If you recall, I was undefeated in the arena.'

'You fought once. And nearly got eaten.'

'Still undefeated.'

She just stared at him, before sighing and rising to her feet.

'I'm going to begin the long climb back into prison,' she said. 'Try not to die.'

Sol watched through the window as the masked men strained against the chain. The body they were hauling was heavy, in part due to its flak armour and reinforced undersuit. The helm was missing, perhaps already reclaimed by the unwashed brethren, but there was no mistaking the armour pattern.

It was an Enforcer.

Exactly which Enforcer was harder to determine. Half his face was missing, replaced by a mess of blood and bone. Probably a dumdum bullet, given the size of the wound. He was far from alone. Other bodies dangled from the fractured walkways and jutting girders like rotten fruit. Sol hadn't seen them before. Perhaps they had blended into the shadows, and it had taken a certain saturation for him to realise, but now he saw they were everywhere. Most had a message scrawled across their chest, though many were too high for him to read. The Enforcer's was clear enough: 'Traytor' was inscribed in poorly formed letters.

He turned from the scene, slipping his robe over his shoulders, wincing as he felt a stab of pain run down his right arm. It had throbbed since he'd awoken, but the pain had started before then. Ever since his arrival in Periculus he had felt something was off. The syphon implanted in his shoulder was used to leeching the pure power of the storm clouds. Down here the flickering thermal energy of Pureburn's braziers was thick with pollutants. It made his head ache and his limbs heavy. Perhaps that was the cause of the outburst. Sorrow's Grinders had dragged him away before he could make more of a scene, and he'd awoken in one of the Corpse Grinder's spare bedrooms. He now wondered if it had been a waking dream, or a hallucination brought about by a combination of Anguis' treatment and the traumas of recent days.

But, even as he departed his room and descended the stairs, he could not shake the image of Lord Pureburn's shadow of other-light.

Voices echoed up the stairway – Sorrow's honeyed tones, and a dulcet whisper he knew all too well. Light was flickering from Sorrow's study.

He entered. A desk-lumen cast a halo around the two figures enjoying a repast at the antiquated table. It was a new addition and appeared to have been carved from silverbark. If so, the wood must have been imported from off-world, and was probably worth more than the building that housed it. A lavish spread was laid before them of sweetmeats and delicacies.

Sorrow rose as Sol entered, spreading his arms in greeting. Beside him Anguis remained seated, longcoat folded over her chair.

'My dear Tempes,' Sorrow said, embracing him. 'How are you feeling? Hungry? I received a shipment this morning and may have sourced some diced grox streak wrapped in vorder leaves. Slightly chewy, I fear, but compared to what we've had to endure so far in Periculus...'

'I thank you, but I am not hungry,' Sol replied, his gaze intent on Anguis. 'I see you found your way here.'

'She did indeed, and I cannot believe you did not introduce us.' Sorrow smiled.

'You may have already met,' Sol said, still intent on Anguis. 'Perhaps she was disguised as a fungal merchant, or an overly friendly waiter.'

'Close,' Anguis replied, sipping her recaff. 'I was actually the entrée. You might have noticed a slightly acidic aftertaste from the micro-explosives I planted in your lower intestine.'

Sorrow laughed, glancing at Sol.

'Oh, I like this one,' he said. 'Your former colleagues were so dour they made servitors seem like good company. A couple of bionic limbs and complete lobotomy could have actually improved their temperament.'

'Sol is still angry because of our little disagreement,' Anguis said levelly. 'How are you feeling?'

'Fine,' he replied, taking a seat and ignoring the throbbing in his temple. 'I am fully recovered.'

'No hallucinations?' Anguis persisted. 'Only, Lord Sorrow was telling me about your outburst. Apparently, he had to have you dragged away before you made a scene? He said you saw something.'

'Did he?' Sol replied, glaring at the Corpse Grinder. 'Because that was information shared in confidence.'

'It was information best not shared at all,' Sorrow said. 'Accusing the most powerful man in Periculus of unsanctioned witchcraft is a death sentence.'

'But it is true. I saw it,' Sol replied, turning to Anguis. 'The spyker showed me somehow, intentionally or not. It took a while to make sense of it, but that was why the interrogation went wrong, why the patient burned and the spyker broke free. Pureburn is a pyromancer.'

Anguis regarded him with her soulless eyes.

'You don't believe me?' he said.

She shrugged. 'What does it matter if I do?'

'There are few greater crimes than witchcraft!' Sol replied, exasperated. 'If we inform the Enforcers he will be arrested. We win.'

'Absolutely,' said Sorrow. 'You should report it to the patrolman strung up outside.' He frowned, glancing to the window. 'He's pretty high up though – you would need to shout.'

'I fail to see the humour in this.'

'As do I,' Sorrow replied. 'If Pureburn's rats can get away with murdering Helmawr's finest, what makes you think you will be listened to?'

'I cannot believe Pureburn would authorise attacks on Enforcers. It's madness.'

'Does it matter what he orders?' Anguis replied softly. 'He unleashed House Cawdor but it does not mean he can control them. He rides their hatred and tries to steer it against his opponents, but the vermin will find their own enemies too. He cannot stop it now – the flame has grown beyond what he can extinguish. All he can do is position himself upwind.'

'Surely there will be conflict between the Enforcers and Pureburn?' Sorrow frowned.

Anguis shook her head. 'There will be no war. Less than a dozen men against an army? With Pureburn now in control of the main gate? Canndis knows he cannot fight this. Some lowly ganger may be charged with the Enforcer's death, but no action will be taken against Pureburn himself.'

'Then what do you suggest?' Sol replied.

'Why don't you just kill him?' Sorrow suggested, taking up his fork. 'Not wishing to brag, but I have previously employed the famed Shadows of Catallus to deal with intransient opposition. I'm sure they could eliminate our troublesome Guilder for a fee. Just say the word.'

'That would destabilise things further,' Sol sighed. 'Cawdor are dangerous enough even when directed. Imagine how they would react to a hidden enemy slaying their prophet? If he is made a martyr we will all burn before their fury is sated.'

'A bullet would not be enough,' Anguis said. 'When Pureburn first arrived, I had an agent stationed here. They made an attempt on his life, but the shell was vaporised before it could strike.'

'Refractor field?' Sorrow asked. 'Not uncommon for a wealthy Guilder.'

She shook her head. 'No. A refractor field disperses the energy, leaving a distinct visual signature, like a bubble. Similarly, a conversion field transforms the kinetic energy into light. This did neither. The shot simply... dissolved, like ice dropped into boiling water.'

'Interesting,' Sol said. 'I know of no device that can accomplish such a feat.'

'Then it must have been sorcery,' Sorrow replied, rolling his eyes. 'Don't pretend you are some expert on force field technology. His throne could contain all manner of archeotech contraptions. One failed sniper-shot proves nothing.'

Sol didn't reply. His gaze was drawn to the window and the masked disciples of House Cawdor, and the still dangling Enforcer.

'We're looking at it wrong,' he murmured. 'If Pureburn is found wanting in his followers' eyes they will remove him for us. The only thing that inspires more hatred than a sinner is the pious turned heretic. We expose him and they shall be our blade.'

'Expose what?' Anguis asked. 'There is no evidence beyond your supposed vision, which was obtained during a psychic interrogation. If you make such a claim you will be branded a liar at best. More likely, they will say you have been tainted by the witch and burn you as the abomination.'

'Then we need evidence,' Sol replied. 'I can at least prove that there is something untoward with the power consumption in the dome – a simple promethium line cannot sustain so many pyres. Perhaps they can be persuaded to investigate. If enough light is shined upon it, the truth will come out.'

'I think your entreaties will fall on deaf ears,' Anguis said. 'But I can set my remaining agents on reconnaissance, see if there is any clue on how he operates the shielding device on his throne, or what secrets he is keeping. But I promise nothing.'

They both glanced at Sorrow. He was chewing absently, seemingly tuned out of their conversation.

He blinked. 'What?'

'How will you contribute?'

'I will keep my head down,' he said. 'Enough people want me dead as it is. I don't seek out new enemies, only friends.'

'Yet you state that many wish you dead?' Anguis noted with a thin smile. 'Were these once your friends?'

'Perhaps,' Sorrow said, returning to his meal. 'But, as any chef will tell you, even corpse-starch has a shelf life.'

11

Palanite Captain Canndis was nervous. It made him angry, which made him even more nervous. Still, his fears were easy to hide behind his ill-fitting helm and battered flak armour. Only his face was visible, his mouth a grim line, daring any to challenge his authority.

The little authority he had anyway.

The Enforcer's body had been recovered, but not before word had spread. He had set two of his best officers to investigate. But given the limited pool he had to draw upon, they were also two of his worst officers. He had his suspicions. He could only pray he was wrong.

He shook his head. He had a court to oversee. The proceedings should have been no more than a blip on his itinerary. As an Enforcer he had presided over countless cases, reviewed evidence that would reduce a lesser man to madness. But, he now realised, his resolve had been bolstered by Helmawr's Law. Logically, he knew it would not stop a bullet or parry a blade. But it had given his words power, his judgements weight.

This deep in the underhive it was different.

Here, there was barely frontier law. His court was a roof-less hovel, his gallery packed with miscreants and outlaws. There were no innocents here, only measures of guilt. Most he knew a little of, by face if not name. But Leara Batrip, Queen of the Acid Drops, and Varl Bloodburn, Forge Tyrant of the Near Dead, were well known to him, and even more to each other. They sat at either end of the gallery, feign-ing ignorance of the other's presence. Varl was intent on his knife, honing the foot-length blade on a whetstone. Leara was inspecting the chambers of her stubber, the shells laid out before her. The rest of the gallery was packed with the usual motley assortment of cutthroats and cred-thieves, but he did not recognise the stranger seated on the central bench. He did not resemble an underhiver, his robes more remi-niscent of a Guilder or priest. A torn strip of cloth covered his left eye, and his grimace suggested the injury was recent.

At the rear of the court was Brother Tritus, the beggar turned deacon, flanked by a pair of Cawdor's most undesirables. Ostensibly, they were acting as bailiffs, but Canndis could not shake the feeling their primary role was as Pureburn's eyes and ears. As Canndis presided over the underhivers' accusations and disputes, so too did they sit in judgement over him. The thought made his blood rise, but there was little he could do about it.

'Silence in the court,' Canndis said, his shock-baton crack-ing against his lectern. 'Periculus is the property of Lord Helmawr. I, for now, am his custodian and will cast judge-ment in his name. All rise for Helmawr!'

The crowd remained seated, though a few had the manners

to at least look awkward about it. Even Tritus just stared at him, his mouth split in a wicked grin.

What could he do? It was a direct challenge to his authority, but the Acid Drops alone outnumbered his Enforcers. He could not stand against them all, not without Pureburn's support. Better to just ignore it, pretend he had not spoken and they had not disobeyed.

'Let's get on with it,' he sighed, motioning to the clerk. 'Gladshiv? Who's first?'

Varl Bloodburn didn't wait for a response. He was already barging his way through the gallery.

'Yeah, I got a problem,' he said as he reached the lectern, jabbing his finger at Leara. 'Her!'

'Is this about the dispute with the Acid Drops?' Canndis said. 'We've been over this. Either I arrest all of you or you resolve it between yourselves.'

'They are trying to take our claim on the northern district. I lost three men clearing it of those pale-skinned things. Suddenly they come in, guns blazing, trying to drive us off. That place is Goliath turf.'

He glared at Leara. She stared back, stubber cocked.

'Well, this is easily settled,' Canndis said, trying not to smirk. 'Lord Pureburn has announced there will be gladiatorial games to celebrate the lighting of the Eternal Flame. I propose you each nominate a fighter. If the Near Dead win then the Acid Drops will withdraw. And if the Acid Drops win... Leara, do you have a preference?'

'I slit his throat.'

'Fine. I will let you work that out between you. You both agree?'

'Whatever.' Varl shrugged. 'I got more to talk about. I want a word about those Cawdor scum pretending they're the law.'

The Forge Tyrant jabbed his thumb at Tritus and his accomplices.

'Two of my lads were flogged just for being in a deserted hab-block,' he said. 'Doesn't sound like justice to me.'

'I see,' Canndis said. 'Well, I am given to understand Lord Pureburn requires additional promethium lines to provide enough power to run the factorums. He has tasked some of House Cawdor with securing the necessary facilities. That is why the serfs have been digging up the western quarter to–'

'They're here for the same reason we are, to see if anything of value survived the fall,' Varl persisted. 'I do not see why the rats get special treatment and can cordon off whole sections.'

'Because Lord Pureburn requires it to keep Periculus running and set up the factorums. If Periculus is to–'

'He's lying.'

Canndis blinked, unsure who had spoken.

The stranger was standing, staring at him with his one good eye.

'Who are you to interrupt me?' Canndis barked.

'I am Tempes Sol of the Mercator Lux,' the stranger replied. 'And there is only one promethium line this deep. Pureburn has already tapped it. If he claims to search for more he is either a liar or an idiot.'

'Hold your vile tongue!' Tritus too was standing, his finger stabbing accusingly at Sol. 'This heathen seeks to question Lord Pureburn?' he said, spitting the words. 'Lord Pureburn, the saviour of Periculus, is not even here to defend himself. How dare he make such accusations!'

'It's a bold claim,' Canndis said, glaring at Sol. 'You got any actual proof?'

'I have schematics that verify my claim.'

'Schematics?' Tritus snorted. 'Maps of the underhive are

forged daily. Nobody really knows what's down here. A picture proves nothing.'

'There is no additional capacity,' Sol persisted. 'There isn't even enough current capacity. I've calculated the flow rates and there is barely enough power to keep even half the braziers burning.'

'And yet there is light,' Tritus sneered, spreading his hands. 'You trying to tell us we imagined that?'

Sol tensed. Canndis had interrogated enough recidivists to know the Guilder was holding something back.

'The man has a point,' he said. 'There is power.'

'Yes,' Sol replied. 'Which begs the question – where is it coming from?'

Tritus swore loudly. 'Lord Pureburn holds true to the only real power, the God-Emperor. With Him anything is possible.'

'The God-Emperor's galaxy has rules,' Sol said, anger creeping into his voice. 'A drop of promethium is a drop of promethium. Faith cannot make it two drops.'

'Blasphemy!'

Tritus surged forward, only to be restrained by his accomplices. One of them whispered in his ear. Whatever he said settled Tritus, though he continued to stare at Sol with undisguised contempt.

'Enough!' Canndis snapped, slamming his shock-baton down on the lectern. 'We are not here to debate theology. Lord Pureburn has brought light to Periculus and you have brought nothing but baseless accusations. The matter is closed.'

Sol shook his head. 'Captain, if I could just have a private word, I can–'

'Get out of my precinct!' Canndis roared. 'I do not expect to hear from you again without proof of your claims.'

Sol glared at him, his one eye gleaming.

'Fine,' he said. 'I will prove him a fraud. I swear it.'

He turned, departing without a backwards glance. Canndis watched him leave before his gaze flicked back to Tritus. His expression said it all. Canndis could hazard a guess at the fate awaiting the outspoken Guilder, but there seemed little point intervening; his men had more urgent responsibilities.

'All right, next case,' Canndis murmured, glancing at his notes before sighing. 'Not this again. You're finding bones in the north quarter? So is everyone else!'

Sol was angry. A little at himself. A lot more at everyone else.

It had been idiocy to approach the Palanite captain. The man had no interest in the truth, merely preserving the status quo. It didn't matter what Sol's calculations showed or what evidence he submitted; Canndis did not wish to hear anything that might require action. In his anger Sol had sworn he would prove Pureburn's deception.

That now seemed a foolish oath. And it was going to get him killed.

He cut left, picking a path between two of the ruins, his flash-lumen revealing the pitted ferrocrete and ankle-deep bone-gravel. In his fury he had stormed off, caring little what path he took. But as his rage abated, he realised he had drifted far from Periculus' centre. Here, the light from Pureburn's braziers did not penetrate as deep. He was at the edge of civilisation, where the darkness concealed all manner of foul creatures.

And he swore something was following him.

Ahead there was the flicker of movement. Whatever it was darted aside, as though fearful of the light, but he caught the impression of pale skin and sharp teeth. It looked almost human, except he'd seen no eyes on the creature.

His mouth felt dry. He had no weapon, so accustomed was he to the protection granted by his status and the backing of the Guild. But he had forsaken the latter, and the former meant nothing to the creatures of the underhive. He was but meat, protected only by a fading light.

He turned, intent on retracing his steps, but the path behind was now blocked. Three figures stood at the alley's entrance. All wore the masks and attire of House Cawdor, and his hand-lumen caught the glint of blades and the gleaming barrel of an autopistol.

'Evenin', your lordship,' the nearest of the trio said with a well-stained smile. 'Bit late to be wandering off on your own?'

'It would seem that way,' Sol replied, glancing over his shoulder. He knew something waited in the darkness behind him, drawn by the prospect of fresh meat. There was no escape.

The trio's leader grinned. 'Still,' he said, raising his pistol, 'perhaps you were guided here by the God-Emperor? Maybe He deems this a good spot for you to face the final judgement?'

'Still think we should burn him,' one of the others muttered.

'Supposed to be clean and quick,' the leader said. 'Besides, he ain't worth the God-Emperor's merciful flames. Not a heathen like him who worships clouds and storms, who dares to mock the great Lord Pureburn.'

'I do not worship storms. I merely seek to understand them.'

'Yeah, well, my old priest always told me ignorance was bliss,' the leader replied, cocking his pistol. 'And he set a fine example. The man knew nothin' but his love for the God-Emperor.'

Sol's gaze was locked on the rusted firearm aimed squarely at his chest. Such a lowly weapon. It seemed inapt that it would bring about his demise.

Was there a little charge left in his neurone circuits? He doubted it; his arm still ached and the trio did not seem inclined to approach close enough for him to use it.

'Any last words?' the gunman asked.

'Nothing of worth.'

'Sad.' The man grinned. 'But honest. I'll give you that.'

He squeezed the trigger. As he did so Sol surged forward, hand outstretched, intent on taking at least one of them with him before succumbing to the hail of bullets.

Then the world stopped making sense.

Agony coursed through his outstretched hand as cobalt lightning engulfed the alley, a micro-storm barely ten feet wide. The three assailants were hurled aside, the bullets scattering like ash on the wind. Sol collapsed, his arm hanging useless at his side, fingers barely responsive.

One of the attackers was down. The others rose groggily, knives drawn. Their leader stared at the fallen Sol with a look of pure hate.

'Witch,' he whispered. 'He's a witch!'

'Not… a… witch,' Sol managed, struggling to form the words. It was hard to think, his thoughts clouded by a colour-scape of other-light. His attackers were stained scarlet, his own fingers tingling a fading blue. He tried to rise as they drew closer, blades bared like teeth. His limbs were unresponsive. He felt exhausted, as though he'd been running for hours.

'Well, this seems rather unsporting.'

The voice came from the alley's end, the words preceding a long-suffering sigh. Sol's attackers turned to face this new threat, knives raised. Between them, Sol could just make out the silhouette of a man in a longcoat, his hair styled in a lopsided mohawk.

'Get out of here!' one of the Cawdors snarled. 'This ain't your business.'

'True,' the stranger said, ambling forward, 'but I am lost and have nowhere else to go. I've already blundered into the web of an orb spider, and nearly been eaten by a swarm of Emperor-knows what. Frankly, I'm pleased to see some human faces. Or close to it, anyway.'

He was nearer now, and Sol could see he was young, though not unscarred; his nose had been broken and fresh scars crossed his cheek. But his smile was at least half genuine.

Sol managed to find a knee. His right arm still hung uselessly, but he grasped a fist-sized lump of broken rockcrete with the other. The stranger was a few paces away now. The second attacker squared up to him.

'You an idiot?' he asked.

'Possibly,' the stranger said, frowning as he studied the man's mask. 'Did you make this yourself?'

'What if I did?'

'Nothing, it's great work. Stylish,' the stranger replied. 'How do you keep it in place? Adhesive? String round the back?'

Before the attacker could reply the stranger seized the leering mask, pulling it over his eyes as he swiftly brought his knee up between the man's legs. The knifeman collapsed with a whimper, clutching his groin. A swift kick to the stomach drove the air from his lungs.

The lead knifeman reached for his fallen autopistol but Sol was quicker, smashing the lump of rockcrete over his head. He fell, Sol collapsing beside him, still struggling for breath. He had never felt so exhausted.

'You all right?' the stranger said, offering his hand. 'I saw the light. Were they trying to rob you?'

'Something like that,' Sol replied as he was helped to his feet. 'I thank you for your help. I am Tempes Sol.'

'Caleb,' the stranger replied. 'And I wasn't lying. I am completely lost. Thought maybe I could find another way out of this place. I've never seen a dome so tightly enclosed.'

'I fear I am also lost,' Sol replied with a tight smile. 'I suppose we are now lost together.'

'Sod that, I need a drink,' Caleb said. 'You want a drink?'

Sol laughed, the sound surprising him. 'Actually, I think I do. But, as noted, we are lost.'

'Not any more.' Caleb grinned, tapping his nose. 'I am a man of many talents. Even if I cannot find a way out, I can always smell out a drink. You comin'?'

Sol glanced over his shoulder. The attackers lay where they had fallen. Behind them he caught the flicker of movement – pale skin and sharp teeth drawing closer.

'I think that might be best.'

Sol glanced up from his data-slate as Caleb emerged from the crowd, clutching two full glasses and one empty. He slumped into the seat opposite, sighing dramatically.

'Busy?' Sol asked as he took up his glass.

'Surprisingly,' Caleb said. 'I had to get an extra drink just to cover the walk back from the bar. I thought House Cawdor abstained from liquor?'

'Most do,' Sol said, glancing to the crowd mustered around the bar. 'But some are probably acting out. This deep, the rules are different.'

'I guess,' Caleb replied, frowning at Sol's notes. 'What are you doing?'

'Calculating electrical current and the magnetic force required to deflect a bullet.'

'You Guilders have some interesting drinking games,' Caleb said, taking a long swig. 'I prefer the classics. Who can down a bottle of Second Best without going blind? That sort of thing.'

'Nothing here makes sense,' Sol murmured, glaring at his notes. 'The numbers don't add up. Even with every circuit running smoothly and charged to maximum capacity, I never wielded that sort of power. There is some additional factor at work. It's like the rules of the universe don't quite apply down here.'

'Can I see?' Caleb asked. Sol slid the notes over to him. 'Hmm.' Caleb nodded, studying the symbols. 'You know what strikes me?'

'No.'

'That I have no idea what most of those symbols mean.'

'It doesn't help that I'm writing with my left hand.' Sol sighed. His right arm still hung limp at his side. He could barely get the fingers to twitch. He took up the glass with his left, taking a sip and almost spitting it out again. 'Emperor's teeth, what is this?'

'Pretty good for down this deep,' Caleb replied. 'I mean, this beer is swill, but I have yet to pass out, or go into convulsions. That's what I look for in an underhive beverage.'

He raised his glass. Sol did likewise. The second sip was more palatable, perhaps due to the first erasing most of his taste buds.

'I thank you again for helping me,' Sol said as he lowered the glass. 'I am in your debt.'

'Really?' Caleb grinned. 'I mean, you Guilders are rich, right?'

'Some of us are,' Sol said, inspecting the vaguely yellow liquid in his glass. 'Certainly I am rich compared to those who dwell down here. Compared to my peers? I am nothing. Is it money that interests you?'

'Always,' Caleb said. 'But actually, there is something else. I need a favour.'

'A favour?'

'I need to get someone out of here,' Caleb replied, leaning closer, voice hushed.

'Then leave.' Sol shrugged. 'The main gate is still open. For now anyway.'

'Yes, but this person might be here against their will.' Caleb winced. 'Maybe they got caught up in something. Maybe they need to slip away quietly.'

'That would be difficult.'

'But not impossible?'

'It would be impossible to depart via the main gate,' Sol replied, choosing his words carefully.

'So you do know another way out?'

'Perhaps. I could not say. I gave my word. I am sorry.'

'I get it,' Caleb sighed, knocking back the last of his drink and rising to his feet. 'Someone who can't keep his word isn't someone I'd want directions off anyway. I'll keep looking.'

'If you do, perhaps you should try somewhere else. Perhaps the eastern quarter,' Sol replied. 'Assuming you have a head for heights.'

'I don't really,' Caleb said, smiling. 'But I know someone who does. I thank you.'

'This person you are trying to free. They must mean a lot to you.'

'Never really met her,' Caleb replied. 'But I owe her grandfather. Good luck with your sums, banker.'

He nodded once, before fading into the crowd. Sol watched him leave. It was difficult to pick much out through the press of bodies, but there was some space on the far side of the room, perhaps due to the three figures clustered around a corner table. Even seated, they were huge, no doubt enhanced by stimms and gene-forging. He did not know two of them, though from their size and attire he assumed they were pit fighters. The third he recognised. Virae of the Mercator Sanguis. The slave who rose to Chain Lord. She was staring at him, though he could not read her expression.

He bent his head, returning to the calculations. But it felt pointless, shuffling numbers between columns, only to be presented with an answer that meant nothing. Perhaps this was how the Council of Light felt when he tallied the Needle's output.

Perhaps he was the aberration. Perhaps the spyker had damaged his mind to the extent that he no longer understood simple arithmetic, and he could not even see that his comprehension was failing. That would be a cruel irony.

'Pardon me, Lord Sol, is this seat taken?'

He glanced up. It was the Chain Lord. He had not heard her approach. For such an intimidating woman she moved silently.

'It is not,' Sol replied, nodding for her to sit. 'I don't attract much company.'

'What happened to the sump trash you were drinking with?' she asked. 'He a friend?'

'No, but I met him this afternoon and he didn't try to stab me,' Sol said, glancing to the masked revellers. 'These days that passes for friendship.'

'Perhaps that will change,' Virae said. 'I heard you spoke out in the courtroom. Not a fan of Lord Pureburn?'

'I'm not a fan of liars and frauds.'

'Yeah, I'll drink to that,' she said with a nod, draining half her glass. 'I'm still waiting on payment for the serfs. When his people requested the workers, all that mattered was getting them here as fast as possible. Now I have arrived there are suddenly issues with payment. I signed everything they put in front of me, but there is always another reason to delay.'

'This is Pureburn?'

'It is.'

'That's somewhat his modus operandi,' Sol said. 'Best way to get rich is not to pay your bills.'

'You think I'll get nothing?'

'You'll get something,' Sol said. 'Probably reduced for various implausible reasons. It depends how much money he gains from this enterprise. He is not by nature generous.'

Virae considered his words, her fingers drumming on the table. 'I could make him pay,' she said softly.

Sol looked at her, before glancing again at the revellers. 'Could you?' he asked. 'You think you can fight through all of them?'

'His guards? Maybe. But all the Cawdor, too?' she asked. 'We'd do better than you might think. But no, I take your point. I cannot best an army in single combat.'

'Perhaps the only way to take him down is to turn them against him.'

'That would take a wiser head than mine,' Virae said. 'But I do know that once the Eternal Flame is lit, Periculus will belong to him. The fire will symbolise both his power and the righteousness of the God-Emperor, the two bound as one. To oppose him will be considered heresy.'

Sol swore, settling back in his chair. It hadn't occurred to him, but she was right. Who would dare extinguish a flame lit from a spark of the God-Emperor's sword? Even Helmawr would have to manoeuvre carefully around that one.

'How long till the ceremony?' he asked.

'Three days. My gladiators are already in training for the fights. He wants blood to consecrate his fire.'

'I cannot convince a mob of anything in that time.'

'Perhaps not,' Virae said. 'But perhaps he will fall by his own hand in time. He holds power, but his control is precarious and built of lies. It will fail.'

'I would like to believe that.'

Virae was staring at him, a slight frown marring her brow. She seemed to be weighing a difficult decision.

'You are a Guilder too, part of the Mercator Lux.'

'True enough.'

'Do you know a means of securing a power supply without going through Lord Pureburn?'

'There are ways,' Sol said. 'Most are illegal and easily detected. But, depending on the location, it might be possible to syphon something from the hive's heat sink. It would be minimal, but enough for some rudimentary environmentals – heat, light.'

'You could assist with this?'

'I could,' he said. 'Though I know not if I should.'

'I will owe you,' she replied. 'If it does all fall apart then you may need sanctuary, or a strong right hand.'

'I certainly lack the latter,' Sol sighed, his gaze falling on his still limp hand. 'But many have already been burned for what you are asking me to do. It is a lot to take on trust.'

'You have my word,' she said, her gaze like steel. 'Once given it will not be broken.'

She held out her chainglaive, hefting the enormous weapon in one hand, the offered weapon a symbol of trust. He took it awkwardly in his right hand, the fingers still numb. The weapon seemed to shudder at his touch, as though roused momentarily from its slumber. A spark danced along its chainblade, the jagged teeth seeming to purr.

'Is that the reason for your moniker, "the Unbroken"?' he asked as he lowered his hand. 'Your word is never broken?'

'No,' she said, her smile fading. 'That name is from my slave life. The Chain Lord who owned me liked my spirit, but only as something he could crush. He was well equipped to break his charges – whips, brands, worse things. But I would not surrender. I would not break.'

'So he named you unbreakable?'

'He did not,' she said softly. 'He decided to scour my hide for a night and a day. Left me bloodied, just a trembling mess of flesh and pain. But still I did not break. He had to repeatedly recharge the shock whip. Maybe that's what caused the accident. Regardless, on the ninth session the whip's power unit exploded. His arm had to be amputated. That broke him. Not the injury, for he could afford to replace the limb. But the story spread of the slave who would not bow, who he whipped until his arm shattered. It ruined him in the end. I was gone by then, fighting in the arena under the name I took from him.'

'You miss the arena?' Sol asked gently.

'No. Those days are done.' She smiled. 'I enjoyed the camaraderie and the discipline, but not the death. My only fight now is for survival.'

12

The pit fighters circled, wielding blunted blades. Still, Virae knew this was no guarantee. The weapons were still heavy, the fighters strong enough to deliver crippling blows. She watched as Gash took the offence, lashing out with his polearm, his opponent parrying desperately, but it was hard to focus. Half her gaze tarried on the line of slaves preparing the grounds. They appeared meek enough, bent to their task, the Shaklemen barely needing to employ their shock-staves.

But something troubled her. It was little more than a feeling, but she had once worn those chains, and knew both sides of the slaver's whip. There was a tension she could not place. And it was not just the slaves.

She glanced to the half-finished amphitheatre, where a score of onlookers sat watching the training, mostly scum and hangers-on, though a Guilder of the Mercator Pallidus was sitting on the upper level, flanked by two enormous guards. All watched intently.

Too intently.

'I'm not liking the audience,' she murmured. Beside her Block glanced away from the combat, following her gaze, his scarred forehead creased into a frown.

'What's the problem?' he asked.

'Why the interest? It's just training. Why so many?'

'Not much else to do.' He shrugged. 'We always get onlookers. A few might be sizing up the competition. Let them, I say.'

He was right. But she could not shake the feeling. They were too intent, like dogs contemplating a prospective meal. It made her trigger finger itch.

'I'm not sure we should be out here,' she said.

'You'd rather be in our new lodgings?' Block asked.

She smiled despite herself. He had a point. They'd been allocated the lowest level of a hab-block that had been ground flat, its sheared roof barely poking above the bone-gravel. Most of the outer building was rubble, but a narrow corridor was still accessible, the only route now accessing the half a dozen rooms that were still intact. It would have been almost secure if they were not directly beneath the suspended slave-block, the two linked only by a rickety service lift of dubious Cawdor workmanship. It fitted maybe twenty serfs, but she wouldn't trust it with more than ten.

There was a roar. She spun round, reaching for the chainglaive strapped to her back. Gash stood over his fallen opponent, but neither seemed injured. Gash's outburst was instead addressed to the crowd. A heckler most likely. No danger, provided the young pit fighter didn't lose his head.

'It's Pureburn,' she sighed. 'Rule by division. The people vent their frustrations in the arena whilst he watches and fattens his pockets.'

'Not a bad plan,' Block said.

'You don't object to being his puppet? Fighting for his amusement?'

'I'm looking forward to it.' Block grinned, stretching his shoulders. 'Been a while since I walked the pit.'

'You sure you're up to it, old man?' She smiled. 'You're the only one of this bunch more decrepit than I am.'

He glared at her. 'I can still swing a blade.'

'So can I,' she replied, tapping the chainglaive strapped to her back. 'Carried that since my first fight and it's never let me down. But I'm not as fast as I was, and I know it doesn't have the bite it once did. We're both good enough to reap the hive's bottom feeders, but a real fight is different.'

'You think I should retire?' Block mused with a mocking smile. 'Maybe start a fungal farm somewhere? Father some brats?'

'No, that sounds far too much like hard work,' she said, grinning. 'Give me a bloody death in the arena any day.'

Lord Credence Sorrow was not a difficult man to find. Sol had spotted him sitting in the upper level of the dilapidated amphitheatre flanked by two of his Grinder bodyguards. The men towered a head above the average underhiver, and were ostensibly tasked with fending off the riffraff. In truth, Sorrow had little to fear as few underhivers would willingly stand too close to a member of the Mercator Pallidus.

Not for the first time Sol wondered if he'd fallen into the right profession.

Sorrow raised his head as Sol approached, offering a thin smile.

'Late night?' he asked. 'My servants say you were out till the early hours. And you seem to be favouring your right arm.'

'I had something of an altercation,' Sol replied.

'Are you injured?'

'No, I was lucky. It seemed House Cawdor did not take kindly to some of my remarks.'

'Yes. I heard you made a bit of a scene. I hear the good captain was not impressed by your charts and diagrams.'

'Perhaps I should have spoken the truth.'

'In Periculus Lord Pureburn decides what is true.'

'You speak as though you admire him.'

'There is much to admire.' Sorrow shrugged. 'He is successful, rich, well respected and crushes anyone who opposes him. He is a role model for any Guilder.'

'I wonder about "rich",' Sol replied. 'I've stolen a glance at some of his ledgers. His financial empire is about as leaky as his pipeline.'

'Wouldn't know it by looking at him,' Sorrow said, adjusting his signet ring. 'And that is all that matters.'

Sol glanced at him, brow furrowed. 'You value appearance more than truth?'

'Appearance *is* truth,' Sorrow replied, his gaze intent on the sparring gladiators. 'If I hoard billions of credits but dress like a beggar I will be treated as such. Likewise, I may be drowning in debt, but if I carry myself as a success then that is how I shall be treated. You obsess over your view of the world, of forcing others to accept it. But you don't realise the world is shaped by perception. If you know the truth, but all others think otherwise, then you are the liar.'

'You are oddly sombre this morning.'

'I am working,' Sorrow replied. 'Making friends.'

'With whom?'

'Possibly this Gash fellow,' Sorrow said, nodding to one of the pit fighters. He was a huge man, gene-forged into a titan.

But despite his bulk the man was fast, his weapon a blur as he knocked another opponent from their feet.

'Doesn't look like much of a conversationalist.'

'Conversation isn't what I want from him,' Sorrow said. 'But I have few men, and the followers of House Cawdor are legion. A seasoned pit fighter or two would be valuable allies. Should something go wrong.'

'I thought you were a connected man,' Sol replied. 'Did you not have the Shadows of Catallus at beck and call?'

'They are assassins, not guards.'

'But you know them?'

'Ah,' Sorrow said with a smile. 'This is the reason you have sought me out on this fine morn? You seek a more permanent solution to your problem?'

'I merely wish to consider all options.'

'Well, I fear they may not be forthcoming. There are whispers that House Catallus has a stake in Periculus. If so, those two will not take any action that might support their former House.'

'I thought Pureburn was aligned with House Catallus?'

'So did I,' Sorrow replied. 'But that may no longer be the case. Like I said – whispers.'

He rose suddenly, breaking into applause. Sol followed his gaze. The pit fighter known as Gash had felled his opponent and was gesticulating obscenely to the small crowd.

'Certainly not a cultured fellow,' Sol observed. Gash was barking something, the words lost. But his remarks were addressed to a figure lounging in the front row of the stands, his boots resting on the rail. He was clapping too, though the movement was agonisingly slow, as though mocking the gladiator.

There was something familiar about his face.

And his lopsided mohawk.

'Does that imbecile have a death wish?' Sorrow frowned, glancing to Sol, who was staring open-mouthed. 'What? Why are you looking at him like that? Do you know that idiot in the crowd?'

Caleb couldn't help but smile as he goaded the pit fighter. He continued his mocking applause a moment before stifling a yawn.

'Sorry,' he said, clamping a hand over his mouth, his voice carrying across the arena. 'I didn't mean any disrespect. You must just be boring me. Please, carry on with your little exhibition. Who knows, maybe you'll find a way to be entertaining?'

'Yeah?' the fighter snarled. 'Think you can do better than me?'

'At putting people to sleep? I doubt it.'

'You want to try me? You want to take on Gash?'

'I'm sorry, what?' Caleb frowned, rubbing his ear with his finger. 'You said your name is *Gash*? Did your vat-mother curse you with that handle, or were you stupid enough to pick it yourself?'

A ripple of laughter flowed through the stands around him. Gash swore, pointing his dulled blade at the smirking Caleb. Behind the pit fighter the slaves had slowed their labours. They were watching. He studied them from the corner of his eye, seeking the familiar crimson-marked eyes of Iktomi.

There. Half swathed in shadows, he saw the ratskin.

She met his gaze and nodded. They were ready.

'Why don't you come in here and say that?' Gash snarled.

'Why should I?' Caleb shrugged, turning back to the gladiator. 'I have nothing to prove. Unlike you, I'm a real warrior, my strength earned, my skills honed. You were gene-forged into that body, the art of combat probably implanted by a data-slug. You're just a weapon crafted from flesh and stimm, a false hope dangled before the serf classes by the Chain Lords. Defeat this monster made man and you too can be free. Except you are not free, are you? You are as much a slave to your artificial body as the rest of us, whilst a sneering Chain Lord yanks your leash.'

He had to speak loudly now, to make his voice heard above the murmur of the crowd. The slaves' work had slowed to a crawl, as they too were watching. The Shaklemen moved between them, employing goad and whip. But there was resistance, and the Chain Lord and her retainers were already making their way over to restore order. Gash was oblivious, his face scarlet. He was a killer, no doubt, and proud of his talent for death. There was no greater insult than to suggest it was unearned.

A flicker of doubt flashed in the back of Caleb's mind as the gladiator strode purposely towards him. But he could not help himself; something about the fighter irked him.

'You're nothing but a coward,' Gash spat. 'Spewing your little words but refusing to back them up. I have defeated a hundred men in the arena, overcome beast and machine alike. You call yourself a warrior, but who have you ever fought?'

Caleb smiled, stretching his shoulders. Slowly, he rose to his feet to a chorus of boos and catcalls.

'Who have I fought?' Caleb said. 'I am the man who slayed the Unseen Beast of Sumptown. I am the one who bested the Badrock Boys singlehanded. I have faced Chain Lord and slave-ogryn alike in the arena, and never been defeated.'

'Yeah?' Gash spat. 'Well, I challenge you to–'

'No,' Caleb said, vaulting over the barrier and striding towards the massive pit fighter. 'I am the one making the challenge. No weapons, no fancy arena tricks. A real fight, one-on-one.'

Gash's face split into a mocking smile.

'You want to challenge me to a fist fight?' he said, raising a massive hand. It was bigger than Caleb's head.

'Last man standing.' Caleb nodded. 'Nothing at stake but honour and bragging rights.'

Gash shook his head, still angry, but an element of his good humour restored at the prospect of violence.

'Who do you think you are?' he grinned.

'I am the Hero of Hope's End,' Caleb replied, playing to the crowd. 'I am the champion of the downtrodden, the under-hive's ninth most dangerous man. I am Caleb Cursebound. And I am going to kick your arse.'

13

Virae barked at the serfs, keeping half an eye on the events happening over her shoulder. Gash was squaring up to the heckler, though neither had a weapon in hand. It was a foolish move accepting a challenge from the crowd, but there was little she could do now. The code of the arena forbade her from interfering, and Gash would never forgive her if she forced him to back down. In any event she trusted the pit fighter would swat the smaller man aside easily enough, but the slaves were the greater threat. They still cowered at her approach, redoubling their labours. But they had listened to the man's words, and something had shifted in their eyes. Behind the fear, anger was rising.

Her gaze darted between them, trying to identify any true threats. She remembered the ratskin, those cold eyes framed by crimson slashes. Was she not part of the work crew? Virae swore she had been there a moment earlier, seemingly labouring without complaint.

But there was no sign of her now.

'Elle?' she barked through the vox-channel.

'Unbroken?'

'Where is the ratskin?' she said, surveying the slaves. 'Tell me someone has eyes on the ratskin?'

'I don't know. I thought she was part of the ground crew?'

'Well, she's not,' Virae snapped. 'Find her. And get some Enforcers down here – tell them there's risk of a riot.'

Caleb wore a self-assured smile as he pandered to the crowd, which was swelling each moment, drawn by the commotion and prospect of blood being spilled.

'You ready then?' Gash said, flexing his massive hands.

'Let's just give them a moment to settle,' Caleb replied, keeping his voice upbeat and free from the fear gnawing at his belly. The cheers were dying now, the onlookers settling themselves for the violence to come. Many were half masked, but there was enough flesh visible to see their faces split by bloodthirsty smiles. There was something deeply unsettling about their collective savagery, but he had no time to dwell on it.

'Iktomi, please tell me you're clear,' he whispered into his concealed vox-bead. 'I'm running out of prefight banter.'

His opponent had discarded his blade and was squaring up to Caleb. Or trying to anyway; Caleb's wilting mohawk barely reached the man's chin, and his shoulder width was perhaps a third of the pit fighter's.

'You got a death-oath or something?' the huge man asked, still smiling like a sumpkroc.

'It does seem like it,' Caleb mused. 'But no, this is all a bit of misdirection. I owe an old man a favour.'

'And this is how you're repaying it?'

'Actually, I'm trying to rescue his daughter from a life of

slavery.' Caleb shrugged. 'But that's hardly here or there. Quick question though – are you willing to take a dive?'

Gash considered this, brow furrowed.

'And lose to a runt like you?' he asked. 'I'd be asking ten thousand credits minimum. And I don't go down until after I've pulled off at least one of your arms. I've got a reputation to protect.'

'Strong opening bid.' Caleb nodded. 'How about thirty credits now, and then we'll sort the rest out tomorrow?'

'How about I just start now with your thumbs?' Gash replied, cracking his knuckles, the sound like a barrage of stub rounds.

'I'd rather not.'

'I'm sure you wouldn't.' The pit fighter grinned, leaning in until their noses were almost touching. 'Tell you what, you can have a free one. Give me your best shot. Then I'm coming for you, and I'm gonna hurt you. But put on a good show, and maybe what's left can keep breathing.'

'Fair enough,' Caleb said. 'Final thought – could I distract you by pointing in another direction and saying "Look over there"?'

Gash sighed, rolling his eyes. 'Why would you think–?'

Caleb's fist smashed into his face.

Sol heard Sorrow wince but did not look round, his focus on the fight. Gash roared in fury, his cry echoed by the crowd. His massive fist swung in a vicious cross, but found only air, Caleb ducking and rolling under the blow, darting out of reach and forcing the lumbering fighter to pursue him. Gash's massive hand seized Caleb's arm, but the smaller man slid from his sleeve at the last second, and the pit fighter found himself grasping Caleb's longcoat and nothing more.

'Caleb, you idiot,' Sol whispered. 'What the hell are you doing?'

Sorrow frowned. 'You know this man?'

'No. But I owe him,' Sol said. 'He took my side during an altercation. It would seem he has a habit of throwing himself into fights that don't concern him.'

'Ah. So what's his real plan here?' Sorrow asked. 'Does he have a secret weapon? Toxic fingernails? Bionic implant?'

'It doesn't seem like he has a plan,' Sol replied, as another roundhouse punch missed by inches.

'You mean he's just some idiot challenging a professional pit fighter?'

'It seems that way.'

'Oh, fantastic,' Sorrow said with a wide smile, settling in his chair. 'Could you introduce us? In the unlikely event he survives.'

Sol didn't reply. He was no expert, but Caleb seemed a competent fighter, quick on his feet and unpredictable. But since throwing the first blow he had delivered virtually no offence, focusing instead on staying out of reach. That was no strategy – at best he could hope for a draw, but the pit fighter only needed one lucky blow to end the fight.

'Looks like this is over already,' Sorrow sighed. 'Bit anticlimactic.'

Gash had Caleb cornered, his back pressed to the chain fence. Words passed between them, though the sounds were lost to the roar of the ever-swelling crowd. But Sol saw Gash snarl in fury. He threw a savage hook, but Caleb ducked beneath it, snatching a handful of bone-gravel and slamming it into the pit fighter's eyes. As the huge man blinked, trying to clear the dust from his face, Caleb suddenly darted upwards, scaling the chain fence like a lizard, until he was hanging at least fifteen feet above the arena. Below, Gash had cleared his eyes and was bellowing for Caleb to come down and face him. Sol could not hear the response, but a ripple of laughter passed across the nearest onlookers, along with a barrage of jeers. The pit fighter swore loudly, attempting to scale the fence, his breathing laboured.

'Too tired and too heavy,' Sorrow observed. 'Surprised the crowd haven't turned on the newcomer though. He's not exactly living up to his threat.'

'Perhaps not,' Sol said, 'but he has made the Guild of Chains look like fools. That's more than most of these piti-ful souls could hope for. Perhaps it's enough.'

'Not for our pit fighter, it seems,' Sorrow replied as Gash suddenly turned, stalking his way back to the centre of the arena, where his chainglaive was stashed. As he seized the weapon it roared into life, hungry for blood. The crowd was likewise; whatever pleasure they derived from Caleb's antics, it palled before the prospect of seeing his bloodied corpse.

Sorrow grimaced as the pit fighter approached the spot beneath the dangling Caleb.

'This will not end well.'

'Iktomi, talk to me,' Caleb whispered into his vox-bead. He was drenched in sweat, and the chain fence was digging into his fingers. He tried to adjust his grip but his foot slipped, almost pitching him to the arena below. He seized the bars, wincing as the metal sank deeper into his hands.

Below him, the pit fighter known as Gash raised his chainglaive.

'Last chance,' he said. 'Get down here and finish it.'

'Sure,' Caleb grunted through gritted teeth. 'Just put the weapon down – this is supposed to be a fist fight.'

'Yeah?' Gash replied, glaring up at him with bloodshot eyes. 'But you ain't fighting. You just run around making me look stupid.'

'That's not true. Your stupidity is a collaborative effort.'

'Whatever, runt,' Gash said, hawking and spitting. 'You're coming down one way or another.'

'*Caleb?*'

The vox-bead hissed into life.

'Iktomi?'

'*It's done. She's safe.*'

'Thank the God-Emperor,' Caleb sighed, as Gash readied his weapon. 'Good to know my impending death was not completely in vain.'

'*You are in danger?*'

'I wouldn't worry about it. You won't make it in time.'

'*I can see you. Try and hang on.*'

The whirling teeth of the blade bit deep, the chain-link offering minimal resistance, the vibrations shaking Caleb to the bone. He could not hold much longer, and even if he could it would be seconds before his refuge gave way.

It was strange. He should have been terrified. But in that moment of certain death there was a tranquillity. As the fence began to tilt forward, he saw the faces of the crowd grinning at his plight. He caught sight of the Guilders on the upper level, recognising the figure of Sol, his expression grim. The other gladiators were cheering Gash on. Only the Chain Lord seemed unsure.

Then he was weightless, the pain in his fingers gone as he tumbled through the sky. He wondered how Iktomi would have handled this – perhaps twisting in the air or rolling through. How did she do it? His limbs just flailed helplessly, making no impression on his flight. He tensed, then wondered at the last second if that would make the impact better or worse.

He landed hard, the air driven from his lungs. Something popped in his elbow, and the corresponding fingers went numb. He tried to rise, spitting out a mouthful of bone-gravel, but a massive hand seized the back of his neck, dragging him almost to his feet before tossing him aside. He tumbled, the world rolling about him, trying to find his feet. Instead, a boot slammed into his chest, pinning him in place. The world above drifted into focus. Gash was staring down at him, face twisted in a mask of savagery more terrible than anything worn by the denizens of House Cawdor. His eyes were bloodshot, almost crimson, and as Caleb watched a single ruby tear welled in the man's eye, leaving a bloody stain as it slid down his cheek.

'Got you now, you little maggot,' Gash snarled, his voice guttural, closer to animal than human. 'Gonna take my time peeling you, gutting out all the good bits. Gonna make them watch as I feed you some of your internal organs. What do you say to that, runt?'

'Just one thing,' Caleb wheezed, his breath restricted by the pressure on his chest. 'This was supposed to... be a... fist fight...'

'So?'

'So,' he gasped, as his hand stretched for the blade hidden in his boot. 'I want the... record to show... I won by disqualification.'

Gash spat in his face before leaning closer, both eyes now openly weeping blood.

'The only records are gonna be written in bits of your intestine.' He grinned. 'You and anyone else who thinks they're better than me. I'll gut you all! I'll–'

He trailed off, frowning despite his bloodlust. For a moment Caleb wondered why, until he realised the crowd had fallen silent. All eyes, including Gash's, were pointed spire-wards.

He followed their gaze. Something was plummeting from the upper levels of the amphitheatre. It hurtled like a missile, and was barely a dozen yards above them when a grapnel-line fired, snagging a strut from the adjoining ruins. The crowd gasped as the figure swung on the line, its momentum shifting. Gash barely had time to raise his weapon before the figure slammed into him feet first, sending him sprawling. Caleb watched as she pirouetted in the air, landing on her feet.

It was Iktomi.

'How… do you… do that?' he asked, struggling to rise. She did not reply, her gaze fixed on Gash. He was already on his feet, brushing off the impact as though it were nothing, his blade in hand. The blood still seeped from his eyes, his face split in a snarl.

'This your woman?' he spat, glaring at Caleb.

'Partner,' Caleb gasped, fighting for air. 'Please, I forfeit. Let this be the end of it.'

'So it's "please" now?' Gash grinned, his metal jaw gleaming as he loomed over the ratskin. 'You worried I'm gonna hurt her?'

'Not even slightly.'

'Walk away,' Iktomi murmured, her hand resting on the pommel of her knife. Besides this, she appeared unarmed.

Gash shook his head, still grinning. 'Not gonna happen. Any last words?'

Iktomi didn't reply. Gash flicked the switch on his chainglaive, the weapon howling back into life.

'Strong and silent type, huh? Bet I can do something about that. We'll see how silent you are with my glaive in your gut.'

Still nothing – no flicker in her eye, no tension in her stance.

'Think you're a contender?' he persisted. 'Think your fancy entrance and a lucky hit makes you a worthy opponent?'

No response.

'Maybe I'll cut you up a little,' he persisted. 'Shave off a limb, or carve up that face of yours. Have some fun with you. What do you think of that?'

Her mouth twisted into something close to a smile.

'I don't like fun.'

His blade sang out. The blow was sluggish, clumsy even. Perhaps he underestimated her, or the kick had hurt him more than he'd let on. But before he could strike, her knife was already buried hilt-deep into his forearm. He screamed, his fingers suddenly unresponsive, the chainglaive falling from his hand. He still clasped it with the other, but was off balance now, stumbling as he tried to recover.

She was already in the air, landing on his shoulders like a phyrr cat. There was a glint of silver, like a strand of steel silk stretched between her fingers. She twisted her wrists, and suddenly he was on his knees, gasping, his good hand clasped to his throat, clawing for relief. But his fingers were huge and could find no purchase on the silken steel, a crimson line forming beneath them as the wire bit deep. As Caleb watched, a single bead of blood welled, falling to the arena's bone-gravel.

Still, Gash was strong. He bucked and thrashed, trying to reach for her with his good hand, but she twisted, favouring his right side where his arm hung useless, her blade having severed vital tendons. He was fading now, slowly pitching forward, lips tinged blue.

It was not a good death. Nor was it quick. The crowd was

silent at first, unsure why the towering gladiator had fallen, the garrotte wire invisible to the spectators. But now they could see what was happening, and the silence was born of unease.

Caleb, still struggling to rise, managed to find his knees. He saw their faces. This was not the bloodshed they craved. There was no clash of weapons, no insults and curses. Gash could not even speak, his last breaths little more than the wet grunt of an animal, his eyes bulging grotesquely as his life faded.

Iktomi released her grip, rising, eyes devoid of regret or sentiment. Around her, Caleb watched a trio of Enforcers advancing, shock-batons raised.

14

The arena was now abandoned, serfs herded back to their duties, gangs and scum retreating to their hideaways. But the braziers still burned, casting their flickering light over the bone-gravel. Soon it would be stained by the blood of winner and loser alike, but for the moment Lord Pureburn felt it a fitting venue from which to deliver judgement.

In a sense, that had been his task since arriving in Periculus. But he had become distracted, his edicts enforced by zealots who were a little too quick to invoke pyres and nooses. He missed the process of considering evidence and weighing arguments as lives and prosperity were decided by his judgement.

It was particularly gratifying when it was two of his peers. Not that either was a true peer, he thought, assessing Virae and Sorrow in turn. The Chain Lord was an upstart, risen above her station through luck and the strength of her arm. Still, while she lacked eloquence she compensated with passion, thumping the table and gesticulating wildly as she made her demands. It seemed excessive. He could appreciate the cost involved in training a replacement pit fighter, as well as the hit her reputation would suffer. But the fervour behind her words surprised him. He half suspected she had held a relationship with the deceased that went beyond mere service.

'Lady Virae,' he said when her rant was concluded, 'I offer condolences for the loss of your fighter. However, I am unconvinced that restitution is required. The death took place in the arena. A challenge had been made and accepted.'

'To that other piece of filth,' Virae replied. 'The ratskin attacked when Gash was already engaged.'

'If I might interject?'

Lord Sorrow had raised his hand, offering a gracious smile of questionable sincerity. Still, at least he understood the game. Lord Pureburn nodded, motioning for him to speak.

'The pit fighter known as Gash had defeated his prior opponent, if not quite dispatched him,' Sorrow began. 'The ratskin should not have been in the arena. However, as she was a hive serf, it was Lady Virae's responsibility to keep her shackled. Once she was in the arena the challenge was issued and accepted. Gash attacked and was bested.'

Sorrow glanced to the fuming Virae, shrugging his shoulders.

'I see no crime,' he said.

'They debased my Guild,' Virae replied, glaring at him before turning to Lord Pureburn. 'His insults are a slur against all of us.'

Lord Pureburn allowed his hand to play across his chin as he considered the point. It was an interesting angle of attack. He had begrudgingly enjoyed some of the insults allegedly directed at the Mercator Sanguis when they were repeated to him, but one could construe them as a wider attack on the Guilds. This was something he could not tolerate; Virae was learning.

'I agree,' Lord Sorrow said. 'But I have uncovered that this is not the accused's first such transgression. A little investigating has revealed a Guilder price was set against him. Apparently, he impersonated a representative of the Mercator Munda, Armitage Rakk.'

'Indeed?' Lord Pureburn frowned. 'That is a serious charge.'

'Quite so, my lord.' Sorrow nodded. 'And, as I am sure a learned man such as you already knows, I have a professional relationship with Rakk. I know how insulted he was by this incident. With your blessing, I would prefer these two to be dispatched to Rakk to receive the penalty for their transgression. I can assure you both that they will never be seen again. Unless it is as a head mounted on a spike.'

He smiled, teeth bright as polished bone.

Virae shook her head. 'Lord Pureburn, they murdered my fighter. They–'

'And they will be punished,' he replied, cutting her off. 'More importantly, they will be punished for an actual crime. The fighting pits are sanctified in the name of the God-Emperor. All combat takes place under His ever-watchful eye. All challenges are made and answered in His name. Frankly, I find this serf's tenacity inspiring. I am surprised you think otherwise, given your history.'

She glared at him. Her hand twitched, and for a second he wondered if she would take arms against him. His Pyromagir must have seen it too, for his head snapped round, the brazier that replaced his arm glowing ominously. Virae's gaze flicked from the monstrous cyborg to Lord Pureburn.

'You will be freeing her then?' she said. 'If they are so inspiring?'

'Of course not. These two defrauded the Guilders and must be executed. But the right of execution would be reserved for an actual victim of their crime. Not you or your incompetent gladiators.'

He smiled, reclining in his throne, Virae's gaze still boring into him. He was tempted to open the cell a little wider, to bring her passion to a boil so his Pyromagir could make an example of her. But the moment had passed, the tension easing from her face as fury was caged by discipline.

'Do you have anything you wish to say?' he asked.

'Yes.' She nodded. 'I am done with your pettiness, old man. You lounge on your throne and play at king. Yet I find my purse empty, my serfs underfed, and your lapdogs bestowing death and pain on a whim.'

'And that is all?'

'No,' she said, glancing to the Pyromagir. 'I would also like to say that, if your pet keeps looking at me like that, I'm going to rip its faceplate off and shove it–'

'Enough!' Lord Pureburn snarled, rising to his feet. 'Your insolence condemns you! You have no serfs. I own them along with every life within this dome and every credit that passes through it. Your liberty is a gift, one I could rescind at any moment. Perhaps you have forgotten what it is like to be the one in chains?'

She glared at him. 'I have not. And never will.'

'Well, if you do not wish to repeat the experience, get out of my sight. Go prepare your fighters for the real battles to come. I just hope they are more competent than that braggart who could not best a scrawny slave.'

* * *

Captain Canndis' recaff was cold.

He sighed, setting down the cup and resisting the urge to light another lho-stick. He was down to his final pack. It needed to last at least four more days, until the next supply caravan. Assuming it arrived; from what he gathered the chance was about fifty-fifty. He resolved to put it from his mind, settling back into work and squinting at the data-screen.

It couldn't be right.

He raised his hand, slapping the terminal in the hopes of coaxing it into providing the information he sought. But there was no change, no list of felonies, no record of incarceration. Not even a public intoxication offence, and he was pretty sure the suspect was currently drunk. He leant back in his chair, unbuttoning his collar, his fingers idly straying into his pocket, seeking the pack on reflex.

'Gladshiv!' he bellowed, his voice echoing down the corridor. 'Get your arse in here.'

The lho-stick had somehow nestled into the corner of his mouth. He shrugged, holding his lighter at arm's length before flicking the flint, the spark exploding like a flash bomb before settling into a more manageable blaze. He lit the smoke, and as he exhaled Gladshiv appeared in the doorway. He looked tired, shoulders slumped, eyes bloodshot. Then again, they all looked like that.

'Yes, sir?' Gladshiv said. There was something in the tone Canndis disliked, but he didn't have the energy to pull the clerk up on it.

'You're a desk-rat and a records-smith,' Canndis said, pointing to the screen. 'Tell me if this looks right to you.'

Gladshiv rounded the desk, squinting at the screen. He frowned.

'No,' he said. 'This is odd. A record has been set up, but it's empty.'

'A clerical error?' Canndis asked, slightly pointedly, but Gladshiv did not take the bait. Instead his fingers danced across the terminal, pulling up an insensible stream of numbers and letters.

'What is this gibberish?' Canndis asked.

'Background code. Every time a record is altered it creates an echo that can be traced.'

'Has the record been altered?'

'Yes, sir. Multiple times. Various precincts have uploaded data, but it has been expunged and the record sealed.'

'On whose authority?'

'I don't know, sir. Proctor or higher.'

'Makes no sense,' Canndis frowned, taking a drag on his lho-stick. 'Why would someone that senior protect a hive scum like that?'

'I don't know, sir. Will that be all?'

'For now,' Canndis sighed. 'Get back to work. And wipe that look off your face.'

Gladshiv bowed stiffly, departing without another word.

There was trouble there. He'd seen it at the first meeting with Pureburn. It had got worse, especially when he'd refused to permit Gladshiv to wear a mask in the precinct-fortress. Perhaps that was a pointless battle, Canndis sighed, rising from his seat. Justice in Periculus was now dispensed by Pureburn's mob. The death of an Enforcer at their hands was dismissed as an unfortunate error perpetrated by the misguided. Perhaps he should just surrender the precinct-fortress too, leave them to murder each other.

He rose, departing his door-less office and descending the adjacent flight of steps, clasping the rusted railings. Below the

precinct-fortress were a handful of still functional cells. There
had been less call for them since Lord Pureburn's arrival. His
followers favoured flamers over shock-batons, and there was
little need to incarcerate ash.

He reached the bottom, rapping thrice on the plasteel door.
There was a brief pause before he heard the click of the triple
locks sliding back. The door ground open, its servo-runners
protesting with a shower of sparks. On the far side Patrolman Sisphant looked dishevelled, panting from the exertion,
his undershirt untucked. Canndis was primed to discipline
him until he remembered his own lopsided collar. What did
it matter anyway; who of worth would see them?

'Patrolman,' he said. 'How was the night?'

Sisphant shrugged. 'The stimm-head in number two died.'

'Good. Saves us a job. What about the others?'

'The idiot with the blue hair won't stop talking. The other
one just sits there. Permission to speak openly?'

'Why not?'

'There's something creepy about her, sir,' Sisphant said.
'I've heard about ratskins. There are tales of them spirit walk-
ing, sending their souls out to strangle you whilst you sleep.
Some say that's how she killed that pit fighter.'

'I watched her throttle him with a garrotte wire.'

'But nobody found the weapon.'

'Oh, then it has to be witchcraft, doesn't it?' Canndis
sighed, pushing past him. 'The only alternative is that you
idiots were too incompetent to find a piece of wire.'

'Sir, I assure you we–'

'At ease, Sisphant,' Canndis interrupted, not looking back.
'It's all you're good at anyway.'

Ahead lay the precinct's two remaining cells, the others
long buried by the fall. He passed the first, where a still figure

swayed on a rope made from boot laces, before stopping
before the second. The accused sat cross-legged on the floor,
a lho-stick tucked into the corner of his mouth. Behind him,
on the cell's only foldout bed, lay the ratskin. She seemed
to be asleep.

The prisoner raised his head as Canndis approached.

'Hello, captain!' he said brightly. 'Any chance of a light?'

'Not for a thief.'

'You sure? You can have one,' he persisted, offering the
pack.

'I will, once the guard has confiscated them,' Canndis said.
'I was just reviewing your record. Never seen anything like
it, Mr Curseborn.'

'It's Cursebound.'

'Not according to your record,' Canndis replied. 'Caleb
Curseborn.'

'Well, we can amend that later,' Caleb said. 'I imagine it
made for some impressive reading.'

'As I said, never seen anything like it,' Canndis said, unfurling a blank scrap of parchment. 'There's nothing there.'

Caleb stared at him, brow furrowed. Canndis suspected it
was the first sustained silence since his incarceration.

'Then you have the wrong record,' he said. 'It's Cursebound.
Try–'

'There are no Cursebounds,' Canndis replied. 'Just a Caleb
Curseborn who matches your description and genetic tags.
From what I can tell it's been tampered with, your crimes
removed.'

'What? But that's ridiculous. I'm a legendary thief. I'm the
man who stole the Hand of–'

He caught sight of Canndis' expression and suddenly trailed
off.

'That is, you're quite right, officer. There is no record because I have committed no crimes. I've always had nothing but respect for the law. In fact, my father is a proctor in Hive City.'

'Is that right?'

'Absolutely.'

'Do you know what I think?' Canndis said. 'I think you've hacked our records, and there is no way you could have done it alone. I think this is part of something bigger. I think you know a lot more than you are letting on, and once Lord Pureburn has released you to my custody I am going to arrange a little interrogation.'

Caleb frowned, seemingly confused. 'Who's this Pureburn? Your boss?'

'Hardly,' Canndis snarled.

'All right! Sorry,' Caleb replied, raising his hands. 'I didn't know you were so sensitive. But, just to clarify, you can only interrogate me if you have explicit permission from–'

'You hold your tongue!' Canndis snapped, slamming his shock-baton against the bars. The sound was satisfying, but not satisfying enough. He fought the urge to open the cell, to step inside and beat some respect into the scum. That was what Caleb wanted, of course, to rile him into making a mistake and opening the door. It was transparent, yet still galling. He smacked the bars one last time for emphasis, but Caleb just stared at him. In the bunk behind, the ratskin made a muffled sound but did not wake.

'You all right?' Caleb asked, a passable expression of concern crossing his face. 'Your eyes are kind of bloodshot.'

'I didn't get much sleep. Too many scumbags like you.'

'I didn't sleep either, thanks to Snorey over here.' Caleb grinned, jabbing his thumb at the slumbering ratskin. 'Any chance I can get a cell of my own? I hear the one next door has just become available?'

'This is a waste of time,' Canndis sighed. 'Talk all you want, but when the interrogation–'

'Oh, do stop blathering about that,' Caleb said, rising stiffly to his feet. 'I have done nothing, you said so yourself. And that little incident in the arena? Lord Pureburn arranged that, wanted to put the Chain Lord in her place. It was inter-Guild stuff – I don't pay much attention to the details providing I'm paid. And he always pays me well.'

'You expect me to believe that?' Canndis replied. He kept his voice level, ignoring the sliver of uncertainty pricking the back of his mind.

'I don't care either way.' Caleb stepped closer to the bars, his fingers wrapping around the rusted metal. 'You'll find out the truth soon enough. But because of our budding friendship, I'm not going to make you apologise in front of everyone. Just your squad. And you only have to do it on one knee, provided you get me that lighter right now.'

He stretched out his hand, snapping his fingers, that smug self-satisfied smile strung across his face.

Canndis stepped forward, throwing a right hook between the bars. Caleb was sent sprawling. He landed hard, clutching his face.

'Why is it always the nose?' he moaned. 'I used to have such an amazing profile. At this rate I'm going to end up as unsightly as you.'

'When I am done, you won't be recognisable,' Canndis replied, leaning closer, until his face was nearly touching the bars. 'I will beat you until you can't pass for human. Then maybe you will begin to learn what respect is, you arrogant piece of sump trash.'

'Well, two things,' Caleb said, rising slowly to his feet. 'Firstly, respect is earned, not beaten into someone. And secondly, whilst insufferable, none of this little exchange qualifies as arrogance.'

'Really?' Canndis said. 'What would you call it then?'

'Misdirection.' Caleb smiled. There was a glint in his eye.

Canndis frowned, unsure.

His gaze flicked to the bunk. It was empty.

There was a sudden tightness about his throat, wrenching him hard against the bars, his shock-baton tumbling from his hand. He scrabbled at his throat with desperate fingers, but the tightness increased, pinning him against the bars. Darkness bled into his vision. Weakly, he reached for his holstered stub gun, but a hand gently but firmly took hold of his wrist.

'In case you are wondering, the garrotte wire is an implant, concealed beneath where her little finger should be,' Caleb whispered. 'We will be leaving now, captain. I would prefer not to kill you, as I see no benefit in murdering an Enforcer. But my partner is… indifferent to that sort of thing. So please cooperate. Just let us out of the cell and escort us past the guard. We will use your data-terminal to correct my name-'

'No.'

The second voice was barely a hiss. It came from right beside Canndis' ear.

'Fine,' Caleb sighed. 'We will just be leaving then.'

Canndis only managed a garbled response. It was hard to think, shadows squeezing his consciousness down to the faintest spark. He would have said anything, agreed to anything, providing that little halo of light was not snuffed out completely. He scrabbled for his belt, desperate to coax trembling fingers into taking the key.

Then he heard a stub gun cocked. Through dimmed eyes he saw two shadows emerge into his vision. The closer of the two he knew from somewhere. The man was dressed in black, his robes adorned with the symbol of the Mercator Pallidus. A Corpse Grinder. Beside him, Enforcer Hendrox had his weapon aimed at the prisoners.

The Corpse Grinder gave an obsequious smile. 'Good day. My name is Lord Credence Sorrow, and I'm afraid the question of your liberty is now out of the captain's hands.'

15

Sol winced as Anguis examined his hand. His fingers had curled back like a claw. He could no longer straighten them.

'What did you do?' she asked.

'What I needed to survive.' Ever since his encounter with the three assailants he'd felt the numbness spreading. It crept down his leg, stiffened his pace, and even his tongue seemed thick and unwieldy.

They were in his quarters, though in truth they were of course Lord Sorrow's. The Corpse Grinder had offered to parlay on Caleb's behalf. Sol had wanted to stay and offer his support, but Sorrow had insisted his presence would only make the situation more complicated. Perhaps he was right, and besides, Sol was too weary to argue. He'd returned to Sorrow's residence and lain down to rest, but his dreams were dominated by flames and blood. When he awoke he could not rise. It was fortunate Anguis had responded to his summons.

'Is this a… common side effect of a spyker attack?' he managed, his words heavy.

'No,' she admitted. 'The nightmares can last years, but this degree of paralysis is unusual. I think it's related to your implants. The modifications have done something to your nervous system. Are you experiencing anything else? Pain? Hallucinations?'

'I…'

He could not answer. For he felt something, a thrill and horror born as one. Whenever he closed his eyes he saw the cracks of other-light, the radiance beyond the physical plane. It felt so real, far more than this material world of ruin and rot. But he knew to speak of it would appear delusional, or even witch-touched. Perhaps he was cursed, but he remained lucid enough to hold his tongue.

Anguis' shadow moved. He craned his head to follow, his movements slowed as though trawling through sump water. There was a second shadow beside her; he had not seen it before. Strong hands seized his collar, roughly hauling his head back and exposing his throat. He saw Anguis retrieve the autosyringe with its vibrant green payload. The liquid seemed to churn, a tempest bound to a bottle. As she raised the needle, doubt seized him. Doctor Caute was right; how could he trust a Delaque? The needle could be infested with nano-tech. Or perhaps it was the true cause of his suffering. A simple poison, administered at intervals so she could watch him die slowly, all the time presenting herself as a concerned medicae.

He tried to fight them, but his flesh was weak and unresponsive, and they pinned him like an insect in resin.

'Keep calm,' Anguis murmured, her fingers pressed to his throat. 'This will help. Just hold still.'

The needle stung more than he remembered, its payload burning as it polluted his bloodstream. He blinked, expecting searing agony or blessed oblivion, but neither claimed him. The two agents stepped back, and released from their grip he swayed, but managed to sit upright. Already sensation was returning to his arm, his clawed fingers painfully unravelling. As his pounding heart slowed, the world of fire and fear faded. It now seemed a dream, senseless and inexplicable. Yet, like a dream, something of it stayed with him. An unease.

'Breathe,' he heard Anguis whisper. 'It's all right. You're safe.'

'Am I?' He coughed, glaring at her through his one remaining eye. The other agent stood beside her, face expressionless. But Sol felt he knew this one, perhaps from the shuttle flight. Perhaps from before.

'You can trust me.' Anguis half smiled.

'I feel someone who is truly trustworthy probably does not need to state that outright.'

'There is a difference between trust and honesty,' she replied with a shrug. 'I may not always speak the truth, but I have never hurt you or brought harm to you through my actions.'

He laughed, but the braying that escaped his throat shocked him. It was like another's voice. It sounded unhinged.

'No harm?' he said, peeling back the bandage and showing her his ruined eye socket. 'Your spyker crippled me and destroyed my life.'

'The spyker you requested?' Anguis replied. 'The interrogation you rushed? Your attack that backfired? These are my failings?'

She held his gaze a moment before sighing, squatting down until her face was level with his.

'We have all made mistakes,' she said. 'But we can only

go forward. We both wish to see Pureburn defeated, even if our reasons are different. We cannot succeed unless we work as one.'

'Easy to say when you have all the answers.'

She smiled her half-smile, but the expression soon faded. She was silent a moment, and quite still.

'Do you know how a spyker is made?' she asked.

Behind her, the other agent stiffened, head tilting as though seeking to engage in silent conversation. Anguis only glared in response.

'Enough of that,' she said. 'There is no time. He needs to know what we face.'

She turned back to Sol, smiling apologetically.

'Spykers are not naturally occurring,' she said. 'The gift is induced, the flame of psychic potential fanned by alchemic concoctions and surgical modification. But the process is unpredictable. Many simply die, or have to be euthanised before they evolve into a threat. Even those that survive are driven quite insane by the process.'

'Like Mr Stitch?'

'Yes, though ironically it was one of our more reliable interrogators. At least, before you happened to it.'

She sighed, glancing to her outstretched hand that still held the autoinjector.

'I trust you have heard of the drug Ghast?' she murmured.

'Heard.' He nodded. 'Never seen.'

'Well, it's the catalyst,' she said, tucking the syringe into her longcoat, her hand lingering in the pocket. 'But Ghast takes centuries to form, and even with it the process is laborious. We do our best to refine it, improve it. But it is inherently unpredictable. We possess neither the time nor resources for cavalier experimentation. But others do.'

'This is more than he needs to know,' the other agent hissed, seizing hold of Anguis' collar. 'You overreach your authority.'

She did not reply. Her hand simply emerged from the long-coat brandishing a flechette pistol. She did not speak, just aimed the weapon and squeezed the trigger. The shots were near silent, the storm of needle-like projectiles a blur of silver. The agent fell without a sound.

'As I was saying,' she said, tucking the pistol into her long-coat, 'it is important we trust each other.'

Sol blinked, unable to process what had just happened.

'I'm sorry you had to see that,' she said. 'It is our way to resolve such disputes in private. But there have been… disagreements about how to proceed amongst my superiors. And I tire of debate.'

Sol could not take his gaze from the body. Part of him thought it must be a trick, a convoluted method of securing his trust. But he could see the fallen agent's face. Their mouth hung slack. There was no sign of life.

'Will you kill me next?' he asked.

'If I desired you dead, I would have left you in the Needle,' she replied, taking a seat beside him on the bed. 'We are both bound to this game now. If Pureburn falls and my House's secrets are kept, then it will not matter how many I lose. But if we fail, both our lives are now forfeit.'

'I know Pureburn's secret,' Sol replied. 'I know what he is. A witch, a pyromancer. His power is abhorrent in the eyes of the God-Emperor he proclaims to worship.'

'Is that right?' Anguis replied, glancing at him. Her artificial eyes were inscrutable, but a ghost's smile played on her lips.

'You are telling me I am wrong?'

'In matters of the metaphysical it is not as simple as right and wrong,' she replied, her gaze falling on the body at their feet. 'I suppose the time for secrets is done. It is time you learned the legacy of Periculus, and why it must remain buried.'

Lord Sorrow stared intently at the brew-pot.

Caleb was unsure what the Corpse Grinder was expecting, though his expression suggested it was significant. He glanced to Iktomi, raising an eyebrow. She shrugged, the gesture causing her manacles to clink. One of Sorrow's guards raised his head at the sound. He glared at her, the lines in his throat taut like steel cables, a flensing knife held tight. Caleb was unsure why; neither of them could be considered much of a threat, and both were bound in a prison far more hideous than that employed by the Enforcers.

The brew-pot hissed softly, a narrow plume of steam ascending from the spout. Lord Sorrow smiled, clasping the handle between thumb and finger and pouring bubbling liquid into three small cups. It was a slightly worrying shade of green.

Lord Sorrow raised his cup, closing his eyes and inhaling deeply.

'Krakian tea,' he said. 'Not strictly contraband, though I might be in a spot of bother if anyone found my supplier. Not quite human, let's put it that way. Please, help yourself.'

Caleb reached for his cup, his movements made clumsy by the thick manacles clamped to his wrists. He took a sniff, then a sip. It tasted like hot water with a subtle hint of old shoes. Still, that was vastly preferable to the smell of their current accommodation.

'Delicious,' he said, cradling his cup. Sorrow nodded, his gaze shifting to Iktomi.

'Please,' he offered. She shook her head.

'I assure you it is not poisoned.'

'That's what a poisoner would say.'

'I suppose they would,' Sorrow said. 'But if I wanted you dead you would already be corpse-starch by now.'

He had a point. It would take little effort. Though the grinding machine that dominated the room was heavily rusted there was no doubt it was serviceable. The blood-stains were evidence of that. As was the smell.

Lord Sorrow nodded to the cup, but Iktomi did not acknowl-edge him.

'Is she always like this?' he asked, glancing to Caleb.

'No. Sometimes she's in a bad mood.'

He sipped his tea. It was starting to grow on him. Sorrow frowned, his fingers drumming on the armrest. Caleb found his gaze drawn to the signet ring. He did not recognise the design; that alone suggested it was valuable.

'Pardon me, Miss…?' Sorrow tried. Silence. 'Fine.' He sighed. 'For expediency's sake I will simply refer to you as Mrs Cursebound. Now, if–'

'Iktomi.'

'That loosened your tongue?' Sorrow grinned, his gaze flicking between them. 'That's interesting. Well, Iktomi, I mean you no harm. In fact, I have taken a great risk bring-ing you here. There are those who would prefer you both suffer for your actions in the arena. Were they to find you still amongst the living we would all suffer. So you need to trust me, just as I need to trust you. And I would certainly not stoop as low as poisoning Krakian tea – that would be a crime against gastronomy.'

He lowered his empty cup and refilled it, before switching it with the steaming cup already placed before her.

'To honest dealings,' he said, taking a sip.

She was still a moment, and Caleb assumed she would not respond. But then she took up the cup, offering Lord Sorrow an almost imperceptible nod before draining the contents.

'Thank you.' Sorrow smiled. 'Well, now we trust each other, I will be blunt. You are both to be executed for the crime of impersonating a Guilder.'

'I see.' Caleb nodded. 'Who am I supposed to have impersonated?'

'Armitage Rakk of the Mercator Munda. A well-known prospector who I gather met a rather unfortunate end.'

'Never heard of him.' Caleb frowned, glancing to Iktomi. 'You remember this? I think they're thinking of someone else.'

'We are not,' Sorrow said.

'It's my word against yours.' Caleb shrugged. 'Is there a trial of some kind?'

'No. The Guilds dispense their own justice. As a representative of Mr Rakk's estate, it would be my responsibility to see the sentence carried out.'

'Then you can grant a reprieve?'

'I could,' Sorrow mused. 'Though I have already made assurances that you will be executed. To go back on that promise would not be in my best interests.'

'They why haven't we been tossed in the grinder?'

Sorrow sighed, a flicker of irritation crossing his face. 'The manufacture of corpse-starch is a refined process. Yes, that process includes some vital nutritional elements extracted from the departed. But we don't simply chuck bodies into a grinder.'

'Someone has been.'

They both glanced at Iktomi. She nodded to the machine.

'Blood smells recent,' she said. 'Month or so at most.'

'Madam, I was not even here a month ago,' Sorrow said stiffly, his gaze flickering just a fraction. 'I only recently reopened this parlour, and I can assure you it was in a vile condition. Quite unsanitary for the preparation of foodstuffs.'

'Someone disagreed.' She shrugged.

'Then perhaps an orb spider made its lair here or something,' Sorrow replied tersely. 'My point is, I do not plan to kill you, providing that you can be of service. Loyal as my Grinders are, they are less suited to tasks that require... precision.'

'Oh, that's us.' Caleb nodded. 'Smooth operations all the way. Everything always goes to plan. You need some scouting done, or someone to run an errand uphive? No problem, we can leave tonight.'

Lord Sorrow smiled, though the expression never reached his eyes.

'You wouldn't miss Periculus?' he asked.

'No, I think we have seen enough,' Caleb said. 'Only came down here because I was curious.'

'Is that right?' Lord Sorrow asked. 'Or was it because you wished to free a slave known as Kallic Stone, and have her sent back to Hope's End?'

Caleb did not reply. Sorrow leant back in his chair, his leg crossed over his knee. He blew across his cup, still smiling.

'Perhaps,' Caleb said. 'But you're not going to find her. We–'

'We already have,' Sorrow said. 'I have an associate in House Delaque, and their spies are most proficient. They still have her, and at present she is quite safe. But that could change. I could change it.'

Caleb glared at him. 'What will it take to free her?'

'Oh, a little of this, a little of that,' Sorrow said. 'In truth, I don't know for sure. In truth, I am more used to dealing with a hired class of assassin. You know of the Shadows of Catallus?'

'The brother and sister who dress in carnival gear? Yeah, they're obnoxious as hell.'

'Well, they get the job done. But I understand you helped a friend of mine, so I'm feeling charitable.'

'So you take us for second best?' Caleb replied. 'I'm not sure I'm interested in such a role.'

'You have no choice. You either agree to my terms or I kill the slave, execute you both, and grind your corpses into tomorrow's repast.'

'Is this how Guilder business is normally conducted?'

'We tend to exchange insincere platitudes first. And perhaps have a couple of drinks and a catch-up. But, for the most part, yes.'

'Sounds like we have little choice.'

'That's the spirit.' Sorrow beamed. 'Worry not. I do not intend to remain in this armpit of a dome any longer than necessary. I have two more shipments of corpse-starch to oversee and then I shall depart. Providing I do not need assistance prior to then, you and your slave will accompany me, and may then go where you please. You have my word that you have nothing to fear from me.'

'And what is your word worth?' Iktomi asked.

'Madam, I am a Guilder of the Mercator Pallidus,' Sorrow replied with a bright smile. 'I always keep my promises.'

'Good. Because so do I, and betrayal will have consequences.'

16

Lord Pureburn watched the flames dance in the crucible. The dome's upper fans were still not operational, and the air was choked with soot and the stench of torched flesh from the executions. But the Eternal Flame burned pure, leaving neither smoke nor ash, and visible even through the billowing smoke.

It was the only part of his world still clear.

He sighed, his gaze creeping over his shoulder to the distant execution pyres, where the condemned had been reduced to powder and bone. The serfs were working tirelessly, employing brush and broom to sweep the pyres clear, heedless of the damage the bone powder would inflict on their lungs. It struck him as a particularly unpleasant way to die, choking on the ash of the recent dead. He watched as two of them backed into one another, the collision quickly escalating into blows. The Shaklemen were immediately on them, respirators down as they employed shock-stave and club to break up the conflict. Even then the serfs had to be beaten to the floor, and still they snarled like dogs squabbling over a bone.

'We are running out of time,' he said, gaze falling to the cell beneath the Eternal Flame. 'Those useless slaves dig like insects, but have found nothing, and the weaker minds already fray. The arena will provide an outlet for their anger, perhaps sate it for a time. But I fear it may not be enough.'

He sighed, rubbing his eyes with his hand.

'I could end it,' he continued. 'I could adjust the filters, seal your presence as much as I can. It would buy time, but then what of our forces? Without you, our weapons would be a liability. There are so many here who wish to see me fall, and House Catallus has yet to act. We must be vigilant. We must be armed.'

He sighed again. He was tired and longed for his throne. But his back would be to the flames, and somehow that felt wrong. He needed to face the danger, to seek guidance in the purifying fires. He knew there would be no spoken response. Not any more. The time they could converse had long passed. But he had faith his voice was heard. Perhaps one day it would be answered again.

'Lord Pureburn!'

He flinched at the sound. He was in a public setting, overseeing the final arrangements for the pit fights. There was no reason for his subordinates not to approach, but it still felt like a private moment violated. He felt a sliver of rage, like a hot needle sliding into the back of his skull. But he ignored it, snuffing out the fury with a flick of his will. The Pureburn blood was stronger, inured to such base urges. He would not succumb, no matter how exhilarating it felt.

He turned. The speaker, Brother Tritus, was doing his best to kneel before him. But his body was twitching, almost involuntarily. His head was bowed and his mask firmly in place, but by the light of the Eternal Flame Lord Pureburn met his bloodshot eyes. The pupils were pinpricks, the veins in the sclera swollen as though fit to burst.

'You have something to say?' he asked.

'Palanite Captain Canndis wants words, milord,' Tritus grunted. 'Keeps insisting.'

'I see.' Pureburn nodded. 'Do you suppose this is because you murdered one of his men?'

'He was a sinner, milord. His death is his own making.'

'Are we not all sinners?' Lord Pureburn asked. 'Do we not all strive for the chance to earn our place at His table?'

'Yes, milord.'

'Then why did this man need to die when he did? The Enforcers preserve order. Sinners or not, they assist in keeping Periculus from descending into chaos.'

'Milord, with respect, they only care for Helmawr's order,' Tritus replied, spitting out the name, as though speaking it left an unpleasant taste in his mouth. 'Before your arrival I watched this so-called Enforcer. He was lax, milord, governed by lust and baseness. There was a woman...'

He trailed off, twitching, as though struggling to compose himself. Lord Pureburn watched the man wrestle for control.

'The woman,' he breathed. 'She was wanton, distracting with her grace and laughter. Even I, milord, was not... she would dance, and sing. Her voice was soft. I remember my mother once sang the same psalms, but even she did not possess such a voice. I-'

He fell silent again, but Lord Pureburn waited, watching the man intently.

'They consorted,' Tritus continued. 'He was too weak to resist her charms. Together, their corruption started to spread, their blasphemies... so I saved him, milord. Perhaps the God-Emperor will grant him mercy. I care not.'

'And the woman?' Pureburn asked softly.

'The fire granted her mercy too,' Tritus murmured. 'I have prayed every day since then that He will find a place for her at His table, craven as she was.'

'I see,' Lord Pureburn said. 'Tell me, Brother Tritus, have you ever worked a mine?'

'No, milord.'

'Neither have I,' Pureburn replied. 'But I heard tell that the more impoverished prospectors, those who could not afford an atmospheric scanner, would bring a small caged animal down into the mine. If the air became toxic the creature's death would provide a warning, perhaps an opportunity for the miners to flee.'

He glanced down at the twitching Tritus, his eyes stained crimson, and wondered if he too should flee.

'Do you understand my meaning?' he asked.

Tritus shook his head. 'No, milord.'

'Hold to that, for as He teaches us, ignorance is strength,' Pureburn said. 'I will speak to Palanite Captain Canndis. But first, tell me – how go the preparations?'

'Pit fighters say they are ready. Plenty wish to fight,' Tritus replied. 'The Chain Lord is still brooding over her fallen fighter, but she has caused no further trouble. The serfs have nearly cleared the execution grounds. Though I still think we should keep some of the remains as an example.'

'Your guidance is valued. But I need the area cleared. Perhaps something can be done with skulls and other bones – see if any of your more artistically minded brethren can come up with something decorative for the gate. But, please, nothing garish.'

Tritus nodded.

'Tell me, Brother Tritus, will you fight in the arena?'

'I do not know, milord,' Tritus murmured. 'I do not know His plans.'

'Perhaps you should pray on it?' Lord Pureburn replied. 'I am sure He will provide an answer. Perhaps not in words, but the pious can always discern His meaning.'

Tritus bowed and rose to depart, but Lord Pureburn raised his hand.

'Please, before you leave, ensure the serfs and Shaklemen depart with you. I would make a prayer of my own, and I wish to do so in solitude.'

'Yes, milord,' Tritus said, tracing the symbol of the holy aquila across his chest before turning to the distant serfs. 'All right, sinners, get out. Our lord needs privacy.'

Lord Pureburn watched the procession of lost souls depart, the serfs dragging bags of ash with them, the remaining bones hauled off in a cart. He waited, until they were long departed and the lights were dimmed, until only he remained. Still, he was cautious, reaching to a panel on the arm of his throne and performing a brief sweep with the bioscanner. No life-forms were detected. He was alone.

Almost alone.

His hand shifted lower, to a gene-locked switch, his thumb poised above the sensor. But he hesitated, stealing one final glance over his shoulder. It was foolish, a needless risk. But it had been so long since he'd seen her, or bathed in her true power.

He opened the gene-lock. A crack of light appeared in the cell beneath the flame, forming the shape of a door. He felt the rush of warmth, the righteousness of purpose, and the comforting fury against any that would oppose.

'We will be reunited,' he whispered. 'We will find the answers. We will find your birthplace, and you will be free.'

He closed his eyes as the passion flowed through him, the light blazing like a fallen star.

Sol frowned. He was still struggling to process Anguis' tale.

'Pureburn is an artificially created psyker?' he asked.

She shook her head. 'I do not know what he is. All I know is what his ancestors attempted before Periculus fell. I do not know what was achieved.'

'And this was why Periculus fell?'

'Again, I do not know,' she sighed. 'My superiors tell me only what I need to know, just as I told you only what you needed. But we are beyond such concerns now. I have one agent left, and their eyes have been on Pureburn all this time. Long ago, his family attempted to induce psychic potential by mass-producing and refining synthetic Ghast. As noted, it is not a reliable process, and the lust for expediency only makes it less so.'

Sol frowned. He understood circuits and current flow, but witchcraft and sorcery were beyond him. He knew the stories and propaganda, that the Imperium's space vessels navigated by a psychic beacon, that sanctioned psychic operatives worked for the betterment of mankind, just as witches and devilspawn sought to tear it down. But it had always seemed a distant thing, something that would never touch his own life.

'I thought I was going mad trying to understand the energy flow,' he said, glancing to his hand, the neurocircuits barely visible beneath the skin. 'How he provided so much power with so minimal a supply. At first I thought a second source responsible, perhaps a tap from another Guilder. But it's more than that, isn't it? He's warping the natural order.'

He held out his hand, willing the syphoned power of Periculus to dance between his fingers. Instead, a flash of cobalt lightning leapt from his hand. It arced through the air, ignorant of every law of conductivity, before striking the ruins and dispersing with another burst of light.

'I cannot explain how wrong that was,' he murmured, meeting Anguis' artificial gaze. 'Electrical energy does not flow in that manner. It follows laid paths, its journey mapped. Everything I have learnt of conduction and current tells me it cannot be directed in such a manner. Yet I see it with my own eyes, and feel it with my own hand.'

'The ways of the witch are anathema to reason,' Anguis said. 'We present the spyker as bound by technology and forged through alchemy, but in truth it is something unknowable.'

'I knew what Pureburn was,' Sol replied. 'I knew it the first moment I saw him. Why can only I see it?'

'Perhaps it was the spyker,' she replied, glancing to a flickering light on her wristguard. 'In the moment you killed it the electrical energy must have briefly created some connection. You saw an echo of what Mr Stitch saw when it delved into your patient's mind.'

'It was Pureburn who scourged the Plains of Salvation,' Sol replied. 'I had thought it some forbidden weapon concealed in his throne.'

'And you were right.'

Sol frowned, glancing to Anguis. She was intent on her wristguard, where pictographs were dancing across the display.

'What do you mean?'

'It would seem Lord Pureburn places too much faith in an outdated bioscanner,' she said, turning to Sol. 'My agent has uncovered the truth. The devilspawn is not Pureburn himself. The true power is bound behind his throne.'

17

'Lord Sorrow, I trust your meeting was productive?'

Sorrow jumped at the voice, slamming the parlour door behind him. He had assumed his office would be empty, but Anguis was sitting upon his desk. She smiled, the expression crooked. He could not understand why she did not have her face fixed.

'Manners. I would suggest you knock before entering,' Sorrow replied tersely, making for the pitiful box-unit that comprised his drinks cabinet. He poured a measure of amasec, swirling the amber liquid about the glass.

'Sol invited me,' she replied. 'He is still recovering from his injuries and wished for me to attend him.'

She still wore that smile, the way another might wear a mask.

'Poor dear Sol,' Sorrow replied, an edge of frustration creeping into his voice. He swallowed it, along with the amasec. 'Perhaps you should invite him down?'

'He slumbers. I fear the poor boy is quite exhausted,' she said. 'But that does not matter. My business is with you.'

'And what could you possibly want from me? Besides a good meal to bulk your skinny frame?'

She tilted her head, as though considering the remark. Her smile shifted, hardening. She reached into her longcoat and he flinched, hand straying to his signet ring, but all she withdrew was a scrap of parchment containing a faded image.

'What do you see?' she said, setting it down before him.

'That someone needs to learn how to use a vid-pict,' Sorrow replied, squinting at the image. 'It's horribly overexposed.'

'No, it is not.'

He peered closer. Though washed out, there was something distinguishable on the page.

'Is that... Pureburn?' He frowned, peering at the image. 'He must be wearing some artisan photocontacts to be able to endure that light. It would be like looking at the sun.'

'Not according to my agent,' she replied. 'The light was not blinding, merely bright. But the energy output is beyond what the human eye can perceive. Even our orbital implants struggled to analyse it. But look carefully. Within the light.'

'This is starting to bore me,' Sorrow sighed. 'The palanquin's flame is bright. Is this such a revelation?'

She leant closer, tracing along the image with her finger.

'This, as you rightly noted, is our esteemed Lord Pureburn. This shape here is his dais, and this is the opened chamber. What do you see inside?'

'I don't know,' Sorrow replied, brow furrowed as he scrutinised the image. 'It looks almost like... a figure.'

Once seen he could not unsee it. Someone appeared seated within the light.

'Yes. This is Pureburn's true power. Not faith, not even

forbidden technology. His throne houses a pyromancer, a psyker who can shape fire with a thought. Sol was correct. Or rather, almost correct.'

'This... this would be a crime beyond any other,' Sorrow murmured. 'Such an act would bring the full fury of Lord Helmawr. But this, this is a picture and nothing more. I cannot... we cannot... to even risk exposing this...'

He trailed off, struggling, unsure what to say or even think. His focus had always been on discharging his duties and departing. The last shipment of corpse-starch was due that very evening. He just wanted to escape Periculus alive, return to the civility of the upper hive. There was an opportunity here; he could see that. But such risk. Such chance of it all exploding in his face.

Anguis smiled without humour.

'Lord Sorrow, you are a most successful businessman,' she said.

'True, and I adore flattery, but this seems painfully transparent.'

'What I mean is, you are not beholden by ideology or blinded by ethos. You are a pragmatist. This is something we have in common. Sol is a smart man, but he is constrained by his desire to prove himself, to be recognised as right. It is not a quality we share. To a Delaque, the greatest victory is when the other players do not even realise you are a participant in the game.'

'And what is your game?' he asked.

'Pureburn and his puppet must die,' she replied. 'Irrespective of collateral damage.'

Sorrow raised a well-manicured eyebrow. 'Surely such an assassination is your House's trade. Why bring this to me?'

'We cannot be seen to be involved. It is already established that a bullet will not end him. And we now know why. But his followers approach the throne all the time, beseeching him for blessing and pardons. Whatever power protects him does not stop them drawing close. Someone could get close. Enough to end it.'

'But the psyker? If it commands this power–'

'House Delaque has technologies that can nullify the witch's power, at least long enough to do the deed. All we need are agents to act as the blade. You said you could call upon the Shadows of Catallus. Surely they would be more than capable, and as mercenaries could not be traced back to any of us?'

'The Shadows are elusive,' Sorrow replied. 'They care more for thwarting House Catallus than coin. It is whispered that Pureburn is set to stand against their House. In those circumstances they will not act.'

'Then what of the scum you liberated from the arena?' Anguis replied. 'We still have their prize.'

'They might be capable and could be pressured,' Sorrow replied. 'But Pureburn knows they were released to my custody. If they were seen, and it was traced back to me...'

'Lord Credence Sorrow advocating caution?' Anguis frowned. 'I thought you the daring entrepreneur?'

'Daring is distinguishable from foolhardy,' Sorrow replied. 'You have the spark of a plan, but the risk is too great. I need time to–'

'There is no time left.'

Sorrow flinched at the sound, turning to see Sol standing in the doorway. He looked awful: skin ashen, deep circles marring his eyes, right arm twitching involuntarily.

'Once the Eternal Flame is lit his control will be absolute,' Sol spat. 'We must act before then. We must expose him, let the Cawdor rats see the truth.'

'I don't think you should be up,' Sorrow replied. 'Anguis said you were injured.'

'It does not matter,' Sol said. 'Because I see everything clearly now. We snatch Pureburn's puppet, right before the ceremony. His fires die, his power ebbs. The rats will devour him, and even if they don't we can present the psyker to the Enforcers. We will have proof of what he is. He will be damned in the eyes of his followers and the law. The only question that remains is whether he is arrested or burned. Or both.'

He was smiling now, his remaining eye glinting. Sorrow glanced to Anguis but could not read her expression.

'Tempes,' he began. 'You are clearly unwell. Let me fetch a medicae – they can attend to your–'

'No!' Sol snapped, fist slamming on the desk and spraying a shower of sparks. 'I cannot live in a world where that man prospers. I have laboured all my life to try to compete with people like him. People who already have all the money and connections, all the power. It was never a fair contest, but I thought we at least played the same game. But, even with every advantage, he still needed more. I am done with it. The hive needs to see what he is... and I am through playing by the rules.'

His breath was ragged, and for a moment Sorrow thought he might collapse. But his old friend steadied himself, a little of the ire fading from his eye.

'I am sorry for my outburst,' he said. 'But I am right. I know it.'

'As do I,' Anguis replied smoothly, slipping closer to Sol and resting a hand on his shoulder. 'I was just proposing your plan to Lord Sorrow. He even offered a pair of agents to take care of the psyker. Isn't that right?'

'If you say so,' Sorrow said. 'But I do not see how they can get close enough to do anything. Have you seen his bodyguard? The one with the metal face? I saw a Goliath direct an offhand remark at Pureburn, and that thing pulled him apart like he was a juve who didn't know which end of the knife to hold. That's before you get to the Cynder guards, the Enforcers, and the Cawdor rabble. There is no way anyone could get close to him.'

'I can jury-rig a conversion field,' Sol said. 'Correctly calibrated, it can siphon power from the shock-batons and release it in a blinding pulse. It will only work once, but even with their visors it should blind the Enforcers and anyone else standing too close, as well as nullify their melee weapons.'

'My agents can assist.' Anguis smiled. 'The Cawdor rats will be spread across the arena, watching the pit fights. A cache of concealed smoke bombs and some long-range suppressing fire should be sufficient. They might be vicious, but they are poorly organised and barely led. If we present multiple threats, they will be unable to prioritise. We only need distract them for a moment.'

They were both facing him now, seemingly united. Except Anguis' smile only extended to one side of her face.

'I admire your dedication to this goal,' Sorrow replied. 'But we have been here before. I did not come to this place to make enemies.'

'No,' Anguis said. 'But it is not somewhere to make friends either. At least not by choice. Perhaps you should tell Lord Sol why you left Hive City. It was certainly not of your own volition.'

Sol frowned, his one-eyed gaze shifting between them.

'What does she mean?'

'Lord Sorrow lives beyond his means,' Anguis continued.

'His fortunes do not equal his debts. He owes much to Lady Anthropopha, and she is not–'

'That's enough!' Sorrow snapped. 'We all have the occasional cred-flow issues. It's nothing more. I am merely here as a favour.'

'Of course,' Anguis said. 'Still, I'm sure such matters are a needless irritant. With Pureburn gone, Periculus would need stewardship. It was a post promised to Lord Sol, but I'm sure he would be willing to share such a burden?'

'I care only for Pureburn's downfall.' Sol shrugged. 'Lord Sorrow, you could claim Periculus for all I care. Providing you help us. Please.'

'I still think this is a fool's errand,' Sorrow said. 'Even were I to help you, even had I the agents to dispatch, how are they supposed to get close enough to take advantage of your little distraction? Pureburn has guards.'

'I have thought of this,' Sol replied. 'The ceremony will have serfs in attendance, either as labour or as witnesses. A handful will be within a stone's throw of the palanquin. Chain Lord Virae owes me a favour. I will speak to her, see if I can–'

'You will do nothing except return to bed,' Sorrow said, and sighed. 'I will speak to Virae.'

'It would be better from me.'

'You have not seen yourself,' Sorrow replied, slipping his frock coat over his shoulders. 'You can barely stand, and I have processed corpses with healthier skin tones. None with any sense would listen to you in your current state. Frankly, you appear more the abomination than anything Lord Pureburn might have under lock and key.'

Virae watched as the crucible was hauled into place, the serfs straining against iron chains. The metal looked as though it might once have formed part of a decorative sphere but had been hastily sewn in half, the edges raw like an open wound. She was surprised Pureburn had settled for the lump of corroded iron to house Periculus' Eternal Flame, and not sought to import something more ornate in gold or silver.

The leftmost chain snapped, sending half the team sprawling in the bone-gravel. At least one rose bleeding, his palm slashed, blood running down his fingers. The team's supposed Shakleman marched over, though it was clear from his snarling mask and ragged attire that he was no member of the Mercator Sanguis. He barely glanced at the wound before hefting his flamer, sending a jet of burning liquid spire-wards.

She was sure the chamber should have emptied, yet the flame continued to soar, as though intent on consuming the hive above. Her gaze flicked to the operator. He seemed lost to the weapon. The serfs watched him, perhaps relieved by a respite from their labours. Or perhaps they too were lost to the flames.

The injured serf let out a moan. The masked Shakleman frowned, glaring down, as though seeing him for the first time. The roar of the flames died, the silence broken only by the hiss of the weapon's red-hot barrel. He barked a command. She could not hear what was said but two other serfs leapt to obey, pinning their injured comrade's arms in place, bloody palm outstretched. He began to struggle, perhaps realising his fate, but they held him tight. The flamer's barrel was pressed to the wound, the sizzle of burning flesh quickly drowned by the injured man's screams as it cauterised the laceration.

'Barbaric.'

She turned. Lord Sorrow stood beside her.

'Pointless too,' she murmured, turning back to the brutal display. 'It was a minor cut. Would heal in a day or so. But now he will be crippled, or die from infection. Yet they expect him to work?'

It seemed so. The Shakleman was dragging the screaming serf to his feet, holding out the chain. The man stared back for a moment, confusion momentarily overriding his pain. He muttered something, though the words did not carry. But the response was clear, the Shakleman slamming his weapon's stock into the serf's face. He fell hard.

'Are you not able to intervene?'

'The Shaklemen are not all mine,' she said. 'I recruited a cohort to bring the serfs here. Some are now aligned to Pureburn, and more still are merely Cawdors taking on the role. Those loyal to me are left garrisoning the slave quarters.'

'If he continues like that there will be no slaves left.'

'They don't care.' Virae winced as the Shakleman delivered a series of swift kicks into the fallen serf's midriff. 'Those trapped at the bottom rarely pray for an end to the system. They just dream of being the one cracking the whip.'

'A cycle of inefficiency,' Sorrow murmured.

'Kill a slave to set an example. Kill a dozen more to make it stick. Then there aren't enough workers, so drag more in from halfway across the hive. Half of them will die on the way, but why worry? Just send for more, twice what you really need, to compensate. The bodies can be sold to the Corpse Grinders, processed, and fed to the next batch anyway, so what's the problem?'

Sorrow smiled, clutching at his chest.

'You wound me,' he said. 'Not all of us are like that.'

'Yet my charges go hungry.'

'You think it's easy for me?' Sorrow replied. 'Shipping

supplies this deep is a nightmare, and I have precious little to work with when the dead are burned. And the living, for that matter.'

'Is that why you are here?' she asked. 'You seek the bodies of my fighters?'

He shook his head. 'Nothing so base. I am, in fact, here on behalf of a prior associate of yours. I understand Lord Tempes Sol assisted you with some... wiring issues?'

'He did.' She nodded, eyes narrowed. 'Enough emergency power to keep the lights on. But that business is between him and me. If he wishes to talk further I am not hard to find.'

'Sol is indisposed,' Sorrow replied, reaching into his pocket and retrieving a flask. He pressed it briefly to his lips before offering it to her. 'Amasec?'

'I'll pass.'

'This is the good stuff,' he persisted. 'Triple distilled, twenty year aged. Notes of citrus and ashwood.'

She hesitated, then took the offered flask. It was exceptional, there was no denying that.

'As I said, Sol is recovering from an assault,' Sorrow continued. 'But I gather you offered him a favour in exchange for his help?'

'That was then.' She shrugged. 'I keep my word, but I am no longer in a position to offer much.'

'The matter is more related to the lighting of the Eternal Flame. I gather a cohort of serfs will be needed for the final procession?'

'Someone needs to turn the taps.'

'Quite.' Sorrow smiled. His teeth were perfect. A little too perfect, particularly for a man with a reputation for gourmandising. For a moment she wondered where he had acquired them. But the answer was all too obvious.

'It must be quite an honour to be chosen,' Sorrow continued. 'I wonder if there is a selection criteria?'

'Beyond a strong pair of arms? I suspect a Cawdor mask is
now a requirement. I care not either way. Once the fights are
concluded I will be departing, whether paid or not.'

'Then you would have no objection if a couple of substitu-
tions were made?' Sorrow persisted. 'I know a pious couple
whose fondest desire is to be part of such a moment. Perhaps
they could be permitted to join the procession? Something
to tell their children one day.'

'And this is Sol's favour?'

'It is.'

'Fine.' She nodded to the slavers' hab-block. 'Hunton is
the Shakleman in charge of selection. I suspect he will want
something for his trouble.'

'My thanks, Lady Virae.'

'Just Virae,' she replied, offering back the flask. He shook
his head, bowing politely as he departed. She turned away
from him, her gaze returning to the crucible's work team. The
Shakleman had given up on the injured serf, who lay quite
still, though whether unconscious or dead was difficult to
determine. The others had abandoned him, returning to their
labours as they dragged the crucible through the bone-gravel,
kicking up a shower of shards. As she watched, the body
slowly sank into the ossified remnants of ancient Periculus.

18

The arena was already heaving when Sol arrived. Stalls had infested the entrance like boils on the sick, offering crispy rat on a stick, or sump jelly rings deep-fried in coolant. He hoped the punters were enjoying the morsels. From what little Sorrow had told him, he gathered Periculus was always a few days from starvation.

He slipped into the crowd, wary of the parade of masks. Ahead lay the entrance, strung with bone and blackened skulls. Two Enforcers were posted there, heavyset men clad in flak armour, their faceplates lowered. Along with a side-arm, each carried a shock-baton, the electrically charged club capable of subjugating even the burliest underhiver. But the weapons were slung, and neither seemed to be doing much to filter or inspect the masses as they poured into the arena.

Sol crossed the threshold, his gaze sweeping the stands. He had to admit Pureburn had done an impressive job pulling the structure together. It had been mere days since he had sat in the crowd, but since then the remaining city blocks had been stripped and levelled until they formed a rough amphitheatre. At the centre, divided from the crowd by a chain-link fence, lay the arena. It was a wide circle, maybe thirty feet across, the traditional industrial sand replaced by ash gathered from those who had opposed Pureburn. It was a bold statement, though Sol wondered how the pit fighters viewed it. He assumed they had their own superstitions, the same as everyone.

The crowning glory was the stage where Pureburn and his dignitaries would sit. Upon it squatted a vast crucible, at least twice his height. It was cold iron now, but in the final ceremony it would be lit by Pureburn's own hand. There were few stronger symbols; the light of the God-Emperor would become a part of Periculus, brought by Pureburn's grace, and any who opposed his rule would be framed as a blasphemer, a heretic against His will.

Except Sol knew the truth. The flames were crafted from foul magicks. Soon all would see.

He heard a shriek and glanced round, sparks dancing between his outstretched fingers. Two children, not even old enough to be juves, were engaged in a mock duel. Their weapons were simple one-piece affairs, purchased from one of the stalls. The larger of the two was laughing as he pinned the smaller child to the ground, sawing his weapon back and forth above the child's neck, miming the severing of their head.

It made Sol uncomfortable in a way he could not quite articulate. He put it from his mind, seeking Anguis. He was confident she would have found a good spot, and he had no intention of missing the opening ceremony. He wanted to see Pureburn in all his glory one final time, before it all came to an end.

* * *

Virae watched the stands filling through the barred gate of the fighters' quarters. Behind her, the gladiators prepared for their bouts. The younger fighters were passing a bottle, trading stories and comparing scars. Block was warming up, silently moving his massive chainglaive through key stances, a red tassel trailing in its wake. It was as much an act of meditation as physical exertion. To a hiver he would probably appear a consummate warrior. But her expert eye saw he favoured his left leg, and there was the barest hint of a tremble in his arm, perhaps from the bite he'd received from the eyeless creatures. She would say he was getting old, but pit fighters did not get old. The arena saw to that.

She glanced back to the crowd, scanning faces, trying to sense the mood. There were smiles and laughter, of course, but there was an edge behind it she knew too well: the sweet anticipation of violence. Lord Pureburn was correct. They wanted blood.

She turned, stamping the pommel of her chainglaive thrice on the ground. The room was silent, the younger fighters lowering their bottle, Block lowering his weapon.

'I'm not going to say much – we've all done this before,' she said. 'In a moment you will enter the arena to salute Lord Pureburn. Then the violence will begin. I remind you that this is no place for showmanship. I don't want you playing to the crowd, or drawing out the fight because you wish to land a particularly memorable deathblow. All that matters is you win and return alive. Remember what happened to Gash.'

She met their gazes in turn.

'The crowd wants to see blood spilt. Let us ensure it belongs to someone else.'

Lord Pureburn smiled as the doors were swept open, his dais suspended on searing jets of brilliant blue. The Enforcer guard advanced before him, their armour resplendent in the light of his Eternal Flame. Canndis was conspicuous by his absence, but even that could not irritate him. Canndis could be dealt with once this was done. Behind him his Cynder guard and Pyromagir marched in unison, even the lumbering cyborg moving with a surprising majesty. The crowd roared at his arrival, a guttural sound like the braying of beasts. But that was just their way – pitiful creatures who knew no better.

He looked to the arena, where the pit fighters were waiting to salute him. The Chain Lord was with them, clad in her arena armour. Unlike the Enforcers' armour, it was marred by combat, whatever decorative adornments it once held long faded. But her helm still bore the impression of a crown. He smiled at the thought; did she consider herself queen of the corpse-ash? He hoped she would do battle, that her blood would be spilled as an appetiser for the ceremony. He could arrange a challenge, of course, force her hand. But no, he was not a petty man. Let her flounder helplessly, bereft of coin and allies. Later she could beg for scraps from his table, along with Canndis. Perhaps he would even offer some, if they were suitably demure.

'Welcome to this historic day,' he said, the vox-amp installed in his throne casting his words across the arena. 'Know now that the Eye of the God-Emperor is upon us, as we prepare to sanctify Periculus in His name. First through blood, then through fire. For within this arena all fight in His name, be they serf or Chain Lord. Any may challenge, and in doing so rise.'

He glanced to Virae as he spoke, but was disappointed to find no obvious reaction. Nevertheless, he continued.

'By the God-Emperor's hand the winners are chosen, and

those who fall are offered to Him and His mercy. Through conflict we grow strong, and in strength we honour His light!'

He sat back in his throne, basking in the crowd's adulation and the glow of the braziers that lined the arena. His worries seemed distant, the threat of House Catallus meaningless, even the failings to uncover his family's former holdings a mere setback. For he had won; Periculus was his to do with as he pleased.

Lord Credence Sorrow was doing his utmost to relax.

It was challenging, even for his considerable talents. He was sitting in his least uncomfortable chair, the vox-speaker beside him spluttering a passable attempt at music. Something about the dome played havoc with the signal, and the sound kept abruptly cutting out. The effect was rather disconcerting. He switched it off, sighing again, as he sipped his Krakian tea. It had begun to cool, but he was loath to finish it, for it was his final cup. Perhaps he could commit the culinary sin of reheating it? Particularly given the dropping temperature.

He shivered, rising from his seat and taking his robe from the door. He'd had little need of it, as Periculus had become consistently humid since his arrival. Yet now he found himself freezing. Perhaps it was the arena, the pit fights drawing power from the rest of the dome; he could faintly hear the crash of weapons and the roar of the crowd. Sol and Anguis would no doubt be there, along with his agents; Caleb and the ratskin had little choice but to agree to the plan.

Or rather, the plans. Sol was insistent on proving Pureburn's crimes, whereas Anguis sought his death.

One was about to be disappointed.

He sighed, glancing to the window and peering through

the boarded glass. Beyond them Periculus was unchanged. The pyres still burned, the braziers spluttering. Was this really to be his domain? He had often thought of owning his own dome, but always imagined somewhere rather more refined and much closer to the spires. Still, one had to start somewhere, and the dome's value could only increase.

He shivered again. What the hell was wrong with the heating units? He reached for the bell on the chair's side table, the chimes intended to summon one of his Grinders to refresh his cup and locate the source of the chill.

The seconds ticked by. His fingers drummed on the armrest.

He rang again.

Nothing.

Where were they? His underlings were under order never to leave him unattended. They were loyal men, to the office if not the person, and more than capable in a fight. It was inconceivable they could have been subdued without at least attracting his attention.

His gaze flicked across the room. Besides the cold it all seemed normal, nothing out of place. The door to the corridor was firmly shut, as was–

The parlour door was open, the lock open.

Impossible. He had the only key, and he would never leave it open, even with his captives now departed for the ceremony.

He crept towards it, mouth dry, nursing the signet ring on his right hand. The amethyst gem concealed a digital weapon, a plasma blaster powerful enough to turn an armoured Enforcer into a foul-smelling stain. But it was a weapon of last resort requiring seven minutes' recharge between shots. One killer could be eliminated via the element of surprise. But what if there were more?

He shivered, and realised he was afraid. It was rare for him. He knew he was not brave, but he had foresight. He was rarely afraid because he was rarely surprised or placed at a disadvantage. Yet here he felt both and it chilled him.

No. Not just him. Ice crystals had formed on the brass door handle, the metal so cold it almost burned his skin. The cold was coming from beyond the door, from the parlour where the bodies were prepared for processing. He glanced through, but it was dark, the lumens extinguished. Yet even in the gloom he saw a shade somehow darker than the rest, a shadow clad in human form.

'Good evening, Lord Sorrow.'

He froze. Not from the cold, but because his limbs no longer recognised his authority. He knew the voice. If in a poetic frame of mind, he might describe it as sharp as splintered bone, or perhaps soft and wet as rotten flesh. But in truth it was neither – almost unremarkable in itself, not cruel or assertive. His terror had nothing to do with the sound itself. No, it came from the base, animal part of him that instinctively knew that the thing that spoke so reasonably was something that should not be.

He mustered himself, and almost kept the quiver from his voice.

'Good evening, Lady Anthropopha.'

19

Sol watched as the body was dragged away, fresh corpse-ash thrown across the bloodstains. The crowd was baying for more, faces twisted in fury, so much so that he struggled to separate the masked and unmasked. All radiated the same hate, their snarling faces etched in crimson. He blinked, rubbing his eyes, but the image lingered. Perhaps the lumens at the lower levels were fading, skewing the light.

His forearm itched. He'd sometimes felt something similar on the Needle, when the perma-storm was poised for a particularly violent outburst. But it was worse here, as though the energies he passively syphoned were tainted by Pureburn's presence.

He scratched it idly, scanning the crowd. Where the hell was Anguis?

'Good evening, Lord Sol.'

He sighed, not bothering to turn. She was, of course, beside him.

'I was worried you had not made it,' he said. 'Is everything ready at your end?'

'My agents have taken the steps needed – your device is stowed beneath the stage, as is a primed cache of smoke grenades. I have a pair of snipers ready for additional disruption as required.'

'And Sorrow's newest hired guns?' Sol asked. 'You think they are up to the task of subduing the psyker?'

'They know their orders. Sorrow has granted me access to their vox-channel. I have instructed them accordingly.'

'And the escape route? Sorrow advised them that the northerly promethium pipe is empty? Once through, they should be able to conceal themselves in the nest of cables feeding the heat-tap until–'

'I would not worry about such details, Lord Sol,' Anguis replied. 'We have made every preparation. Remember the God-Emperor is watching. He will ensure the right outcome.'

'Your facilities would benefit from some attention,' Lady Anthropopha murmured. 'The decor is… uninspired.'

Sorrow found he could not reply, his eyes fixed on the figure before him. She was tall, perhaps taller than any human he'd ever met, but skeletally thin, and clad in shadow, her robes midnight black, shoulders and torso adorned with stylised armour crafted from polished bone and studded with amethyst gems. Her face was mercifully concealed by an elaborate mask, nothing like the sneering grimaces of House Cawdor. It was cast in flawless ivory, its expression serene.

'It has been challenging to source the right materials,' he stammered.

'Did you not get my gift?' she said.

'Yes. Most kind of you… I believe I left it in the other–'

Lady Anthropopha held out her hand. In it was the archeo-tech jar Sorrow had been using for a parchment-weight.

'You know what this is?' she asked.

'I... it resembles a Mung vase.'

'Indeed,' Lady Anthropopha said, her fingers curling around the jar like the legs of a spider. 'I do not begrudge the scepticism. There are precious few pristine examples left. There were, after all, only some scions of House Mung who were able to preserve their brains in these stasis jars. In their arrogance they hoped that House Mung would one day rise again, thanks to their conserved wisdom.'

Lady Anthropopha's blank face examined the skull-shaped jar.

'A specimen like this could fetch a million credits,' she murmured. 'But there is a complication. Once the jar is opened the contents quickly spoil. Thus, each poses a conundrum – to truly authenticate its value, one must open it. But once opened, its value is spent. Each brain is, after all, only large enough for one sublime meal.'

There was something off about the voice; he could hear it now. Lady Anthropopha's delivery was almost too polished, as though the tone did not quite match the emotion behind it. And there was the barest trace of feedback loop. It sounded almost as though the voice were synthetic. Could he smell something? Rotten flesh? Preservative fluids? Or merely his own sweat?

'A truly bounteous gift,' Sorrow said, barely keeping his voice steady. 'I thank you again. But I confess I am surprised to see you. I understood you were delegating responsibility for Periculus. Have I failed in some way?'

Lady Anthropopha glanced at Sorrow from behind the mask, the Mung Vase still nestled in her palm.

'You need not fear me, Lord Sorrow. I am merely here to free you of your remaining debts.'

'My debts?' Sorrow swallowed, unsure of her tone. 'But... We are talking the full amount? Every credit?'

'Indeed.' Anthropopha nodded. 'Your service has been exemplary, despite some very trying circumstances. I am more than happy to write off your liabilities. I require but one final task before the matter is closed.'

Sorrow's mouth was dry. Freedom from his burden was so very tempting, but such a princely sum would require no minor task. Still, he forced his brightest smile, offering a deep bow.

'I await your instruction, my lady.'

'You scheme against Lord Pureburn.'

It was a statement, not a question.

'My lady, I am not sure what you have heard, but I do not–'

'You would not lie to me, Lord Sorrow?'

The voice was soft, the mask's blank face calm. But Sorrow had spent his life learning the language conveyed by a turn of the head, or an errant tapping finger. He knew the danger he suddenly faced.

'Forgive me, my lady,' he said, bowing his head. 'I feared you might object to our plans.'

'Yes. Plans,' she said. 'You find yourself in a difficult situation, Lord Sorrow, serving two masters. Tell me, have you advised your dogs that they are to retrieve their target, or eliminate it?'

'The latter. The Delaque is right – the threat must be ended. The risk is too great.'

'A reasonable position. Tell me, Lord Sorrow, have you unloaded the latest shipment of supplies?'

'No, my lady. They have yet to arrive.'

'If indeed they are coming at all.'

'My lady?'

'Ours is a difficult trade,' Lady Anthropopha replied. 'Power is a one-way conduit, as is water and air. There is a commodity and a demand. The one feeds the other. But our business is more… cyclical. The people must be fed. But what can we feed them when supplies are low?'

'There is a shortage of corpse-starch?'

'That need not concern you,' she said. 'All you must do is contact your dogs. Tell them the plan has changed. Tell them to take the psyker prisoner and flee. It does not matter where. I care not if they are found, only that their capture is delayed.'

'And for this you would cancel my debt?'

'You have my word.'

'And I could leave this place?'

Lady Anthropopha did not answer for a moment. Instead she glanced to the rusted meat grinder dominating the room. Her gaze then slid back to Sorrow.

'My dear Lord Sorrow, why would you leave?' she said. 'Just when we are poised to resolve our supply problem?'

Virae was sweating. Mostly it was the heat, the dome's questionable atmospheric regulators unable to cope with the tightly packed crowd. There was something particularly unpleasant about the heat generated by the press of human bodies; it felt wet, as though it were seeping into the skin.

But she was also nervous. Not that anyone could tell. She stood like a general at the head of an invincible force, her fighters untouchable. They might find their match in the wilds of the underhive, but within the confines of the arena, in one-on-one combat, few could match them.

Gash had been just as confident…

At least she had no stake in the current bout. It would be fair to describe it as a clash of styles. Dunder, the hulking Forge Boss of the Near Dead, bellowed as he swung his massive renderiser. The axe screamed in fury with each blow, the whirling teeth of its head hungry for blood. But his opponent, Flatline of the Acid Drops, was always just out of his reach. Her own blade shimmered with a faint blue glow, etched in a disruption field powerful enough to destabilise matter.

It was an interesting conundrum, Virae mused, as the fighters traded blows. In theory, Flatline's power sword could slice the renderiser in half, but the blow would have to be precise. A misstep, and the force of the axe could shatter Flatline's arm, even if she succeeded in damaging the weapon. And, unarmed, it was unlikely she could overcome the Forge Boss' superior strength and toughness.

The crowd roared as she ducked a vicious swing, lunging forward, intending to drive the blade through Dunder's chest. He stepped aside from the thrust, moving with surprising speed, the weapon glancing from his side. But she saw his furnace-plate armour bubble at its touch, metal droplets dripping onto the arena's corpse-ash. Flatline grinned, circling her foe, seeking another opening. Virae wondered if the Escher thought her victory would settle the long-standing grudge between the gangs. It did not work that way in her experience; the loser would inevitably find a reason why the victory was tainted, and it would provide yet another rationale for future conflict.

She turned from the contest, her gaze falling on Block. He lay on the bench, a fellow fighter stitching his wounds. He was lucky to have survived. Virae had seen the danger the moment the contest started. Block was the more experienced warrior, but the young Goliath was stronger and faster.

He dominated the fight, brandishing a roaring chainsword in each hand and unleashing a flurry of blows. Most would have fallen in moments, but Block knew to slow the flight, using his weapon's superior reach to keep the Goliath at a distance, ignoring the jeers of the crowd.

Virae squatted down beside him, examining the deep wound in his chest. Block had refused to engage until the Goliath began to lose his temper. His attacks grew faster and bolder, but the blows were sloppy and off-balance. Still, they seemed too much for Block. He faltered, stumbling to a knee. The Goliath youth gleefully seized the opening, only to find he had fallen for the veteran's feint. A flick of Block's wrist drove the chainglaive's curved blade through the Goliath's abdomen, the younger man erupting in a shower of gore. But one of the chainswords had slipped through, tearing open Block's sternum. She was not sure if he would fight again. She hoped not.

The crowd exploded into thunderous applause. Her head snapped round to see the remains of Flatline crumpled at Dunder's feet. His skin was stained red by gore, the render-iser axe having apparently found its mark. He wiped his face, bellowing a bloody yell to the roaring crowd.

Blood. That was all they hungered for.

Block groaned. He needed better care than could be offered here. She glanced to Hunton the Shakleman, and the score of serfs awaiting their moment in the spotlight. They would be the ones to turn the promethium lines that would sup-ply Periculus' own Eternal Flame. All wore masks adorned with flames.

'I'm taking Block back to our quarters so he can be properly tended to,' she said. 'Make sure the ceremony goes smoothly. No mistakes.'

Hunton nodded, barking at the serfs to form a line. As they moved, something caught her eye. The fourth slave from the right – something about the way they moved was familiar, each footstep precise. Perfectly balanced…

Block groaned. She shook her head, pushing her uncertainty aside.

Whatever happened now was not her problem.

Lord Pureburn found his gaze wandering. In the arena below, a burly pit fighter was playing to the crowd. He was even vaster than his peers, his muscle growth bordering on abhuman. His opponent was of House Van Saar, clad in an advanced combat rig to compensate for his own wasted frame. His face was almost level with the pit fighter, suspended on multiple insectoid mechanical limbs, each ending in a blade tip.

He stifled a yawn. The games were beginning to bore him, the bloodshed uninspired. Perhaps the ceremony could be moved forward? The crowd had surely had their fill. But no, they continued to shriek as the brute struggled against the cybernetic contraption, his stimm-enhanced sinews straining against the plasteel carapace.

He glanced over his shoulder. The serfs were in place, each standing at one of the taps ready to spill the sacred promethium into the crucible. They all watched him intently, ready for his signal. His Pyromagir stood ready, its brazier fed by the Eternal Flame, poised to light Periculus' own crucible.

It was his moment of triumph, and even though the spilling of blood was laying its groundwork, it irked him to share it with these gladiators.

The crowd roared suddenly. He turned back to see the pit fighter howling in triumph, arms raised high, each clasping a mechanical leg. His opponent was in pieces at his feet. The armour was mangled and bloodstained, though it was unclear whether the occupant was still alive.

Pureburn rose from his seat, feigning breaking into applause, though his hands never quite touched. This would do.

'Periculus, with blood and flame we are born anew–'

All went white, a blast of light bright as the fabled sun. Blinded, he reached to hold on, scrabbling. Gunshots followed in an instant, from different directions, and his nose was suddenly filled with the acrid burst of smoke grenades. Screams, both close and far, filled the amphitheatre.

Then, he felt the whoosh of a jet of flame, followed by a different sort of scream, closer still. His Pyromagir, fighting? Someone was trying to board the dais.

Impossible!

He could see nothing, but as he groped his way towards the chamber at the back of his palanquin, he felt rough hands seize his person. Before he could draw a weapon, or resist, he was forced forward and off balance. He struck the floor with a thump, before being drawn back to his feet. Like a vice, hands grasped his wrist and forced his palm against the concealed gene-lock behind his throne.

There was the hiss of the door unsealing and beginning to open, before he was thrown aside. He tried to cry out, but his voice was lost to the chaos.

Then the white became red.

ACT 3

1

Canndis shouldered open the fortress-precinct's entrance, half ducking and half falling through the doorway as stub rounds thudded into the frame above. He bled from a dozen wounds, his helm cracked and armour studded with stray shells. He rolled to his front, kicked the door shut, stub gun raised and trained on the now-closed door. His shock-baton hung lifeless at his side, but the pistol still held four rounds. Or was it three? He could not remember.

What the hell had happened?

Whatever it was, it was still happening. He could hear screams and the rhythmic thuds of autogun volleys. Worse was the stench of burning promethium mingled with the scent of burning flesh. At least with the door sealed the smoke was thinner; he'd lost his helm's respirator to one of the Cawdor filth. The thief's brains now stained his shock-baton, but there'd not been enough time to restore his gear with more rats closing in. His weapon lacked charge but could still crack skulls.

A sound behind him. Footsteps? Something else?

It didn't matter. He spun, rising to a knee and scanning the room, back pressed to the fortress-precinct's main door. It was dark, the lumens now extinguished, and the only light was that which bled from the madness beyond the door. His heart pounded. That was fear in part, but anger in the main, a simmering fury threatening rational thought. He forced it down, drawing on his training, and on reserves he'd thought long squandered. Anger led to mistakes. Mistakes got you killed.

'This is Palanite Captain Canndis,' he barked. 'You have one chance to surrender or I will open fire!'

As he spoke he recognised the absurdity of the threat; who exactly was he planning on shooting? Or did he just intend to spray the inside of his precinct house with his three remaining bullets?

'Please, sir, don't shoot!'

Hands appeared from the gloom behind the reception desk. The face that followed was hidden by a cracked mask.

'Take that off!' Canndis roared, cocking his pistol. But beneath his fury he recognised the wearer. As the mask was discarded he found himself face to face with Gladshiv's bloodied cheeks and haunted eyes.

'Please,' he said, voice trembling. 'I just... don't shoot, captain.'

'I can't spare the bullet,' Canndis replied, lowering his weapon. He exhaled for what felt like the first time in hours, his shoulders slumped.

'Any patrolmen made it back?' he asked.

Gladshiv shook his head. 'No, sir. I... Are they still out there?'

Canndis did not reply. He could picture the last of the squad, their stubbers spitting rounds, their shock-batons reduced to clubs. Still they fought as the Cawdor rats swarmed over them, their rusted blades seeking the cracks in the patrolmens' flak armour. Mere hours before, the team had been designated as Pureburn's escort during the lighting of Periculus' Eternal Flame. It should have been juve's-play, and the closest any of them had come to leave since being dispatched to Periculus.

He glanced at Gladshiv, who was staring blankly at the fortress-precinct's main gate, his eyes wide and bloodshot.

'Did you see it?'

'I… yes,' Gladshiv said. 'I only stepped outside for a moment. Climbed one of the hab ruins. I just wanted to see the flame.'

'Well, mission damn well accomplished,' Canndis spat. 'Take a look outside, boy – plenty of fire to go around. Blood too, if that's more your taste.'

'How did–? What happened?' Gladshiv frowned, as though unable to hold the idea in his head. 'I heard shots, and suddenly… I couldn't see.'

Canndis remembered that well enough. There had been a flash of light. He had been some distance from the rest of them, his weapon powered down, but it still pierced even his photovisor. All was reduced to a searing blur of shape and colour; he barely made out the two shadows darting through the patrol, intent on Lord Pureburn. His guard, that hideous fusion of man and metal, had tried to intervene, but it could not see to aim. Its blast of flame had engulfed the half-blinded throng of worshippers. Canndis felt some satisfaction at that last part. Some justice had been done, albeit of the poetic nature.

As the shadows reached the dais Lord Pureburn was still standing there, seemingly too stunned to react. Canndis was racing towards them, stubber drawn, but he knew he was too late to intercept a blade or bullet. But the would-be assassins made no such move, instead unceremoniously dumping Pureburn from his throne. Then a crack of light pierced the cell mounted on his dais' rear. Bright, though not blinding. And then–

The next thing he recalled was the bloodied face staring up at him. It must have been screaming, but the sound was inaudible against the blood pounding in his ears. His hands tightened about its throat, but still it fought, clawing weakly at his face, no fear in its bloodshot eyes, just hate and hunger. He kept squeezing, so hard that tears of blood stained the dying man's cheeks as his eyes bulged, life finally leaving him. Canndis tried to tell himself it was self-defence, that the bruised and battered face belonged to a dangerous killer who needed to be subdued. But as the light died in the man's eyes his expression softened, and Canndis recognised the face of Palanite Sergeant Hendrox.

He still did not know why he'd killed him.

He'd run then, volleys of auto-fire breaking the screams, wicked blades scoring his armour. Everywhere was darkness or fire, the lumens across Periculus suddenly dark and the braziers that had once symbolised Pureburn's power now toppled, spreading pools of burning promethium. He fired blind at any and all who crossed his path. Something had struck his head, knocking his helm askew and staggering him. He'd turned, and found himself facing the hulking form of Varl Bloodburn, Forge Tyrant of the Near Dead. The giant was stained crimson, droplets of blood evaporating from the cracking head of his power-hammer.

There was nowhere to run. Canndis watched the Goliath raise the weapon. But before the fatal blow was struck another figure burst from the shadows, screaming in fury as she plunged a stiletto blade into Bloodburn's chest. Canndis caught a fleeting glance of Leara Batrip, but as the two figures grappled he ran on, oblivious to the outcome.

He blinked, trying to focus. Gladshiv was still slumped behind the desk, mask cradled in his hands. The clerk was not an ideal ally, but he was all he had.

'Get up,' Canndis snapped, rising. 'We need to secure this door. Then I need an inventory of weapons and supplies. Sooner or later someone will come and we need to be prepared. Gladshiv, you listening?'

The clerk did not reply. Canndis considered striking him, hoping to rouse the man, but what would be the point? There was no pain he could inflict that would compare to the horrors already witnessed.

'Gladshiv?' he tried, adopting a softer tone. 'Gladshiv? We need to work together. I don't know if any of the others survived, but it's hell out there, and–'

'They took it.'

Gladshiv was not looking at him, addressing instead the world of fire and smoke beyond the gate. The adjacent window was sealed, but flickering light bled through the cracks as flames consumed the ruins of Periculus.

'What do you mean?' Canndis asked. 'What did they take?'

'The fire,' the younger man whispered. 'The God-Emperor's flame. They snuffed it out, and with it stole His light.'

'Who? Who took it?'

'Now He will punish us,' Gladshiv whispered. 'Now we are truly in hell. We failed Him. We deserve to burn.'

'Nobody needs to burn, not if we get out of here,' Canndis

replied. 'We just need something to clear a path. A cache of smoke grenades or flash-bangs, just enough to reach Periculus' main gate. We can regroup uphive, gather our forces and counterattack. Or... there must be a vox-transmitter somewhere. One of the Guilders, maybe. If I can send a message uphive we can show these degenerates Helmawr's justice!'

He slapped the man on the shoulder. Gladshiv swayed slightly but did not otherwise react. Perhaps he was catatonic. Canndis had seen it before – weaklings stretched beyond sanity by the violence of the hive bottom. If so, the clerk was useless to him.

He stepped behind the desk. There were a handful of slugger rounds as well as a pack of lho-sticks. He pressed one of the latter to his lips, raising his lighter with shaking hands. He leant back as he lit it, expecting a now familiar surge of flame, but there was barely a flicker.

'Blasted thing,' he muttered, shaking it. 'Gladshiv, I will promote you to sergeant if you can find me a damn lighter. Gladshiv?'

He glanced to the spot on the floor where the clerk had been sitting. But he was moving, striding towards the precinct-fortress door, his mask secured in place.

'Gladshiv?' Canndis asked. 'Where are you going, you idiot?'

The clerk turned, glancing back. His expression was hidden.

'All must burn,' he whispered, before he crossed the threshold and stepped into hell.

There was a thud at the door.

Sorrow jumped, his data-slate falling from between his fingers. He glanced to the doorway, now flanked by two of his burliest Grinders. Assuming they were his Grinders, of course; their marked absence during Lady Anthropopha's visit suggested a split loyalty. Still, they tensed, expectant, flaying knives poised.

Sorrow retrieved his data-slate, nervously adjusting his signet ring. He was attempting to review his holdings in the upper hive, but had barely managed a page. It was difficult to concentrate, particularly when the lights suddenly cut out. The backup generators had quickly kicked in, just as Sol had assured him, but the light was not the same: flickering and indecisive. The screams and explosions had not helped his concentration either, or the glow of firelight bleeding between the cracks in the blinds.

Not his problem, of course. What happened out there was the choice of the people out there. He was busy working, minding his own business. Whatever transpired was not his fault.

Another thump, louder. Then a voice.

'Sorrow!'

He pretended he did not recognise it. Better yet, that he did not even hear it. Because if he did not hear it, he could not be blamed for the door remaining locked.

'Sorrow!'

Another cry. Plaintive, almost begging. He had never heard his friend sound like that. One of the Grinders glanced at Sorrow, a frown carved into his slab of a face. He nodded silently to the door in the corridor beyond, motioning with his blade.

Sorrow glared at him, mouthing 'no'.

'Credence, please! They're coming!'

It felt low, using his given name in that way. Cheap.

He twitched, fingers drumming on the armrest. He did not want to think about it. But he knew the voice would stay with him. It would hollow future triumphs, haunt him in moments of weakness. It was not a burden he wished to carry.

He sighed, nodding to the Grinder and motioning to the doorknob. The man raised his blade one last time, a hopeful expression forming on his face. Sorrow shook his head again. The Grinder nodded, disappearing from sight. He could hear heavy footsteps as the Grinder made for the entrance, but ignored the sound of the door opening and the screams that accompanied it, his focus on dishevelling his robes and hair. Seconds later his study door burst open, to find Sorrow stifling a yawn and blinking blearily, as though just roused from deepest slumber.

He was unsure whether Sol noticed the performance, but he staggered in regardless, robes torn and bloodied, half carrying the stumbling Anguis, her arm slung over his shoulder. Behind him came the screams and the thud of stub rounds.

'Close it!' Sorrow snarled, grasping Anguis' other arm and helping Sol lower her to the couch. Sol's wounds seemed superficial, barring the gash on his forehead. His patch was gone, exposing the ruined socket that once held an eye.

'Is she injured?' Sorrow asked, glancing at Anguis.

'I don't know. I don't think so. Check her back – we need a medi-kit.'

Sol seemed frantic, torn between his injured comrade and whatever it was that was happening outside, his gaze flicking to the sealed blinds. Sorrow tentatively laid a hand on his shoulder, but the man flinched as though struck.

'What happened?' Sorrow asked.

'What happened?' Sol snarled, turning on him. 'Were you not out there? Did you not see?'

'No,' Sorrow replied. 'My part was done. I thought if something went wrong it would be prudent to be as far away from Lord Pureburn as possible.'

Sol glared at him a moment longer, then sighed, the anger draining from his face.

'You were wiser than I. I wanted to see the look on his face. But all I saw was fire and blood. Something went very wrong.'

'Our agents failed?'

'Oh, they succeeded,' Sol replied. 'The Delaque provided the distraction and the conversion field took out his guards. Your people got to the target. They opened the cell. And then–'

He trailed off, perhaps still in shock. As the Grinder reappeared with the medi-kit Sorrow bent down to Anguis.

'How was she injured?' Sorrow asked.

'Electric shock,' Sol replied. 'I held back as much as I could.'

'You did this? Why?'

'Because she was trying to kill me.'

Virae slammed shut the storage crate she used for a desk, employing her weight to force the lock. She had little idea what was in it, having scooped up the contents of her office in great armfuls. Block had been stabilised; once the others returned she saw no reason to stay. Pureburn would never pay, only find more ways to kill her men and humble her before them.

'Festering waste of skin,' she muttered, her gaze scouring the walls for any last possessions. Her chainglaive was mounted on its fittings, and she was clad in her armour. She would bear both as she departed the dome, her head held high. The slaves were someone else's problem now. They could starve or rise up and overthrow the old fool; she cared not.

But she could not leave without her badge of office. Where the hell was it?

Her gaze flittered to the hastily packed crate.

'Stupid old woman,' she muttered, tearing off the lid and rummaging through the contents. 'Elle? Elle, where is my damn badge of office?'

Footsteps came from the adjacent room. Elle emerged. She looked downcast, perhaps pouting because Virae had refused her request to attend the Eternal Flame ceremony.

'I don't know,' Elle said. 'Have you looked in the crate?'

'That's what I'm doing, idiot!' Virae snapped. But as she spoke she felt her anger ebb. The girl was barely older than a juve, young and sometimes thoughtless. Raging at her achieved nothing. Anger should be used like a furnace to temper a blade, not an inferno to rage unchecked.

'Elle,' she sighed. 'I'm sorry. I–'

The lights flickered.

She frowned, glancing at the ceiling-mounted lumen. There had been a surge maybe an hour ago, the slave-block suddenly swamped in darkness, but whatever adjustments Sol had made seemed to have worked.

But something felt off.

She glanced to the window. Any view of the ceremony was obscured by the crumbling hab-blocks, but she could make out a faint orange glow framing the ferrocrete edifices. It was getting brighter.

'Elle, would the Eternal Flame be lit yet?'

'Should be.'

'Hmm. It's brighter than I expected.' Virae shrugged, returning to the open crate and fumbling through assorted weapons and trinkets. She hauled aside a harpoon launcher, seeking the box containing her vox-bead.

'Virae!'

Her head snapped up, just in time to see Block stumble round the long corridor leading to her office. He was bleeding, his chest reopened. As he lurched forward she saw another blade was lodged in his shoulder.

'Run!' he snapped to Elle, before a figure pounced on his back, pitching him to the floor as a dozen more rounded the corner. Then they were on him, stabbing with rusted knives.

'Elle! Get back!' Virae barked. But the girl was paralysed, just as before, transfixed by the scene. The lead attacker raised its head and screeched, the sound inhuman. For a heartbeat Virae was back on the road to Periculus, with the terrible creatures crawling from the shadows. She felt a chill run through her, but it was soon swallowed by her anger.

'Out of the way!' she snapped, shoving Elle aside as the killers surged towards her, their knives stained crimson. There were at least half a dozen, more following behind them. As they closed the distance she stood, waiting, until they were scant feet from the doorframe.

Then she seized the harpoon launcher, aiming it at the lead figure. The barbed spear, almost three foot in length, gleamed.

'Vermin!' she spat, squeezing the trigger. The steel harpoon tore into the horde, impaling the lead attacker and punching into the next, piercing flesh and bone. Both were hurled into the attackers, scattering them, the passageway partially plugged by the dead and maimed.

But on they came, clambering over the fallen, unconcerned by the blood and bodies.

She snatched up the chainglaive, the weapon roaring into life as the first attacker reached her office's threshold. He leapt for her, only to be cleaved in twain, her return stroke disembowelling the next attacker. More followed, but their howls were drowned by the whirling teeth of the chainglaive. The corridor was narrow, the path impeded by the bodies and slick with blood. Their numbers meant nothing; one by one they reached her, only to be cut down.

But the sheer press of attackers forced her back a step. Then another.

Another step, and they would surround her in a circle of blades. Then it would be over. Still she waited, chainglaive whirling around her, seeking an opening.

There. A heavyset ganger, wide enough to near fill the corridor, lunged for her. The glaive sliced him open, but his weight pitched him forward. She stepped back as the body fell. They pressed in behind him, filling the doorway and corridor beyond.

She flicked a switch at her belt.

Her view was obscured by the press of bodies, but she felt the tremble as the frag grenade mounted on the harpoon detonated, the blast sending shrapnel scything through the corridor. The nearest attackers suddenly lurched forward, thrown off balance. It was all she needed; her glaive swung in a savage arc, the whirling teeth reaping flesh and bone.

Suddenly it was still, silent barring the hum of her weapon.

She stepped over the rent corpses, scanning the corridor. The walls were stained crimson, the floor concealed by broken bodies. Somewhere in the press of death was Block's massive frame, concealed by blood and bile.

A hand grasped weakly for her leg.

She glanced down to the creature sprawled at her feet. He was missing half his torso, but still clawed at her with his remaining limb. Somehow his mask had been blasted clear, his face marked by dust and shrapnel, but she could not take her gaze from his eyes. The whites were now crimson, bloody tears staining his cheeks.

'What is wrong with you?' she murmured. He gave no response other than a pitiful howl, more frustration than fury, his anger fading as his life ebbed. She brought her foot down hard, silencing him, before glancing back. Elle stood rigid in the doorway behind her, her face blank.

'Elle?'

'Unbroken?' the girl replied, her voice monotone. It seemed the cogitator was speaking for her.

'Fall back. Get anyone left to the service lift and slave quarters.'

'Understood.' The emotionless Elle nodded. 'When can we-?'

But her voice was drowned out by the distant howls of rage. Distant, but rapidly drawing closer.

'Go!' Virae snarled, as the next wave rounded the corner.

2

Lord Pureburn knew she was gone. Even before his eyes opened he could feel the shift, the intoxication of righteous fury supplanted by the cold, hard rage of loss and failure. A lesser man would be consumed by it, but his will was iron. Even when his mother had been claimed by the family's tainted blood he had accepted it. Not a tear had stained his cheek during her entombment, or two years later when she had finally died. He was only eight then, but already understood. Emotion was a weakness, a tool the strong used to shape the soft of mind.

But this rage was different. It was not a fury that warmed the belly. It was a cold void seeking to consume everything it touched.

He groaned as he sat up, his aged body beset by aches and bruises. Pain was a constant, but the arbitrary studding of injuries to his arms and knees was almost a novelty. He had felt paralysed during the attack. He had wanted to issue orders, demand reprisals, but he could not get past the absurdity of it. Who would orchestrate so blatant an assault? In the heartbeats between the blinding light and the two figures unceremoniously ejecting him from his throne, he'd considered myriad possibilities. His own followers may have turned on him, or lesser members of his family undertaken a coup. House Catallus might have finally struck, though he suspected they would be both subtler and more effective.

But they had spared his life, taking perhaps the only thing of equal value. His own trembling hand slapped against the hidden gene-lock on his dais. They had known of her. It was his failing. He had been overconfident, thought himself unassailable.

He wiped the dust from his eyes, leaving an ugly brown smear on his sleeve. It was dark, the lumens dead and braziers toppled, precious promethium soaking the ground. But fires had been cobbled together from scrap and detritus, enough to give him an impression of his surroundings. He was laid out beside his fallen throne, its crucible now empty, the rear-mounted cell torn open like a wound. It felt obscene, the unwashed masses granted a glimpse of so sacred a place. A handful of Cynders surrounded him, his Pyromagir maintaining a silent vigil. He held no warmth or gratitude to them, but there was a certain satisfaction in knowing that, even now, his servants fulfilled their function.

He motioned to one of the Cynders to close the dais, another assisting him to stand as he surveyed the surrounding flames. There were six in total, forming a rough circle, the fallen throne at its epicentre.

'You're finally awake then, milord?'

Lord Pureburn stiffened at the words, turning as a score of

his followers emerged from the shadows. He recognised Tritus, but the rest were interchangeable, hidden behind their masks. It was odd though; in that moment, the snarling grimaces seemed a more sincere representation of their souls than whatever lay beneath. Each carried a haul of scrap and detritus, and all were bloodied, though whether the blood was their own was unclear. Each regarded him as though in judgement, a thought that sickened and angered in equal measure. He was tempted to signal his Pyromagir to burn respect into them; a less temperate patron would no doubt have done precisely that.

'I am alive,' Pureburn said, regarding each man in turn. 'It would seem the assassination attempt was unsuccessful.'

'Perhaps.' Tritus shrugged, slinging a pack from his shoulder and laying it by his feet. 'I'd say they got exactly what they wanted.'

All eyes were upon him. Lord Pureburn maintained his composure whilst his mind raced. Were these men responsible for his fall? Did they know his secret? Did they still have her?

No. He would not succumb to paranoia. These simpletons fetishised scrap and filth as divine relics. They were too small and stupid to see the truth.

'It would seem much has been taken from us,' Lord Pureburn noted, surveying their ruined surroundings.

'Traitors, that's what it was,' Tritus spat. 'All those sinners adopting their own masks, trying to integrate themselves into House Cawdor. Half have turned on us, or on each other. But we ain't so stupid – killed a bunch before they could lure us in. Some weren't even human – I saw it beneath their masks. I warned you, milord. I told you dark things waited in the shadows.'

Lord Pureburn did not reply. Instead his gaze slipped to the refuse dumped at his feet. There were familiar shapes tucked into it. Some had fingers.

'Need to keep the fires burning,' Tritus said, apparently following his gaze.

Pureburn frowned, unsure of his meaning.

'The Eternal Flame,' Tritus grunted. 'Before they stole it the flame fell, starting these pyres. So long as we feed them, the God-Emperor's flame is not extinguished. Not yet.'

Pureburn glanced to the circle of fire.

'Well done, Tritus.' He smiled. 'You are correct. I thank you.'

'Yeah, well we did our duty to the God-Emperor whilst you rested,' Tritus said, turning to his lackeys, the largest of whom had a body slung over his shoulder. 'Lost some good men though. Look.'

The man staggered forward, laying the corpse at his feet, its funeral shroud a torn blanket. Lord Pureburn could not help but notice its boots were missing. The feet were blackened, and the cause of death clear enough from the smell.

'This was Hoyke,' Tritus said. 'Knew him for years, back when Isaiah recruited us. Show Lord Pureburn how he died.'

'I am familiar with the scent of burnt flesh.'

'Yeah, he burned.' Tritus nodded. 'Wasn't them though. The weapon you issued exploded. Poor bastard was a walking inferno. Had to shoot him in the head, deliver the God-Emperor's mercy.'

'Unfortunate.'

'Is it?' Tritus said. 'Two more of my lads' flamers failed as they were swallowed by the mob. Bit of a coincidence, don't you think?'

Lord Pureburn stared at the man. Slowly, he stepped forward, until his face was inches from Tritus'. He could smell smoke and sweat on the man's skin, see the bloodstained eyes behind his mask.

'No,' he said softly. 'Not coincidence. Consequence. Tell me, Tritus, who is the Master of Mankind?'

'The God-Emperor,' Tritus replied. He glared back, suspicious, but that did not matter. There were only two types in House Cawdor: those enslaved by their faith, and those who used faith as a tool to enslave. Tritus was one of the former; he just needed an appropriate whip to remind him of his place. Pureburn held his gaze a moment longer before turning to the ruined dais and empty crucible.

'My family was entrusted with the God-Emperor's sacred flame,' he murmured. 'We guarded it since before His ascension to the Golden Throne. For tens of thousands of years, the fire has burned. Until now.'

He turned back to Tritus, his face sombre, regret crafted into every crease.

'We failed,' he said, glancing to the others. 'I failed. And each of you failed. You think He does not see this from His throne? You think it coincidence His favour has been withdrawn? Your weapons failing is not my doing – it is His punishment.'

He could see Tritus twitch. It was dangerous, provoking him. But the risk was calculated. Despite his rage Tritus was a follower, his faith in the God-Emperor absolute. He already considered himself fallen; it took little to convince him he had failed.

'We have all been found wanting,' Pureburn continued. 'But this is not the end. Our faith is true. Our enemies, those who did this, they are the true heretics. We must make them repent before we deliver His mercy.'

'But how?' Tritus replied. His tone remained surly, and

Pureburn had to repress the urge to strike him for his insolence. But the words were telling. No longer accusatory, now with a problem to solve and an enemy to conquer.

'He has taken our weapons,' Pureburn replied, touching the man's chest. 'But the fire here, in our hearts? That blazes stronger than ever. If we cannot burn the sinner, we beat him down until he is naught but bloodied meat. Seal the dome, none in and none out. Whomever is responsible will be found, for only their death can redeem us in His eyes.'

Tritus still seemed unsure but nodded slowly. 'Aye,' he said. 'In His name.'

'In His name,' Pureburn replied. 'Rally your men, kill any who fail to fall into line. There are only two sides now – His followers and the faithless.'

He watched them depart, their fury tempered by purpose. He must keep them busy; he needed time to figure out how to proceed. All was not lost. He still held power. He would find them, those that had taken her. He could feel her power, unfiltered by the dais. The anger was raw, but still it could be shaped, used to guide his followers. This setback would make him stronger in the end.

A flicker of doubt marred his thoughts, as some small part of him pondered the consequences of the Eternal Flames' keeper no longer being confined to the cell. But it was a small voice, and shrinking all the time. His thoughts had shifted to power. To vengeance.

His eyes itched. He wiped them again, untroubled by the blood now staining his robe's sleeve.

Sorrow's hand trembled as he tried to sip his tea. The other cup rested beside Sol, untouched. His focus was the window and the nightmare unfolding beyond. So far attacks were minimal, feral gangs armed with little more than clubs and hatred. Most had given up at the threshold, lacking the tools to penetrate Sorrow's abode. The more determined had been dissuaded by frag grenades his Grinders dropped from the upper levels.

'You should drink your tea,' Sorrow heard himself say. It was an idiotic statement. That was what he was reduced to: platitudes.

Sol did not reply. He had been quiet since his arrival, but Sorrow was starting to wonder whether it was more than just shock. The way his fingers tapped a rhythm on the armrest suggested he was thinking, and Sorrow was not sure if that was a good thing. Sol was not intuitive but had a gift for analysis.

'How is she?' Sorrow asked, desperate to fill the increasingly oppressive silence. Sol glanced at him.

'Stable,' he said. 'It would seem I restrained the blast.'

'Why did you attack her?'

'I did not. She attacked me,' Sol replied. 'When the dais opened. I... I thought it would be simple. I could not have seen this, I–'

He trailed off, frowning.

'I did see this...' he murmured. 'I thought it was an echo of the before, of those who burned on the plains of Salvation. But it was a warning. Not of what had happened, but what would happen. The door wasn't really open, and the veil still closed. It was I who tore it clear. And now I cannot put it back.'

He sighed, staring at Sorrow with his one good eye.

'All because I wanted to win,' he said sadly. 'No, it wasn't even that. Not just win. I needed him to lose.'

'We are all slaves to our desires,' Sorrow replied. 'But, even if you were selfish, you did not intend this. This is not your fault. You could not have known.'

'Yes, I could have,' Sol replied. 'I took a risk once before, cut corners, tried to do things too quickly. It cost me my eye and the man who named me. I fear this time it will cost us all.'

'There is no time for self-recrimination,' Sorrow said. 'We need to flee before someone has the bright idea of seizing the main gate. If that gets sealed we will be trapped in here.'

Sol glanced to Anguis. 'What about her?'

'Take her? Leave her to her people?' Sorrow shrugged. 'Either, but we cannot stay. If Pureburn is alive then he will be seeking out who is responsible. If he is not then the madness will continue unabated. Either way, there are too many mouths and not enough supplies. Sooner or later he will come for me.'

'I thought we were resupplied?' Sol frowned. 'Were you not just waiting for some paperwork?'

'I doubt very much those supplies survived the fire,' Sorrow replied, barely hesitating. 'In fact, now I think of it, I wager that whatever was shipped has been consumed by flames.'

Sol frowned, glancing at his friend. 'Why so sure?'

'Because that was my warehouse,' Sorrow lied, pointing at a distant plume of smoke. 'It happened quickly, while my Grinders were securing the building. It matters not. Either way we must leave.'

'We can't leave.'

It was Anguis who spoke. She had sat up, and was clutching her head.

'God-Emperor, my eyes hurt,' she said, rubbing the implants imbedded in her orbital sockets. 'Left one doesn't seem to be working.'

'I had to subdue you. I might have damaged it.'

'I suppose that's why I feel like I've sucked on a power-tap?'

'Perhaps. Can you stand?'

'I think so.' She nodded, her fingers stealing into her long-coat, emerging with a small metallic box. She popped it open with her thumb, revealing a series of minuscule tools, and began making adjustments to her damaged ocular implant.

'How long was I unconscious?' she asked.

'A few hours,' Sol replied. 'Do you remember much?'

'Everything until the attack,' she murmured, ripping clear some loose wiring. 'The last thing I recall clearly is Sorrow's agents opening the cell. Then it's black. Well, actually, more red than black.'

'You remember attacking me?'

'A little?' She frowned. 'I was just... so angry. I can recall flashes, but it was like being drunk. My thought processes were... I don't know. They make so little sense I struggle to recall.'

'Why did it happen?' Sorrow asked. 'Is this some weapon? Or a contaminated air supply?'

'It's because we opened the door,' Sol said. His fingers were still tapping a rhythm on the armrest; Sorrow saw a spark jump between them.

'Please ignore Sol,' Sorrow said, turning to Anguis. 'He has decided we should alternate between wallowing in guilt and masochistic self-flagellation.'

'He is not wrong,' Anguis sighed, detaching one of the lenses and blowing on it. 'We were so caught up in Lord Pureburn's little secret, in the psyker powering his empire, we neglected to ask if there was another reason he kept it locked up. The cell was more than a conduit for Pureburn's power – I suspect it restrained the psyker, or perhaps harnessed it. When opened, the full, unfocused power was unleashed.'

'And that is the source of the violence?'

'Yes.'

'But you seem lucid,' Sorrow replied. 'Perhaps it is temporary?'

'I would suspect that depends on whether the psyker is still alive,' Anguis said, glancing at Sorrow. 'Did your agents do what we agreed?'

'I cannot contact them. Perhaps they fell in the chaos.'

'I see,' Anguis said. 'Well, whatever they unleashed, it's not over. I can still feel the anger. Part of me wants to hurt Sol, even though rationally I can see he had to subdue me. And part of me wants to hurt you, because I can.'

'You seem calm.'

'I am House Delaque.' Anguis smiled, reaffixing her lens. 'My House prides itself on restraint and patience. Yet even I struggle. House Cawdor was founded on religious ferv-our. They worship hate and anger as expressions of the God-Emperor's will. Restraint is an unknown concept.'

'What about Sol and I? We seem unaffected.'

'You were far from the source of exposure,' Anguis said. 'Besides, you seem to carry little anger. Perhaps you are difficult to enflame?'

'And Sol?' Sorrow said. 'He is always angry. It's repressed, along with most of his personality. But I still see it. It makes no sense that you would become homicidal whilst he was practically untouched.'

They both glanced at Sol. He was still staring from the window, his fingers drumming. As Sorrow watched, another spark jumped between his fingertips, the electrical charge a cyan blue veined with amethyst.

'Sol?' he asked.

'There is a storm coming. I can feel it. Almost see it, like forgotten embers. They are everywhere, tiny particles of energy. Linked to everything. To everyone.'

'All right.' Sorrow nodded, glancing to Anguis. 'That's… interesting. But do you feel calm?'

'Yes.'

'No anger?'

'No more than usual.'

'Then you are unaffected?'

Sol glanced at them. His lost eye was still unbandaged, but the socket was no longer empty. A spark must have jumped from his finger, because for just an instant Sorrow swore he could see a tiny light blazing in the socket, like a lone star shining bright against the encroaching void.

'I think that might be an overstatement.'

3

'Do you think we can eat this?'

Caleb poked the bud suspiciously with his boot knife. The flesh of the plant was a faded green, studded with little black seeds that glinted malevolently in the dappled light.

'Iktomi?' he said, raising his head. The ratskin was further ahead, scouting a route through the jungle of cable-vines. He'd seen his share of interesting underhive flora and fauna, but nothing quite like the forest in which they were currently stranded. From what he could tell, the vines were once cables or pipes, perhaps transporting promethium or similar. But they had long since fallen into disuse, and the plants had found a niche, growing through and within the cables, swelling until they split, revealing luminous bulbs of acid green and barbs the size of punch-daggers. The canopy stretched as high as he could see, sealing them in. Most curiously, it was lit by what appeared to be a network of grow-lumens, the light possessing a certain ethereal quality apparently intended to mimic daylight.

He glanced back to the bud, prodding it. It looked tough as rockcrete. Still, in his experience most things could be eaten, providing they didn't eat you first.

He sighed, rising to his feet and tapping the vox-unit provided by Lord Sorrow. He'd done so thrice already. No reply. He was not wholly surprised; the last-minute change to their orders had roused his suspicions. Sorrow had provided a laudable account of why the assassination had become a snatch and grab. He was no doubt a talented liar, but then again so was Caleb.

Of course, that had not been the most surprising part of the enterprise.

She was sitting a few feet from him on one of the smaller bulbs, seemingly taking in the forest. She wore the whitest robes he had ever seen, but had no adornment besides that, lacking gang markings, hair and even eyebrows.

He frowned, pretending to still examine the bulb whilst watching her from the corner of his eye. There was something unsettling about her that he could not place. She seemed young, little older than twenty cycles, but her eyes told a different tale. They had seen things. Done things, perhaps. She had not spoken. He'd expected tears or threats, but she seemed calm and appeared no threat whatsoever. He found that particularly worrying.

Still, he was relieved he had not been expected to kill her. When the cell opened, she'd been sitting cross-legged, eyes closed, at peace. He knew he could not have pulled the trigger. Iktomi had no such reservations, stabbing the autosyringe into her throat before the girl even opened her eyes. She'd slumped and he'd slung her over his shoulder, the two of them racing from the scene. He'd heard the screams and explosions, and glanced back just once. What he'd witnessed would take a significant amount of liquor to erase.

He sighed, tugging at the headband wrapped about his temple. It was supposed to provide some resistance to psychic intrusion, though he had no way of knowing if it worked. It felt warm to the touch and irritating to the skin. That probably counted for something.

'Iktomi?' he called, feeling stupid as he did so. But he did not like being left alone with their captive.

There was a rustle ahead as Iktomi emerged from the undergrowth. She barely acknowledged Caleb, shouldering him aside as she dumped a spun sack of sliced fungus at his feet. Provisions, albeit not particularly appetising ones.

'We need to move,' she said without looking at him.

'We were supposed to hide in the cable-vines. We should wait.'

'They're not here. And this is not a safe place.'

'So where are we supposed to go?' Caleb said. 'We have no idea of our location. Is this even Periculus? We could place ourselves in greater danger.'

'We stay? We die,' she replied, glaring at him with blood-shot eyes. He reminded himself she was tired. They both were. That must be why she was so irritable.

'All right,' he sighed. 'But if we do go, what do we do with her?'

They glanced at the captive.

'Leave her.'

'We cannot do that.'

'She will slow us down. And someone wants her. They will come for her.'

'What if they come for us and we don't have her?' Caleb countered. 'Perhaps there was a delay, or perhaps the–'

'If they come for us, they mean to kill us,' she snapped. 'Our best hope is moving quickly. If they hunt her then we leave her behind.'

'But… she's defenceless,' Caleb said. 'Look at her. We cannot just abandon–'

'This isn't a discussion!' Iktomi snarled, their eyes barely a knife's width apart. 'Do as I say or I leave you both.'

Caleb met her gaze. It was not reassuring. Her eyes had a glazed quality, as though intoxicated. But she never drank, never touched a stimm. It had to be the heat. They were both sweating profusely.

'I don't leave people to die,' he said. 'You should know that better than anyone.'

Freedom. She had never known its meaning. Not until now.

She still felt sluggish, mind muddied by the sedative. But without the walls of her cell she saw so much further. It had seemed a haven from the hive's incessant chatter. Perhaps she had needed it, once. But it had been a world of shadow and echo. Now her mind was open. She bore witness to a billion souls, each a beacon, each fascinating in its own way.

Her warp-sight fell upon the two who had liberated her: the woman who barely spoke and the man who never ceased. They argued; it was what they seemed to do. The altercation was barely a flicker on her consciousness, a drop against the sea of souls. But, she realised, there was much to be learned from the microcosm, just as a humble hydrogen atom contained the essence of a supernova.

She watched them. She watched the man run his mouth, his soul myriad colours: fear manifesting as jaundice-yellow, hope the blue of an untouched sky, his love a fierce cerise veining every other thought.

But beneath it all there was an unfamiliar constant, a sliver of silver that remained immutable. It was a little thing, like a loose nail, but whatever flowed through him, however disjointed his thoughts became, it remained, a pin holding his mind together. Odd.

But the woman...

Her soul was nothing like his. It appeared a black and jagged thing, like a barbed prison spun from the shadows of blades. But within, straining against the shackle of self-restraint, was a presence, a pent-up ball of pain, rage and hate that glowed like a furnace. With each exchange the soul-prison buckled, the bars straining against the fury burning within.

She frowned, and without thought or intent beyond satisfying her curiosity, began to pick at the bindings that held the rage in check.

Sorrow knew he should leave it all behind. His entrepreneurial instincts, honed through years of profit and survival, screamed at him to flee, to trample over any who sought to slow him.

And yet he could not get over the table.

It was such a beautiful piece, carved from silverbark, the grain of the wood glimmering in candlelight. The cost of acquisition had been significant, as had the risks of importing it from off-world. It had been a mistake sending for it, he saw that now. Likewise, the compulsion to keep it was irrational, a manifestation of fear and guilt.

But, by the Throne, it was a nice table. Probably the third best he owned.

A Grinder entered, carrying a pack swollen with Sorrow's most prized possessions. It was probably heavier than he was, but the Grinder was unperturbed by the weight. Two others stood in the doorway behind him, similarly equipped.

'Well?' Sorrow asked. 'Are we ready?'

The Grinder nodded, his gaze shifting to the table. He raised an eyebrow.

'We can dispose of it if it becomes a burden,' Sorrow replied, glancing to Anguis, who was seated at the far side. 'Dear lady? I apologise, but I must ask you to sit elsewhere.'

She barely glanced at him, rising and silently vacating the table as the Grinders rushed to retrieve it. Sorrow was fairly sure she was voxing with someone, but it was no longer his concern. Whatever her suspicions, she could take no action with Sol in the room.

'Well, I suppose this is goodbye,' Sorrow said, addressing no one in particular. Sol was seated with his back to him, intent on the darkness beyond the window, fingers still drumming on the armrest. If he heard Sorrow speak he did not acknowledge it. Anguis at least made eye contact, or seemed to, her ocular implants temporarily directed his way. She nodded. Presumably it meant something.

'Well, I hope to see you somewhere closer to the spire,' Sorrow sighed, turning away.

'You will not.'

Anguis had spoken. He glanced back.

'Excuse me?'

'Pureburn is alive,' she said. 'He has sealed the main gate. There is no way out.'

'For you? Perhaps,' Sorrow replied. 'My Grinders will cut down any rabble that oppose me.'

'There are six manning the main gate. Two groups of four in ambush. All armed. Two heavy stubbers,' she said. 'So far, eleven have tried to cross. Would you like to know what happened to their remains?'

'No.'

'Are you sure? Given your profession it may interest you.'

'Do you have an alternative suggestion? Other than waiting to die.'

She shrugged. 'It requires less walking.'

'You intend to just give up?' he asked. 'Fine. But I refuse to.'

'I'm not sure you understand the situation,' she murmured, glancing to the window. 'Whatever we unleashed is beyond anything I have encountered. I know of no spyker or psyker with this kind of power. Perhaps one or two of those employed by Helmawr might approach it. But they would not risk unleashing something like this.'

'Why?'

Anguis hesitated. Sol's drumming had ceased.

'I only know stories,' she said. 'But I know we have spyker contingency protocols for a reason. Our House would not terminate valuable assets unless the risk was severe. All I know is they draw their power from somewhere else. Too much, and it can start to bleed through on its own.'

'How do we know Pureburn's witch is even still alive?'

'Because it's getting worse,' Sol murmured, not looking round. 'The saturation is increasing, perhaps exponentially. I can see it. Feel it.'

Sorrow sighed. 'Sol, I love you dearly, but I fear recent setbacks have had a detrimental effect on your judgement.'

'Is that a polite way of questioning my sanity?'

'If you would like me to be crasser, you need but ask.'

'I believe him,' Anguis whispered, appearing to gaze into space. 'My agent says the madness is spreading and becoming more pronounced.'

'Wonderful,' Sorrow said. 'Anything else?'

'Only that flesh-eating ghouls are invading Periculus.'

'Madness!'

'Exactly.'

'I feel this strengthens the case for running.'

'It will spread uphive.'

'Then I will retreat to the spire until Helmawr stamps it out.'

'If it reaches the spire it will be too late,' Sol said, his voice soft, almost tranquil. 'If the hive falls, the spire falls with it.'

'Then I flee to a different hive, or off planet,' Sorrow replied. 'The joy of running is that there is always further to run.'

Anguis shook her head. 'Not with the main gate sealed.'

'There is the other way,' Sol murmured. Anguis glared at him, but he continued. 'We entered through another path. Dangerous, but probably safer.'

'Excellent,' Sorrow said, clapping his hands. 'It is also information which would have been more pertinent an hour ago, but still great news. Let us set off now and you can show me the way.'

'Anguis can provide a map.'

'No,' Sorrow said. 'No, don't be stupid. Tempes, look at me.'

Sol turned in his chair, glancing to his friend. There was no doubt now; his ruined eye blazed like a plasma coil.

'Come with me,' Sorrow pleaded. 'Martyrdom is the province of priests. We are Guilders. Entrepreneurs. Businessmen. Not soldiers. This is not our fight.'

'I can't leave,' Sol said softly, rising to his feet and nodding to the window. 'I look out there and I see something I have sought my whole life.'

'Devastation? Death?' Sorrow snapped as Anguis handed him a torn scrap of parchment marked with hastily scrawled directions.

'The truth,' Sol said. 'There is an order behind everything. I can see it now, like sparks of inspiration. Particles of understanding. Other-light. It's unstable, dangerous. But it does not have to be. We only need to find the psyker, end her corruption. We can still fix this. I will fix this.'

He glanced at Sorrow, smiling. The expression would have been less disconcerting if his eye were not shining like a supernova.

From his fallen throne Pureburn watched the Cawdor dump another haul of detritus onto the spluttering pyres. There seemed little thought behind the process; human remains and scraps of food were equal boons to the ravenous flames.

By the Throne, they sickened him, diseased and debased mockeries of the human ideal. The irony was not lost on him that these pathetic creatures, weak of mind and body, considered themselves exemplars of humanity. They took arms against heretic, mutant and witch. But, if elevating mankind was their true goal, they would have better success by first eliminating themselves.

He watched them shuffle away to secure more supplies, stooped like beasts. One even scuttled on all fours, his sharp nails dirtied by the corpse-ash. Another was infested with vermin, the creatures scurrying beneath his clothes, emerging occasionally to feast upon a titbit or enjoy a scratch behind a mangy ear.

This was his army. This was how he would resist House Catallus and restore his family's legacy.

He laughed. It was an ugly sound: the cackle of a lunatic. But he cared not. His kingdom was whatever the spluttering braziers still lit, his throne a broken relic.

Yet relic it remained.

He glanced over his shoulder at the cell, where his Cynder attendants were still trying to restore some semblance of power. It had been the vessel for her energies, harnessed as required. But it now occurred to him she was a passive component. Mere fuel, for want of a better term. It was his intellect that channelled the power, his will that shaped an army and forged an empire. If the power had now been released, if the curse now infested Periculus, could he not still shape it?

He wiped his sleeve across his face, peering through the firelight. There was movement in the shadows, masks picked out by the flames. Most were bloodied, or cracked under the impact of a particularly vicious blow. They were somehow viler in the dark, adorned by cruel fangs or blackened eyes. But they came to him. They came because his power called, because they recognised their master.

That was the truth. Only he could command the power and remain uncorrupted by its influence.

'Tritus!'

His lackey's ears pricked like a well-trained dog, all evidence of his earlier sedition gone. He scurried to the throne, bending his knee. Blood was dripping from beneath his mask. Not that it mattered.

'Tritus, until my throne is restored you must be my herald,' Pureburn murmured. 'Tell my congregation what has transpired. Tell them of the dark forces that tried to extinguish the God-Emperor's flame. Tell them they have failed, that we have kept it burning. But the fire cannot go out, and those who did this cannot go unpunished.'

'Yes, milord,' Tritus hissed, his voice a muddied blade. 'They say all is dark now. Except the slave-block. They have light.'

'Do they?' Pureburn murmured, rubbing at his eye with a yellowed nail. 'Virae's serfs. You know she challenged me, Tritus? Threatened me, even?'

'Blasphemy, milord.'

'Do they refuse us entry?'

'So far, milord. A handful of pit fighters have retreated to the slave quarters and sabotaged the service lift. For now, they hold.'

Pureburn shook his head, rising to his feet.

'I own those slaves,' he snarled. 'Upon their backs Periculus will be reforged. From their blood, industry will rise. Take it back. Take it back or bring it down. They will serve in chains, or they will die in flames.'

At his words, black smoke began seeping from beneath the dais. There was a flash of fire, as one of the jets found a semblance of power.

He smiled. All the proof he needed. The true power was his – the divine spark bound to bone and meat, fire made flesh.

He would still rule. And they would still burn.

4

'Hold!' Virae roared. The serfs redoubled their efforts, straining against the bulwark. Beyond it was the walkway, one of three supporting the slave-hab. And it was infested by the screaming hordes of House Cawdor.

The line lurched, the serfs buckling.

'Hold!' she snapped, shouldering her way forward and throwing her weight against the bulwark. Those around her strained as one. They held, but the attackers were relentless, willing to crush themselves in their determination to break the barrier. She heard the snap of bone and tear of flesh, even as her own body began to fail. Her back was agony, needles of pain piercing her left knee. An old wound, earned a lifetime ago. She wondered if now it would be her undoing, the weak link in the chain that would see her fall.

'Move!'

She did not know the figure pushing his way through the crowd, though his garb and bulk spoke of House Goliath.

He bore the same swollen frame as the rest of them, but his face was void of malice, or thought for that matter. A melta-gun was clasped in his hands. Perhaps there was a chance.

'Need to… seal this,' she grunted, straining against the metal.

'Hold it still,' he replied, raising the weapon in a leisurely manner. 'You need to 'ave it in place.'

'We're trying!' she snapped. 'Fancy helping?'

'No,' he said with a grin. 'I can hardly weld it if I'm holdin' it shut.'

Virae swore, drawing on the last of her reserves, her knee screaming, daggers of pain piercing her spine. But something shifted beyond the gate, the attackers stumbling or falling. For a moment the pressure eased. The bulkhead slammed into place, and the Goliath levelled his weapon.

'It's gonna get hot,' he warned, pulling the trigger. There was no flash of light, merely a hum as moisture in the air evaporated. The bulwark was already glowing; she could feel the heat against her forearm, an unpleasant tingle rapidly escalating.

'Keep going!' she bellowed. Beyond, the rats of Cawdor hammered against the metal, self-immolating in their hunger to kill. The tips of her fingers burned, even through her gloves. Beside her, one of the elder slaves was moaning softly with each breath. But still he did not yield. None of them did. They would not break.

'For Helmawr's sake, go faster!' Virae roared, but the Goliath ignored her, slipping with surprising agility through the press of limbs as he traced a line around the bulkhead, fusing the metal. Painstakingly, the pressure eased.

'Done.'

She stepped back. The rim of the bulkhead still offered a

fading orange glow. Would it hold? Perhaps against reclaimed autoguns and improvised firebombs. But what if they found something heavier?

She turned to the Goliath. He too was breathing heavily, and there were burns on his forearms.

'Virae,' she said. 'I'd offer my hand, but my fingers are burnt.'

He grinned. 'Rivv.'

'You got a gang?'

'Had. The Stolen Sons. Guess I'm in charge now.'

'All dead?'

'Think so,' he sighed. 'I killed three of them. Had to.'

'Lot of that going round,' she said. 'You're with me now. Fall in.'

He nodded. She turned, glancing to the serfs. Most were shuffling from the door, uncertain. At least two were lying prone, clutching burnt limbs.

'Anyone with medical training?' she asked, surveying the room. 'Cleaned up after a doc or anything?'

Stillness. Then a hand raised. And a second.

'Get the wounded down to level fourteen,' she said. 'Whatever medical supplies we have are there. If you can't treat them, get them drunk. The rest of you begin a sweep – you see a crack, I want it sealed. They might find another way across. Scrounge whatever weapons you can find – I want snipers in the windows above each walkway. Tell them to focus on heavies and anyone carrying grenades or melta weaponry.'

She glanced around, meeting each of their gazes in turn. Lost, scared. Like dogs missing their owners.

Except one. Bloodshot eyes glaring back in challenge.

'You got a problem?' she said.

'Yeah,' he said, squaring up to her. 'Don't see why you

should be giving the orders. World's ending. Every hiver for himself.'

'Should have said something a minute ago,' she said, shrugging. 'I could have dumped you outside and had one less mouth to feed.'

'We carried the food,' he snarled. 'Not you, slaver! It's your fault we are trapped down here, your fault–'

She backhanded him. Hard. He spun in the air, landing face down, and did not rise.

'Take him too,' she said, nodding to the newly appointed medi-serfs. 'If he acts up, hit him again, harder.'

She turned before they could question her, stalking down the corridor, Rivv falling in behind. They must not see her exhaustion, or the stabbing pain in her knee, or her fear. Sealing even a factory-pressed hab-block was virtually impossible, like trying to render a sieve watertight. The fact her castle did not touch the ground was an advantage, but piecemeal attacks could still come from above and below.

And if one of the walkways were to breach…

She passed serfs and gangers, scum and work crews, all now apparently under her jurisdiction. Some had slunk in during the chaos, or retreated from adjacent buildings before they sealed the entrances. Escher and Goliath stood shoulder to shoulder with Orlock and Van Saar. It was strange; ancient rivalries were as nothing against the current threat.

Ahead lay her laughably designated command centre. It was formally the Shaklemen's quarters, though few of them remained. Whatever madness had consumed Periculus had spared most of those locked in the slave-block, but many Shaklemen had still been dragged down by frenzied serfs before order was restored. Still, the room had weapons and surveillance. It was a start.

'Status?' Virae barked as she entered the room, Rivv a few paces behind.

Elle, alone, glanced up from the data-terminal.

'All three entryways are sealed. We found a few long rifles, enough to set up some snipers. They are returning fire, but casualties are light. It's too dark to confirm numbers.'

Her voice was flat, the cogitator still speaking through her. Her own voice had not returned since the attack that had claimed Block.

'This is no mere madness,' Virae murmured. 'At least, not the madness of beasts. They are becoming organised, sending feints. Planning. We can hold them, I think. But what if they decide to blow the walkways?'

'They wouldn't,' Elle murmured, the barest hint of emotion creeping into her voice. 'Nothing is stable. If the slave-block were to fall it could collapse half the dome.'

'And kill us all,' Virae replied. 'Even beasts would not think that way, at least not deliberately. But I know Pureburn is behind this. He considered us his property, and our refusal to bend the knee a grievous slight. If his choices are relinquishing control or killing us all he would not hesitate.'

'Then what do we do? How–?'

There was a tremor. It was near nothing, little more than the vibration of a passing rail-engine. Then there was a second. Closer.

They exchanged glances.

And suddenly the vox-channel was filled with screams.

Caleb knew Iktomi was angry. What was worse, she was also right.

They should have cut and run. But he could not bring himself to leave their captive to die. It had not been hard to persuade her to follow, trotting behind him as he navigated a path Iktomi carved through the vines. But she slowed them, and it was already heavy going. He wiped his brow, muttering as his sleeve caught on his headband. It was getting hotter.

He glanced to their captive. She seemed unconcerned by the heat, unconcerned by anything. He'd tried sparking up a conversation a few times, but she did not respond, or seem especially interested in his words. It was as though she occupied another world.

They had walked for hours. Iktomi claimed she followed a path, but it was difficult to differentiate between cable-vines. They could have stumbled in circles for all he could tell. That was why he was so relieved when they came across the clearing. At least, at first.

The cable-vines receded, in their place a barren semi-circle of a hundred yards or so that jutted from a metal cliff-face. The ground was like nothing he had seen, a brown mulch that crumbled at the touch. Soil, he'd heard it was called. Handfuls were sometimes exchanged in the underhive for princely sums. It came from off-world and was apparently used for farming.

Or gardens.

Above them, the glow-rig was infested with cable-vines, casting long shadows over the ruined building. It was a small build, at least for the hive, barely two storeys high and a dozen or so yards wide, a framework of rusted struts jutting from its roof like the spines of some beast. It was built against a cliff-face of blackened metal, but the ruins were corroded a colourful buckshot of orange rust and dulled iron. Its main entrance hung open, leading to what might once have been an atrium, but the remaining inner doors were long sealed by corrosion. Caleb suggested they shelter and rest before moving on. Iktomi had not argued, but neither had she agreed, instead muttering something about scouting a perimeter before stalking off.

He'd strung enough glow-rods to light the space and tried to sleep. It was uncomfortable lying on the cold metal grating, and the headband itched terribly. He debated taking it off; surely they were far enough from whatever threat warranted such additional protection?

Yet he kept it. He was unsure why. Perhaps the discomfort was why sleep proved elusive. Perhaps he snatched a few moments of slumber, but his dreams drew him back to the jungle of cable-vines. They writhed like a living thing, thorns stained with blood. He tried to run, but rotten hands reached up from beneath, dragging him down into the underhive.

He awoke to their captive watching him, her expression inscrutable.

Why was she a target? Ransom?

She had the look of a priest, except the eyes. Her gaze was unsettling, but he could not think why. His mind kept drifting, unable to focus. He lay back down, closing his eyes.

But the disquiet lingered.

Eventually he gave up, rising and stepping outside. Perhaps it was the silence that unsettled him. He was used to the hum of the hive, the echoes of distant engines resonating through the metalwork. But wherever they were, it was too deep for such sound to carry. Too well hidden.

But something had been built there.

He frowned, glancing to their adopted shelter. It was too corroded to discern the building's original purpose. But whoever had built it had prized secrecy above anything else. Had they discovered the forest of cable-vines, considering it a perfect hideaway? Or did the construction come first, the land subsequently shaped to conceal it?

Were they even still in Periculus?

He frowned, trying to recall their flight. They had taken the pipe as instructed, the cable-vines thickening to block their passage. He had just slung the captive over his shoulder and concentrated on keeping up with Iktomi. She had torn through the throng of screaming masks and the cables just as easily, her knife carving a path. Then there had been tunnels, a mad scramble through waist-deep sump. Running. Reacting.

He had no idea where they had ended up. At the time it had felt like chance. But now he looked at the building, and their captive so calmly nestled within it.

And he found himself wondering.

He needed Iktomi.

He turned back to the wall of cable-vines. The light was waning, perhaps a part of the grow-rig's cycle, but his photo-goggles pierced the gloom, picking out the cable-vines in a sickly green.

There. She sat hunched by the forest's edge, knees drawn to her chest, back to him. He approached slowly. He knew she heard him, even if she did not react.

He cleared his throat. 'Iktomi?'

She glared from over her shoulder, irritated by the inter-ruption. Her knife was drawn, held in her left hand, her thumb and three remaining fingers curled about the handle. Her right hand was laid out before her, fingers spread like the legs of a spider.

'What?' she hissed. Her eyes were more bloodshot than ever. He wished she'd slept.

'I'm starting to wonder how we ended up here,' he said. 'There is something strange about… what are you doing?'

She had turned away, ignoring him as she raised the blade, right hand outstretched.

He seized her wrist.

'Do not touch me!' she snarled, pulling away, but he held tight.

'What are you doing?'

'They are out there,' she murmured, tearing her arm clear and nodding to the wall of vines. 'All around. Hunting us. Can't go back – they followed. Three sides, a wall behind. They herded us here. They are waiting. Something calls them. We need to draw them into the open. I need bait.'

'Bait?'

'They are flesh eaters.' She nodded, as though the rest were obvious.

He glanced to her outstretched fingers.

'You're planning to feed them your hand?'

She rolled her eyes like a petulant juve. He'd never seen such an expression before. It would have been comical were he not so terrified.

'No, just a finger,' she muttered. 'I'll cut it off just like the other one. Better they match anyway.'

Caleb gingerly lowered to his haunches, so he was squatting beside her.

'You're going to cut off your finger and feed it to cannibals?' he said softly. 'And, as a bonus, it means your hands will match.'

'Yes,' she said. 'Eight fingers. Neater. Blood. Then I–'

She trailed off, frowning, as though hearing her words for the first time.

Caleb licked his lips, his mouth dry. 'Please don't kill me for saying this,' he said. 'But that sounds a little insane.'

'A little,' she conceded, her focus now shifted to the cable-vines. But she still held the knife.

'Is it possible you're not thinking clearly?' he ventured.

'Possible.'

'You could have been exposed to a toxin in the jungle,' he said. 'Hallucinogenic spores or something. We should head back to the–'

'There.'

Her knife pointed to the forest of cable-vines. All he saw was darkness.

Except…

Except there had been a flicker. Nothing substantial, a shadow slipping from sight.

'I suspect there are rats and bugs creeping around in there,' he said, hand edging towards his holstered laspistol. 'But we should head back to the shelter. We still have some supplies. A little food and sleep will clear your head.'

Gently, he took hold of her shoulder. She stiffened at his touch, but rose, her gaze lingering on the encroaching cable-vines, and the shadows between them. Her face kept twitching, and there was an ugly red mark on her forehead.

He frowned. 'What happened to your headband?'

'It hurt.' She shrugged, her focus still on the cable-vines. 'Didn't like it.'

'Let's just get back,' he murmured, glancing back to the ruins. Their captive was standing in the doorway, watching them. It was odd, perhaps a glitch in the photo-goggles. But at that moment it was almost as though her eyes were shining, like dying stars.

5

Lord Sorrow stumbled on, hands bound, his Vermisian robes stained and rent. Two masked figures flanked him, pinning his arms in place. Behind, he could hear the muffled tread of his Grinders. They were similarly bound, shotguns pressed into the smalls of their backs. The last two, all he had left.

Perhaps he should have followed Anguis' directions, or even accompanied them on their fool's errand. But he did not trust her motives, or Sol's judgement. He'd never reached the main gate. One by one, the Grinders had been taken, gunned down between alleys, or dragged into the shadows by pale, grasping hands. He had lost his antepenultimate minion to the silken strands of an orb spider. Still, he did not go easily, silently hacking at the creature's carapace even as it sank fangs into his shoulder. Sorrow had fled, his final two Grinders close on his heels, and almost barged into an Enforcer slumped at the alley's edge. His helm was dented, the faceplate missing, and Sorrow thought he recognised the jawline of Palanite Captain Canndis. The man opened his mouth to speak but they ignored him, pressing on. The rule of law meant nothing. The Enforcers no longer mattered.

A hand slammed into his back, pitching him forward and back to the present. He fell face first into the corpse-ash, but they hauled him upright. His Grinders no longer tried to assist; the brands of House Cawdor had imparted restraint. As his vision cleared he saw something ahead, the gloom broken by a circle of fallen pyres. The air stank of industry, but beneath the fumes he detected a familiar aroma.

Death.

Ironic. Until that moment it was a smell he associated with success.

They led him between the flames, his skin tightened by the heat. The air was choked with sulphurous smoke, but he could make out a figure at the circle's centre. His throne was no longer suspended on flames, instead belching smog. The crucible was cold, his vestments torn. But, even with his face hooded, Sorrow recognised Lord Pureburn in all his faded glory.

'Lord Sorrow,' he said, leaning back in his chair, his fingers pressed together. 'Once again, I sit in judgement as you plead your case.'

'Lord Pureburn,' Sorrow replied, bowing his head, arms still pinned. 'I am so relieved to find you alive.'

'As you are. For now.'

'I had pressing business and could not attend the ceremony,' Sorrow said. 'I was most disheartened at the time. In hindsight, I suppose I should thank the God-Emperor for my good fortune.'

Pureburn seemed to stare at him, but his eyes were still hidden by his hood.

'Why would the God-Emperor waste His favour on you?'

Sorrow smiled, gaze flicking between the pyres, where hungry eyes waited.

'Well, in any event, I am alive. How may I be of service?'

'You ran. None may leave Periculus without my permission.'

'I feared you dead, my lord. Of course I ran.'

'I am warden of the God-Emperor's flame,' Pureburn said, spreading his hands. 'I am of His will. I cannot die at the hands of a traitor.'

'I am relieved to hear that, my lord. Forgive my foolishness.'

'Are you a traitor, Lord Sorrow?' The voice was soft and inviting, like spider's silk.

'No, my lord. I am loyal to the God-Emperor and to his rightful champion.'

'So you say!' Pureburn hissed, his finger stabbing out accusingly. 'Yet you went into hiding. Two assailants attacked me, Lord Sorrow, thieves who struck from the shadows, fled before I could retaliate. Did you know this?'

'No, my lord.'

'It took some time to come back to me,' Lord Pureburn continued. 'But then I remembered the tale of those aspirational pit fighters released into your custody. Tell me, do you still have them?'

'No, my Lord. I ensured they were shipped out to face Guilder justice.'

'Interesting,' Pureburn said, his smile glinting beneath his hood. 'And what would you say if I told you some claim they were responsible for this blasphemy, that they stole His Eternal Flame?'

'I would be horrified and at a loss, my lord,' Sorrow replied. 'If you wish, I could try to contact my partners. However, I understand there is confusion surrounding the event, no doubt because some pathogen or toxin was unleashed as part of the attack. I would therefore humbly suggest that such recollections are, at best, suspect.'

'A reasonable point.' Lord Pureburn nodded, fingers idly stroking his beard. 'Fair. Very fair. And civilised men should consider carefully before making accusations or threats.'

'Wise words, my lord.'

'Sadly, I think the time for civilisation is over.'

Pureburn's finger tapped thrice against his wrist, and the Cawdors started to move. An instant later Sorrow heard a grunt as his Grinder smashed the guards aside, sweeping up a fallen polearm as he made for the Pyrocaen Lord.

A blast of flames swallowed him, transforming the brute into a living inferno. The second Grinder leapt forward, using his body to shield Lord Sorrow from the heat. It spared him the sight of the first Grinder being roasted alive, his bones blackening and fat bubbling. But he could still smell it, the scent of scorched flesh somehow appetising and sickening all at once.

As the flames died and the body crumbled to ash, the towering Pyromagir stepped forward. Smoke seeped from its brazier-arm, its tip tinged a burnt orange by the heat.

'We are done with platitudes and negotiation,' Pureburn said, advancing on him. 'Those who set themselves against the God-Emperor's light will not hide in the darkness. For I am His fire. I am His vengeance.'

Sorrow found his feet, his final Grinder stepping between him and the Pyromagir. Not that it would matter; even armed, his minion would have stood no chance against the cybernetic monstrosity. Sorrow still had his ring, and the digi-weapon contained within. A single blast would obliterate Pureburn, or his foul underling. But then the rest would swarm in, and Sorrow would fall beneath their rusted knives.

Pureburn halted a foot from him. 'I ask you again,' he said. 'Where are they?'

Sorrow was close enough to see the Pyrocaen's eyes. They were stained crimson, tears of blood marring his cheeks, his pupils constricted to pinpricks, like the needle-marks on a junkie's arm. One misplaced word would spell Sorrow's end.

'Forgive me, my lord,' Sorrow pleaded, bowing his head as his mind raced. 'I delivered them in good faith to a colleague from the Mercator Sanguis. He assured–'

He trailed off, frowning, as a realisation suddenly dawned. He had to sell the lie. His life depended on it. But he could sell anything.

'My lord,' he said, a look of horror forming on his face. 'I delivered them to a colleague from the Mercator Sanguis and was advised they would be transported to Rakk. But I now wonder if Virae the Unbroken intercepted them, or had already bought their cooperation? Perhaps she wished to defy your orders and deliver justice herself, only for the two of them to escape. Unless–'

He bit his lip, as though afraid to speak.

'Out with it!' Pureburn roared.

'My lord, what if she never planned to execute them?' he whispered. 'What if they were always in her employ? The arena contest may have been a cunning ruse to mask their true intentions.'

It was a stretch. But a lie built on existing prejudice was the easiest to swallow, and Sorrow still recalled Pureburn's heated exchange with the Chain Lord. His head was still bowed, but he risked a glance at the old man, maintaining a facade of confusion, as though seeking guidance from his superior.

'Forgive me, my lord,' he said. 'She outsmarted me. I was a fool.'

Pureburn was not looking at him, his gaze intent on something beyond the circle of flames. Even his Pyromagir seemed hesitant, its brazier smouldering.

'I suspected her treachery,' Pureburn murmured, rubbing his face. His fingers were stained red, the nails clotted, his bloodied gaze lingering on the distant light of the slave-hab.

'You will remain at my side,' he murmured. 'You can, at least, carry a conversation. Your Grinder will be needed to provide sustenance as our supplies are low. Sadly, most of our produce is somewhat charred, but we must make do with what we have.'

'I thank you, my lord,' Sorrow said, nodding. 'But I will need the equipment housed in my accommodation. Corpse-starch must be sanctified, the purification rituals vital to prevent possible... corruptive elements. We cannot simply carve flesh from the bodies of–'

'Do not think me a fool, Lord Sorrow,' Pureburn said with a thin smile. 'I know your hand is somewhere in this mess. All of you are threatened by me, envious of my power. You would be wise to shut your mouth and follow my orders. And, for your sake, let us hope your role in this affair is that of naïve simpleton. Otherwise I shall see you carved up and fed to the deserving.'

Anguis shouldered Sol to one side, her flechette pistols spraying needle-like slivers into a snarling face. He staggered but she grabbed his arm, dragging him on.

'Which way?' she barked. He gestured ahead. The path was clear to him, the glow left by the psyker clearly visible and so bright that it blinded him to the dangers in the shadows. But shadows were Anguis' job; he just found them tiresome, a distraction from the other-light.

It was everywhere and nowhere, like clouds on the wind. There was no single source, tiny stars manifesting spontaneously and fading just as fast. It reminded him of the perma-storms – eternal yet mercurial. And, like them, there was a direction to the flow. It was that they followed.

'Stig-shambler!' Anguis barked.

Sol blinked. A hulking figure blocked their path, a swarm of Cawdors clustered at its feet. It was big, and would have dwarfed even a Goliath were it standing upright. Instead it shuffled on all fours, scarred knuckles scraping the bone-gravel, face hidden by a burlap sack. A platform was bolted to its shoulders, upon which a diminutive figure was hunched behind a double-barrel heavy stubber.

'Down!' Anguis shouted, hurling herself behind a mound of rubble as the weapon spat a hail of armour-piercing rounds.

Sol raised his hand.

The shots scattered, repelled by the electromagnetic shield, ricocheting between the ruins. Two of the swarm fell to the stray shots, and a round thudded into the hulking Stig-shambler's shoulder, drawing blood. The brutish creature barely seemed to notice, braying as it charged, the dwarf on its shoulders spraying shots indiscriminately at enemy and ally alike.

Sol stepped forward to meet it, bracing himself against the rain of shells, his good eye on the beast, the ruined socket staring only into the other-light. He felt wind on his face as he drew the tiny stars into his palm. A halo coalesced around his fingers, narrowing to a blinding pinprick, before surging forward as a bolt of searing light. It struck the Stig-shambler, scourging flesh and frying synapses. It fell, a nimbus of lightning arcing from the body, seeking the surrounding Cawdors. As they twitched and stumbled Anguis darted forward, her flechette pistols euthanising any who still clung to life. She lowered the weapons, regarding him with an eyeless gaze.

'How did you do that?'

'I don't know,' Sol murmured, staring at his hand. 'It wasn't lightning. It wore its shape, but a storm seeks the easiest path, the quickest route. It does not discriminate, or kill with intent. This other-light is different.'

He glanced to Anguis. She wore that same inscrutable expression, her face somehow always in shadow. But he saw more now. There was light within even her.

'I think I understand,' he murmured, an unbidden smile spreading across his face. 'This is it. The Motive Force. One energy uniting everything. I knew it was true. I felt it. I always knew.'

'Sol, you need to calm down.'

She flickered. Perhaps it meant something? It was hard to focus on both at once; the other-light was blinding when he stared too hard, like a torch from a mirror, shadows reflecting... along... what to...

The ground suddenly lurched towards him. Anguis grasped his arm, steadying him. He looked at her. She was a shadow again. The other-light had faded.

'Breathe. Slow,' she whispered. 'You need to stay focused.'

'But I saw it,' he murmured. 'I was so close. There is a greater truth, but I cannot hold it in my head. It's too much. It hurts.'

'You are trying to comprehend too much too fast. Find a focus. Make it a frame of reference.'

'What?'

'It's part of the initial spyker conditioning process,' she said. 'Just close your eye a moment. Focus on a symbol, or an idea.'

He closed his good eye. But the ruined one still saw her: other-light bound to shadow. The glow flickered as she spoke, like a sparking circuit. He saw her reach into her longcoat.

His hand shot out, seizing her wrist. She held a familiar-looking autosyringe. The sickly green liquid within seemed to shimmer.

'What is in that vial?' he said.

She smiled. As much as she could, anyway.

'It's a neuron-cleanser. It aids recovery after psychic attack.'

A flicker.

'My present condition does not seem much like recovery. Try the truth this time.'

'I do not know for sure,' she said. 'I am no scientist. But I do know that without this you would still be paralysed in a medical unit in the Needle. If you want to continue, you need this.'

Her other-light was faint. But it shone without a flicker.

He sighed, releasing his grip and offering his throat. The syringe stung, but he was accustomed to it now, and already the other-light was bright again, the path clear – were it not for the shadow looming before them.

They had reached Periculus' Wall, the impregnable barrier to the world beyond. And their quarry lay on the other side.

Caleb felt a drip on his cheek.

His eyes snapped open, hand darting to his boot knife, but something seized his throat, squeezing tight enough to deaden his limbs.

His vision swam into focus. Iktomi.

She straddled his chest, one hand clasped to his windpipe, the other clutching a length of cable-vine. The glow-rods were fading, but he could just make out her eyes. The sclera were stained red, blood flowing down her cheeks like tears. He tried to speak, to raise his hand, but her grip tightened. He almost lost consciousness.

'Still,' she said, slurring as though drunk. She was shaking, muscles twitching of their own accord, like a stimm-head's withdrawal.

'Listens now,' she hissed, releasing her grip a fraction. 'Listens.'

'I'm listening,' he croaked.

She peered at him through bloodied eyes, seeking sign of deceit. Finding none, she released her grip, standing up and wiping her eyes on her hand. Behind her, Caleb could just make out their captive, watching. He rose slowly to a sitting position.

'Iktomi, we need to find a doc. This–'

'Shut up,' she said, striking him across the face. He rolled with it, barely keeping his footing. The punch had been pulled, but not by much. He glanced up. She was shaking, her left hand seizing her right, fighting for control.

'You need... restrain,' she said, nodding to the vines at his feet. 'No argue.'

'Then what?'

'You figure out!' she snapped, crossing her arms behind her back and dropping to her knees. 'Always me. Always I fix your mistakes. Would be better if you were gone. Freer.'

'Probably,' he said with a nod. 'But we're bound together by oath.'

'Stupid,' she said, voice breaking. 'Stupid oath. Stupid child's oath. Foolish.'

'But you made it,' he said, taking a step closer. 'Your word. You swore to protect me. You cannot relinquish that promise. Your word is your bond.'

She twitched, the veins in her neck pulsing. Her breath a hiss.

'I'd like to kill you,' she said softly. 'All of you. You took my home and my people. You birthed this nightmare world from greed and hubris. You still live because I once gave my word. But I care less and less for words.'

'You want to kill me. Kill us all?' Caleb murmured, glancing to their captive.

'Yes.'

'Her?' Caleb said. Iktomi frowned, following his gaze.

'No,' she murmured, studying the girl, as though seeing her for the first time.

'No anger? No murderous rage?'

'No,' she said softly. 'No rage.'

Her eyes narrowed.

They moved as one, Iktomi leaping to her feet, snatching her knife. But Caleb blocked her path, laspistol raised. She stared at him, almost amused, her mouth splitting into a vicious smile.

'You think you can stop me?' she said.

'Oh, I don't *think* I can stop you,' Caleb replied, his pistol aimed square at her chest.

'That's it?'

'Yep,' he said. 'I don't think I can stop you. You could kill me in a heartbeat. Please don't.'

'Out of my way.'

'Can't.'

'Why?'

'Because I can't let you kill her.'

She glared at him, head swaying back and forth. It reminded him of a phyrr cat he'd seen in the outskirts of Hive City.

'She is doing this,' Iktomi snarled.

'You don't know that.'

'I don't want to kill her. That's not normal.'

'She's unarmed. We don't just kill unarmed people. There is a code.'

Iktomi burst into laughter. He had never heard the sound before, and hoped he never would again. She was also surprised by the outburst, frowning. Hesitantly, she lowered the blade.

'Maybe you are right.'

'Thank you,' he said. 'Now I–'

The floor struck his face, and a second later he felt the punch. His pistol was gone. He glanced up and saw she had it, the weapon aimed squarely at the captive's face. Too fast. He could not stop her.

'Don't–'

She pulled the trigger. The target was mere feet from her. It was impossible to miss. Yet the blast never reached her, detonating inches from her face.

Caleb glanced to Iktomi. She squeezed off another shot. It too never reached the target.

'It's her,' Iktomi murmured, tossing him the pistol. 'Bind me. Now.'

'No,' Caleb replied, rising, pointing towards the door. 'We just need to get out of here. We–'

But the shelter's entrance was sealed, the bolts fused into place by heat or acid.

'Can't go out there,' Iktomi murmured. 'They are coming. I tried to lock them out, but now we are trapped. With her. Didn't see her as a threat. Stupid. Too angry to think straight.'

'That's why we need–'

She stared at him, blood flowing freely from her eyes.

'Too late to stop her. Should have acted sooner. Now we can't.'

She dropped to her knees, hands clasped behind her back, still staring at him.

'Don't make the same mistake with me.'

6

Sorrow swore as the data-slate's display died. He glanced over his shoulder, expecting at any moment to be confronted by Pureburn's thugs. Still, his Grinder's broad shoulders concealed him, and the Cawdors were occupied with their bloody work. An execution, or possibly martyrdom. It was harder to find reasons for the violence. Whatever madness had consumed the dome was getting worse. Anguis was right.

He tapped the data-slate, his fingers slick with sweat. Was it the heat? Nerves? Or something more insidious? He'd thought himself immune to the madness, either through force of will or his minimal exposure. But perhaps he'd merely delayed the inevitable. He caught his reflection in the data-slate's screen, tugging at his eyelid, inspecting his sclera. It did look bloodshot. Then again, the air was choked with the smoke from burning corpses.

He tapped at the screen, keeping half an eye over his shoulder. Tritus was addressing a wizened old man, his

373

rags twitching with a seeming life of their own. As Sorrow watched, a rat emerged from his sleeve. It had an unlit candle taped to its head.

Truly, they were mad.

Abruptly, the data-slate hummed into life. Two figures stared back at him, though neither showed their face. They wore exquisite masks of unblemished ivory, nothing like the twisted visages of House Cawdor. Each was sculpted to mimic a perfect human face.

'Mr Sorrow,' said the first mask, her voice soft and erudite. 'You are well, I trust? You seem a little… dishevelled.'

'We have a situation,' Sorrow replied, smearing back his hair and forcing a smile. 'It's urgent.'

'Yes. Periculus is quite the talk of the spire,' the second mask said. 'House Catallus seems especially flustered. And, of course, that pricked our interest, as we do so enjoy seeing them flustered.'

'An informant has kept us abreast of the situation,' the first mask said. 'And quite a situation it is.'

'Indeed,' Sorrow replied. 'A pity you were unable to take the initial contract.'

The masks exchanged glances.

'We are happy to do business,' the second mask said. 'But publicly attacking a Guilder during a quasi-religious cere-mony? Surrounded by the filth of House Cawdor? Only a fool would consider it.'

'Well, it did not go well. There are loose ends that I would very much like tied.'

'I see. What are the targets?'

'Three. One primary, two secondary. Have you heard of Caleb Cursebound?'

The sigh was audible over the data-feed.

'You are referring to that little upstart who claims to be responsible for House Harrow's decline?' the first mask said disdainfully.

'Not that we have love for House Harrow.'

'Certainly not. They are little more than House Catallus' vassals. But the idea an underhiver could assassinate the head of a Noble House, even one as lowly as House Harrow?'

'It's preposterous,' the first mask said. 'A fiction spun by a braggart and liar. I find it insulting.'

Sorrow smiled, his good humour restored, if only for a heartbeat.

'Well, that braggart is currently in danger of opening his mouth about matters I would prefer were kept quiet. He and his partner are the secondary targets.'

'And the primary?'

'Their captive. I would advise you not to engage directly. Pick them off from a distance, and–'

'I think we know how to conduct our business,' the second mask said, his fingers straying to the ornate handle of his sheathed blade. 'All we require from you is the location.'

'I planted a tracker on their equipment. I can provide details of where they fled. You should be able to follow the signal from there.'

'Then we have an accord.'

'Excellent. How soon can you be here?'

'How soon?' the second mask replied with a haughty cackle. 'Lord Sorrow, my sister and I are the Shadows of Catallus. We live to snap at their heels. We are already here.'

Virae could barely follow the vox-chatter. Even Elle was struggling, the cogitator whirring ominously as it processed the data. She coughed, smoke seeping from her lips.

'They've broken the east gate,' she murmured. 'There were explosions from within the hab-block. Heavy casualties, though we have fallen back to the second line. Hold. Reports of additional explosions across multiple levels. No pattern, random. But all internal. They found a way in.'

'How?' Virae snarled, her fist slamming against the wall. She didn't know what to do. She was no general. Her battles were in the arena, one on one. This was like fighting a swarm of insects. Elle was babbling now, her vocal cords unable to keep pace with the reams of data. Rivv stood by the door, meltagun held ready. He was calm. It was unclear what else he offered.

'They got in,' Virae murmured. 'Not just a few. Enough to attack multiple levels without being detected. How could they get in?'

She studied the data-screens, seeking a clue but finding only smog and flame. There were three entrances to the hab-block. All sealed, yet they had snuck through. How? House Cawdor was not renowned for stealth and subterfuge. There were cracks in the outer wall, but none sufficient for a human. Did they send children scurrying into the firefights?

Something flickered in the corner of her vision, the flutter of a tiny flame. As she turned it vanished behind the equipment store, but she heard the skitter of tiny claws.

What was it?

She peered into the shadows. There was a glint of red, needle-like eyes, and the flick of a worm-like tail. A rat. Not even an especially big one, no more than a foot in length. But something was strapped to its back – a crude chamber housing a flickering candle stub, and next to it a small container of–

'Bomb-rat!' she bellowed, seizing Elle and diving for cover as the blast detonated, the force slamming her into the far wall. She landed heavy, but her groan was deadened, the explosion momentarily deafening her. Through the smoke and flames she saw a second creature scamper closer. Its whiskers twitched as it regarded her, seemingly oblivious to the blast charge strapped to its back. She could not hear the timer, but she could see it tick down. There were seconds left.

She tried to rise, but her leg was pinned. It was the end.

Then suddenly Elle was lunging past, scooping up Virae's cracked helm. She dived onto the rodent, just as time ran out.

Caleb pressed his shoulder to the door, straining, sweat dripping from his forehead.

Nothing. Iktomi had chemically fused the bolts into the frame; he found two broken vials beside the door. A krak grenade might dislodge it, but they would be too close to the blast.

He glanced round. Iktomi sat cross-legged in the corner, arms bound behind her back. Her eyes were squeezed shut, cheeks stained crimson. She was chanting something in a language he did not understand. She too was stained by sweat.

Their captive was inspecting the walls. Her finger brushed lazily against the corrosion, which promptly ignited in a shower of blue sparks. She blinked, slightly surprised. It wasn't just the walls either. He'd noticed that if she stood too long in one spot the metal beneath her feet began to warp, as though superheated.

His gaze crept to the laspistol at his hip. If she were dead, perhaps it would all return to normal?

'It's not as though I could kill you even if I wanted to,' he murmured. 'Not with this. Perhaps a choke grenade might do it? Or, if I set off enough explosives, I could collapse this place.'

She did not respond. But he did not expect her to.

'I don't like killing,' he sighed. 'Never really got the hang of it. But I also don't like dying. Don't have the hang of that either, but from what I gather it's easy to pick up.'

His gaze had drifted back to the door. He frowned, concentrating, forcing himself to focus on their captive. There was little of note. Though hairless, her skin was unusually smooth, unmarked by scar or blemish. By a certain light she might have been beautiful, but there was a wrongness too. He felt nothing, looking at her. He tried, but was unable to hate her, even with Iktomi's blood staining the floor. He wasn't even sure why he was helping her; he felt no love or kinship. She just kept fading...

'You're influencing me, aren't you?' he murmured, feeling at the silver headband still clamped around his head. 'Is this doing anything? Even with it, you're in my head. Are you even doing it consciously?'

His gaze slid to the bound Iktomi.

'She could find a way,' he murmured. 'She can kill anything, given time. Of course, she'd probably die in the process. Or kill me first. Or both of us.'

The captive still did not acknowledge him, her focus on a twisted frame that had once been an interior door. She prodded it with her finger. There was another shower of sparks, revealing a silvery layer of metal beneath the corrosion. She frowned, pressing her palm to it, the suggestion of a scowl forming on her face. Caleb felt the heat radiating from her, the air shimmering. But the door did not yield.

Caleb frowned, stretching out his fingers, seeking the point where temperature shifted from oppressive to searing. He unsheathed his laspistol, firing a tentative shot. It burst into sparks several feet from her. Before, it had been inches. The aura was growing, but the shelter was not. He was already sweating. How long before his hair began to burn? His skin singe?

He glanced to the outer door, a trio of krak grenades dangling from his fingers.

They were out of time.

He gave it no further thought, magnetically clamping the grenades to the door's centre, forming a rough triangle, and setting the charge.

That was the easier part. Iktomi was the challenge.

He approached her, slow but deliberate. She still seemed lost in a trance, but she tensed as he drew closer, muscles coiled like a spring. Gently, he took hold of her arm.

The chant ceased. She gave a low growl.

'We're just moving a little this way,' he murmured, edging them along the far wall so their captive was between them and the sealed exit. She was still straining against the interior door, unaware of or unconcerned by their presence.

Caleb gritted his teeth and squeezed the detonator.

The implosive charges tore the door into jagged shards, spraying them in all directions. Caleb and Iktomi would have been shredded had it not been for the captive, the fragments bursting into sparks around her. She barely acknowledged it.

Caleb gave her a wide berth as he waded through the smoke, Iktomi in tow and respirator in place. The door was split, the crack wide enough to squeeze through. It was cool outside, the stale air of the underhive never smelling so sweet.

But they were not alone.

A figure stood at the vine-cable forest's threshold. It strode slowly towards him, blade glinting in the fading light.

7

Canndis could run no more. He'd been slowing before that thing seized his leg, its nails scoring his undersuit. He'd struck it with the impotent shock-baton, expecting to crack the hideous, eyeless mask. Instead the creature's face split open in a shower of gore. But its mouth still held enough fangs to sink into his ankle. He'd howled in pain, finishing the creature with a second blow, but from then on he was reduced to a hobble.

Perhaps he could move faster without the riot shield. It was all he'd salvaged from the fortress-precinct before it was over-run by the Cawdors. He had no proof of who'd led them to him. But he was pretty confident he recognised the scrawny figure urging the killers on. He'd voxed a message to central command, pleading for reinforcements, but there had been no response. He was on his own.

Where was there to run? He had plunged on into the dark, stumbling through firefights, his armour and the God-Emperor's grace saving him a dozen times over. But this was the end. The Wall loomed before him, the great barrier that separated Periculus from the hive. It was said that only Lady Wirepath knew the secret to piercing it, and she had disappeared before Canndis had even arrived. Claimed by Periculus.

Behind him came the screams and howls. Distant once, but closer now. But ahead there were also voices. He slowed, straining an ear. Not the shrieks and liturgies of violence. A conversation, albeit a heated one that made little sense.

'This is the only way.'

He recognised the man's voice, but could not place it.

'There is no way through,' a woman replied, her voice barely a whisper. 'The Wall is virtually impenetrable. We were lucky to discover the crack in the upper levels. But we cannot pass through. We must find another path.'

'We know it can be broken. Nothing is immutable.'

'Yes. By someone who knows how, or–'

She suddenly fell silent. Canndis frowned. Had they seen him? Impossible, and he had made no sound. Was it something else? Perhaps–

'Do not move.'

He glanced up. The Delaque was crouched on a ledge above him, little more than a shadow. The light gleamed from her flechette pistols, both aimed squarely at his heart.

'Put away your weapons. I am Palanite Captain Canndis,' he barked. He half expected her to kill him where he stood, but after a moment she lowered her pistols, tucking them seamlessly back into her longcoat.

'Apologies, captain,' she said, suddenly demure. 'These are strange times.'

'True enough.' He nodded. 'What are you up to? Trying to break out?'

'Something like that,' she said, a smile flashing on the right side of her face. 'But there is no means to–'

The blast of light near blinded him. The Delaque threw her hood over her face as the brightness intensified. He felt his hair rise on his arms, his teeth tingle. There was another violent pulse of light and the roar of thunder, before all was dark.

'Sol?' he heard the Delaque say, disappearing over the ruin blocking his path. He stumbled after her, struggling, his night vision stolen by the blast. She was bent low, her longcoat spread across the bone-gravel and blocking most of his view of the second figure. He could just make out a man on his knees, clutching his right hand with his left. Sparks of blue light danced between his fingers. The Delaque moved to one side, and Canndis saw the man's empty eye socket blaze with the same glow.

'What in the God-Emperor's name are you?' Canndis roared, brandishing his weapon.

The fallen man smiled through gritted teeth. He was clearly in pain.

'Lord Tempes Sol of the Mercator Lux,' he said. 'We met once before, captain. I claimed that Lord Pureburn was involved with something untoward and you asked for proof. I vowed to find it, but I fear I was too late.'

'And what is that?' Canndis asked, nodding to the light playing about his arm.

'Neurone circuits, mapped along my nervous system and my eye. It's advanced Guilder tek,' Sol replied, displaying his wrist and the thin metal slivers imbedded into the flesh. 'I was trying to find a weak spot, a way through the Wall.'

Canndis shook his head. 'Forget it, that stuff is stronger than adamantium. No idea what it is. I bet plenty would pay a tidy sum if anyone could figure out how to carve off a slice.'

'We have to get through. We have to find the–' Sol hesitated.

'Find what?' Canndis frowned. 'Get to who? What is happening?'

The Delaque sighed, stepping forward.

'Lord Silas Pureburn was secretly employing the skills of a pyromancer,' she said. 'That was the true source of his power. Somehow, it broke free, and it's causing all of this. We have been tracking the psyker, hoping to put an end to this before it is too late.'

She smiled, the expression reserved for one side of her face.

'A psyker?' he said, before turning to Sol. 'You're sure this Delaque is on the level?'

'On this I am,' Sol said. 'Believe me, I'm as surprised as you are.'

'Pureburn,' Canndis snarled. That smug old man, looking down on him, letting his patrolmen be murdered in plain sight, all the time harbouring an abomination.

His fingers tightened about his shock-baton.

'Suffer not the witch to live,' he murmured.

'Indeed.' The Delaque nodded. 'But we cannot kill her unless there is a path through.'

'Then it's over,' Canndis said. 'The Stolen Sons say they spent the better part of a day trying to melt their way in. But then Lady Wirepath used some device – apparently made their ears bleed, but it opened a crack. Barely.'

Sol frowned, the spark in his eye faltering like a dying candle.

The silence was broken by a hateful scream. Then a second. They were getting closer.

'We need to get out of here,' the Delaque said. 'Seek higher ground before they pin us down.'

'I ain't climbing far with this leg,' Canndis grunted.

The Delaque glanced to his hobbled ankle. 'Looks like you won't be running either. Sol?'

The Guilder was intent on the Wall, running his fingers along its matt-black surface.

'It's been tempered,' he murmured. 'I can feel it. Whatever this substance is, it was created *after* the Wall was built. Something transmuted it into this state. To keep something out. Or something in.'

'There is no time to speculate,' the Delaque said, pistols in hand. 'I can hear them. They are close.'

He didn't reply, pressing both hands to the wall, his shoulders tensed. Light shimmered about his fingers, but not as bright this time, less a flash-lumen and more a cutting torch.

Another shriek, loud enough to pick out the gutted remnants of words, accompanied by the muted thud of boots on bone-gravel.

'They are coming,' Canndis snarled, raising his shield to face the impending horde. 'The light is drawing them!'

'Sol, give up. You can't–'

There was a thunderclap, the force throwing Canndis forward, his shock-baton falling from his hand. Shards of glass-like metal pattered from his armour before rapidly collapsing into powder. He glanced over his shoulder. Sol was bent over, breath a shudder. But the Wall was split, pierced by a crack barely wide enough for a man. Beyond was darkness.

The Delaque darted forward, grasping Sol's arm and dragging him upright. Canndis lurched for the split in the wall, but it was too tight, his armour's bulk preventing his passage. The Delaque glanced up, training a pistol at his head.

'Step back or I end you!'

'I'm stuck!' he grunted, dropping his shock-baton and trying to force his way through. It was no use; the chest plate was too wide. With the yelling in the distance, there was no way he'd have time to remove it before they were upon them. He stepped back, defeated.

'I'm sorry, captain,' the Delaque sighed. 'But there is no time. We need to get through and conceal the entrance. And you need to run.'

'I can't,' he said, nodding to his leg. 'What part of that don't you get?'

She shrugged. 'The bit where it's my problem?'

'At least leave me a weapon,' he pleaded. 'My baton has no charge!'

Behind her, he saw Sol hesitate. He pushed past the Delaque, glancing down at Canndis' fallen shock-baton. He stooped to retrieve it, wincing in pain as his fingers closed around the handle. Canndis heard the weapon hum softly, as though awakening from slumber.

'There is always a reserve to tap,' Sol said, smiling weakly as he handed Canndis the weapon. 'I'm sorry, this is all I can give you. Hold the line, captain. Pureburn will pay for his crimes. I promise.'

They both vanished through the gap. He heard the scrape of metal as something was dragged over the other end.

He was alone, except for the screams, and the hunters at his heels.

'Milord!'

Pureburn's head snapped round at the cry. At the movement, his Pyromagir lurched forward, hissing steam menacingly from its jaw-plate as Tritus approached the throne. The Cawdor ignored the creature, dropping to his knees. His shoulders shook as he fought for control.

'What it is now?' Pureburn snarled, irritated at the

interruption. He had been engaged sanctifying the cell behind his throne, one of the Cynders assisting. It was challenging work. The dais was wreathed in smoke that tightened the throat and choked the lungs. But he'd made progress, crafting a vessel to complete the circuit. Then the Eternal Flame would blossom again, he was sure of it.

'Lies, milord. Lies and blasphemy!' Tritus thundered, as Pureburn returned to his work. 'We have broken through the slaves' lines. But there are whispers, my lord, plots and lies sent against you. They call you a monster, sir.'

'To the poor and weak, the rich and powerful will always be villains,' Pureburn murmured, wiping a bloodstained arm across his face as he scrutinised his bloodied work.

'They say you–'

Tritus choked on the words, clearly struggling.

Pureburn frowned, turning from the cell.

'Tell me, Tritus,' he said softly.

'They claim you traffic with foul magicks, milord,' Tritus said, each word a weight upon his tongue. 'They call you witch, claim your flames are hell-spawned. They say your works are tainted.'

Lord Pureburn regarded the man trembling before him, shoulders shaking in silent fury.

'And what say you?' he whispered.

'They lie!' Tritus snarled, meeting Pureburn's gaze. His mask was stained, the eyeholes marked by bloody tears. Strange, such a thing might once have troubled him, but he no longer knew why. For, behind his mask, Tritus regarded him with the eyes of a zealot, one who knew the truth in his heart and required no other proof.

His eyes were beautiful. Those of a servant of perfect loyalty.

'It won't stand, milord,' Tritus muttered. 'I've sent out

runners. Trusted soldiers. They'll bring word of what's happened here to the rest of House Cawdor. Once the thane
hears of these blasphemous words there will be no escape.
Periculus will be cleansed of heretics.'

He continued to babble, but Pureburn paid no heed. The
man was a servant, not an orator. But he served the cause,
and would do so in this life and beyond.

'Assist me, Tritus,' he said, offering his hand. 'Let me show
you my work.'

Tritus reached out, hesitant. Lord Pureburn raised him to
his feet, escorting him to the fallen dais.

'You see?' he said, nodding to the smoke-wreathed cell.

Tritus leant forward, struggling to see through the smog.

'Milord, I… what is this?'

'A realisation,' Pureburn replied, unable to hide his smile.
'I realised the organic component is a necessary cog in the
machine. The flames must be fed – then she will be restored.'

He nodded to the crimson-stained cell, the steaming flesh
and jagged bone, before glancing to Tritus.

'I thought He sought the impure, Tritus,' he said. 'Power
from the sacrifice of the unworthy. But that was foolish, I
see that now. Only the faithful can restore the flame. Only
those who embrace His light.'

Tritus' gaze flitted from the bloodied flesh to Lord Pureburn, desperate to understand. It was unsurprising, given his
minuscule intellect. But, despite this failing, there was no
doubt in his eyes, no hint of guile. Only faith.

Pureburn smiled back benevolently, his fingers closing
about the handle of his dagger.

8

Virae's eyes snapped open.

For a moment she wondered why she lay prone. She tried rising, but her leg was pinned. She grunted, straining against the weight and coughing a mouthful of dust and blood. Her head pounded, eyes aching as though fit to burst. She clawed rubble and blood from her face, and peered through the dust and smoke.

Something lay crumpled in the dark.

Elle.

Virae groaned, fingers scrabbling at the floor's rusted sheet metal as she tried to drag her leg clear. A sharp pain dug into her calf. She ignored it, grasping the grating with both hands. She took a deep breath and pulled, tearing herself free. Blood ran freely down her leg, but she ignored that too, crawling forward on hand and knee. She tried to call out, but her mouth was still choked by dust.

Elle's eyes were open, her body cradled about Virae's

shattered helm, hands and arms a bloody mess, breath shallow and fading. She should have been in agony, but when she met Virae's gaze the sweetest smile crossed her lips.

'I saved you,' she whispered. 'Unbroken, I did something right. I saved you.'

Virae shook her head, eyes brimming with tears as she sought words that would ease the girl's passage. She had none.

'Don't cry,' Elle murmured, trying to reach for her face with ruined fingers. 'It's all right. You did everything you could. There were... worse lives I could have lived.'

The light died in her eyes. But, obscenely, her lips continued to twitch, the damaged cogitator attempting to animate her.

Virae felt tears stain her cheeks. Dimly, she was aware of Rivv groaning on the far side of the room, but the sound was distant. She just kept staring at the dead girl. She'd promised she'd save her, give her a better life than a serf. Instead Elle had died in agony on a cold slab of metal deep beneath the hive.

Just like Block. Just like Gash. All condemned, just to line the pockets of a bitter old man.

She wiped her face again, frowning momentarily at streaks of blood left on her hand. Some small voice within wondered why her eyes were bleeding. But it was inaudible against the thud of her heart and the roar of her blood.

Beside Elle's body lay her fallen chainglaive.

The stranger was taller than Caleb, an effect exacerbated by his headdress. It would have looked comical: two dangling lengths of cloth adorned with tinkling bells, mounted above a stylish ivory mask concealing all but nose and mouth. But Caleb recognised the contempt in the man's swagger, the way his hand rested on the pommel of his blade. He was a noble, and a killer at that.

'Good day. I am Aramista Dae Catallus,' the nobleman said, stopping a dozen feet from Caleb and offering a mocking bow. 'I am here to claim the life of Caleb Cursebound.'

'Thank the God-Emperor,' Caleb breathed, gesturing to the forest of cable-vines. 'He went that way. If you hurry, you'll catch him. Can't miss him really – he's about eight feet tall, and his eyes burn like–'

The nobleman lunged forward, his blade singing. Caleb ducked as the weapon sheared the top from his mohawk. He rolled to his feet, pistol raised and aimed at the nobleman's chest.

'One warning,' he said. 'Back off.'

Aramista Dae Catallus did not reply, instead charging forward, rapier poised. Caleb fired, but as the bolt flashed the nobleman was gone, space seeming to fold around him. From the corner of his eye Caleb saw the blade thrusting from his left. He hurled himself aside, firing wildly. But the nobleman was gone again, reappearing several yards away, closer to the cable-vines. Their shadows had grown long, the light cycle slipping towards darkness.

'Good trick,' Caleb murmured.

'Displacer field.' Aramista smiled pleasantly, resting the blade against his shoulder.

'Seems cheap,' Caleb said. 'That's all right though. I can do cheap.'

At his words the flash bomb struck Aramista. Even through his photo-goggles, Caleb had to shield his face from the searing flash of light. But Aramista seemed unaffected, glancing to the smoking patch on his chest where the weapon had detonated. He raised his head, eyes hidden by the mask.

'I see,' he said. 'An attempt to blind your opponent to gain the advantage? Hardly seems sporting. Does that often work?'

'Fairly often,' Caleb said, retreating a step. From the edge of his vision he saw their captive emerge from the shelter. She wore a frown, surveying her surroundings, disturbed by something. That was a first.

'Ah, the primary target, I assume?' Aramista said. 'I'll collect her bounty once we are done.'

'Or we could make it really sporting?' Caleb offered. 'How about we settle this fist to fist?'

'I don't brawl like an animal,' Aramista replied, advancing. 'In truth, you should be honoured that I am willing to debase my blade with your mongrel blood.'

'Words can't express my gratitude.'

Aramista laughed, bringing his sword up in mocking salute before launching a devastating thrust. Caleb snatched his boot knife, deflecting the blow more through luck than skill. The second thrust was leisurely, Aramista either taking his time or feeling Caleb out. He barely avoided it, stumbling, trying to keep some distance between them. Even had his bladework been Aramista's equal, his opponent's reach would have made all the difference. The rapier flicked out and Caleb dodged again, the sword tearing a chunk from his greatcoat. An elbow hammered into his face and he fell, barely avoiding a slash that would have pierced his heart. Aramista was no longer playing.

'This is embarrassing,' he said as Caleb rose. 'I'd heard tell of a mighty warrior, a man who slayed the great Lord Harrow. Do you not claim the title of the underhive's ninth most dangerous man? Aren't you–'

He trailed off, distracted, his head tilted as though listening in on another voice. Caleb's gaze flicked to the shelter. Their captive was leaning against the doorway, her forearms resting on the frame, face hidden by her hands. She looked unsteady.

Aramista spoke suddenly.

'Please, sister, calm down,' he muttered, presumably into his vox. 'I will settle it. Be calm. You are not usually so easily shaken.'

He glanced at Caleb, shrugging almost apologetically.

'There is nothing out there... We will talk later,' he said, apparently switching off the vox and focusing on Caleb once more. 'Forgive the interruption – my sister does not appreciate the art of combat. She's a stickler for efficiency, would rather just shoot you in the head and be done with it.'

'Unlike you?'

'I think in any trade the personal touch is important. It helps with the brand.'

'Interesting,' Caleb said, edging towards the shelter. 'Perhaps we should grab a couple of shots of Wild Snake and discuss the matter in extensive detail?'

'A kind invitation,' Aramista replied. 'But I am now working against the clock.'

He darted forward. Caleb raised his pistol, firing. Aramista disappeared, his form folding into nothing, only to rematerialise a dozen strides to the left, as though emerging from shadow. His back was to Caleb but he turned seamlessly, barely breaking his stride. A second shot saw him reappear a scant foot away. Caleb ducked a strike, leaping back, feeling heat on the back of his neck from the captive's presence.

Aramista launched a blistering attack. Caleb barely deflected it, the impact jarring his knife from his hand. He fired another shot, the nobleman reappearing a yard to the right. There seemed little discernible pattern to the jumps;

Aramista recovered rapidly but did not appear to choose his destination, otherwise the fight would already be over.

The blade again. It seemed to be everywhere. Caleb leapt back, gritting his teeth as the heat washed over him. He could smell hair singeing on his arm. He risked a glance. The captive was intent on Aramista, her flawless face stretched in an expression of abject horror.

There was no time to think of it. Aramista was on him, blade gleaming in the dying light. Caleb dropped to a knee, unleashing a last volley. The nobleman flickered in and out of existence as he raced closer. As he thrust, Caleb twisted from the blade's path, firing point-blank into the soulless mask. Aramista faded like smoke, materialising behind Caleb, poised to deliver a coup de grace.

Instead he screamed as his finery was engulfed by a sudden inferno. The blade tumbled from his fingers and he threw himself to the ground, desperate to beat out the flames. The captive had also collapsed, hands clutched to her head, but Caleb could not attend to her. Aramista was already rising, his shaking fingers reaching for the knife at his hip.

Caleb tackled him. The two fell sprawling, tumbling through the dirt, Caleb emerging on top.

'Not so tough now, are you?' he snarled, smashing his fist into the masked face. 'Not without all your fancy tricks. Not when you fight like a mongrel!'

Aramista retaliated, a glancing blow that bruised Caleb's cheek. He ignored it, striking again and again at the smug, silvered mask, ignoring the pain in his hands. He felt something pop beneath the metal. It did not slow him.

Iktomi shrieked. A wordless, guttural sound. He had not seen her emerge from the shelter, but the sound reached him through the red haze. He seized Aramista's collar, throwing himself to one side and using the semiconscious nobleman as a shield. As he rolled, a shot skimmed his shoulder.

It must have come from the trees. The sister – she was out there.

Aramista was stirring. Caleb rolled away from him, snatching his knife from the ground and backing as close to the captive as he dared, in the hopes she could shield him. The girl was bent double on hands and knees, her white robes billowing about her, as though caught by an unseen wind. Iktomi seemed intent on her, though her face was so bloodied he could not tell if her eyes were open or closed.

'I think you were right about us being hunted,' Caleb conceded, trying to keep a tremble from his voice. 'But there were only two of them. We're all right.'

Iktomi did not reply. But her head turned towards the cable-vines. She murmured something, the words lost in a guttural snarl. Aramista had found his knee, mask torn clear, face bloodied beneath. He might have been handsome once; it was hard to tell now.

'How dare you?' he said, stooping to retrieve his blade, his eyes blazing with fury. 'How dare a miserable piece of hive trash lay his filthy hands upon–'

Caleb held up a flash bomb. Aramista was suddenly silent.

'I'm guessing this might be more problematic without your mask?' Caleb said. 'How good do you fight blind?'

'You can barely stand,' Aramista spat in retaliation.

'Maybe, maybe not.' Caleb smiled. 'But I still beat you. Would have finished you too if your backup hadn't weighed in. Is this how it works? You issue your little challenge, knowing that if things don't go your way a sniper's bullet is always an option?'

'I don't need her help to deal with you.'

'I think you just did.'

'You are trying to bait me,' Aramista replied. 'I do not know how you pulled that trick, disrupting my displacer field, but this ends now. Sister dear? Kill them.'

Caleb scanned the cable-vines, but even with his photo-goggles it was too dark to make anything out. The lumen-rig above barely glimmered, the light almost gone.

They all heard the shot. Caleb flinched, but no bullet struck.

Another shot. But not a rifle this time. Pistol rounds.

Aramista frowned, turning his head a fraction. 'Sister?'

A woman burst from the forest, sprinting, a long rifle slung over her shoulders. She held a pistol, firing blind at the shapes emerging from the cable-vines behind her. They ran bent double, loping on all fours. Two fell to well-placed headshots, but a dozen more followed, and more still after that – a tide of pallid skin and bloody maws.

Aramista didn't hesitate, turning his back to Caleb and sprinting towards his sister, the bounty seemingly forgotten. The woman was veering from the shelter, sprinting towards the right side of the clearing.

More creatures were emerging from the shadows before her, but Caleb did not see what happened next. The horde were racing towards them, devouring the distance to the shelter. Their captive was still prone, fingers digging into dirt. It was bubbling at her touch. Her head snapped up, her eyes blazing like a blast furnace, the air shimmering about her.

He glanced to the shelter. There was no way to secure the door in time. His gaze then shifted to Iktomi. Her face was a bloody mess. He could not even tell if she knew what was happening.

But the grapnel-launcher was still slung about her waist.

He raced to her, ignoring the low growl as he wrapped his arm around her, his fingers struggling with the grapnel's trigger. He could hear the snarls drawing closer, the sounds horribly close to human.

Suddenly it fired, a cable spiralling upwards, finding purchase on the frayed struts jutting from the shelter. As they were drawn up he felt clawed fingers snatching at his boots, but they were hauled clear, landing hard on the roof.

He glanced back just in time to see a blast of flame arcing spire-wards.

She lurched into the shelter, staggering. She knew not where she was. Something had felt off since her removal from the palanquin, but she had ignored it, relishing her freedom. But that was before the fool with the blade had torn the material world apart. He did not understand the tool he used, and was heedless of the damage it inflicted on the veil. The beyond bled through, and it bled through her.

One of the eyeless things lurched for her, but its flesh was scourged from its bones. Not that she chose its death. She had no choice any more; she could not control the power spilling through and from her. It lashed at the external doors, sealing them against the horde.

It was not supposed to be this way. He was to take her where she could be fixed, made whole. And she had found it, the lost garden. It was supposed to make her better.

There had to be something.

She grasped the internal door that once resisted her touch, channelling her power, burning the corrosion away in moments. The metal beneath proved more resistant, but power was everywhere now. She redoubled her efforts, drawing upon the maligned energy. Slowly, droplets of metal slag began to trickle from her fingers.

9

Beyond the Wall was darkness.

Sol had expected the break to lead them into the wider underhive, but instead they seemed to have passed through an interior wall into an unlit structure beyond. Anguis appeared unconcerned, her optical implants capable of piercing the deepest shadows, whilst he was left stumbling behind her. He tried to summon a spark of light, but there was nothing left, the muscles in his arm throbbing from exertion. He had only the barest impression of his surroundings. It smelt stale and decayed. He ran his hand along the nearest surface, the outer layers crumbling at his touch. Rust. Centuries worth.

'Where are we?' he asked, addressing the shadow that was Anguis. 'Tell me what you see.'

'Nothing,' she replied. 'An old facility. No idea as to its original function. You led us here – what can you see?'

'Nothing,' he murmured. There was only darkness. Either

the other-light could not penetrate the facility, or he could no longer perceive it.

'Pity,' she sighed. 'Perhaps we need to… oh.'

'What?'

'There is a body. Two, in fact.'

'How long dead?'

'I'm not sure,' she murmured. 'Recent. Days perhaps? Less than a lunar cycle.'

'Any idea what killed them?'

'No,' she said. 'Though I think one of them is your kind.'

There was the flash of a glow-rod. By its halo he saw Anguis crouched by the bodies. Their backs were propped against the wall, heads bowed as though at rest.

'See if you can identify them,' she said, laying the glow-rod beside the corpses. 'I will search for a way out.'

He approached gingerly. He did not know the woman or her servant, though she had the look of a Guilder, her bodice adorned with gems of pure melerithyst, her cloak comprised of chain-linked keys. Her badge of office hung about her neck, her name inscribed in Guilder-tongue.

Lady Belata Wirepath of the Guild of Coin.

He saw no obvious wound or sign of attacker.

'It seems we have solved the mystery of the disappearing colonist,' he murmured, raising his head. Anguis was visible in the room's corner, lit not by the glow-rod but the flicker of a data-terminal. She seemed absorbed by the information, her fingers expertly navigating the console.

He frowned, unable to recall a time she had not heard him. House Delaque, after all, placed great value on eavesdropping.

He remained silent a moment, watching her dissect the data-stream.

'Anguis?' he said, raising his voice. 'What have you found?'

She stiffened. Her fingers slowed, now haphazardly tapping the keys, as though unfamiliar with their function.

'Not much,' she murmured without looking round. 'I was hoping to restore a semblance of power, but the cogitator has slept too long and does not wish to be woken.'

She seemed to flicker as she spoke. Perhaps it was an optical effect caused by the display.

'I see no wounds on our Guilders,' Sol murmured, watching Anguis from the corner of his eye. 'Perhaps they became trapped in here? Starved?'

'Perhaps.'

'Presumably, if they found a way in, there must be a way out?'

'Agreed. I suggest you search for it whilst I try to rouse the cogitator.'

She still had not turned. Her fingers were dancing again.

'Seems a poor use of our skills,' he ventured. 'You're more likely to spot an exit, and I should have better luck restoring power.'

No response. Just the click of keys.

'Anguis?'

'A moment,' she murmured. From over her shoulder he saw reams of data flash across the terminal: alchemic equations he could not follow, blueprints and manuals for unknown machines.

He rose, approaching the console, all the while her fingers moving faster, the display a blur. He was close enough to touch her when suddenly it went dark, rebooting, a single flickering pixel-gram inviting him to input his access privileges.

'Damn,' she said, glancing to him. 'I appear to have locked us out.'

She seemed to flicker as she spoke.

'Careless of you.'

'I'm tired,' she said with a shrug. 'Let us keep searching. No point wasting more time here.'

'I wish to try,' Sol replied. 'You look for a way out.'

'Of course,' she said, rising as he took her seat at the console. It was vaguely familiar, a layout he had seen if not used. He tapped a few pixel-grams, but the display seemed reluctant to respond.

'Only one door. Rusted to slag,' Anguis called from behind him. 'Nothing I carry could open it.'

He nodded, still intent on the screen. Though she could move near silently, he had the distinct impression she was standing just behind him, watching. He resisted the urge to turn his head.

'There is still the way we entered,' she said. 'But if Pureburn's followers find it we will be trapped. Perhaps we should retreat?'

He did not reply, raising his hand and pressing it to the data-display, fingers tingling at the static charge.

'Sol? Help me move this. I think we need a barricade.'

The screen flickered, the display shifting. A symbol flashed on screen, a doubled-bladed knife bathed in flames. He'd seen it before. Somewhere.

There was an ear-splitting crash behind him. He spun in the chair to find Anguis beside a broken shelf, its contents strewn about the floor.

'Apologies,' she said, tucking something into her longcoat. 'Clumsy of me. However, I have stumbled across an exit.'

She held out a glow-rod. By its light he saw a maintenance ladder, and above that the faint etching of a long-sealed access port.

* * *

Canndis had quit trying to run. There was no point, not once he realised the swarm was ahead of him. He'd tried to cut across, sneak through their lines, but the corridor he'd chosen, a crevice between two ruined hab-blocks, ended in a still smoking pile of rubble. They were close, snapping at his heels. It seemed he could no longer pick the place of his death. Only the method.

He still had his stubber, one round in the chamber.

Part of him wanted to do it just out of spite, to render the chase futile. But some would call it cowardice. That alone stayed his hand. He would not cower before the scum of Cawdor. He would go down like his patrolmen, weapon in hand and a curse on his lips.

He glanced over his shoulder. They were gathering at the passage's end. No hurry now; they could take him at their leisure. It was funny, of all the Houses they were in some ways his favourite. Their crimes tended to be big and obvious. There was little need for detective work when a fanatic with a flamer stood next to a smouldering corpse, ranting about how all sinners must burn. Few put up a fight, and once they'd exhausted the initial fervour, relished the opportunity to be punished for their sins, welcoming death as a chance to become one with the God-Emperor.

He missed those simple days.

Canndis turned to face his pursuers, riot shield in hand, shock-baton humming. It usually carried enough charge for six blows. Of course, that was with a normal charge. He doubted the Guilder had been able to provide even half of that.

They were drawing closer, the alley swollen with cracked masks and dull blades. But he recognised the scrawny figure at their head, even behind his mask.

Gladshiv.

'There you are, captain,' Gladshiv said, and Canndis could hear the grin in his voice. 'Are you starting to regret your lack of faith?'

'My faith is in order. In law!' Canndis snarled. 'You are all guilty of crimes against Lord Helmawr, the man appointed by the God-Emperor Himself to rule this planet in His stead. Surrender now, and perhaps your lives can be spared.'

'Blasphemer! Heretic!' Gladshiv roared, stabbing an accusing finger at the Enforcer-captain. 'Helmawr is no ruler. He is the worst heretic of all! Under his watch the sinners rise to power whilst the righteous are left persecuted and destitute.'

'Being poor and gullible doesn't make you righteous,' Canndis spat, his gaze flicking through the swarm. They were twitching, knives bared like fangs. Gladshiv wanted to gloat. The rest desired only blood.

He tightened his grip on the shock-baton, barely listening as Gladshiv babbled about oppression and faith. He wagered the hunched figure on the left would be first to charge. But a trio broke ranks as one. Canndis braced himself as they surged forward. His back leg was no good, his arm already aching. But he would take at least one of them with him.

The lead figure leapt to meet him, his cracked mask revealing a pale face stained with blood, its teeth bared like a dog. Canndis swung the shock-baton, putting what little he had left into the blow. As it struck, lightning flared, engulfing the weapon in a nimbus of energy. The blast hurled the snarling attacker twenty feet into the air. His body crashed to the ground, his head joining it a few moments later, whilst the other two attackers convulsed before him, smoke seeping from their lips before they were still.

Canndis glanced in disbelief from the devastation at his

feet to the crackling head of his shock-baton. If anything, it was even brighter than before.

He grinned. Gladshiv was silent. Around him, the Cawdors chittered uncertainly.

'For Helmawr!' Canndis roared, raising his weapon and breaking into a stumbling run.

Caleb lashed out as the pale, eyeless creature clambered onto the roof, his boot connecting with its fanged jaw. Its head snapped back, the force sending it tumbling into the arms of its fellows.

A second was scrabbling at the edge, nails scoring the metal. He stamped hard on its fingers, sending it tumbling, his gaze sweeping the roof. He did not think the beasts could jump high enough to reach, but when enough pressed together they could create a sort of ramp, allowing another to ascend on their backs. So far, it seemed to be happenstance. But if a couple of them were bright enough to make the connection he would be finished.

He needed Iktomi.

She was sitting at the roof's centre. He'd cut her restraints, but she no longer responded, head lolling on her shoulders. He'd tried begging, yelling at her, even removing his headband and placing it about her forehead. But nothing roused her. In the end he'd circled her with the last of his glow-rods. The creatures seemed repelled by light, but the rods were fading, sufficient to hinder but not stop them.

And there were so many.

They encircled the shelter, and he could not shake the sense that more were still emerging from the dark. Drawn to them. Or, more likely, drawn to his former captive. He knew she was still alive. He could feel it through his boots.

The roof was barely warm, but it had been cold an hour ago. There was no way off. They were surrounded on three sides, and the wall of black metal at the rear was as impregnable as Periculus. He'd found an access hatch further along the building, but the rust had sealed it shut, and he had no krak grenades left.

'Need some help here,' he murmured, glancing to Iktomi. 'You better snap out of this on your own. Don't expect me to start talking about feelings and gak. Nobody wants that.'

There was a scratching to his left. He turned, blade extended, wishing his laspistol still had charge. A pair of creatures were hauling themselves up. One was naked, the other clad in a scrap of cloth and, strangely, a cracked mask. Both bared their fangs, edging round him, one at each side.

He leapt at the first, taking it off guard, his blade piercing its throat. But the second was on him, talons scoring his shoulder. He connected with a glancing blow as it brought him down, teeth snapping for his throat as they rolled across the roof. He heard the pop of implosive charges and saw a flash of smoke, but knew not the source. The creature's face was inches from his own, its eye sockets staring down at him, maw snapping like a servo claw.

'Down!'

The voice was barely a whisper, but somehow he heard it, ducking. The creature's flesh was suddenly torn apart, as though sliced by a thousand razors. He turned to see a figure emerging from the ruined access hatch, her longcoat stained with blood, a flechette pistol held in each hand. Both were trained on him.

'Hello,' he said. 'Listen, I would like to surrender to literally anyone who–'

Her hand snapped up, spraying a burst of needle-like

shards over his head. He glanced round just in time to watch another creature tumble from the roof.

'Thank you,' he said, turning back as a second figure emerged from behind her. His face was bloodied, one eye an empty socket. It took Caleb a second to recognise him.

'Sol?'

10

Sorrow watched the detonations tear through the slave-block. Around him, Pureburn's court roared in approval at each explosion, as though they were enjoying fireworks on the festival of Sanguinala. Certainly, they were enjoying a repast, though to Sorrow's culinary eye the preparation left something to be desired. For one thing he could still make out toenails.

The explosions were focused on the three fortified gateways. Each, of course, was connected to one of three walkways that suspended the bottomless hab-block above the bone-gravel. The only thing keeping hundreds of tons of rockcrete suspended above them.

Pureburn was going to kill them all.

His followers had already breached one of the gates. From there, they could have taken the slave-block level by level. But they persisted in attacking all entrances, determined to tear down any obstacle and kill all who opposed them. Swarms of bomb-rats had been driven into the confines of the block. Who knew where they would end up before detonating? Though they were not situated directly beneath the block, its fall would tear Periculus open, causing further quakes, perhaps sending it plunging even deeper into the hive bottom.

'Something troubles you, Lord Sorrow?'

He flinched, forcing a bright smile before glancing to Lord Pureburn. He sat at his fallen throne, Pyromagir bodyguard beside him.

'My lord?'

'You seemed troubled by the fireworks?'

'Not exactly troubled. I just fear that in their zealousness your followers may end up slaughtering most of the slaves.'

'They chose their lot,' Pureburn said. 'They could have embraced righteousness. I shed no tears – my followers are legion. They are not needed.'

'Very true, my lord.' Sorrow nodded. 'I do wonder whether there is a risk of damaging Periculus further, should the hab-block collapse?'

Lord Pureburn laughed, the sound a foul hiss, like leaking air escaping from a pressure line.

'I am the only power that matters in Periculus. Nothing will fall or stand without my permission.'

'A great comfort, my lord,' Sorrow murmured. His fingers kept straying towards his signet ring. The temptation to use it was growing. It would be simple enough to incinerate the demented old fool. Of course, there was a distinct possibility Sorrow would then be torn apart by his deranged pack of sycophants. Still, there was probably an equal chance he could assume Pureburn's place on the throne without most of them realising.

Except the Pyromagir.

Whatever madness had infected the dome, the hulking

creature seemed immune. The alterations made by the Pureburn clan had rendered it barely human, untouched by the madness.

Perhaps he should kill it first. Then the rest of them.

No.

He took a deep breath, fighting for calm. His eye itched, but he resisted the urge to scratch it. He didn't want his fingers to come away bloodied. He didn't want to become one of them. It started with the eyes, that was obvious. But it did not end there. They were changing. It was slow for some; they were still clad in their House's vestments, though now torn and bloodied.

But others.

They crept through the shadows on all fours, like beasts, masks cracked, robes mere scraps. One sat hunched by Pureburn's throne, sinking half-rotted teeth into a charred lump of flesh. As Sorrow watched, it raised its head, sniffing like a dog. It growled, and it was not alone in its displeasure. A ripple of dissatisfaction was spreading through the rest of the court, though Sorrow was unsure of the cause. Not until he realised the explosions had ceased.

He glanced up. Smoke still emanated from the slave-block, but it had fallen silent, at least for now.

Pureburn glared at him.

'Where is the Keeper of Vermin?' he snarled. 'Finish them! Bring it all down!'

'My lord, I know of no vermin keeper,' Sorrow replied.

The Pyrocaen Lord just stared at him, his bloody eyes unseeing. He did not seem to hear the words.

'Bring him to me!'

'My lord, I am Lord Credence Sorrow of the Mercator Pallidus. I do not train rats.'

But it did not matter what he said. Pureburn's fury demanded an outlet, clouding whatever reason remained. The creature by his foot turned its head, regarding Sorrow from eyes that were now little more than bloodied sockets.

It was over, he thought, feeling the weight of the ring on his finger. Still, at least he would have the satisfaction of killing–

The head tumbled by their feet.

All stared at it. The decapitation had not been clean, the neck frayed and torn. The mask indicated its wearer was once of House Cawdor. The stains of rat urine suggested that the errant vermin keeper had been located.

'Pureburn!'

The voice was thunder. As one, they turned to the woman advancing through the smoke, her armour battered and torn, a broken helm slung at her waist. She favoured her left leg, and bled from a score of wounds, her greying hair stained crimson. But her face was fury manifest, eyes bloodshot and mouth a bitter line.

Pureburn rose as she drew closer, a sadistic smile swelling on his face.

'Virae the Unbroken,' he said as she halted before his throne. 'You finally muster the courage to emerge from your hiding hole and face me.'

'Took some time – had to carve a path,' she spat.

'I once swore I'd see you in chains if we met again,' he said. 'But I've reconsidered. Instead, I am going to torture you. Perhaps snip off an ear, then maybe a limb, until all that remains is a blinded, crippled thing that lacks even the tongue to beg for death.'

As he spoke the court drew in around her like a noose, cutting off any escape, whilst Pureburn's Cynders formed a protective screen between the Guilders. Virae slowly turned, taking in the horde. The flames caught her face and Sorrow saw that madness had found her, bloody tears running down her cheeks.

Still, there was steel in her eyes, her rage a cold, hard thing, sharp as Fenrisian ice. Slowly, she raised her weapon, the tip of the chainglaive pointed towards Pureburn.

'I am here to issue a challenge.'

Pureburn frowned, his anger momentarily giving way to confusion.

'Challenge?' He laughed. 'On what grounds? Do you still dispute the contract you signed?'

'No,' she said. 'I challenge you to face me in the arena. I challenge you in the God-Emperor's name.'

Pureburn laughed again, his court joining him, though to Sorrow's ear they sounded more like a braying pack of waste-dogs.

'Why would I entertain such a challenge?' Pureburn said, his Pyromagir stepping forward, brazier-arm raised.

'Because you gave your word.'

It was not Virae who spoke. Instead, all eyes turned to Lord Sorrow. It took him a moment to realise the words had come from his mouth. A sliver of consciousness, observing from a deeply entrenched corner of his mind, marvelled at the audacity inspired by the madness. The rest of him silently screamed in terror. He had seconds before Pureburn's surprise became violence.

'Forgive me, my lord,' he continued with a deep bow. 'But did you not state that you sanctified the arena in the name of the God-Emperor? That all combat took place under His ever-watchful eye, and all challenges were in His name? You said a serf could challenge a Chain Lord if they wished. It would appear instead that a Chain Lord is challenging you.'

Pureburn stared at him, eyes hooded and hidden by blood. Sorrow knew he was unsure. The challenge could have been deflected by art and artifice, but Pureburn only ruled now because he had ruled then, because the pack recognised him as alpha. None had thought to challenge this hierarchy. Not until this moment, anyway.

'Ridiculous,' Pureburn snapped. 'This is not the arena.'

'Yet there is corpse-ash beneath our feet,' Sorrow murmured. 'And we bathe in the light of His Eternal Flame. Do you claim the God-Emperor is not watching, even here?'

'Silence!' Pureburn snarled. 'Her first, then him. Kill them!'

But the court hesitated.

It was one of the Cynders that stepped forward, blade raised. Virae met him, her chainglaive a blur. As his blood stained the corpse-ash and his body crumpled she stepped forward, meeting Lord Pureburn's gaze.

'I say again, I challenge you in the God-Emperor's name,' she whispered. 'Do you refuse Him?'

'Who are you to invoke His name?' Pureburn snarled. But there had been a shift amongst his followers. Few would see it, but Sorrow knew how the body betrayed intent; a tilt of head or shuffled foot could say much. They did not stand with Virae, but it seemed not all stood with Pureburn either. His rule depended on strength. Despite his madness, the old man could sense it. He slowed, considering.

'Very well,' he said with a smile. 'We could do with some sport. I see you have your glaive. Tell me, how long have you carried that weapon?'

'Since the arena. My first fight.'

'Does it have a name? A personality? A rich, exciting story?'

'No.'

'Good,' Pureburn said. 'Such sentimentality is nauseating.

Well, I, like you, have a weapon. And, like you, it does not require a name or personality. It just kills.'

He raised his hand and the lumbering Pyromagir stepped forward, squaring up to Virae. It stood at least a foot taller than her, its shoulders twice as broad. Steam hissed from its face-grate, burning promethium dripping from the brazier mounted on its arm.

Virae glanced from the monstrosity to Lord Pureburn.

'We do not allow such weapons in the arena.'

The old man smiled, settling back in his throne as his court formed a wide circle around the fighters.

'This is my world and my arena,' he said, raising his hand. 'In the God-Emperor's name, begin!'

'This psyker is going to explode?' Caleb said, resting his head in his hands. 'Just to be clear – she will explode?'

The Delaque known as Anguis shrugged. 'Perhaps. Physically or metaphysically. The power is building beyond control. Either way, all of us will be dead, or wish we were.'

'Great,' Caleb said, glancing to Sol. The Guilder had said little. He was intent on the darkness beyond the glow-rods' halo. Where the eyeless things waited.

'But if I can get close then, with Sol's help, I should be able to neutralise her. But we have to get inside before she goes critical.'

'You came from inside,' Caleb replied, nodding to the hatch. 'I vote that way.'

'Do you have a meltagun?' Anguis asked. 'Because, otherwise, there is no way through.'

'So your plan is to try the front door?' Caleb replied, nodding to the shadows. 'Good luck with that.'

'From what you said, it's barely standing. One krak grenade should be enough.'

'That's not the part of the plan I'm questioning,' Caleb muttered, glancing to Sol. 'And what are you so obsessed with? This can't be your first horde of eyeless blood-drenched cannibals.'

'It's… there's a tear.'

Caleb frowned. 'What, to the shelter? The door?'

'Everything,' Sol murmured. 'There's… it's like someone has taken a knife to a canvas, but then smoothed the two pieces back together. You would not see it from a glance, but the damage is there. All it needs is someone to peel it back, let the other-light bleed through.'

Anguis glared at him. 'Don't think that way. Your focus is clearing a path.'

'I used up my power breaching the Wall. I don't have enough to stop more than a handful. Not unless I pull back the tear…'

'Do not do that.'

'You wouldn't say that if you could see it,' he whispered. 'It's like the sun behind an ash cloud.'

'Only saw the sun once,' Caleb said. 'From what I recall, looking directly at it was a bad idea. And visiting it a worse one.'

Anguis nodded. 'Yes. Listen to the idiot.'

'Do you have an alternative?' Sol frowned, his right eye blazing. 'Can you think of another way of holding them off long enough to get inside?'

'How long?'

They both turned to Caleb. He had unsheathed his knife and was tucking the spluttering glow-rods into his longcoat.

'How long do you need?' he said.

'I don't know,' Anguis replied. 'Long enough to get to her. Once close, her light should repel them. A few minutes?'

'And this is our only chance?'

She smiled, though only half her face moved. 'Chance is a strong word. But it would not guarantee our deaths, which is an improvement on the current situation.'

'Good odds then,' Caleb said, reaching for his fallen laspistol, before remembering it had no charge.

He glanced to Anguis. 'I'm out. Do you have a gun? I might not give it back.'

Sol approached him, retrieving the fallen laspistol and unclipping the power pack. He cradled the device in his hands, blowing on it, as though coaxing a fire to life. The ammo sensor flashed green.

'You Guilders scare me.' Caleb frowned as Sol returned the weapon. He glanced to Anguis. 'Any spare flash grenades? They don't like light.'

'All out.'

'It's fine, I have three left.' Caleb sighed. 'Listen, I can't promise anything. I might last seconds. I'm not really... this is more her area.'

He nodded to Iktomi. She was still slumped, like a puppet without strings.

'I'm going to die now,' Caleb called to her. 'Thought you might like to know.'

No response.

'It's just that you had that oath. Something about protecting me? Remember that?'

Nothing.

'I'm not saying it,' he warned, turning his back on her and glancing to Sol and Anguis. 'When I jump, make for the door. I'll make a break for it, try to cause as much distraction as possible. You will only...'

He trailed off, gaze flicking over his shoulder to the fallen ratskin.

'Just go when I go,' he murmured, turning towards her. She did not react as he drew near, her head still bowed, face marred with dried blood. He retrieved a stained handkerchief from his longcoat, lifting her chin and wiping some of the red from her cheeks. Her eyes were still closed, breath short and ragged.

'Well, if this doesn't work, we will both be dead anyway,' he said. 'So, seeing as how it is a bit like the end of the world, and our last chance to lay cards on the table... Well, if we die, perhaps we can meet on the other side?'

He rested his forehead against hers, forcing back a tear. She smelt awful, like an abattoir. He took a deep breath, cupping her chin with his hand, brought his fist back, and punched her in the face as hard as he could.

The blow sent her tumbling but he was already running, sprinting for the roof's edge and the waiting jaws of the eyeless monsters.

Behind him, he heard a low growl.

And footsteps. Running.

11

Virae avoided the Pyromagir's talon, her chainglaive biting into the creature's abdomen. It drew little blood, and what did flow was a deep purple and thick as wax.

The Pyromagir raised the brazier, belching a stream of flames. She ducked beneath it, the burning promethium clinging to her shoulderguard. But there was no time to smother the flames. The claws lashed out again, wreathed in the blueish haze of a disrupter field. She parried with her blade, throwing a shower of sparks as the field tore into the weapon's haft. She was lucky to escape with that; formidable as the chainglaive was, a direct hit from the Pyromagir's claws would simply split it open, slicing between the molecular bonds.

She sidestepped the next strike, spinning on her heel and bringing her weapon round in a decapitating blow. It bit deep into the Pyromagir's neck before slowing, struggling to chew through the steel cables underlying its flesh. The creature knocked the weapon aside with the back of its hand, wax-like blood staining its shoulder, its brazier aimed directly at her face.

Her elbow hammered into the creature's forearm, the spiked guard driving into its flesh. It did not bite deep, but she must have struck something, for there was no spark of ignition, the weapon spluttering promethium but nothing else. The Pyromagir glanced at its arm, puzzled. She took the opening, bringing the glaive round in a savage strike, aiming for the torn flesh of its neck.

The claws lashed out, severing the chainglaive just below the head.

The whirling blade spun through the air and struck the corpse-ash, falling silent. Virae barely hesitated, plunging the broken haft of the weapon into the Pyromagir's midriff. It did not even flinch, its brazier hand smashing into her chest plate, launching her into the air. She smashed into the congregation, scattering them. Her vision was clouded, but she could make out Pureburn smiling in triumph, the wretched Lord Sorrow standing beside him, head hung. No doubt he would be next.

The cybernetic monstrosity was advancing stiffly, dragging its heels as it loomed over her, its taloned hand twitching as it raised its claws.

She had damaged it then. Just not enough.

Anguis took the lead, flechette pistol in hand, her ocular implants navigating the darkness easily.

Sol followed. His eye was useless but it did not matter; the other-light was stronger here. It softly radiated from Anguis, so the black of her longcoat was somehow bright against the shadows. It tarnished each footstep left by their quarry, and the metal warped and blackened by her passage. But, strangely, what shone brightest was something in Anguis' inner pocket. Whatever it was seemed to writhe, as though desperate to escape its confinement. The other-light was drawn to it, like corpse-moths to an open flame.

The further they pressed, the brighter it grew, the other-light around almost agitated by its presence. Or excited – but neither made sense. Energy was dispassionate, despite Pureburn's claims. It did not have agency. It followed laws of conduction and dissipation. Fire did not choose its path. Lightning did not strike with intent. That was true. It had to be true.

Except the other-light discriminated. Even now, an unfelt wind drew it into a channel between him and Anguis. It lapped at his fingers, as though urging him to strike. It would be so easy to reach out and remove her. Almost easier than staying his hand...

'We are close,' she whispered. 'Though from Caleb's words I don't know what we will find.'

'But you can stop her?'

'Maybe. With your help,' she said, glancing at him. 'How do you feel?'

'Dangerous.'

'Hold on to that, for we are close,' she whispered. 'Just save the danger for her.'

She was right. Ahead lay an intersection. As they approached, he heard a scream like a lead furnace, and a backdraught of flames erupted along the corridor.

Except they were not true flames. He could see beyond the mimicked form. The other-light might appear as fire, but it was closer to fear and anger made manifest, its given form a cloak. For the flames hungered, desperate to consume and propagate. He saw it. He saw all.

'Anguis,' he murmured, but she bolted round the corridor, raising her flechette pistols and unleashing them on full auto. It felt like she moved in slow motion; he could almost see the needle-like slivers liquify in the air as a second rush of heat engulfed them. Anguis barely darted aside in time, the blast catching the train of her longcoat. She tore it off, stamping out the flames.

'No good,' she said. 'She's about halfway up the passage. She looks immobile, but I can't even get close. No bullet or lasblast can penetrate that inferno.'

'Then what?' Sol asked. 'Don't you have some anti-spyker tek?'

'Not exactly,' she said, reaching into her longcoat. Her hand emerged clutching an ornate needle pistol. Within its ammo chamber, a crystallised neurotoxin glimmered purple. The other-light clawed at it, as though desperate for the weapon's contents.

'This gives us a chance, albeit slim,' she said. 'She is drawing energy, but if we can re-channel enough of it she might weaken enough for me to finish it.'

'How?'

She looked at him. 'How else? You syphon the energy, just like you did with the storm clouds.'

'No,' he said, stepping back. 'I don't understand any of this, but I know I was wrong. This is not the Motive Force I sought. It is not rational. It does not unify anything. It mimics and lies and hungers. It's malignant. I cannot just syphon it like a stray storm cloud.'

'Then we shall die,' she said simply.

He swore. 'Can you even tell me what I am supposed to do?'

'No. Trust your instincts,' she said. 'We just need to get a little closer. I'll be right behind you, ready.'

He crept forward, back pressed to the wall. It was hot to the touch. Ahead lay the intersection, the heat radiating from his left.

'Now what?' he asked.

'Can you feel it? The energy flowing through her?'

'Yes. I feel it.'

'Hold it close, let it flow through you. Just a little. Taste it. Know it.'

He closed his eyes, breathing slow. He let the heat envelop him, soak into his skin, till the fire found veins. Sparks danced between his fingertips, etched in crimson.

'Do you have it?' she asked.

His eyes opened, the right shining like a star.

'Yes,' he said. 'I have it. Now what?'

'This,' she said, stabbing the needle pistol into his throat, and she thrust him into the inferno.

Caleb slashed with his knife, firing wildly from the laspistol, each blazing bolt briefly revealing a horde of mouths and claws. The light disorientated but did not stop them, the glow-rods tucked into his long coat ever fading. He had no idea if Sol and Anguis had made it. He just kept running, for behind him came the snap of bone and spurt of blood. He glanced back, just in time to see Iktomi's blade tearing through the sightless beasts.

His distraction cost him. One of them pounced, pinning him, claws grasping at his flesh. He set off the final flash-bang, illuminating the scene for an instant. The creature howled, clutching at its eyeless face. His knife opened its jugular, but more were closing, stumbling but unbowed. He fired the pistol, but a clawed hand seized his wrist as fangs sought his throat.

A strand of silver wire caught the creature's wrist. It tightened, severing the hand, a boot simultaneously shattering the creature's mouth. Iktomi's knife took another even as one lunged for her back. He tried to scream a warning, but she had already ducked, seizing the creature's jaws. She twisted, tearing its head clear, and for a moment her gaze met his. Her face was stained crimson, but her eyes were clear, the irises almost purple in the faded light of the glow-rods.

She regarded him, knife in hand. He dared not move.

Then a score more leapt for them. Caleb had time for a single shot before she was amongst them, blade a blur, the silver wire weaving between them, snapping necks and spraying gore. He'd always known she was dangerous, but this was beyond anything he'd seen. There was no thought left, just an instinct to kill. Given time and space, she could have perhaps claimed them all.

But the glow-rods were dimming. And their numbers were endless.

All was fire. All was agony.

His skin blistered, bones boiled. But even as his robes burned around him, he felt the fire flow through him, exhilarating and horrific, lost in a hurricane of screams and prayers, his own voice one with the torturous choir. He saw the truth now. The other-light was not of this world. What he'd thought of as glimmering stars were eyes from beyond the veil.

They saw him. They hungered, but were little more than apparitions. It was the flames that granted form, shapes coalescing within the fires. They were indistinct, inverted shadows. But he saw a glimpse of blood-red skin, skull-like faces framed by dark horns. Blades that glimmered with baneful runes.

They were close. The tear was opening. And they hungered for him most of all.

He tore his gaze back to the material world. Was that the psyker? The woman crumpled on the floor? She was beautiful – a star dressed in human form. She raised her head, his mismatched eyes meeting hers. He felt her pain, confusion, and a strange kinship. Then she screamed again, other-light radiating from her like a sun. He felt his skin charring. He fell to one knee.

It was too much. Even with whatever Anguis had given him, he could not endure her power. Not without an outlet.

His fingers clawed at the metal, throwing up sparks as the other-light spilled from him, the heat channelled into lightning. It arced across the corridor, the lumens above bursting.

But still he burned. More flowed through him, beyond the confines of the corridor, his consciousness now a storm of light.

He saw Caleb and the ratskin surrounded by the horde, their strength fading, the last glow-rod going dark.

He saw Canndis, surrounded by broken bodies, laughing as blood poured from his eyes, and the Cawdors fell beneath his crackling weapon.

Beyond, he saw a ring of flames, where Pureburn's monster stood over a prone figure. He struggled to recognise them, struggled to make sense of anything. He wanted to let go, be washed away, let the flames consume Periculus.

No.

He was done being a pawn, done with failure and powerlessness. It did not matter what the other-light was, or the horrors that it brought. It was still power. He had channelled it before and could do so again. No machines, no politics. Just him. His will. His refusal to let them win.

He could cling to his flesh again, what little of it lingered. He felt the flames rage through Periculus, and the lives they sought to consume. Most of all, he felt the Wall surrounding it, the cage holding it all in. It had been warped by the dome's fall, forged into its current state through foul magicks, perhaps by chance, or perhaps to keep what Periculus' fall had unleashed caged.

But nothing was immutable. Change was the only constant. What had been forged could be remade. He'd done it already, even with the little he'd had. He'd broken the Wall. Now he had too much power to contain. It had to flow somewhere. Something vast enough that Anguis would have her opening. He could not hold it. But perhaps Periculus could.

His soul reached for the wall of blackness. Across the dome, even over the savagery and screams, there came the sound of thunder.

Virae rolled aside as the claws struck the corpse-ash, the disruption field causing it to explode in a shower of dust. Her fist hammered into the side of the Pyromagir's head. It was like punching rockcrete. It turned to face her as she retreated, steam hissing from the metal grate in place of its face.

She had nothing left, her weapon broken, her opponent seemingly invincible. It lurched after her, still slowed by its leg. But she was slower still, adrenaline beginning to fail, only her anger fighting against fatigue and injury. But fury did not bring victory.

It must have a weakness. Everything did. She needed to think. She needed an opening.

'Finish her!' Pureburn roared as his Pyromagir lumbered closer. She retreated as far as she could, but now her back was pressed to a ruined section of the hab-block. Nowhere left to run.

The claws lashed out. She ducked, the talons piercing the rubble behind her. The rockcrete wall crumbled at its touch, momentarily trapping the Pyromagir's wrist. It screeched in fury, steam hissing from its mouth grate. Its face was etched by firelight, and she saw the flesh around the metal grate was scarred, scorched by the steam it belched.

It tore its hand clear, but she had already leapt upon its back. The creature snarled like an angry furnace, but its bulk hindered it; it could not reach her. Still the beast bucked, seeking to slam her into the rubble, smoke hissing from its face.

She gritted her teeth, reached out and seized its mouth with both hands, her fingers wedged into the grate, ignoring the pain as the steam scoured her flesh. Both knees were pressed into the back of the creature's neck, forcing its head up.

The claws were reaching for her, but she barely saw them. All she could picture was Elle, dead mouth twitching as the machine drove her corpse. Even death was not an escape from this world, where bodies were ground and baked into bread to slake the hunger for industry.

Virae screamed, her fingers digging into the torn flesh of the creature's throat. With a savage wrench, she tore the metal from its face. Smoke billowed from the wound, its tar-like blood spilling down its face, and Virae leapt clear. It lunged for her, blinded but no less lethal for it. She side-stepped, seeking a weapon, anything that could finish it. All she saw was the head of her broken chainglaive. She seized it, brandishing the weapon as a club.

The creature lurched after her, its eyes blazing with fury, the lower half of its face a mess of wire-stretched sinew. It roared, the sound like thunder.

No. The thunder was elsewhere. She could feel its weight in the air. The hair was standing on her forearms.

The broken weapon gave a faint whine. She frowned, glancing at it. There was no power pack connected, but she saw sparks dance between its teeth.

As the Pyromagir reached for her, half blinded by the steam belching from its wound, she thrust the blade upwards into its ruined face and squeezed the trigger. Her glaive howled with joy as the teeth bit into flesh. The force ripped the blade apart, its teeth tearing the Pyromagir's head open.

It fell, soundless. She swayed, falling to a knee and glancing up at the incredulous Pureburn.

'Your weapon is broken,' she said. 'As is mine.'

He shook his head, unable to process what was happening.

'No,' he said. 'No, this changes nothing. I am appointed by the God-Emperor. I am His champion.'

'Then why did you lose?'

'I did not lose,' he shouted, rising. 'Periculus is mine! I am the–'

Thunder again, louder. But this time it brought the lightning. It arced above and around them, tearing through Periculus. The ground trembled, pitching Pureburn from his feet. She staggered, glancing up, expecting the slave-block to come crashing down.

But it was not the slave-block. It was the Wall.

It was cracking, jagged lines scoring the metal, the faded light of the underhive piercing the gloom. Pureburn's followers scattered, some screaming as they shielded their ruined eyes from the light.

She looked for the Pyrocaen Lord himself. But he was gone, swallowed by the smoke billowing from his fallen throne.

ACT 4

1

The six pyres were long extinguished, the corpse-ash swept. But Pureburn's throne still stood where it had fallen, even though its flames were spent. Canndis stared at it, struggling to light his lho-stick. Most of his cuts had healed, but his right hand was bound in a sling, the wrist cracked. Too many split skulls, according to the medic. Not that he recalled exactly what happened. Then again, few did, or at least claimed amnesia. Now the Wall was cracked, and disparate flickering lights of the underhive spilled into Periculus, it was harder to face the acts committed in the dark. Better to discard the memories entirely, just as easily as the cheap, crude masks.

He shook his lighter, cursing.

'Allow me, Proctor Canndis.'

He turned at the voice. Lord Credence Sorrow, acting governor of Periculus, approached, flanked by two of his enormous bodyguards. Canndis made to bow, but Sorrow shook his head.

'Please. The hero of Periculus need not bow to a humble bureaucrat.' He smiled, as one of his attendants lit Canndis' lho-stick. 'You are the man who held the hordes, who had the forethought to request reinforcements when it was clear Pureburn had gone mad. Your promotion to proctor is well deserved. If anything, I should bow to you.'

'Just my job, my lord,' Canndis said, taking a draw on his lho-stick.

'Well, it's why I requested you stay on,' Sorrow replied. 'I need men of conviction, not the weak-minded sort who can easily be manipulated. It will take a great deal to restore Periculus, but with stout hearts we will succeed.'

'How goes the rebuilding, my lord?'

'It's pretty grim,' Sorrow sighed, surveying the slave-block looming high above them. 'Pureburn's men penetrated the slave-hab. Casualties were serious. What remains of my team have processed most of the bodies, and by doing so solved the supply problem. So, some good news.'

He glanced to Canndis and offered a broad smile. 'We are turning it around, proctor.'

'Some decent patrolmen would be a start.'

'Indeed,' Sorrow said. 'We need law here. Not that superstitious nonsense. The God-Emperor is the Master of Mankind, and our shield against the dark. But, frankly, I think in matters of business He prefers pragmatism over ceremony.'

They both glanced to the fallen throne.

'Tell me,' Sorrow murmured, 'have your men had any luck finding our lost Pyrocaen Lord?'

'Not yet. But we will,' Canndis said. 'That is, unless the underhive takes care of the problem.'

'Good.' Sorrow nodded. 'That man is responsible for so much pain and loss. All because of his avarice.'

Canndis frowned, exhaling a cloud of smoke. 'I thought that was the lot of Guilders?'

'Acquisition of credits is certainly important,' Sorrow said, smiling. 'But a business model in which you kill all your customers for coin is, frankly, unsustainable. First rule of the Mercator Pallidus is you need supply and demand, because sooner or later the one will become the other.'

'So, will you take the throne?' Canndis asked, nodding to Pureburn's fallen dais.

Sorrow laughed lightly. 'I think not. I cannot decide whether to leave it there as a reminder or just demolish the whole thing. It smells awful, like something crawled inside and died.'

'Taint of the witch, my lord,' Canndis said. 'Not uncommon. We've kept the cell sealed until a priest can sanctify it.'

'Well done, proctor.'

'Standard procedure,' Canndis said. 'We are just lucky that friend of yours eliminated the psyker before it was too late.'

'Yes,' Sorrow said. 'A shame Sol was so badly injured. I had hoped to find a place for him here. Still, I have spoken to his colleagues from the Mercator Lux, and Lord Adūlator is inbound to assist us with our power shortages. Once that is finalised I will liaise with the Mercator Sanguis to provide fresh serfs. But not until the factorums are ready – that was Pureburn's other error. He rushed things. We have time to do this right.'

Canndis did not reply. He was staring past Sorrow. A score of figures were approaching. For the most part they were skinny, malnourished. But their eyes were hard, and they were led by a tall woman in battered armour, its golden veneer stripped by fire and blade, revealing cold iron. Her head was bare, greying hair bound in a tight plait, and a massive chainglaive with a curved blade was slung over her shoulder, a red tassel hanging from beneath the head.

'Chain Lord Virae.' Sorrow nodded as they drew closer. 'Are you taking some of our serfs for an excursion?'

She stopped, glaring at him. The look made Canndis wish he carried his stubber.

'I am done with this place,' she said, nodding to the hab-block, or perhaps the entire dome. 'We are leaving.'

'You are free to do so,' Sorrow said, before glancing to her entourage. 'But I am afraid they must remain behind. Those serfs belong to Periculus.'

'Pureburn never paid. They are still mine.'

'Periculus needs workers. You will be reimbursed.'

'It has workers,' she said, jabbing her thumb to the slave-block. 'Most chose to stay. These few felt there was a better chance out there.'

'Chain Lord Virae,' Sorrow began, 'we owe you a great deal, but–'

'Do you know how I earned that title?' she asked.

Sorrow shrugged.

'Because I was the only one left,' she said softly. 'The Shakle-men. The pit fighters. Once our craft went down, the ash wastes claimed them one by one. Chain Lord Garak survived longer than most, and that was because he was too frail to walk. I carried him on my shoulders most of the way. Didn't realise he'd died until we reached our destination. But some-one had to oversee the transaction, and they all looked to me. I think it was less work for everyone if I assumed the title and his badge of office.'

'Such an inspiring story,' Sorrow replied. 'A meteoric rise from the bottom through strength of arm and determina-tion of spirit. Helmawr's Law, in action.'

'That's what I told myself,' she sighed, glancing to the serfs. 'That I had risen. That life would be better holding the whip.'

She looked at them, her eyes cold as she unhooked her badge of office from its chain.

'I was wrong,' she said, handing it to Lord Sorrow.

'Nevertheless, you will–'

'I will go where I please,' she said, glancing to Sorrow and Canndis in turn. 'I walked through the flames. I broke Pureburn. I would advise you both to stand aside or I will break you too.'

'Stand aside?' Canndis spat. 'If you think you can just deny–'

Sorrow held up a hand.

'This has been an unprecedented incident,' he said. 'My people are still calculating and processing the dead. Perhaps the numbers have yet to be finalised. Perhaps another, say, fifty slaves and one Guilder were lost to Pureburn's madness, their bodies consumed by the flames.'

'Lord Sorrow?' Canndis said. Sorrow smiled.

'I have no interest in forging enemies,' he said simply. 'This woman is as responsible as anyone for our freedom. If the only reward she asks is to disappear with a handful of slaves, half of whom I'd wager would not survive a day in a factorum, that seems a small price.'

He turned to the former Chain Lord.

'You may leave, Virae. Consider it my parting gift.'

She glanced at him, nodding once. The slaves shuffled past them, led by a burly Goliath carrying a meltagun. Virae made to follow, but hesitated, glancing back at Sorrow. She tossed something at his feet. He glanced down. It was a shattered helm that still bore the impression of a broken crown.

'It is heavier than you think,' she warned, before turning

her back on Periculus and departing for the depths of the underhive.

'You sure about this, lord?' Canndis asked as she faded from sight.

'Oh yes,' Sorrow said. 'As you say, the underhive will no doubt take care of the problem, and who cares about a handful of slaves?'

Caleb threw more briquettes onto the fire, the flames greedily devouring the fuel.

'You're overfeeding it,' Iktomi warned, not looking up. She sat cross-legged, slicing a three-foot tentacle into rings.

Caleb shrugged. 'Forgive me if, given our recent troubles, I seek the comfort of a very bright fire.'

She shrugged in return. 'Don't complain if the meat burns.'

'You're not scared by what happened?' Caleb asked, glancing into the darkness beyond their little fire.

'No.'

'Not even a little affected by it?'

She raised her head, frowning as she considered his question, the blade tapping absently at her boot.

Then she shook her head. 'Not enough to waste fuel.'

'Ah-ha!' Caleb grinned as she returned to slicing. 'So, you were affected?'

'Everything we undergo changes us.'

'What do you remember?'

She glanced at him.

'I remember that you were annoying me,' she said. 'I was thinking about how best to stab you. Quick and clean, or slow and lingering?'

'Fair,' Caleb said. 'Was this when you were tied up?'

'No,' she said. 'This was when you suggested we descend

to the underhive to rescue a slave girl and get paid a pittance for our trouble. From then on my mood only soured.'

'Hilarious,' Caleb sighed. 'You make jokes now?'

'Maybe I made them before. You just understand them now.'

She speared three of the rings with her blade, holding them out to the flames.

'You think she made it?' Caleb asked. 'She must have, right? Sorrow said he would free her if we did as he asked. He wouldn't lie about that, right?'

'We could ask him.'

'I think Periculus is best behind us,' Caleb replied, stretching out on his back. 'I don't know what happened back there and I'd prefer it stays that way. We are a day's travel from Sifter's Gate. There are some exceptionally fine drinking establishments and I intend to get drunk enough to forget all this ever happened.'

'Good plan.'

'Really?' He frowned, glancing at her. 'I'm surprised. I thought you'd be seeking vengeance or settling unfinished business or something?'

'Perhaps I saw a reflection I didn't like,' she said. 'You can go drink. I have some thinking to do.'

Caleb grinned. 'Listen to you – all introspective.'

'Or I could gut you and leave you to the scavengers,' she warned, removing her knife from the fire and flicking a ring into his outstretched hands.

'I'd survive,' he said, tossing the morsel between his fingers as it cooled. 'I always find a way.'

'It was a good trick with the Enforcers,' she conceded, biting into the meat. 'How did you erase your record?'

'I didn't,' he said, his smile fading. 'That was someone else.'

'Still, you have no record,' she persisted. 'The Enforcers will never come after you. This is a good thing. Isn't it?'

Caleb shrugged again, turning away, intent on the flames. From the corner of his eye he could see she was watching him.

'Isn't it?' she repeated.

'Sure it is,' he said, forcing a smile. 'I don't want to get on the wrong side of the Enforcers. After all, my father is a proctor.'

'Does he protect you?'

'No. He has never protected me,' Caleb replied. 'Could we enjoy the quiet for a moment? For once, I don't feel like talking.'

2

Pureburn found himself staring at the scrap and bone relics on the makeshift altar. They seemed different since he'd last visited the shrine. His reception had certainly changed. The priest did not fawn at his arrival, instead practically cramming his followers inside the church, as though scared to be seen with them. All Pureburn had requested was supplies and a secure vox-channel. Neither had been forthcoming yet. Why was it taking so long?

Then again, his prior visit had been when he was enthroned and empowered by the God-Emperor's Eternal Flame. Now his robes were torn and stained, his army reduced to a trio of Cynders. He appeared little more than a pauper. Periculus had cost him nearly everything.

It had been a mistake; he saw that now. He had tried to move too fast. That was why he lost control. Or rather, why he was unable to prevent her from losing control. That was the truth of it. The girl, like her mother, had been gifted with the power, but lacked the will to harness it. Had the fire burned in him as it did in her, it would have been different. He could have channelled it. He knew this.

It was strange – he should have felt incensed by her failure. But he was just exhausted, hollowed, as though when the Eternal Flame went dark a piece of him was lost with it. His eyes still ached, even the flickering light of the altar candles almost painful. He just needed rest, time to recover.

Where the hell was the priest?

His mouth still tasted of… well, that did not matter. He had decided the last few days were a blur, that he could not recall exactly what had transpired. No one could with any certainty, and there was no point dwelling on it. He needed to move on, rebuild and consolidate his empire. House Catallus would support him. They had to; he knew their secrets.

Behind him, he heard the church's main door creak open.

'Finally,' he snapped, turning. 'Where–'

But the man standing at the church's entrance was no priest. He wore a ragged cloak that glimmered in the candlelight, shards of glass and metal sewn into the lining so they sparkled like stars. And, even in the half-light, Lord Pureburn could see his mask had an odd, leather-like quality, almost as though it had been stretched from skin.

'Good evening, milord,' the stranger said. His voice was base, guttural. Yet there was a trace of an accent, one Lord Pureburn could not quite place.

'How dare you enter unannounced!' he snapped. 'Do you know who I am?'

'Oh, I know all about you, Lord Pureburn.' The stranger smiled. 'My name is Isaiah. I used to keep company with a man called Tritus. I believe you are acquainted?'

'That is not your concern.'

'Well, Brother Tritus thought it was,' Isaiah replied, as he crossed the threshold. 'His messenger had all sorts of strange tales to tell, including some about you. Tritus was most distressed. That was the last I heard of him.'

'I fear Brother Tritus was not a well man.'

'That might be true.' Isaiah nodded. 'Seeing your family eaten in front of you can have that effect. But, for his flaws, he was a pious man. And he believed, which makes me believe him in turn.'

His gaze fell to the altar as he traced the wings of the holy aquila across his chest.

'The thane of Cawdor was most concerned to hear tell of witchcraft in Periculus,' he said, glaring at Lord Pureburn from behind the leather mask. 'That is why I must ask you to come with me, so you can provide a full account of what transpired.'

Something had shifted as he spoke, his voice shedding the guttural twang of the underhive.

'I do not answer to the likes of you.'

Isaiah spread his hands. 'I must insist.'

'Dispose of him,' Pureburn said, nodding to the nearest Cynder.

Before it could move, a shot shattered its kneecap, pitching it to the floor. It came from above. Pureburn glanced to the rafters. There was the impression of a tarnished ivory mask, and the gleam of a long rifle.

'My apologies, Lord Pureburn,' Isaiah said, his voice lacking any hint of remorse. 'Sister Harriette is a fine shot but can sometimes be trigger happy. I would suggest no more sudden moves, and your hands remain where I can see them. Because she can take them at the wrist. Believe me, I've seen it.'

Pureburn did not reply. His gaze was drawn to the shadows,

where more masked figures waited. They were all around him.

'This is ridiculous,' he said. 'I am Lord Silas Pureburn, Pyrocaen Lord of the Mercator Pyros. I have led armies against heretics, attended the spires of House Catallus. I supped with Lord Helmawr less than half a cycle ago.'

'Well, that sounds very grand indeed,' Isaiah said, as his followers closed in. 'Tell me, Lord Pureburn, are any of those people here now? To stand with you? To defend you? To protect you?'

He looked left to right, before glancing at Pureburn and shrugging his shoulders.

'You cannot do this,' Pureburn snapped as rough hands seized his arms. 'I will have words with the thane!'

'Yes, you will,' Isaiah said. 'But you will speak to me first. You must confess your sins.'

'I will not be judged by the likes of you!'

Pureburn spat in the Cawdor's face, his spit staining the leather. Isaiah smiled, wiping the cheek of his mask. This close, Pureburn could see that the flayed skin still bore the features of its previous owner.

'The God-Emperor will judge you,' Isaiah said, smiling. 'But first, we must show Him your true face.'

Sol opened his eye and saw nothing.

The room was dark, the only light the green hue of the medi-unit's display. By its glow he could barely make out the bedframe on which he lay. His right arm was bandaged, angry scars peeping from beneath the dressing. He flexed his fingers, trying to lift it, but the limb hung useless by his side.

'I am afraid surgery was required.'

The whisper came from the shadows. His eyes were

adjusting, and by the stolen light of the medi-unit he could just make out Anguis' face.

'That hardware in your arm had to come out,' she continued. 'The wires were fried, and there may be some neurological damage. But you did it, Sol. Your storm ended Pureburn's rule. He is finished, and even House Cawdor now speaks of the God-Emperor's tempest that freed Periculus.'

'How... we won?'

'Oh yes,' she said, stepping closer. 'You almost killed yourself channelling her power, but you gave me an opening. I took care of everything else.'

'The psyker. She's dead?'

'Yes. Don't worry, I took care of it,' Anguis replied. 'You just need to rest. Pureburn has fallen, Periculus is saved and Lord Sorrow has stepped in as governor. He asked that I pass along his best as he's quite busy at present.'

Sol nodded, head lolling, as though he could not quite support it. She leant closer, helping him settle against the pillow.

'Poor dear,' she sighed, wiping his brow with a cloth. 'It's all been a bit too much, hasn't it?'

'I... it's gone,' Sol said. 'I can't see... whatever it was I saw. It's hard to explain, like I no longer even understand what happened. I just feel empty. Like I lost something profound.'

'Better that way,' she said. 'I'm relieved there is no sign of permanent corruption. Your power is spent now. The sense of bereavement is a common side effect of Ghast withdrawal, but it will pass. I am afraid you are stuck with the dreams though. Those never leave completely.'

'Is that what you were injecting me with?'

'More or less. It was a little more... refined than something you might find on the street.'

'You took it from the ruins, didn't you?' he said. 'I know you found something.'

'Ruins?' she said, frowning. 'I'm not sure what you are referring to, because if you returned to the site of our triumph there would be no trace of any building, merely a forest of cable-vines and a large pile of eyeless corpses.'

'No evidence?'

'Evidence of what?'

'You played me.'

'I play everyone.'

'Lied to me.'

'That's true,' she said. 'I did once say you would make a passable Delaque. But you are right, it was a lie. You are too honest, Sol, too trusting. Go back to chasing storms and making little gizmos. It's a simple life, and you will be happier for it.'

'I would be happy with the truth.'

She sighed, resting her weight against the bed rail, head bowed.

'What would you like me to say?' she asked. 'That, long ago, House Delaque conducted experiments in Periculus that contributed to its fall? That, when it was rediscovered, we had to remove all evidence before Pureburn's blundering revealed our dirty secret to Lord Helmawr? That I arranged an accident, directed your apparent rehabilitation, arranged your escape, all as part of a plan to get you where I needed you? That I used my contacts to manipulate you, even faked an agent's death to buy your trust. That you were merely a tool that got me where I needed to be? That all of it was just as planned?'

He suspected that, if she had eyes, she would have rolled them. As it was, she merely smiled her half-smile, but it looked odd. He did not know why.

'I just want the truth,' he said.

'The truth?' she replied, the smile fading. 'The truth is my masters tell me little beyond where to be and what to do. From what I gleaned, Periculus' rediscovery was seen as a threat to our spyker operations. Believe me, they are delicate. That is why you were marked for death when Mr Stitch was lost, but I convinced them that you could help. I was confident you could earn the contract with a little assistance. So I protected you, cared for you as best I could, even killed my own agent to keep you safe. I followed you through the hell of Periculus, using whatever scraps of information came my way. In the end I found something in the ruins and took a chance. It was a risk, but it saved us both.'

She looked at him. Perhaps there would have been tears in her eyes if she still had them.

'I waited by your bedside,' she whispered. 'Night and day, praying you would wake. You mean a great deal to me. You must know that? How much I care for you?'

'Perhaps.' He frowned. 'Or perhaps you only arrived an hour ago and asked them to take me off the sedatives?'

'It is possible,' she said, the half-smile playing on her lips. 'Which account do you prefer?'

This time he saw what was different.

'Your smile,' he said. 'It's on the wrong side of your face.'

'Is it?' she said, coyly touching her cheek. 'How very odd.'

'And that's all you'll give me?'

'I gave you a great deal,' she said. 'Your Guild has secured the contract with Periculus, and I hear Lord Severior wishes to welcome you back with open arms. You know of the newly promoted Proctor Canndis, the hero who held off the hordes and liberated Periculus? Well, he claims you were the one who handed him his weapon. When the legend of Periculus is told you will be a not insignificant footnote.'

'And you will never even be mentioned?'

'Exactly.'

'You spoke to Severior?' Sol asked, trying and failing to sit up. 'Doctor Caute – did he survive?'

She sighed. 'I am sorry, I forgot to ask. But you will find out soon enough. Now I must take my leave.'

'You think you can just walk away?' he spat as she made for the door.

'One of us can.'

He tried to rise but collapsed, grasping his right shoulder and moaning. She glanced back, and for a moment a pained look crossed her face. For just an instant, her face flickered. She looked older, harder, and so very sad. Then the light shifted. The expression was gone.

A moment later, so was she.

He waited, leaning back in the bed, hand clutched to his shoulder, as though he were in agony.

He waited that way for some time.

Only when he was certain she had gone did he straighten, rising smoothly from the bed. It was still dark in the room, the medi-unit the only source of light.

He held out his bandaged hand, examining the scarred fingers, now stripped of wire and circuit. No energy syphon, no neurone circuits. Only flesh remained. Only Sol.

He was just human now.

Yet, above him, the lumens flickered. Slowly, light bled into the room. It was enough to catch his reflection on the medi-unit's screen. His face was scarred, burns running across forehead and cheek. His lost eye was covered. He concentrated, for a moment, on a now familiar feeling. Beneath the dressing, a light sputtered into life, shimmering.

He held out his palm. Within, a tiny star glimmered into being.

He smiled. Perhaps he would make a good Delaque after all.

EPILOGUE

Lord Credence Sorrow, acting-governor of the Fallen Dome of Periculus, smiled at the flickering face of Lord Severior on the vox's screen. The old man was less disagreeable than Sol had indicated, though Sorrow would have preferred that he not lean so close to the data-screen. His crystal-blue eyes were merely disconcerting, but the plumage sprouting from his nostrils was positively off-putting.

'We have an accord then?' Sorrow said. 'The Council of Light will satisfy Periculus' power needs?'

'We are delighted to,' Lord Severior said. 'Though I feel sadness for dear Silas Pureburn. Although we were rivals, I cannot deny he was a great man. A pity he fell so far.'

'Indeed.' Sorrow nodded. 'I count myself fortunate that I had the chance to work with him, albeit briefly. But I think he was the wrong fit for Periculus. I see the Forbidden Dome as the cutting edge of fashion and culture. The veneration of a fire is, frankly, something better suited to the more backward zones of the hive. Periculus will be a beacon of enlightenment.'

'I could not agree more.' Severior smirked. 'For too long the Mercator Lux have been considered secondary to the Pyrocaen Lords of the Mercator Pyros. I welcome the opportunity to prove our value to Periculus.'

'And, perhaps, improve your own status within the Mercator Lux?'

'If that is the God-Emperor's will,' Severior replied, bowing his head and crossing his wrists. 'His Light Binds All Shadow.'

'From Darkness We Ascend,' Sorrow said, smoothly returning the gesture. 'I look forward to Lord Adūlator's arrival.'

'You are content that Lord Adūlator remains the liaison? I gather you and Lord Sol were close?'

'We were acquainted,' Sorrow said, his smile fading. 'But when I recently floated the idea of a partnership he made his opinions known. I am sure there is other work he could undertake once recovered.'

'Certainly,' Severior said. 'In fact, I intend to make the Light-touched his official title. He will be an ambassador to those more backward zones of the hive. Places where settlers might struggle to understand our work, but have heard tell of the God-Emperor's holy storm.'

'I'm sure he will embrace the appointment with his usual gusto.'

'Quite so.' Lord Severior smiled. 'I do look forward to working together.'

The data-screen faded to black. Sorrow rose from his chair, smoothing his freshly laundered robes as he surveyed his new home. It had once housed Lord Pureburn, and Lady Wirepath before him. Neither left much impression on the place.

'That's a cycle we shall need to break,' Sorrow murmured, half addressing himself and half the two Grinders guarding the door. Yes, much would change. The tyranny of Pureburn had not only been cruel, but short-sighted and self-defeating: hive serfs starved to the point of worthlessness, until their flesh hung from their bones. When they died there was little to harvest, the corpse-starch provided by their bodies thin and innutritious.

That would not be the case in his Periculus. His workers would be well fed, cared for, and enjoy an extra thirty minutes of sleep a day. And when they passed on, their bodies would provide sustenance for the next generation. More than that, as each generation fed the last, they would grow healthier, more productive.

'Perhaps entertainment too,' Sorrow said, glancing to the Grinders. 'Pureburn was right about–'

But his guards lay crumpled.

Sorrow blinked, unable to process what he was seeing. Both men were hardened killers. Each must have weighed over three hundred pounds. He had heard neither of them fall. Yet they were dead, and beside them a shadow stood, blade glinting in its hand.

'Guards!' Sorrow snapped, tapping a button on his belt.

The shadow shook its head.

'Who are you?' Sorrow said, retreating. He felt the reassuring weight of his signet ring. One shot. He had to make it count.

The killer stepped from the shadows. He caught a flash of red about her eyes, and for a moment thought it was one of Pureburn's followers, still consumed by the madness. But, as the light fell on her, he realised the crimson stains were not blood.

They were tribal markings. Ratskin.

He remembered those eyes. Black. Soulless. But he could not recall her name.

'So, you have returned?' he said, putting on a welcoming smile. 'I was concerned when we lost contact with you and Caleb. Where have you been?'

'Thinking,' she replied. 'About how our deal changed, and how you double-crossed us. And how I warned you what would happen if you broke your word.'

'I did no such thing,' he said, shifting away. A few more steps and she would be framed between two pillars. No room to dodge.

'You're lying.'

'And how could you possibly know that?'

'I can smell it.'

'This is foolish,' Sorrow replied. 'Where is your partner? Perhaps he and I can discuss an additional fee. What is it you want?'

'Nothing you can offer.'

'Everyone wants something,' Sorrow persisted, slowing. She was almost in place. 'There must be something important to you?'

'Yes. My word. I gave it to you. I intend to keep it.'

With that she surged towards him. As she stepped between the pillars, he activated the ring. A blast of plasma spat from the weapon, forming a crackling ball of super-heated matter over two feet across. It was on her in a heartbeat, no time to dodge or duck.

She did not break stride, kicking against the pillar as she leapt, twisting through the air. It was impossible, but somehow she arched her body over the miniature sun, pirouetting on the wind, her blade glimmering with stolen light.

As it swept towards him, he found he could not take his gaze from her eyes. Perhaps it was the reflected glow of the plasma bolt, but they seemed to burn amethyst in the fading light.

ABOUT THE AUTHOR

Denny Flowers is the author of the Necromunda novel *Fire Made Flesh*, the short story 'The Hand of Harrow' and the novella *Low Lives*. He lives in Kent with his wife and son.

YOUR
NEXT READ

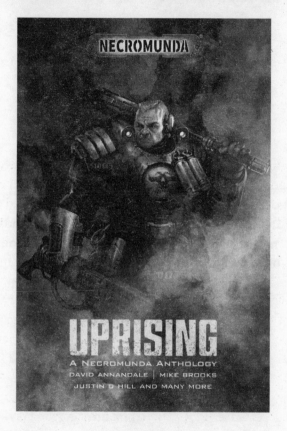

UPRISING
by various authors

Venture into the underhive of Necromunda with a collection
of action-packed tales encompassing gang war, strange events,
desperate escapes and cunning schemes.

An extract from
Low Lives
by Denny Flowers
taken from the anthology *Uprising*

Four hunters departed Slag Row. Five if you counted the
unbloodied rookie, though none of the others did. The trail
was not hard to follow; wherever their quarry passed there
would be stories, improbable deeds and daring feats. It did
not concern the hunters that the accounts were mired in con-
tradictions. All that mattered was the hunt.

The five suffered their first casualty just outside Sump
City. Whilst the rest slept, Bor Meathook pressed on alone,
intent on being the sole claimant of the bounty. The other
hunters found his body a day later floating in a pool of
refuse, unharmed if you discounted the knife wound in his
chest. They knew Meathook had been arrogant and at times
sloppy, but he was no amateur. Lars the Sly, the group's
self-appointed leader, had seen him break a man's neck with
a backhand slap; had seen him dislocate a shoulder with a
vigorous handshake. The former Goliath had been a moun-
tain of muscle, and surprisingly quick for someone his size,
but his life was still ended with a single thrust. The rookie
obsessed over the injury, measuring the length of the incision and the path of entry, as though cataloguing the killer's

methods. The rest of the party silently paid their respects, each recalculating their share of the bounty now it would be split three ways. Four if you counted the rookie, though none of them did.

The remaining hunters continued, more cautious now. Since Meathook's death the trail had vanished, their quarry aware of the pursuit. Perhaps they would have escaped had it not been for Garak the Seeker. The old man struggled to keep pace with the younger hunters, but he had the uncanny ability to know where their prey would flee to. It would sometimes be the smallest clue – a stray hair or errant boot print. More often there was no real sign at all, and the old man would consider each route in turn before inevitably guiding them down the right path. He'd smile when they asked how, exposing a motley collection of ill-formed teeth, and explain that he'd spent most of his life running; he knew where they ran because it was where he would have run.

The hunters lost him just outside Sinkhole, the sump lake that had long since swallowed the Orlock territory of Iron-crown. The old man had been so intent on the trail he had failed to spot yellow eyes bobbing just above the surface of the toxic waters. He screamed as the sumpkroc seized him, his fingers scrabbling on the bank as he was dragged below. The rookie fumbled for her weapon, but Lars held out his hand, motioning her to be still. There was no need for a tracker now; there was only one path left.

A few miserable souls scratched out an existence on the sump lake, cultivating fungus and trawling the waters for scraps. A handful of credits bought information, confirming their quarry's flight across the lake, and a handful more secured passage on one of the trawlers' barges. The two remaining hunters, three if you counted the rookie, wordlessly gravitated to the centre of the vessel, backs pressed together, gaze intent on the emerald waters. The trawler was unfazed, propelling the makeshift craft with a sculling oar that ended in a barbed hook. He would pause occasionally, reversing his oar to haul some trinket from the sump.

No one knew how far the lake extended. The trawler claimed to have sailed further than most. He told of a forgotten shore where twisted creatures wore the faces of men. When asked whether their quarry had headed for those shores, the trawler laughed, and told them that none dared cross the lake, for those who once tried had never returned. The rookie rightly asked how he knew of the creatures on the far shore if no one had ever returned, and the trawler smiled, his teeth surprisingly white and just a little too sharp for comfort, and said these were but stories.

Still, neither the hunters nor their quarry were interested in crossing the lake. Their focus was the island that lay at its centre.

The land mass was unstable, little more than jetsam drawn together by the currents, the toxic waters fusing it around a steel cylinder, perhaps ten feet in diameter and that much again in height, the top sealed by a bronze cap with a rich turquoise patina. Before the hive quake, back when Ironcrown was a centre of industry, the shaft had been one of a dozen used to haul valuable ore from the mines below. Now it was all that remained; the final passage through Sinkhole to the last remnant of the lost empire. It was their prey's final refuge.

For a modest fee, the trawler promised to return in three days to retrieve them. Lars threatened that reneging on the deal would have dire consequences, though in truth he knew that this would be a difficult threat to enforce.

Within the former mineshaft, a cage of corroded iron and tarnished copper was suspended on frayed cables and worn chains. It was barely a few yards across, and heavily worn by corrosion and filth. The motor had long since fallen into disrepair, so they alternated operating the winch, two hauling on the rusted chain whilst the other rested. A single spluttering lumen was their only source of light, like a candle in darkness. Not that there was anything to see, suspended in a steel shaft deep within the sump. But they were not alone in the waters. Occasionally something would brush against the metal of the shaft – perhaps a trailing tentacle or malformed fin – and the cage would rock, the chain creaking as it sank deeper.

Their third loss came during the descent. The rookie awoke to find Lars pulling on the chain alone, the body of Scrag Dry lying at his feet. Psychosis, Lars would tell her, no doubt brought on by the confines of the mineshaft and the dangers lurking in the sump. Lars had been forced to act in self-defence. A pre-emptive defence, admittedly, but defence nonetheless.

The rookie said nothing.

At the next waste valve the two of them flushed the corpse. Through the viewport they could just see it floating, suspended in the iridescent sump. Then there was a shadow, and a flash of teeth the size of a Cawdor polearm. The body vanished.

They both set to work on the chain, redoubling their efforts.

Eventually they came to a juddering stop at the bottom of the shaft. When they stepped out of the cage, they emerged into a vast cavern, having left the sump far above them.

Lars stepped from the cage, rifle slung low but always to

hand, his olive-green greatcoat buttoned tight, his pock-marked face set in a sneer. The rookie followed close behind, her long-las strapped to her back. Before them lay all that remained of the Ironcrown of old: a subterranean desert of ash and crumbling stone, pierced by vast stalactites the size of mountains. They grew from the dome far above, the tips having long since pierced the ash dunes. A few rusted gantries linked some of the larger stalactites, and far above he could just make out the glow of the remaining dome lights. It was hard to imagine that above those lights were the festering waters of Sinkhole. He wondered how large a hive quake it would take to open a crack in the dome and drown them in the sump, and decided it would be best not to dawdle.

The rookie was studying the maps, trying to pinpoint the under-realm's only remaining settlement. She'd survived longer than he'd expected, outlasting three seasoned hunters, and had acquitted herself admirably during their travels. He would still most likely kill her once they had claimed their bounty, but she was worth keeping around for now. If nothing else she might catch a stray bullet intended for him.

She caught his gaze and pointed. Before them, shrouded in smog, he could just make out the settlement of Hope's End – barely two score buildings, some welded from rusted bulkheads, others carved directly into the spoil heap. To his left a workshop was stacked with minecarts and drilling equipment. On the far side was some form of distillery, which at least raised the possibility of getting a drink. Centrally, one building stretched slightly higher than the others, presumably belonging to whoever ran the place. A crowd was gathered outside of it, and he could hear the distant echo of voices.

Lars raised his rifle, adjusting the telescopic sight. He was too far to risk taking a shot, but he could at least see clearly now. The settlement was indeed in the throes of some celebration, though it did not appear planned. People were still emerging from some of the buildings, converging on an improvised stage assembled from rusted bulkheads. On it, a bottle of Wildsnake clasped in each hand, a lone figure was addressing the crowd. He was average height, clad in a fraying shirt and tattered green scarf that had probably been the pinnacle of fashion a couple of cycles ago, his hair worn in a fading blue mohawk. His face was unremarkable until he smiled, the warmth of the expression either genuine or a flawless facsimile. Lars had the bounty in his pocket, but he didn't need to check it. The face was all too familiar.

'Caleb Cursebound,' he whispered. 'Nice to see you're enjoying yourself.'

Satisfied, he turned to the rookie, who was still adjusting the scope on her long-las.

'Quickly,' he snapped. 'Our boy seems to be making a spectacle of himself. I think we should put him to bed. Permanently.'

He grinned, pleased by the joke. Still, Caleb was only half the problem. There was a secondary target, Caleb's accomplice. He had neither her name nor picture, but he knew the ratskin would be close, even if she was proving rather elusive. He could not find her on the stage nor in the crowd. It was only when Caleb concluded his speech, his closing remarks eliciting a roar of approval, that Lars noticed a flicker of movement on the roof of the central building. There she was, barely visible in the shadows, but he could just make out her face, the eyes framed by crimson markings that looked a little like tears. She was scowling.

'Not enjoying the party?' he said, grinning, and displaying an incomplete set of rotten teeth.

As he spoke her head snapped round, her gaze meeting his own. He flinched involuntarily. There was no way she could mark him; even a bionic eye could not spot someone at this distance, but he still felt a shiver of fear scurry along his spine. He would enjoy making her pay for that.

'You think you could make this shot?' he asked, turning to the rookie. She was still struggling with the long-las, displaying an unusual level of incompetence.

'Give me that,' he snapped, snatching the weapon from her hands. It was still a long shot. He was confident that he could pick off either of the duo, even at this range, but doing so could reveal his presence and potentially give the other target the opportunity to escape. The ratskin would be the better choice, he decided. Alone on the rooftop there was a good chance nobody would spot her fall. That would give him time to adjust his aim and take the second shot at Caleb.

He barely felt the rookie's blade slide across his throat, effortlessly parting skin and flesh beneath. He managed a gurgled scream before folding to his knees, clutching weakly at the gushing wound. Then he fell forwards and was still.

Elissa wiped her blade on Lars' shirt, sweeping up the long-las with practised grace. Through the scope she could see Caleb on the improvised stage. He raised his hands and the crowd roared again, the sound carrying to the hilltop. She felt a bubble of hate swell within her chest. For an instant her finger tightened on the trigger.

But she stopped, lowering the weapon, taking a deep, slow breath.

No.

She had pictured his death a thousand times. It would not be quick and not be clean. His last moments would be as a broken man, a pariah to the pitiful underhivers whose approval he so desperately craved.

Her fingers danced over a silver vambrace on her forearm, the metal smooth and unadorned barring the symbol of a golden dagger set against a field of blood. The holo-matrix display blossomed into life, and she pulled up a set of coordinates half a mile hence. She slung her weapon over her shoulder and set off, leaving Lars' corpse sprawled in the ash desert.

Her pace was methodical. There was no hurry. Not yet.